ASHES OF FIERY WEATHER

Ashes
of
Fiery
Weather

Kathleen
Donohoe

Houghton Mifflin Harcourt

BOSTON   NEW YORK

2016

For information about permission to reproduce selections from this book, write
to trade.permissions@hmhco.com or to Permissions, Houghton Mifflin Harcourt
Publishing Company, 3 Park Avenue, 19th Floor, New York, New York 10016.

www.hmhco.com

Library of Congress Cataloging-in-Publication Data

Names: Donohoe, Kathleen, author.
Titles: Ashes of fiery weather / Kathleen Donohoe.
Description: Boston : Houghton Mifflin Harcourt, [2016]
Identifiers: LCCN 2015037241 | ISBN 9780544464056 (hardback) | ISBN
9780544526693 (ebook)
Subjects: LCSH: Women — Fiction. | Fire fighters — Fiction. | Irish American
families — Fiction. | BISAC: FICTION / General. | FICTION / Literary.
Classification: LCC PS3604.O5646 A89 2016 | DDC 813/.6 — dc23
LC record available at http://lccn.loc.gov/2015037241

Book design by Jackie Shepherd

Typeset in Adobe Jenson Pro

Printed in the United States of America

DOC 10 9 8 7 6 5 4 3 2 1

To Travis and Liam,
the two I cannot do without

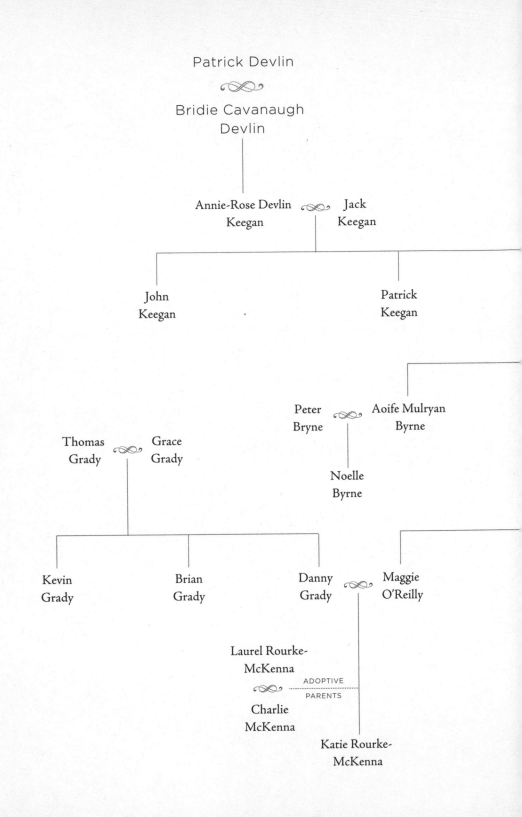

Patrick Devlin

Bridie Cavanaugh
Devlin

Annie-Rose Devlin
Keegan ⁓ Jack
Keegan

John
Keegan

Patrick
Keegan

Peter ⁓ Aoife Mulryan
Bryne Byrne

Thomas ⁓ Grace
Grady Grady

Noelle
Byrne

Kevin
Grady

Brian
Grady

Danny ⁓ Maggie
Grady O'Reilly

Laurel Rourke-
McKenna

⁓ ADOPTIVE
PARENTS

Charlie
McKenna

Katie Rourke-
McKenna

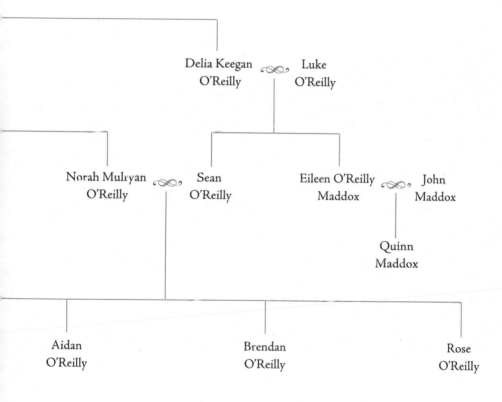

Delia Keegan ⚭ Luke
O'Reilly   O'Reilly

Norah Mulryan ⚭ Sean
O'Reilly   O'Reilly

Eileen O'Reilly ⚭ John
Maddox   Maddox

Quinn
Maddox

Aidan
O'Reilly

Brendan
O'Reilly

Rose
O'Reilly

These are the ashes of fiery weather,
Of nights full of the green stars from Ireland,
Wet out of the sea, and luminously wet,
Like beautiful and abandoned refugees.

— Wallace Stevens, "Our Stars Come from Ireland"

CHAPTER ONE

Norah O'Reilly

April 1983

THE BAGPIPES TOOK UP "Going Home" as the firemen bore the coffin out of the church.

Norah O'Reilly paused on the threshold of the heavy double doors, thrown open as they'd been on her wedding day, a gray November morning, altogether better suited to the end of the story than this soft April afternoon. A warm spring rain had begun to fall during the Mass.

Norah scanned the faces of the assembled firemen, three deep from the curb to the street, skipping the mustached, the older guys, the not-tall, the dark-haired, the obviously non-Irish, the ones in white caps, who were the officers. She didn't see Sean. She saw Sean a hundred times.

Cameras flashed as she stepped fully outside. For ten years, she'd been an understudy in this play, but she'd never once rehearsed. She didn't know her lines, forgetting the names of longtime friends, missing cues, blinking stupidly at outstretched hands and stepping into hugs moments too late. Wherever she went, she left whispers in her wake. *Poor Norah.*

This morning, while savagely biting the tags off her new black dress, she'd resolved not to cry in public. She would be brave. Not like a fireman, but like a Kennedy. The Kennedys were always burying each other. They knew how it was done.

In the crowd, Norah spotted Amred Lehane with his hand over his heart. He knew, of course, that civilians were not supposed to salute. Amred, the buff. She recalled Sean explaining that to her. A buff was a fire department fanatic. They often knew more about the history of the department than the guys themselves. Some buffs were attached to particular companies, like Amred, who belonged to the Glory Devlins and whose insistence on calling them by the company nickname instead of the number was so strong that the men had caught the habit.

The firemen who had not come into the church for Mass, the ones who hadn't known Sean personally, and those from other cities surely spent the service having a breakfast beer across the street in Lehane's, the bar Amred and his sister owned. Amred would have told them how Sean used to bartend there, that he and his Irish wife had met there. *Poor Norah*. She supposed that was her name now.

The men eased the coffin down the steep steps of Holy Rosary. Norah knew that they would not let go of Sean, but rather than watch, she lifted her face to the sky. *Happy is the soul rain falls on*. An Irish proverb. Rain on the day of a funeral was good luck.

She sensed her brother's eyes on her. All three of her brothers had traded Galway for England. Two had called to tell her how they'd liked Sean the time they met him. Only Cathal got on a plane.

Norah told their parents not to come. Her relieved mother promised to have a Mass said for Sean in their own church. Her sister, though. On the phone, Aoife made no mention of emergency passports and plane tickets. She only cried and said she'd have Noelle make a sympathy card for her cousins. Aoife's daughter was ten, a year older than Maggie.

Norah started, then looked for the children. There were three, yet in four days they seemed to have multiplied, surrounding her with their confused blue eyes and moving mouths. Four-year-old Brendan was clinging to the skirt of her dress. Surely she'd had hold of him most of the way down the aisle. When had she let go?

She pried the fabric out of Brendan's fist and grasped his hand so hard he looked up at her in surprise. His hand was mucked with chocolate licorice, which she'd trusted would keep him occupied during Mass, even though the smell made her sick. Her dress, long-sleeved and too warm for the day, was tight over her breasts, which were already fuller. Nobody knew.

Aidan stood beside Brendan, wearing the suit and tie he'd worn this past Sunday, for Easter. Aidan would turn nine two days before Maggie turned ten. Irish twins. Norah located Maggie slightly behind her and reached back with her free hand, but Maggie shied away and then stared back at Norah, daring her to beckon again. Maggie, as the only girl, believed she was Sean's favorite, but it was Aidan who was his heart.

Maggie and the boys had Sean's eyes, a striking blue a shade darker than her own. Maggie glanced at her grandmother, wanting to be her ally instead of Norah's, but Delia, her gaze fixed firmly ahead, didn't seem to notice.

Suit yourself, Norah thought and turned around.

Sean's eyes were his mother's eyes. Delia O'Reilly, beautiful still at sixty-five. She'd been an elementary school principal, formerly a teacher, and there was something in her bearing that suggested it, Norah thought. She expected to be listened to. Sean had often called his mother brave. Back in the 1950s, not many people got divorced. Sure as hell nobody Catholic, he'd say. Many of her students had come to the wake, clearly self-conscious in their dress-up clothes, passing right by Norah. The boys kept their hands in their pockets as they mumbled that they were sorry. The girls had more poise, but it was easy to tell the ones who'd never been to a wake before by the way their wide eyes couldn't leave the open casket. Former students had come as well, college-aged if not in college, and they shook Norah's hand and told her they remembered Sean coming to their classroom in his uniform, and they remembered visits to the firehouse.

Norah, too, remembered Sean saying these kids pulling the fire alarm boxes accounted for probably half their runs. Delia would say that's why it was important that he talk to them. He would shake his head, but he never said no to her.

The coffin arrived at the bottom of the steps and Norah started down, going slowly, for Brendan. She sensed her brother tense. Cathal was ready to grab her arm if she stumbled. The cameras clicked in chorus. Aidan pressed Sean's helmet against his stomach. She made a mental note to be sure to let Brendan get a chance with the helmet. She would make Aidan give it to him as they were leaving the cemetery, when the pipers began "Amazing Grace."

A few members of the FDNY's pipe and drum band had played at their wedding too, though Sean hadn't been a fireman yet.

He'd been waiting to get on the job, increasingly worried that the city's money troubles would keep it from hiring more firemen, needed as they were. When he did get called, only a few months after the wedding, Norah had been too relieved to fret about his safety. A better paycheck and a steady one, she'd thought, as though he'd been hired to sell insurance. They could move out of his mother's house and into an apartment before the baby came.

Cross Hill Cemetery had been closed to new burials for a decade at least. But an exception was being made so Sean could be *laid to rest*, as the priest put it, near his grandfather and great-grandfather, firefighters both. The newspapers were making much of it. "Legacy of Bravery," said one headline.

And, of course, Eileen was in the papers too. The articles about Sean all mentioned that his sister had joined the class-action lawsuit against the FDNY and that she'd graduated from the academy last year, in the very first class to include women.

The procession halted. Three times, Monsignor Halloran blessed the casket with holy water, his spotty hand quaking. He'd baptized Sean too.

The firemen lock-stepped a turn and hoisted the coffin onto the pumper. The honor guard took up their places, four on either side of the pumper and two standing on the back. Firefighter Eileen O'Reilly was one of the four.

Her red hair was pulled back in a tight bun at the nape of her neck. When she got on the job, she'd cut it so it was above her shoulders, but she refused to have it short-short. She was already being called a dyke, she told Norah with a crooked smile. Couldn't give them more ammo. Norah laughed and felt she was betraying Sean, who'd found nothing funny at all about his sister's new career.

The pipers started "Garryowen."

Eileen's back was straight, her face impassive. Eileen looked like she was playing dress-up, as though she'd stolen Sean's Class-A uniform for the occasion.

Joe Paladino was escorting Delia. Sean, apparently, had left instructions with this request. But it was Nathaniel who should have been beside her, and Sean should have realized this. Nathaniel Kwiatkowski, whose gentle voice was accented with both Poland and Brooklyn, had known Sean his whole life. That should have trumped the goddamn holy fire department. Nathaniel was there, of course, not far behind Delia, but like an ordinary mourner.

Indeed, Joe startled Norah in all ways when, straining for composure, he explained Sean's wishes to her.

Sean never told her any details about his funeral. Firemen loved to say you never know when you get on the truck what you'll find when you get there, but Norah had spent her marriage convinced that none of them believed they might die on the job. That it was possible, that they very well might be, she'd thought a secret kept by the wives.

But choosing Joe to escort his mother at his line-of-duty funeral meant that Sean understood. And if Sean had, then all the guys from Sean's firehouse — the funny ones and the shy ones and the ones who bullied the probies worse than if the firehouse was a frat house, the swaggerers, the ones so kind they were like Irish priests in old movies — then all of them knew that they might, one day, go to work and get killed.

At the bottom of the steps, the fire commissioner shook Norah's hand and then Delia's. Then Mayor Koch did the same.

Both the mayor and the fire commissioner retreated, and Norah herded the children to the limousine, and as they climbed in, followed by her brother, she and Delia faced each other on the sidewalk.

"I will never —" Delia began, but then pressed her lips together and turned to Joe, who helped her into the car. Norah followed.

Norah didn't want Act II. She badly needed the curtain to come down and take the audience away. Then Sean could appear from the wings, grinning and carrying a bouquet of lilies.

"You did good," he'd say.

"That Mayor Koch," she'd say, "he's like an egg with ears."

And Sean would laugh.

The morning after the fire, before the children emerged from their rooms, she'd sat at Sean's desk and used his calculator. Possibly she'd never touched it before. He was the one who paid the bills and balanced the checkbook. She was almost thirty-four years old. Suppose she lived to be seventy? 70 − 34 = 36. Thirty-six years without him. More than half her life without him. She got up and lay down on his half of the bed.

Norah had the limousine drop them at her own house first so the kids could change their clothes. The after-funeral should have been at her and Sean's, but Delia insisted that her house would be better.

Though Cathal told her to stand her ground, Norah said she didn't want an argument. Delia owned the three-story brownstone that had belonged to her grandparents. It was the only one on the street that had not been cut up into apartments. Delia had grown up there herself, and after her husband left, she had taken it back from the tenants so she could raise Sean and Eileen there.

It was far bigger than Norah and Sean's two-story three-bedroom, just three blocks away. And Norah knew Sean didn't choose to live close to his mother so he could be there if she needed him. Delia didn't, as far as Norah could tell, need anyone. It was the house.

Sean had formally explained to the kids that Aunt Eileen had been adopted, and that it didn't matter. She was his sister and their aunt.

Norah knew he meant it. Yet. When Norah asked him to please consider moving to Long Island because they needed more space, or even upstate, a town that wouldn't be too bad of a commute to the firehouse, Sean refused to discuss it. He was still the older child, and the boy. The brownstone certainly would have come to him, and he would have moved them into it someday.

Norah didn't change out of her funeral dress, much as she wanted to. Aidan threw on jeans and an FDNY T-shirt. After warning Maggie, who was staring fixedly into her closet, to be quick about it, Norah brought Brendan back downstairs to find Cathal standing before the small gallery of family pictures that were clustered on top of the bookcase in the front room.

Aidan went to the front door, and about every five seconds, they heard him kick it hard. Brendan dashed into the dining room to plunder his Easter basket.

"Aoife should have come," Cathal said. "And I'll tell her that next week."

"Next week?" Norah asked.

"I'm going home for a few days before I head back."

Norah felt a rising panic. Of course Cathal would be leaving. He wasn't about to take up permanent residence on her couch.

"You should go to Ireland, once the kids are out of school," Cathal said gently.

But she wouldn't be doing any traveling this summer if things remained as they were. She had the urge to tell her brother that she was pregnant. It would be like jumping off a cliff. Or backing away from one.

Instead, she shook her head. "Airfare for all of us."

"We can help with that."

"We?"

Though Cathal never spoke of anyone, Norah suspected that he had a girlfriend he couldn't bring home. A non-Catholic. A black girl.

"Me and Eamonn and Donal," Cathal said after a hesitation.

There wasn't any way he'd meant their brothers, but Norah let it go. "We'll see."

She went back to the foot of the stairs. "Magdalena! Pick any shirt!"

When she got back to the living room, Cathal said, "I hate to bring this up today, but the fire department, they *will* take care of you?"

"Three quarters," she said, and then, realizing he didn't know the lingo, she added, "Three quarters of Sean's pay for life."

Cathal nodded, and Norah read his thoughts: that can't be much for someone with three kids. It wasn't. Even with his full salary, Sean had still worked odd jobs as a carpenter when they came his way through the firehouse.

Maggie arrived in the living room still wearing her dress.

"Can I stay home?" she asked.

"You are not sitting around the house by yourself," Norah said. "You'll come to Gran's and get something to eat."

"I'm not hungry."

"You'll come to Gran's and not eat, then."

"Can I read?"

"You can stand on your head in the backyard if you like," Norah said.

Maggie noticed Brendan in the dining room and charged, shrieking, "Just because you ate all yours already doesn't mean you get to take mine!"

Brendan dove under the dining room table and scooted out the other side, bolting as Maggie frantically inventoried her Easter basket.

Brendan threw his arms around Norah's waist. Norah licked her thumb and rubbed away the chocolate from the corners of his mouth. She didn't spoil him — she didn't — but today she couldn't deal with it.

Maggie stomped into the living room. "Three of my chocolate eggs are gone."

Aidan shouted from the front door. "They're all waiting for us."

"For God's sake, Aidan, it isn't a surprise party." Norah pressed the heel of her hand into her firming belly and pushed a little. There was no Sean to cut them down with his decisive "Knock it off!" She was never the bad cop.

Norah put her narrowed eyes on her daughter. "Are you going to change?"

The front door banged. Aidan leaving. Norah shut her eyes.

"Norah?" Cathal said quietly.

She opened her eyes and said to Cathal, "Can you go with him? I'll sort this out."

During the Mass, the other wives had gone to Delia's house and set up. The food was arranged on the dining room table. Plates were out and napkins and plastic utensils. The refrigerator was stocked with Budweiser and Schaefer and Coke and ginger ale. There were stacks of plastic cups. Folding chairs set up. Ashtrays placed about.

Though she kept the black dress on, Norah discarded the stockings and heels. She would be a bohemian widow. When she thought the word "widow," it didn't seem as though Sean had died, only that the alphabet went mad after the first two letters of "wife."

Need anything? You're all right? He was, I know. Thank you, yes. He was.

I'm fine, thank you. I'm fine, really. Thank you. We'll be all right, thank you.

The rituals of the wake and funeral had let Norah hide the rattling of her bones. But now that they were nearing the end of the scripted part, her hands were being taken by fits. The right kept reaching for the left and clasping it tightly enough to hurt. She twisted her wedding ring around and around and kept grasping the gold replica of Sean's badge that she wore on a slim chain around her neck. Sean had given it to her not long after he'd transferred to the Glory Devlins.

Norah, near midnight the day of the fire — after Delia had left and she'd made Eileen go with her, which neither of them wanted, but Norah was too tired to care, after the children were finally in bed, and quiet, though maybe crying into their pillows (she refused to look) — she'd remembered Sean's wedding ring. Firemen weren't allowed to wear jewelry on the job, and she was forever telling Sean to take off the ring before going to work. It was a silver claddagh, of which hers was a more slender version. But she looked, and it was not on top of his bureau or hers. In a panic, she'd called the firehouse. *Check his locker,* she begged whoever answered the phone.

It was Frank Burkell who walked over. Norah opened the door before he could knock. Frank uncurled his fist, and after Norah snatched the ring, in the porch light she saw that the crown had left an impression in his palm.

A hardware store. Combustibles in the basement. An explosion. The floor collapsing. Sean plunging into the basement. But not before shoving the probie behind him to safety.

Norah could not stop her mind from chasing itself. The shove meant he'd realized it was about to go bad. For at least a few seconds, he'd known. It had taken the men almost a half hour to get to him. The collapse had blocked the only door to the basement. She hadn't asked if he'd radioed a mayday from the basement as it filled with water from burst pipes.

An hour before the wake began, she'd added Sean's wedding ring to the necklace. When she hurried up or down stairs, the Maltese cross and the ring clinked together, a sound almost a musical note but never quite.

Norah could not sit still. Conversations dove in each ear, swooped up her nose. She walked a circuit from the living room, on the parlor floor, and down the stairs to the garden floor, where the kitchen was. The door opened into the backyard, which abutted the yard of the firehouse, where Delia's father and maternal grandfather once worked. A ladder leaned against the wall that separated the yards, and as a child, Sean used to climb over it and hang out at the firehouse.

Sean's first permanent firehouse had been in Brownsville. During those years, Norah hadn't worried about him being killed in a fire so much as being shot running into one.

After three years, Sean had put in for a transfer, and got sent to the Glory Devlins. I did my time, he said. Norah assumed he made a few phone calls to make it happen. She never asked. It wasn't her business.

Delia sat in the blue easy chair, Sean's chair, and Nathaniel sat beside her on the ottoman. Her face was turned away. Nathaniel was leaning forward and speaking, too softly for Norah to hear.

She moved away without disturbing them.

Need anything? You're all right? He was, I know. Thank you, yes. He was.

She saw a tall man with dark blond hair standing by the front windows, and she took two steps toward him, ready to shout "Where have you been?" before she realized it was Keith Powell, the company chauffeur, the one who'd written the song about women firefighters. He'd sung it at the picnic last year. Norah recalled only two lines:

> *We used to sleep without any covers,*
> *Can't now in case they become our lovers.*

She'd laughed with a little bit of guilt, but she couldn't for the life of her understand why any woman would want to be a fireman. Eileen was out of her head.

She watched Eileen navigate the rooms. The men stopped talking as she came near, and most looked away.

Back in 1977, when women were allowed to take the test for the FDNY for the first time, and Eileen decided to do it, Sean laughed and said no way in hell would she pass the physical. Indeed, not a single woman had.

One of the other women who failed, Brenda Berkman, also happened to be a lawyer, and she filed a lawsuit, *Berkman et al. v. FDNY*. Eileen was informed by mail that she was one of the "et als." She'd said in amazement that suing never would have occurred to her. None of the men imagined the FDNY would lose the lawsuit.

But the judge ruled that the current physical test was unfair and that the department had to design a new one that actually tested the skills used on the job. That is, a test that didn't rely almost entirely on upper-body strength. Bullshit, Sean said. How the fuck could firefighting not require upper-body strength?

Eileen and fifty-two other women passed the new test.

Yeah, Sean said, and all the guys said, because they made it easier, not better. If the women had passed the same physical as the men, fine. Let them on. But they didn't. They passed *the soft test*.

Eileen had graduated from the fire academy last year, a full five years after she first applied. So did eleven other women.

Norah tried to slip past Grace Grady with a quick nod, but Grace put a hand on Norah's shoulder, her pretty green eyes lit with sympathy. Norah barely stopped herself from slapping her hand away. Grace was the girl at school who was lovely without trying, and you'd hate her for it if she weren't so nice.

It was Grace who'd taken charge of setting up the house this morning. If the power went out, Grace would have candles and extra batteries for each flashlight. She'd probably never used her sleeve to wipe her kids' noses, and she'd surely never had to pull the Halloween decorations off the windows because she'd run out of candy. Norah bet that on the nights her husband worked, Grace still cooked meatloaf or chicken for her three boys, not hot dogs or grilled cheese the way Norah did.

Grace had a small stack of dirty paper plates in one hand.

"Norah, don't forget we're right up the street. Kev said to let you know that he already takes Danny to baseball practice and he'd be happy to bring Aidan along too. Danny said he didn't mind losing out on playing first base because it was Aidan . . . And Brian's my soccer player. He said he'd teach Brendan a few tricks. Whatever you need."

That's just what we need, Norah thought. Football tricks for my four-year-old. Not soccer but football. All her years in the States and she still turned things Irish in her mind. She nodded, and Grace pulled her hand back.

"We'll miss him, Norah," she said. There were tears in her eyes.

Norah thanked her and continued on. She felt Grace's gaze between her shoulder blades.

She went down to the garden level again, intending to step outside for some air. She recalled how strange it had looked to her when she first arrived in Brooklyn to see doors built into the sides of stairs, as if to some kind of secret passageway. As soon as Norah opened the door, she heard the voices of firemen and smelled the cigarette smoke.

— that story, right. With Sean and the guy who gave us the finger?

Norah, though she'd been about to slam the door in frustration, stopped.

Nah, I don't think so.

I know it. It's fucking funny.

This was a couple years ago. We're heading back to the firehouse after another fucking false alarm and Tommy's driving. It's got to be eleven at night.

We're coming to the light and this asshole in a Toyota shoots right in front of us, cuts us off. Tommy slams on the brakes and hits the horn, and the prick sticks his hand out the window and gives us the finger.

Asshole.

Yeah, so, Tommy, he's pissed as shit. He floors it. He goes around the corner, goes around the corner, we're hanging on in the back. I don't know how he does it, but we beat the guy to the next intersection. He's sitting there at a red light. Tommy stops the truck and gets out. You know him, he's a big fucking guy. He goes over to the car and opens the door and pulls the guy out and he says something we can't hear.

So he gets back in the truck, we're heading back and it's dead quiet. Then Sean goes, "Hey, Tom, you misunderstood the guy. He wasn't flipping us off. He was telling us we're number one."

Norah smiled into the general laughter. Sean never told her that but then he'd never talked much about work. There had to be a lot of stories, she realized. Stories starring Sean. Sean, alive. Stories that would come to Aidan and Brendan someday.

Norah went back upstairs and into the living room, trying to prepare for the onslaught of pity. Brendan scampered over and declared he was hungry. She didn't see the other two, but she knew Aidan would be in the center of a pack of boys, with Cathal nearby, she assumed. If they weren't in Delia's yard, it was because they'd already gone over the fence to the firehouse. Aidan would want to show his uncle Sean's locker, which still had to be cleaned out, and then no doubt he'd take Cathal up to the bunkroom to visit Sean's bed.

Maggie might be with Joe Paladino's daughter, Isabel, who was her age, though they weren't quite friends, mostly due to Maggie's reserve, a thing that had puzzled Sean and frankly annoyed him. More likely, Maggie was in her grandmother's bedroom, with Delia's books. If Sean were here, he'd say, "Put the book away, Magee." If he were here. If it weren't his funeral.

Grateful for a job, Norah took Brendan's hand and led him to the dining room. The smell of cheese always got to her in the first two months. She'd been avoiding the dining room, though if she threw up, surely it would be put down to nerves.

Ray Cavalieiri had handled the food. He owned a deli with his brothers, and he told her not to worry, they'd get everybody fed. Indeed, Cavalieiri's supplied trays of ziti, lasagna and meatballs, and cold cuts for sandwiches. Roast beef and ham and Swiss and American cheese. There were rolls and Italian bread. Salads and olives and pickles. Norah wasn't sure if the deli had also taken care of the soda and beer and ice, but somebody certainly had.

Seeing the abundance of food made Norah suddenly wonder about the cost. Was Ray expecting to be paid? Would he bill her? Or was he donating the food?

There was maybe a twenty in her wallet. The morning after the fire, she'd snatched the checkbook from the drawer of the desk in the corner of their bedroom where Sean sat and paid the bills every month. She hadn't recorded the checks she'd written for the funeral home and for the casket. She'd ordered a wreath from the children and one from herself. *Beloved Father, Beloved Husband.* But she'd put those on the credit card, as well as her black dress and a navy-blue one for Maggie, whose only other dress was her Easter dress, and she wore that on the second day of the wake. The boys wore the same suits for both.

Nobody had ever told her that you spent the day after a death shopping. When was the credit card bill due? Norah felt a shot of panic. She'd never thought of herself as a helpless sort of wife. But when was the electric bill due? The mortgage? The phone bill?

Would she get Sean's paycheck on his usual payday? Would it be his last full paycheck? It would have to be. Would they keep her and the children on his insurance?

The FDNY had assigned her a liaison, but so far they'd only talked about the funeral.

If she couldn't keep up with the mortgage, would she have to move all of them into an apartment? Stuff all the kids into one bedroom and keep the other for herself? She could divide the kids between the two bedrooms and sleep on a sofa bed.

The questions were like bees diving at her head. She always waved her hand frantically when a bee got too close, and Sean would laugh and tell her that was exactly the way to get stung.

Norah swallowed hard, fighting the rise of sick.

There would surely be a lot of leftover food. She would donate it to the nuns of St. Maren's, the cloistered convent in the neighborhood, and that would be her last bit of shopping for them. Buying groceries for the nuns who had retreated from the world had seemed little enough money to spare before, but not now.

It wasn't long after she was first married that she accompanied Grace on a shopping trip so Grace could take her through what to buy. Oatmeal and fruit. Milk and juice. Bread and cheese. The nuns never said what they liked to eat. They simply accepted what they were given. She went with Grace to the convent, around the back to the one public room, the turn room, and watched Grace place the grocery bags in the turn, a revolving cabinet in which the parishioners left their offerings for the nuns in exchange for their prayers.

For prayers, people tended to leave sweets, cakes and cookies they bought at the bakery.

Grace had explained that it was the wives of the firemen who took care of the practical side of things. The founder of the convent was Saint Maren of Ireland, the patron of those in danger of drowning and those in danger from fire. There was Saint Florian, the patron of firefighters, and it was his medal the wives all wore. But there was no patron saint for the wives.

"The wives of firemen don't need a patron saint. They're saints themselves."

That was the joke they told now, and maybe it was as old as the custom, which Grace said went back at least to her grandmother, but probably further. The wives of the Glory Devlins had adopted Saint Maren as their patron.

Norah had done her duty by the saint, hadn't she? She'd gone to the grocery store and filled a basket with things for them, even if she'd never actually prayed to Saint Maren. It should have been enough.

As if her thinking of the nuns had conjured their presence, she saw on the table of food a plate of soda bread, each slice wrapped individually, and wondered who had brought it. The soda breads were baked by the nuns and sent out of the convent wrapped for sale at Agnello's bakery. The nuns used some of the money to pay for the upkeep of the convent, and the rest they gave away.

One slice from every batch was blessed, and whoever ate it would have a prayer answered. There were stories of women conceiving who had not been able to. Letters arriving from husbands away at war.

Norah wondered if the person who'd brought the bread knew of the blessing. Surely they knew the only thing Norah would want was Sean to be alive. Not the only thing. Perhaps not. She picked up a piece of the soda bread and held it for a minute. What if she ate it and ended up with twins? What if two babies instead of one was considered a blessing, and never mind what she actually wanted?

Her hands shaking, she made Brendan a cheese sandwich on a pumpernickel roll, spread thickly with mayonnaise. Brendan dove under the dining room table to eat it. She tried to coax him out.

"It's hot under there! Brennie, you can go outside on the stoop and eat."

Brendan mashed his hand into his sandwich to flatten it, ignoring her. She felt the heat rising in her face as people turned to stare. One of the other wives nudged her husband.

Kevin Grady, who was standing nearby, said, "Hey, Mrs. O'Reilly, I'll keep an eye on him if you want."

Grace's oldest son was fifteen or sixteen, and was no doubt used to keeping his two younger brothers in line. The middle one, the football player, was about thirteen, she thought, and Danny was in Maggie's class. The boys all favored Grace, with her green eyes and very dark hair from the Italian side of her family.

"I guess he's all right." Norah pushed her hair out of her face.

"Yeah, sure he is." Kevin squatted and peered under the table. "Hey, Bren, man, you setting up camp under there or what?"

With a failing smile, she thanked Kevin and abandoned Brendan to him. She envied the Gradys the simplicity of their family. She'd often wished her own children were better organized, with the two boys close in age but Maggie had been born on June 21, and a year later Aidan, on June 19. Which made them the same age on June 20. For the first three years, they'd had a co-party on that day, but after that it became impossible to please them both, and so she had to organize a boy party and a girl party on the nearest weekend, one held on Saturday and the other on Sunday.

The long break between the boys was her fault. She thought sometimes that her Big Irish Family was one of the things Sean had been attracted to when they first met. He had this idea that families with lots of children operated like baseball teams, with everyone bonded together for a common purpose. He'd never thought to wonder how well you could know older brothers who were gone to another country by the time you were eleven.

When Brendan turned two, Sean began to suggest having another. But the thought made Norah restless. Without pregnancy stretching her in ways she shouldn't be stretched, she might take an interesting job doing something or other, or write a children's book, something Irishy but nothing to do with leprechauns. Or maybe she would take some college classes.

Sean never asked about her day. He didn't understand how much of her life was simply boring. When he worked twenty-four, Norah felt abandoned in this foreign country.

But once Brendan started half-day nursery school, she'd begun to weigh the odds of her actually doing any of those things against how happy Sean would be. She'd been hoping the new baby would be a uniter, someone they could all root for. Another girl.

Slightly stupefied, her eyes gritty as though sand had blown in them, Norah wound through the rooms again, moving with pretend purpose. She stepped out of the living room and bumped into Amred Lehane, studying the family pictures in the hallway.

"I can hardly believe this has happened for the second time in five years," he said. "The grandson of a fireman who died in the line of duty has also died in the line of duty."

"The second time?" Norah asked, confused. A mistake, she knew as soon as she said it. Amred was a walking encyclopedia of FDNY history.

"Bill O'Connor, who died in Waldbaum's," Amred said. "His grand-father died of burns. Delia's father, Gentleman Jack Keegan, in 1941. Now Sean."

Norah began edging away. She had no place to put other people's sad stories.

"Bill O'Connor's wife was there, you know, at Waldbaum's."

"I know that," Norah snapped.

The men talked ceaselessly about what caused the roof of the Wald-baum's to collapse in August of '78, and how the six men who'd been up there venting the roof fell into the fire.

The wives, though, talked about Louise. How Louise came by the firehouse early in the morning, right as the night tour was ending, with the kids in the car, to pick up Bill for a trip to the beach. She'd followed the rig to the fire. From the roof, Bill waved to Louise and their three children. Minutes later, he was dead.

Norah left Amred and took off upstairs to Sean's old bedroom, be-cause if she didn't get ten minutes alone, her bones might dissolve, and then what would happen to her kids? But in the bedroom, Eileen was standing at the window, her shoulders slack beneath the blue shirt of her dress uniform, her eyes red-rimmed. She didn't turn when Norah came in.

"They wouldn't let me dig for him, you know. We'll bring him out, Sean's captain says to me."

"I'm sure he didn't want you to see, Eileen," Norah said sharply. "You're his sister."

"I'm a firefighter," she said stubbornly.

Are you? Norah thought. Hasn't this gone far enough? She'd gotten Sean's attention and her mother's. Now Sean was gone, half the audience.

"I said, That's my brother, and they said, He's our brother. And you know what?"

Eileen paused so long that Norah didn't think she was going to continue.

"I left. I walked away. Sean didn't want me on the job."

"Eileen, please." Norah wondered how many beers she'd had. Three at least, no doubt.

"I've been thinking about quitting."

Norah was surprised, though Sean had predicted she would, once she realized that very little about firefighting was romantic.

"I love the job. I fucking love it," Eileen said fiercely. "But the bullshit? Fighting fires is easy compared to living with firemen. I know some guys were giving Sean a hard time too. Saying he told me to take the test or some crap like that."

Norah rubbed her eyes. He certainly had not. One Thanksgiving night, long after Delia had left and the children were in bed, Sean and Eileen were still drinking, and Sean began teasing her about failing the physical. Eileen, not amused, recited the points of the lawsuit. Soon they were both yelling, and then Sean stretched out on the floor and, tucking his arms behind his head, told her to go ahead and drag him out of the fire — unless women were going to specialize in rescuing kids and pets? Eileen aimed a kick at his head, and Norah had to get between them, hissing that if they woke the kids, she would set them both on fire and they could have fun putting each other out. Why, she thought now, would she ever have said such a thing?

Thankfully, in the past few months, Sean had been less furious and more worried about how the men were treating her. For the first months on the job, firefighters rotated from firehouse to firehouse. Wherever Eileen worked, they'd have her back at fires; it wasn't that. But in between runs, in the firehouses, what the fuck was going on? When he asked Eileen, she'd only say that she was handling it.

Two weeks ago, Eileen was assigned her permanent firehouse, and Sean, satisfied, told Norah that Eileen would be okay there. The captain was a law-and-order type who wouldn't put up with any bullshit.

Norah didn't ask, but she assumed Sean had pulled strings to get Eileen in there, and that Eileen didn't know it.

"Sean would have been all right, Eileen."

"Yeah?" She looked at Norah hopefully.

Norah hesitated slightly. "I think so."

Eileen yanked her hair out of its bun. It fell down around her shoulders. She was thirty-three but looked like a college girl.

Norah often forgot that they'd once been close. Before she'd taken up with Sean. Her wedding day, the way it came up so quickly, like a storm, and her own family not there, for much the same reasons they hadn't come to the funeral, though she and Sean had pledged to travel to Ireland in the summer. Her parents had been pleased with that idea, because the neighbors would turn out to see the American husband and baby without knowing when, precisely, the wedding had taken place.

Eileen had been her bridesmaid. Norah had been happy to have her best friend in America as her sister-in-law, but somehow their own friendship had fallen away, leaving only the sister-in-law part. Eileen was still single and Norah was not, but Norah thought it was also that she couldn't talk to Eileen about Sean. Eileen shrugged or took his side whenever Norah issued a complaint. He left early for work, Norah would say. Just to get out of the house, away from the chaos. And Eileen would defend him, saying that he liked to get to the firehouse before nine to bullshit with the guys coming off the night shift. They all did. On St. Patrick's Day, he left at eight in the morning to march in the parade and didn't stagger in until almost three the next morning. Well, it's St. *Patrick's* Day, Eileen would answer.

"Eileen, I need to lie down for a minute," Norah said.

"You okay?" Eileen asked, standing up straight.

Never again, Norah thought. She said, "I just need a minute. Can you go find the kids and see if they're okay?"

"Right, right."

"And check on your mother."

"Sure," she said with much less vigor.

Eileen left, shutting the door behind her. Norah jammed the desk chair under the doorknob. She curled up on the bed. Sean had slept in this room through his whole childhood, never imagining he'd be given only thirty-five years.

Sean had passed the lieutenant's test, and she'd already been told that he would be posthumously promoted. All well and good. There would be a nice ceremony, but the pension she would get as a fire widow was based on the money he'd been currently making.

A job would probably be easy enough to come by. Some fireman or some fireman's wife or sister-in-law or fourth cousin would know someone who needed someone who could type or answer phones. She wondered about Irish Dreams, the travel agency over in Park Slope, and the position there that had been waiting for her upon her arrival in New York thanks to her aunt, who'd been the office manager. Helen, her mother's sister, had left Ireland when she was barely twenty. She'd come over just in time for the Depression. Depressed America, she'd liked to say, was better than any kind of Ireland.

Norah knew that her own former co-worker Marian Clark ran the place now, but she could hardly ask her for a job. It was altogether possible that Marian had been at the church today, somewhere in the back. Glad, finally, that Sean had never looked twice at her?

The Glory Devlins would no doubt organize a fundraiser that might bring in enough to pay Aidan's and Maggie's tuition at Holy Rosary for the next year. Brendan would be in public school for kindergarten, since Holy Rosary didn't have one. A year's grace there.

If she had to, she'd put them all in public school. Sean and Eileen had gone to Catholic school, and Sean insisted their children would as well, too bruised by the stories of his mother's years as a public school teacher and principal.

Norah agreed. She didn't much buy the claims of being scarred for life by nuns and priests. Eileen went on about it now and again. Delia would say sharply that if she'd been better behaved, they'd have left her alone. Norah secretly agreed.

Still, her children ending up in public school was hardly adding to the tragedy.

At the Mass today, Father Halloran told the congregation how impressed he was by "Norah's strength" when he went to see her the afternoon of the fire. Norah did not recall saying much of anything. She'd been watching the front door for Sean. Father Halloran told her to come by the rectory if she needed to talk. His own parents were from County Down, he added.

Norah wondered what the priest would do if she did indeed appear in the rectory office, if she sat down in a chair opposite him, if she crossed her legs and explained that she'd lost the member of her family she loved best and now she didn't want to be the mother anymore. Not of three children, and sure as hell not of four. He'd probably stammer and say, "Most widows keep their children, Norah." Then maybe he'd jump into a verse of "The Mountains of Mourne."

Here in the United States, a woman could. Nobody needed to know, ever, and were it to be discovered, surely her grief would excuse her.

"I was out of my head," Norah said aloud, rehearsing.

Sean would never forgive her. Maybe she could plead ignorance, like Mary. The Immaculate Abortion. An angel would appear and say, I'm taking it back. And Norah would answer, Take all of them back.

Set free, she would go home to Ireland, and back in time, find her twenty-year-old self, which held like a pearl the twenty-year-old soul who knew hardly anything at all. Somehow, she'd displace that girl, slip back into her childless body and her childless mind. She would never take the life handed to her by her sister when it became clear that Aoife herself couldn't have it. America would remain untouched by them both.

On Saturday afternoons, Aoife and Norah rode their bikes out to the farm where their father had grown up, the only boy in a family of eight. His two oldest sisters, the ones who'd neither married nor gone to America, lived together in the house. The land was leased to a neighbor who farmed it.

Even when they were very young, Aoife and Norah knew the town was divided over what her father had done. Jimmy Mulryan sold the family farm out from under his sisters because he knew he'd do better as a shopkeeper. Ambitious, he thought too much of himself to be a farmer.

Veronica Daley was a pretty girl, but wasn't her father's grocery prettier? Some thought it was a sin how Jimmy Mulryan made his two sisters tenants on what had been their family's land. Some said he'd seen his chance and he'd taken it. He'd hardly turned the sisters out.

In their bicycle baskets, Aoife and Norah had bread, cans of soup, sausages and a few other items their father thought his two sisters might like.

The farm was at the edge of Ballyineen. Aoife rode ahead and Norah pedaled behind her. At the foot of the drive, they hopped off their bikes, and after taking the grocery bags out of their baskets, they set the bikes on their sides and walked up to the house. One of their aunts would be watching from the window and would have the door open before they reached it.

Aoife and Norah took off their shoes, even if it wasn't raining. Every week, they said they weren't hungry as they'd just eaten, and the aunts would exchange a glance and sniff.

You like what your mother makes for your tea, then?

Norah said nothing, too afraid, but Aoife always said they did, they liked it very much. The aunts would share another sour look. One would begin unpacking the groceries. Now and again she would hold up an item for her sister to see.

"The other brand costs ten cents more."

"Too much for himself to spare."

When the groceries were put away, one aunt or the other would say, "And how much does his lordship want?"

Aoife would say what their father told them to say. "He doesn't want anything. It's for you to have."

It would go on for another few minutes, the aunts trying to get Aoife to take their money, though Norah noticed that neither ever reached for her pocketbook.

Aoife and Norah would ride home, lighter without the bags in their baskets. Norah was so relieved to have it over for another week, she sometimes laughed aloud, and Aoife would turn her head, eyes off the road, against the rules, and she would laugh too.

When it rained very hard and the road was too muddy to ride, they had to get off their bikes and walk. They should have gone back to wait it out, but neither could bear the thought of sitting with their aunts in the cold front room.

"Don't you feel sorry for them?" Norah asked once. "Even a little?"

Aoife was twelve and Norah was eleven. Aoife had the answers.

They were at the top of the hill, Ballyineen in view, before she answered.

"I don't feel sorry for them," Aoife said. "They should have gone away."

Their mother's sister was the one relative who'd left Ireland and kept in touch.

When they were girls, Aoife and Norah stayed awake long after the light went out and whispered across the lane between their beds.

Their aunt Helen worked for a travel agency in New York City, and along with letters home, she often sent brochures from the trips they offered.

Their mother asked what good it did her, working in that place, when she never took the trips herself. She could have, Veronica said forcefully. No husband, no children. Helen could have gone anywhere she liked, whenever she liked.

"We will," Aoife told Norah. They'd go together to Italy and Spain and France and Greece. They studied the pictures of sunny beaches and the ocean that didn't look at all like their ocean. The blue made it look like a painting. Often the brochures had small maps on the back that said things like *Places of Interest. Local Attractions.*

But then, when Aoife was thirteen and Norah was twelve, one of the travel agents Aunt Helen worked with started his own business and asked Helen to come with him. In her letter home, she wrote, "Mr. Fitzgerald has stolen me away."

The new office was not in Manhattan but Brooklyn, because the rents were much cheaper. Most of their business was conducted over the phone; nobody had to come to Brooklyn to book a trip. And Mr. Fitzgerald was looking to target those who'd always wanted to visit Ireland, and those perhaps because they'd seen *The Quiet Man.* Those who'd left decades ago and had not been back. The new agency was called Irish Dreams.

The brochures Helen began sending from Brooklyn were of the Ring of Kerry and the Burren. Aoife always took a quick look and flung them to the floor. Norah took Aoife's side, but she did think that it wasn't as though Aunt Helen herself were getting on a plane and flying to Ireland again and again. She'd left at nineteen and had only come back one single Christmas.

Mr. Fitzgerald had stolen Aunt Helen away for her brogue, but before long she was doing far more at Irish Dreams than answering the phone.

From spring through fall, not so often in the winter, tourists who'd booked through Irish Dreams arrived in her hometown. It had been Helen's idea to send the groups over to Ballyineen, or, in Irish, Baile Iníon, which meant Town of Daughters. Americans loved the strange story about how no sons were born in the town for almost a hundred years after the famine.

The itinerary suggested a meal in the pub, or that they go to Mulryan's grocery and buy sandwiches for a picnic. Helen instructed her sister to have sandwiches made and wrapped, ready to buy. Ham and cheese or roast beef. Make them thick and don't butter the bread. Americans don't care for that. Have packets of mustard or mayonnaise available for them to choose from.

Norah's father objected.

"Across the ocean, and she's still the boss of you?" Jimmy said.

"It's for the boys," Veronica answered. "To build up the business for them."

"Any one of them comes back, he'll be lucky to get a job off me," Jimmy said.

But he never spoke another word against it.

Norah thought it was when Cathal left that their mother and father started living in separate parts of the house, meeting for tea in the kitchen.

"We won't see the boys again," Aoife said scornfully of their three brothers. "Not for good. Why would they come back here when they've got the run of London?"

Aoife and Norah made the sandwiches, first under their mother's eye and then, when she was satisfied, without her supervision.

Americans turned up in the store, often muddy and wet from walking around the hills and the small cemetery beside the church.

"Helen in the office said we should say hello to you," one or the other visitor would say, followed by a look, like they expected something.

Norah never had a guess as to what until the night her mother, talking about the man who wanted to record them all saying things like "Top of the mornin' to you," said, "Helen's made us into characters, like in an American film."

In 1967, when Norah was eighteen, she went into the grocery, working the cash register. It was important to have one of the family back there, her father thought. Saying hello and the like. Norah did, and she smiled, but her tongue often pressed at the back of her teeth as she lis-tened to the old ones complaining about the price of this or that. Jimmy also hired their neighbor's youngest son, Hugh Quinlevan, to stock the shelves and make deliveries.

Two years later, Norah still hadn't thought of anything better to do.

By then Aoife had a job in Butler's dress shop, where she persuaded women to buy more than they came in for, like a top to match the skirt they were getting or stockings with a pattern on them.

Aoife wasn't prettier than Norah. It wasn't that. They had the same fine brown hair with some sparks of red from their father's mother. Their own mother's small nose with its light freckles. But Aoife was livelier. Somehow, she got more out of her face, her voice, her hands.

During her Christmas Day phone call in 1970, Aunt Helen asked if Aoife would like to come and work in New York for a year. She'd spon-sor her for a visa.

Veronica and Jimmy didn't feel they could say no when Helen asked for their daughter. Not after all the business Helen had sent them.

So it was arranged that Aoife would go over in late June 1971, just af-ter her twenty-third birthday. Helen offered to send the fare, but Veron-ica said half would be fine. She would match it, and Aoife herself would pay for new clothes and other expenses.

After that, Aoife talked of nothing but America. Peter Byrne, who wanted to be Aoife's boyfriend, didn't understand why she was going when she had a job at home. He himself had been running Byrne's pub since his father died the year before. People spoke well of Peter because he canceled his own plans for university, just for a bit, until his two youngest brothers were grown. Aoife told Peter she wanted adventure, and though Norah pretended to be on her sister's side, in secret she agreed with Peter.

In their room at night, Aoife drew New York from her imagination. The bigness. The excitement. The freedom to go anywhere and not have to tell your mam and da where you were and when you'd be back.

"You'll be living in Aunt Helen's flat, though," Norah said.

"She's different than Mam."

"You can't know that," Norah said.

Aoife laughed. "I do, though. Didn't she agree to write and offer me a job?"

Norah sat up in bed. "You asked her to do it? Why?"

"God, Norah, I don't have the money to pay for a trip to America," she said. "I knew Mam and Da would offer to pay if Aunt Helen asked for me. Mam won't ever say no to her."

Norah said nothing.

"But listen, Norah, I won't leave you stuck here. I'll save what I can and help you with the airfare," Aoife said. "It'll take no time."

"I can't leave," Norah said, appalled. "We'll all be gone then."

The bedclothes rustled as Aoife turned over. "There may be jobs in Ireland these days, but there's still no air."

"I might go to Dublin and live for a bit," Norah said.

"Why settle for Dublin when you could go to New York?" Aoife said. "Is it Hugh?"

"Hugh?" Norah felt her face heat. They had been seeing each other for a while but hiding it because, without having to say it aloud, they knew it would get her father's hopes up.

"He's boring as butter, Norah."

"I can live without taking myself off to New York for a year," Norah said.

Aoife said nothing.

"It's only for a year, isn't that right?" Norah said.

"I'm going to see how things develop."

Norah turned her back to her sister.

In May, Aoife went to visit her friend Cynthia, who was attending University College, Dublin. She said she was going to spend the weekend shopping for clothes to take to America.

It wasn't her idea, Aoife later said. She'd never heard of the Irish women's liberation movement, and Cynthia had to explain it twice at least before she understood what it was about. But once she knew, Aoife admitted that she'd agreed readily enough to board a train to Belfast with Cynthia and about fifty other women, to buy contraceptives and carry them back to Dublin, daring customs officials to arrest them. They waved the packets of condoms and diaphragms and spermicides in the air and declared to the customs officers that they were on the Pill. They were bringing contraband into the country. Shouldn't they be arrested? But they weren't. The customs men waved them through, embarrassed, wanting the scene to be over.

Much had been made of it in the newspapers. There was great disapproval all over Ballyineen. Father Dillon declared that they were going against God and against nature.

When Jimmy called Aoife downstairs, both she and Norah were in their bedroom, waiting to be called for tea. Norah was on her bed with a book, but Aoife wasn't even pretending to read. At their father's sharp voice, Aoife stood and headed for the stairs. Norah followed, half expecting their father to tell her that this didn't concern her and to leave.

Jimmy was beside the counter and Veronica across from him, at the sink.

Aoife took her usual place at the kitchen table, and so Norah did as well. They sat across from each other. Norah tapped Aoife's foot with her own.

Veronica began. She wanted to know if it was true, what Mary Mahon had heard.

"Mary Mahon?" Aoife repeated, as if she didn't know their neighbor.

Aoife was going to be the ruin of them, didn't she realize? There was no telling how many customers would go all the way down the hill to McDermott's now.

"Women should decide how many babies they'll have," Aoife said.

Jimmy looked away but said, "You've disgraced this family."

"It's 1971 for God's sake!" Aoife said.

"If this is how you behave at home, what'll you get up to in America?" Veronica said. "If you go at all. I don't know now if you should."

"You're right. I'll not be going." Aoife tried to keep her voice casual, but she couldn't hide the tremor.

Beneath the table, Norah put her foot over Aoife's foot.

"What are you talking about?" Jimmy said.

"Peter Byrne and myself have decided to get married in June."

Jimmy made a low noise in his throat.

Veronica said, "Next June?"

Norah had to look down, away from the last speck of hope in her mother's tired face.

"This June. In two weeks." Aoife folded her hands on the table.

That night, in their bedroom, Norah said into the dark, "Aoife?"

"Hmm?" Aoife said as if she were half asleep, though Norah knew she wasn't close.

"He's nice, Peter is," Norah said.

"He is."

Norah listened to her sister's breathing.

"I said no to him fifty times before," Aoife said, "but I didn't want to get to America and be some stupid Irish girl with no experience at anything. So I thought, just the once. It'll be goodbye to him."

"Is there any reason you wouldn't go to England before you go to New York? Visit the boys, maybe?" Norah asked.

"Why don't I take care of it in England and be on my way to New York?" Aoife put a laugh after the words. "I don't know."

"But —"

"I don't know, Norah, I don't. And that's all I'm going to say to you. Good night."

The next morning at the breakfast table, Aoife, reaching for the milk, said, "Since I won't be going to New York, I think Norah should."

Jimmy looked up from his newspaper and Veronica turned from the stove, where she was frying the rashers.

Norah put down her spoon. She could guess her parents' thoughts. If they were to simply substitute Norah, there didn't need to be an embarrassing admission. They could let it be known that Norah was the more responsible one. Helen wouldn't be left telling her American boss that the Irish niece wouldn't be coming.

"I don't have a passport. The visa, all that," Norah said. "I'm sure Aunt Helen can find someone before I can get it all. Long before then."

"If she needed to, she could," Veronica said, her shoulders gone straight with hope. "But she could say it's just until her niece comes."

Norah looked at Aoife, who lowered her eyes.

March 1972

To get a better look at him, Norah leaned forward until the bar pressed against her ribcage. Handsome wasn't the right word, somehow, for Sean O'Reilly. But he had a face that you wanted to keep seeing. He was tall. If she were standing beside him, Norah would just reach his shoulder. He accepted money and left the change on the bar, giving a nod and quick smile when greeted by name.

Marian jabbed her in the spine. "Don't stare."

So Marian had a crush on him. Norah nearly laughed.

Marian Clark was one of the three travel agents employed by Irish Dreams and the only one Norah's age. William was a bachelor and Patricia was divorced. The two shared a host of inside jokes and all their cigarette breaks. Often, they went out for a drink after work, calling goodbye to Norah and Marian as they left for Lehane's together.

Today, though, William called, "Come out for a St. Paddy's Day drink, girls?"

It was shortly before closing time, six p.m. Norah's own relief at being asked was reflected in Marian's face. It was ridiculous. Weren't they the young ones? But Norah herself was new to the country, and Marian was plain and serious.

Lehane's was jammed. The jostling crowd seemed a wave that might break over Sean O'Reilly at any minute. A skinny man who might have been anywhere between forty and sixty was perched on a stool behind the bar, surveying the crowd with a bemused expression. He sipped from a glass that might have held either soda or whiskey. He made no move to help Sean, who was pouring a set of shots.

William and Patricia were guarding the small table they'd managed to snag. Norah spoke over her shoulder to Marian in as near a whisper as she could and still be heard.

"What's wrong with the other bartender? Why isn't he helping?"

"That's not a bartender," Marian said. "That's Amred. His sister runs the place."

Norah nodded. Marian had a way of speaking that suggested you should know the answers to your own questions. Marian had been at "the agency" for almost two years. That was what Helen called Irish Dreams. When William and Patricia said it, they put an emphasis on the word: the *ay*-gency. Norah was sure they were testing her, to see what they could get away with saying about Helen in front of her. No doubt they were outright mean behind Helen's back.

Norah felt sorry for her aunt, something she could never have imagined the day she got on the plane in Dublin. Helen didn't speak badly of a single member of the staff, but she ate her sandwich and drank tea from a thermos by herself at her desk in the corner instead of the small lunchroom in the back.

At home, nobody wore green for St. Patrick's Day, and Norah had appeared for breakfast in blue. Helen, who was not good before eleven a.m. and rarely spoke to her in the morning, went into her own closet and reappeared with a green sweater that had white shamrocks embroidered on the cuffs. If Mr. Fitzgerald came in, he would be very annoyed to see Norah not in the spirit of the day, Helen said as she handed it to her.

At only six-thirty in the evening, everyone was well into it. The noise level seemed to rise by the second. Patches of song broke out around Lehane's.

"Sean's been quiet since he got back," Marian said. "He works here, but he doesn't hang out when he's off."

Without taking her eyes off Sean, Norah asked, "Back from where?"

"Nam," Marian said, and Norah looked at her to see if she was serious.

"Vietnam?" Norah had barely paid attention to Vietnam at home, but since coming to America she heard about it constantly.

"I wrote to him when he was over there. He never had time to write back, but then, when he was in Arizona — that's where he finished his tour after he got injured." Marian smiled. "He sent me a postcard."

Sean was making his way down to their end of the bar. That he'd been in a war made him seem a real grown-up, while the rest of them were just pretending.

"How do you know him?" Norah asked. She hoped she didn't sound rude, but she could hardly imagine.

Marian spoke close to Norah's ear. She and Sean had gone to grammar school together. Norah had already heard the story of how the nuns had given Marian's father a hard time about enrolling her and her sister at Holy Rosary because their mother was Jewish.

Marian's mother and father had been disowned by their families when they eloped just two months after they met. Three years later, when her mother took off, Marian's father brought her and her sister back to Brooklyn. Their grandmother let them move in only after the two of them were baptized. In fact, their father had to leave their suitcases on the stoop and take them to the church, where Father Halloran interrupted his own dinner to toss water on their foreheads. Sarah tried to bite him. Marian didn't remember any of this, but her sister said that was the night their father went into the drunk he never quite came out of.

Marian kept her eyes on Sean as she explained to Norah that there were a few other kids in the neighborhood who had one parent. Mostly, the fathers had been killed in the war. But Sean's father had left his mother. They had that in common.

Norah watched as a girl with long red hair muscled her way up to the bar.

"Sean!" she called.

Sean kept working, though he had to have heard her, even over the din.

The redhead rapped on the bar, hard, three times. "Sean! Come on!"

Norah couldn't believe the rudeness. Didn't she see there were a dozen people ahead of her?

"Knock it off, Eileen," Sean said, his eyes on the glass he held beneath the tap.

"Mick's not coming," the redhead — Eileen — said. "Jackass is probably passed out already and you know it. Let me come back there and help."

Sean pushed fresh beers across the bar. "Five," he said.

Eileen raised her voice. "You can't handle this crowd alone all night. Amred? Tell him!"

Amred said, "Let her, Sean. This way, if Mick does show his face, I can get Lizzie to toss him out."

Sean glared at Eileen, then jabbed a finger at her. "I get half your tips."

"Fair enough." Eileen disappeared into the crowd. Seconds later, she popped up behind the bar.

"Hmm. I heard they weren't even talking," Marian said.

"Did they break up or something?" Norah asked.

"Break up?" Marian snorted. "No, that's his sister."

"His sister?" Norah repeated. They weren't remotely similar.

Eileen handled her end of the bar as expertly as Sean, who moved down so that he was taking the order of the blond girl beside Norah and Marian. The blond leaned forward for the occasion, pressing her cleavage against the bar. She ordered a gin and tonic and a vodka and cranberry.

"For my girlfriend," she said hopefully.

Marian made a small noise of disgust in the back of her throat as Sean started to make the drinks.

"Sean," Marian said. "Hi."

Sean glanced at her. "Hey, what's up?"

Norah flinched at the flatness in his tone. She willed Marian to notice and be quiet, but Marian said, "Work was crazy today. St. Patrick's Day is like Christmas Eve in Santa's workshop for us." Clearly, she'd rehearsed the line.

A flicker of a smile crossed Sean's face. "I bet."

"I have this couple celebrating their fortieth wedding anniversary and they want to go to Belfast. I keep telling them that might not be a good idea. Better than asking, Do you want to get killed?"

"Crazy shit going on there, yeah," he agreed. "Ten," he said to the blond, who then handed him a crumpled twenty.

"I don't think you've met Norah?"

"Don't think so," he said.

"She works with me at Irish Dreams. She's Irish."

Norah nodded, and Amred Lehane said, "Ah, Helen's niece!"

Sean gave the blond her change. She fanned the bills and carefully placed them on the bar. Sean gave a quick nod of thanks and turned away from her and looked at Norah.

"From Ireland Irish?" he asked.

Norah nodded. "I came over in January. It would have been a little sooner but my sister was having a baby, so we all figured I should wait." She stopped and directed her gaze at the bar.

"Well, Irish, what can I get you?" Sean asked.

Norah raised her head to see Sean looking at her expectantly, not annoyed but smiling.

She ordered four pints of Guinness. If he poured them right, she'd have a few minutes near him.

"Where in Ireland are you from?" he asked as he flipped two glasses upright.

"Galway," she said. "Ballyineen. You've probably never heard of it."

"Not on any maps?" he said.

"I don't know. I've never had to look."

Sean laughed, and after a second Norah smiled as though she *had* made a joke.

"My mother is Galway on both sides, she thinks. Way back, though," Sean said.

After two and a half months, she'd gotten used to the way Americans insisted on telling her where their families were from, as if she might nod and cry, Oh, yes, the O'Malleys from Mayo! The McCanns from Kerry! The Delaneys from Roscommon!

"Where in Ireland was your father's family from?" Marian asked. "Mine's from Cavan. That's the smallest county."

Sean shot her a look that Norah couldn't quite read. But he answered as he filled their next two pints. "Sligo. So my mother always said."

"And she's a fountain of information," Eileen called.

"Shut up," Sean said back, but without rancor.

Eileen laughed. "Up Sligo!" she shouted at the bar in general, getting more than a few shouts back.

"What brings you to America?" Sean asked. He set the finished pints in front of her and Marian.

"It's a bit of a long story." Norah handed him a twenty, hoping it was the right bill.

Sean smiled as he accepted her money, and Norah's stomach dropped the way it did when she took the subway by herself, certain she would be lost in spite of the careful directions on the folded piece of paper tucked in her pocket.

"Do you know when you're getting on the fire department?" Marian asked. "Anna told me you and her brother took the test."

"No, no word yet," Sean said.

"Firefighting is in Sean's blood," Amred said. "His grandfather died at a fire."

"He had a heart attack at the scene," Sean said. "Amred likes to make it sound like he jumped out a window with a kid in his arms."

"He rescued a woman once who was, ah, expecting," Amred said. "And a heart attack counts. Firemen are always having heart attacks."

"So are old men," Sean said.

"He was still fighting fires?" Norah asked.

"He was a captain. He was outside managing the scene," Sean said.

"My father remembers the day he died," Marian said. "He said the bars around here were all packed. Everyone came out to toast him. Gentleman Jack Keegan."

"Things were different back then," Sean said to Norah. "Firemen lived near where they worked, because they weren't allowed to live on Long Island or anywhere out of the city. The boroughs only."

"The neighborhood," Norah ventured. The neighborhood was something she couldn't quite get her head around. There were no marked boundaries, no signs, yet everybody seemed to understand where one ended and another began.

"Exactly," Sean said.

Marian looked down at her clasped hands.

"Sean! Come on, man. I'm fucking dying of thirst!" a man shouted from the far end of the bar.

"Good!" he shouted back. He looked at Norah. "Talk to you later?"

Norah nodded and Sean moved on.

Norah and Marian took two pints each, and Marian let her take the lead through the crowd. She glanced back and saw Sean angling a glass beneath a tap. Aoife would have gone for him, Norah was sure of it.

Irish Dreams was closed on Mondays, since it was open on weekends. Norah tried to think of things to take her out of the apartment on Mondays, to give her aunt a few hours alone. Norah went to the library or on idle walks through Prospect Park. Once she'd made the mistake of accepting an invitation to go to the movies with Marian, but when she went by Marian's to call for her, the grandmother wasn't feeling well, or said she wasn't. They ended up spending an incredibly dull afternoon playing rummy with the old lady, who cheated.

The Monday after St. Patrick's Day, late in the afternoon, Norah arrived back at Helen's and immediately sensed her aunt's disappointment. So Norah asked if she could go into the office. There she could use a typewriter to write a letter home. They'd all be impressed. Helen gave her the keys eagerly, but as soon as they were out of her hand, she seemed to regret it. Three times she told Norah to be sure to lock the door when she left.

Norah did owe Aoife a letter. She hadn't answered the last one, which was full of boring paragraphs about the baby. Noelle was lovely, but she didn't care for sleep, Aoife wrote. The two of them together saw every sunrise. She'd be glad when Norah came back home. None of her friends who were still home had children yet, and they didn't visit much. Norah had read this with mounting anger. Aoife made her go to New York because she'd ruined her own chance, but her sister hadn't thought for a second that Norah might make a life for herself.

She hadn't written to Hugh Quinlevan lately, which was almost embarrassing because, before she left, he'd told her he thought he might be in love with her, and she'd thought, Why not propose, then? She'd get to stay home. Imagine if he had.

At her desk at Irish Dreams, Norah's gaze was fixed on the front door. She tried to think of a way to tell Aoife that she liked working at the agency, speaking all day to people who were excited to be fulfilling, yes, a dream that they'd had for years. Americans were so funny in the way they spoke of Ireland, as though it wasn't a real place and they'd be taking a plane into their imaginations.

She would write that she was making friends without mentioning the dull specifics of Marian. Let Aoife wonder.

Norah had just set her hands on the typewriter keys when the red-head appeared, first peering in the window, then grinning and rapping on the glass. She pushed the door, and when she found it locked, she mimed opening it. Norah jumped up and did so, a queer feeling in her stomach, as if she'd been waiting for something exciting to happen since she'd arrived in America, and it just had.

Eileen O'Reilly came in. "I hope you don't mind. Your aunt told me where you were. Which is actually perfect, because I wanted to ask you about a trip to Ireland."

"I'm not a travel agent," Norah said. "We're closed today, actually."

"I know. You're the secretary or something. But you must have some idea of stuff. I didn't feel like coming in when Maid Marian was here."

Eileen made a quick face and flung herself down in the chair beside Norah's desk. "We all thought she was going to be a nun."

"A nun? Why?" Norah asked.

Eileen shrugged. "She just has that look. And she used to work for the convent on Cross Hill Avenue."

Helen had told Norah about the cloister, St. Maren's. The mother-house, Helen said with something like pride, had been in Ireland. Galway, in fact. In Ireland, the order had died out in the decade after the famine.

"What did she do there?" Norah asked.

"Who the hell knows?" Eileen said. "We all figured she was sorting their mail and answering the phone. She was all secretive about it, like she was in the CIA. We figured she might just go in there one day and never come out. I can't see her selling Irish vacations."

"I thought the same thing," Norah said. "But Aunt Helen gives Marian the nervous people. She said nobody would believe Marian was trying to cheat them out of their money." Norah hesitated. "She said, 'No charm, no swindle.'"

Eileen laughed and Norah felt a twinge of guilt. It was hardly Marian's fault that she longed for a more exciting American friend, the sort of bold, confident girl you saw in films.

"I'm wondering how much these trips cost. I tried to get my mother to buy Sean a ticket to Dublin, but she said he doesn't need to be far away from home all by himself right now, and I said, So buy a ticket for me too, and she just looked at me like I was crazy. I thought if I had a price to tell her, she might listen."

"Why do you want Sean to go to Ireland?" Norah asked.

"He was in Nam. Marian told you that?"

"She did."

"I bet," Eileen said. "He always talked about traveling when he got home but all he does is work. He barely goes out with any girls. Sean always had a girl. Or three. If he's gonna travel, I figure he should do it now while he's waiting to go on the fire department."

"But what's he waiting for? If he wants to be a fireman, why doesn't he just do it?"

Eileen laughed. "You've got to wait to be called," she said. "You take the written test and you get put on a list according to your score. When the city's hiring, they go to the list and it's those with the highest scores who get called first. Sean got one hundred on the test. I'm not sure if he gets legacy points."

"Legacy points?"

"For having family on the job. Sean's father wasn't a fireman — he was an asshole — but his grandfather and great-grandfather were. They might be too far back, though. When they do call him, he'll go for training. When he passes the physical, he graduates."

Norah placed her hands on the edge of her desk. She felt that she'd just been asked to save a life. She quoted Eileen a few packages.

"Shit." Eileen blew out a breath. "That's a lot."

"Those prices include airfare and the tours and some meals and transport and lodging," Norah said.

"Tours." Eileen made a face. "Sean would probably hate being led around. I guess he could skip those."

Norah felt a flash of irritation. If Eileen knew being on a tour was something her brother would hate, what on earth was she even doing here?

"Who's that?" Eileen pointed to the picture on Norah's desk.

"That's my sister, Aoife, and her husband and their baby."

Eileen looked up. "What's her name?"

"Noelle Mary."

Aoife hadn't wanted a holiday name. She said it would be like being dressed up all the year through, but Peter insisted, and as Aoife told Norah, she was exhausted, her breasts were leaking, she had stitches in her bum.

"No, no. Your sister. Ee-fa? How do you spell that?"

Norah, mystified, spelled it for her.

"An A? That name begins with an A? It's Gaelic, isn't it?"

Norah nodded.

"What about E-i-l-i-s?" Eileen leaned forward in her chair. "How do you say that?"

"Ay-lish," Norah said.

Eileen jumped up and began to prowl the office. "I always said it E-liss. Say it again?"

"Ay-lish."

"Ay-lish," Eileen said. "Ay-lish."

"Do you know a girl who's called that?"

Eileen turned from the front door. She was in silhouette against the gray light, as though she might vanish through the glass. "I was called that."

After that, Eileen and Norah were friends, going out on Friday and Saturday nights to bars or parties in the apartments of people Eileen knew, or said she did. Norah went out on two dates but then told the guy (lads were guys in Brooklyn) not to call her again while Eileen listened in, mouthing words Norah should say. At first, Norah made a point of being home by midnight, much to Eileen's scorn. They weren't teenagers. Eventually, Norah followed Eileen's lead and stayed out later, always careful not to wake Aunt Helen when she slipped in, quietly exhilarated from the events of the evening.

Once, Marian asked her if she wanted to go see the movie *Slaughterhouse-Five*, and Norah stuttered an excuse. Marian nodded, a blotchy blush on her neck.

One evening, Eileen went to Irish Dreams at closing time and insisted Norah come to her house for dinner. The reason for the dinner invite, Eileen explained as they walked toward her home, was that she was sure her mother was due to lecture her about the direction her life was going in. Which was no direction. She had to think about getting her own place.

Norah wondered how she knew it would be tonight, and why at dinner? But she didn't ask. Eileen's mother, Delia, was composed and polite. If she was angry at her daughter, she kept it to herself. Her friend Nathaniel, whose long last name Norah forgot as soon as she heard it, smiled at her warmly.

Norah sat beside Eileen and studied her and Delia O'Reilly. If she hadn't known Eileen was adopted, she would have assumed without too much thought that Eileen looked like her father.

Sean came to the table after they were all seated. Both Delia and Eileen looked up in surprise as he sat down, but neither said anything. He looked like he'd just woken up.

Delia asked questions about the town Norah was from, then asked where Norah had gone to college, and Norah swallowed a bite of fish and said that her oldest brother had gone to university, but she herself had gone right into the family grocery. She didn't mention the long hours at the cash register, hoping to give the impression she sort of managed things.

Delia glanced at Sean and said she didn't understand young people. When she was eighteen, she'd wanted nothing more than to go to a four-year school, but her father hadn't let her. She'd gone to a two-year college to become a teacher instead.

Nathaniel smiled and said that his father had brought the family over from Poland and built his business while supporting them with other jobs on the side. He, Nathaniel, had taken it over. To walk away from your own dream was one thing, but to do the same to a parent's was another.

Norah was about to ask what kind of business it was when Eileen announced, "I'm thinking about taking the test for the cops."

Delia set down her fork.

"You're too short," Sean said.

"They're doing away with the height requirement. The Hispanics sued," Eileen said. "Where have you been?"

"Southeast Asia," Sean snapped.

"You should both have college degrees," Delia said.

"You don't need a college degree to be a fireman," Sean said, an edge to his voice.

Eileen grinned. "What if you fall out a window and they don't let you back on? What'll you do for a living?"

"If I'm dead, nothing. If I land on my head, nothing," Sean said. "If I shatter my legs, then I'll have plenty of time to go back to school."

Eileen laughed. Norah wasn't sure if she should, so she didn't.

"That isn't funny, Sean," Delia said.

Nathaniel said, "It's a little bit funny."

Delia smiled slightly at him and he winked. Norah bent over her plate to hide her raised eyebrows.

After dinner, she and Eileen had the living room to themselves. Delia and Nathaniel were in the kitchen playing cards. Norah asked how they met, and Eileen laughed and told her to stop thinking dirty thoughts. They'd been friends forever. Since the forties.

At ten o'clock, Norah said she had to get home. It had been a long day at work and tomorrow would be another. The advertising for summer trips had gone out; they were getting a lot of phone calls.

Norah insisted on going into the kitchen to say goodbye to Delia, in spite of Eileen's insistence that it was hardly necessary. Delia said it was nice meeting her.

Nathaniel held up his hand of cards. "Tonight is my night," he said.

"Isn't it always?" Eileen said, laughing.

"Therefore, one of these days I will be right," he said, holding up a finger. He smiled at Norah and she smiled back. There was something calming about him, almost priestly, though she knew he was Jewish, since Eileen had mentioned that instead of ham for Easter dinner, they'd always had roast beef, for Nathaniel.

Delia put down her cards. "Norah, I'm going to have Sean walk you home."

"Mom, come on," Eileen said. "Don't bother him. I'll walk her home."

Norah wanted to say she knew the way herself, and she did, but truthfully, the thought of being on the street alone in the dark did unnerve her.

"And so all three of you will walk Norah home, and then Sean can walk you back."

Home. An image of her and Aoife's bedroom rose in Norah's mind. She saw the twin beds with the matching white bedspreads and the chest of drawers they'd divided down the middle, Aoife getting the extra drawer because she was older. The room, dark and lifeless as a museum exhibit. Norah had to make herself call to mind the room she'd been given at Helen's, which was so small she'd taken to shutting the door with her foot after she climbed in the narrow bed.

"It's not the middle of the night!" Eileen said.

"It's late enough."

Delia disappeared up the stairs to the middle floor, which Norah now knew was called the parlor floor. The bedrooms were another flight up.

"He's going to be pissed," Eileen said.

"There are worse things," Nathaniel said mildly.

Delia came back downstairs. "Go on, girls."

Eileen left the kitchen without another word, and though Norah wanted to thank Delia, she didn't, following Eileen's lead. Her own mother would be horrified at her manners.

The O'Reillys rarely used the big double doors at the top of the front steps. They came and went by the door beneath the stoop. Norah had learned fairly early on in Brooklyn that the stoop was like another room of the house. Sean appeared, shrugging on his jacket and scowling.

"Okay, future cop. Let's go."

"I haven't got a gun yet," Eileen said.

They reached the corner, Sean walking ahead of them, practically daring them to keep pace, when Eileen called, "Hey! So this is where I get off."

Sean turned around and Norah looked at her, alarmed.

"I've got a date." Eileen pulled a lipstick out of her purse and wiggled it at them.

"With who?" Sean asked.

"Madd," she answered.

"John Maddox? That explains the sudden interest in law and order. Fantastic."

"He said he thought I'd be good at it," Eileen said.

"I'm sure it wasn't to get you into bed," Sean said.

"He's already gotten me into bed." Eileen laughed. "I'll call you tomorrow, Norah."

She crossed the street and hurried up the block.

Norah turned to Sean. "Ah — you don't have to —"

"No, now I really do," Sean said. He turned right and she followed, prepared to nearly run, but he was walking more slowly now.

"Sorry about that. If I weren't here, I'm pretty sure she would've walked to your aunt's before taking off."

"I know where I'm going," Norah said. "You don't have to —"

"Nah, my mother's right. Our block's okay but you can't walk alone around here. Not anymore."

"Eileen told me she's a teacher."

"Principal now, but she taught fourth grade for twenty-whatever years. This neighborhood didn't used to be too bad but—" Sean shrugged.

"Oh." Norah wondered why they didn't move but it seemed rude to ask.

"Did you come here for work?" Sean asked. "That's what I always hear the Irish say."

She couldn't tell him about the Contraceptive Train. He would think her family was mad.

"I did," she said. "I came to take a job with my aunt. She's been here a long time."

They approached the next corner, where they should have gone left, but Sean said, "Want to see something? It's not far."

"Okay."

"It was my great-grandparents who came over from Ireland. Mom's grandparents. I swear, sometimes I wish they never left," Sean said.

"If you were there, you'd be leaving," Norah said. "My brothers did."

"How many brothers do you have?"

She told him, and he said, "It's just me and Eileen. She was adopted, from Ireland."

"She told me."

Sean glanced at her, his eyebrows raised. "Yeah? She doesn't usually go into it."

"I get the feeling she thinks I can tell her — I don't know, something," Norah said. "She's asked a lot of questions about Ireland and what we eat for breakfast and our schools, that sort of thing."

"She's hoping to go over there someday and see where she was born."

When they reached the corner, there was a break in the row of houses. By the streetlight Norah could make out a small grassy area and, in its center, the silhouette of a Celtic cross. She stopped.

"Is that a *grave?*" she asked.

"That? No. It's a monument to a Civil War soldier. There's a name on there but I don't think anybody's ever been able to find a record of him.

The story goes that he was a paid substitute. That's when a rich man got out of the draft by paying a poor guy to fight for him. Then, poor usually meant Irish. This soldier was supposedly a substitute who got killed and the rich man put up this monument, out of guilt. Nobody knows if it's true. We're on Cross Hill Avenue. This is the spot that the neighborhood get its name from."

They walked in silence for a moment, then Sean stopped in front of a three-story firehouse that had a tower on the left side with tall windows in it.

"My great-grandfather, the one from Ireland, pretty much founded this fire company," he said. "His daughter was born here, up on the third floor, where they lived."

"Born in the firehouse?" Norah said. "That must have been fun for everyone."

Sean laughed. "She married one of the men, Jack Keegan. Her and him are my mom's parents. Look at this." He walked over to a plaque on the brick wall between the big garage doors and a regular-size door.

Norah squinted at it but couldn't read it in the dark.

"James Walsh. Died December 28, 1884. That's the night my grandmother was born."

"That's sad," Norah said. "Will you work here when you're a fireman?"

Sean said, "You go where they assign you. I could end up anywhere. But yeah, it'd be nice to work here."

Norah remembered what the man at the bar had said. "The fire department's in your blood."

"Fucking Amred," Sean said, the affection in his voice at odds with his words. "He turns up at fires and takes pictures. He's pretty good."

"Did you always want to be a fireman?"

"Sure. I'd go nuts sitting in an office all day." Sean paused. "Some girl once told me I could be an actor, so for a while there I had fantasies about heading out to L.A."

"Why didn't you?"

Sean frowned. "You heard my mom tonight, about college. I figured,

I'd do the two years she asked me to and then maybe give acting a shot. Then a guy I knew got killed in Vietnam. I started thinking, Why the hell should I sit on my ass trying to earn a degree I don't need? I enlisted. I'm pretty sure I'd hate L.A. anyway."

"I thought I'd hate New York," Norah said.

Sean looked directly at her, and Norah forced herself not to duck her head like a schoolgirl.

"You don't?"

She thought for a moment of explaining how she'd nearly run to Helen when she saw her in the airport because she'd thought her mother had somehow arrived ahead of her to tell her the whole thing was canceled.

"I don't hate it here," she said. "You could still go to L.A. If you didn't like it, you could just come back."

"True. They won't close New York behind me."

The door next to the garage doors opened then, startling Norah. Sean grinned when a fireman appeared.

The smile transformed his face, took away the faint lines around his eyes that made him look older than twenty-four.

"O'Reilly? I thought that was you," the fireman said.

"What's going on? You got housewatch?" Sean asked.

"Yeah," he said. "Slow night so far. Nothing doing."

"This is Joe Paladino. Joe, this is Norah. Whose last name I don't know."

"Mulryan," Norah said.

Joe grinned. "You don't know your girlfriend's last name? Jesus, Sean."

Sean didn't look at her. "I'm walking her home. She's a friend of Eileen's."

"Eileen! How is Eileen?" Joe said.

"Hanging around with John Maddox."

"Nice enough guy," Joe said. "A little fucking nuts."

"He's a cop." Sean shrugged.

"Where you been anyway?" Joe asked.

"Me? Bartending at Lehane's. You're the one who's never around."

"Yeah, I was dating a girl from Queens."

Joe studied Norah. "Where you from? Not around here."

"I'm from Ireland. I'm staying with my aunt here in Brooklyn."

"Irish?" He sounded pleased. "I brought an Irish girl home once. Mary O . . . Mary O'Something. My ma said if I married her she'd kill herself and then kill me. She tells me this in English and Italian so I know she means it. My dad's more practical. He goes, Why you want to marry a girl who can't cook?"

"Why, ah —" Norah stopped.

"Because she was Irish. That's all he meant," Sean said, and Norah must still have looked confused, because he added, "It's a dumb thing between the Irish and the Italians around here."

"Only an Irish guy's gonna call food a dumb thing," Joe said.

Sean laughed. "All right, enough of this. I've gotta get Norah home."

"Nice meeting you," Norah said.

"You too, Norah from Ireland. You get tired of this galoot, come find me."

"So your mother can kill herself?" Sean asked.

"She's lived a long and full life."

Two days later, Sean called and asked her to a nun's funeral.

The phone rang at eight o'clock at night, startling Helen so much that it rang five times before she managed to answer. Norah quickly calculated: it was two a.m. in Ireland.

Helen handed the phone to Norah, her eyebrows raised. With no more than a hello, Sean explained that he had a job as a pallbearer for Reliable's, the funeral home next to the bar. He and a couple other guys carried coffins in and out of the church at the Masses, and then again at the cemetery. In movies, friends and family members do it, but most people can't. Coffins are heavy.

"I know you been to Mass a million times, and there's nothing special for the nuns, but the cemetery where they bury them is pretty cool. If you're interested in that kind of thing. I am."

Norah said she'd love to go.

She sat alone in a pew in the middle of the church. There were a few old ladies scattered among the back pews, bent over their rosary beads. Across the aisle and a couple rows ahead of Norah was Sean's mother, sitting very still, eyes fixed on the altar.

Up in the choir loft, the organ began to play and the doors of the church opened. Sean and three other men carried the coffin down the aisle and set it in the center, up front, close to the altar. Then Sean came to her pew. Norah saw the surprise on the faces of his friends. One of them called in a loud whisper, "Hey, Sean!" and another guy punched him in the shoulder. They went to a pew a few rows ahead. His mother, too, was watching. Without changing expression, she faced forward again.

During his homily, Father Halloran praised Sister Magdalena, who had been in the cloister for over thirty years, for devoting her life to God in the purest form possible.

Norah blinked. Good God, thirty years. How did you not go insane?

After the Mass, outside the church, Norah stood at the bottom of the steps, watching Sean and his friends place the coffin in the hearse. She turned when Delia O'Reilly came to stand beside her.

"Sean told you about this?" she said lightly.

Norah nodded. "He said the cemetery was interesting."

"If you like cemeteries," Delia said.

"I do," Norah said.

Sean came over. "We gotta go." He took Norah's elbow and said to his mother, "You're not coming to the burial, right?"

"Do I ever?" Delia said, inclining her head. "Have you seen your sister this morning? I know she's not working."

Norah assumed Delia was asking if Eileen had come home the night before.

"I'd say she's probably hanging around with a bunch of other twenty-two-year-olds."

"Thank you, Sean. Helpful as ever."

He grinned, and Norah watched her expression soften and saw at once that Sean was adored. Norah hadn't been sure, but she surmised now that his mother was simply better than most at hiding it.

Delia turned to Norah. "You should see the Green-Wood if you like cemeteries. There are a lot of famous people buried there."

"O'Reilly, come on!"

At the cemetery's chapel, where Father Halloran said a final blessing, it was just Norah, Sean and the three other pallbearers. There was no graveside ceremony, Sean explained. The coffin stayed behind in the chapel, and the cemetery crew took care of the rest.

Outside the chapel, Norah stood back a little from Sean and his friends as they finalized some complicated plan Norah couldn't follow, but it had to do with baseball, the Mets and opening day at Shea Stadium. When it seemed to be settled, Sean told his friends to go home without them.

"Whoa, O'Reilly, you know how to show a girl a good time."

"Be sure and snag some flowers offa the grave."

The three of them walked off, laughing.

The cemetery was small. Sean told Norah it had only ever been used by the parish of Holy Rosary. Nobody was being buried here anymore.

Sean brought her to where the nuns were buried and where the new grave would be dug, probably later today. The nuns' gravestones gave their nun name and the date of death, but no birth date, and not their real name, whatever they had been called before entering the order.

Sean pointed to the high stone wall and explained that the convent lay right behind it. There were stories of nuns leaving the convent at night to put flowers from their garden on the graves, but that was probably bullshit.

"My grandmother was one of them. In the cloister."

Norah looked at him, ready to laugh but uncertain. "A nun? She left the convent to get married?"

"Other way around. She went in after she was widowed. This is the one who was born in the firehouse."

Norah stared at him. "Is she still in there? Or —"

Sean shrugged. "We don't know. They don't have any more contact with their families. Mom never saw her again. I'm sure she's here by now." A wave of his hand encompassed the neat row of graves. "Whenever one of them dies, Mom goes to the funeral. Come on." Sean started walking, and Norah had to run a little to catch up.

They crossed the cemetery and came to a corner separated by a low wrought-iron gate. At the center of the enclosure stood a statue of a mustached, helmeted fireman holding a child whose head was buried in his shoulder.

"Fireman's Corner," Sean said. He took Norah's hand and led her to the statue. She read the inscription, focused more on Sean's warm hand than on the words.

PATRICK DEVLIN

A SON OF IRELAND
WHO BRAVELY FOUGHT FOR THE UNION
AND FOR 30 YEARS BATTLED FIRES FOR
THE CITIES OF BROOKLYN AND NEW YORK

Two headstones lay flat against the ground in front of the monument. One said *Patrick Devlin* and the other *Brigid Cavanaugh Devlin, Beloved Wife.*

"They're my great-grandparents," Sean said. "My mother's grandparents. The ones from Ireland."

Norah thought for a second. "The nun's parents?"

"Yeah. My mom's dad is here too. Jack Keegan. Right over there." Sean waved a hand. "But you don't have to meet my whole family on our first date."

Norah laughed.

"Actually, it's not the whole family. My mother had two brothers who died in 1918, before she was born. They're not here, and Mom's not sure what happened to them. It was the influenza epidemic, and she thinks maybe the city was cremating the dead to try and get it under control. Even if you were Catholic."

"That's awful." Norah rubbed her arms.

"I'm probably boring you," Sean said.

"No, no," Norah said. She kept wondering what it meant that he would bring her here and tell her about his family. Surely he didn't do this with every girl he met.

"Do you want to go get something to eat? Somewhere besides Lehane's? I'll know everybody in the place. Nobody'll leave us alone."

Norah agreed and they started the walk back. The ground didn't give beneath their feet. The trees were still bare, though it was already April.

"Working at the travel agency's what you want to do?" he asked.

Norah had been hoping he wouldn't ask. "It's a good enough job, but travel agencies don't get in the blood, like being a fireman." She tried to laugh but he took it seriously.

Sean rested his hand on her lower back. "Something'll come to you," he said.

The heat startled Norah when it arrived in early June. In Ireland, if it went to eighty degrees, people complained they were boiling. She was not prepared for ninety-degree afternoons and nights that didn't feel much cooler. All through the summer, she lay on Sean's bed, facing the fan.

Norah shouldn't have been in Sean's room. In Ireland, she'd believed that what her parents thought counted more, but she understood now that she was old enough to do what she liked. Still, it was Delia's house. Each time she and Sean went out, Norah told herself she would have him leave her at the door of Helen's building. Yet again and again she followed him inside the silent brownstone and up the stairs, trusting the sound of his footsteps to hide her own.

Together, they got into his bed. Mornings, Eileen went downstairs to distract Delia, usually by picking a fight, so Norah could slip down to the parlor floor and go out the heavy double doors that opened onto the stoop. Which was the same as climbing out a window, Eileen said wickedly one night when they were drinking together at Lehane's while Sean was behind the bar. Don't think the neighbors don't notice. Though, to be fair, there were only a couple of families they knew left on the block. All the other houses were chopped up into apartments. Norah tried to summon a sense of shame but couldn't.

When she arrived back at Helen's in the morning to shower and change her clothes for work, Helen never said anything, except on the Fourth of July. Irish Dreams was closed. Norah, Sean, Eileen and a group of Eileen's friends were going to Breezy Point Surf Club, in Rockaway, which was in Queens. Later, when it got dark, they'd be able to see the Macy's fireworks from something called A Court.

On the Fourth, after Norah showered and changed, she was ready to rush out the door, but Helen had made a fresh pot of coffee and Norah stopped and poured herself a cup. She'd never thought to make coffee at home, but here everybody drank it. Helen stood in the kitchen doorway and told her that though certainly she, Helen, was not one to give romantic advice, she had one thing to say.

Norah held her steaming mug and waited, curious, already rehearsing the story for Sean. She and Sean had a running joke about Helen being in love with Mr. Fitzgerald.

"I know Delia O'Reilly from the neighborhood, more or less. Well enough to know that if it comes down to it, she raised Sean right and he will do the right thing by you. But isn't it better not to begin like that?"

"This isn't Ireland, Aunt Helen. You don't have to rely on prayers alone." If Norah could have done it unnoticed, she would have crossed her fingers as she said the last bit.

Helen nodded and retreated.

But after that, Norah started thinking about the future in earnest. Whereas she'd been deliberately steering her thoughts away from her return to Ireland, she began imagining herself stepping off the plane, greeting her parents, walking in the front door of the house. In each scene, she felt acutely the emptiness beside her, in the place where Sean would be.

"You're not going back," Sean always said.

"I'm only here for a little while."

"Just tell them you're staying."

To stay in America for no reason except that she wanted to? Sean had gone to war against his mother's wishes. How could she explain that with the boys gone and Aoife married to a man who had his own business, it was expected that she, Norah, would bring in the son-in-law who would take over from her father?

A brave daughter would have written a letter saying that she wanted to try some other kind of job, or take college classes. Travel, like Sean was always talking about. Boston, Maine, Florida, California. She might have said outright that she had a real boyfriend. An American. An American who was Catholic, but whose mother was divorced. An American who hadn't seen his father in twenty years.

About his father, Sean would say only that his parents had met right after Pearl Harbor. They'd married; his father had gone off to fight in World War II, came home. Eileen told Norah his name, Luke, and that when Sean was four, he'd left Delia for an Englishwoman he'd met during the war.

Norah did ask Sean if he'd ever tried to contact Luke O'Reilly.

"We're right where he left us," Sean said with the same expression he gave Norah when she tried to ask him about Vietnam, although he turned aside those tentative questions with even less patience. "I was there, now I'm back," he'd say.

Norah was sure a better girlfriend could have gotten him to talk about it. When he rocketed out of bed, drenched with sweat and sometimes shouting, she didn't do anything but crouch by the bed, afraid his mother would break through the barred door.

Delia only ever knocked, though, and never hard enough to dis-lodge the chair Sean had jammed beneath the doorknob. He would snap that he was fine. Sometimes he leaned his forehead against the door as he said the words.

His mother would go away. Norah would climb back in the damp bed and wait for him to leave the window where he always went to stand. Early on, she tried to hug him, but he would shove her away, once hard enough so that she stumbled back into the desk. It left a bruise on her lower back. Sean never apologized or even mentioned it. She didn't know if he remembered. She learned to lie down and wait, and when he returned to bed, sometimes he wanted to go right to sleep, but often he didn't.

Those nightmare times, she never asked him to use a rubber, as he called them. She thought of Aoife, who assumed a baby couldn't result because she had fantastic plans. But how could she have? Norah wondered. The danger was like standing on a ledge. Like changing the course of a river or calling the moon to a new orbit.

On Halloween, they settled on Sean's stoop with a bowl of candy for the trick-or-treaters. Norah hadn't planned to tell him on Halloween. He might think she was joking. They sat handing out Hershey bars and Milky Ways to the kids. The little girls singsonged his name, drawing out the one syllable to three. "Hey-y-y, Sha-a-awn, this your girlfriend? She from Ireland? You gotta accent? Say something!"

Sean grinned at Norah. "Say something, Irish. Say 'Top o' the mornin' to you.'"

Cringing, she did it. The children hooted, and Sean, she could see, was proud of her for playing along.

In one group of four kids there was a guy with them who greeted Sean by name.

Sean grinned. "Hey, Freddy. Sorry — no costume, no candy."

Freddy waved a hand at a little boy wearing a Batman cape. "That's my nephew."

The little boy, about seven years old, held open his bag and Norah dropped two candy bars in.

"At least you got a nice girl."

Sean laughed. "She is. This is Norah." He turned to her. "Freddy and me were in high school together."

"Hi," Norah said, and he nodded at her and turned back to Sean.

"How long you back from Nam?" he asked.

Norah sensed the tension that ran up Sean's spine, pulling it straighter.

"Long enough."

"The beaches were luxurious, weren't they?"

"I found the food magnificent," Sean answered, and they both laughed.

"You a fireman yet?" Freddy asked as the kids ran to the next house.

"I'm waiting," Sean said.

"Maybe I'll be a fireman too. Maybe I'll change my name to McLewis and make that my *career*." He grinned.

Sean was no longer smiling, and Norah tensed, not sure what had just changed.

"Take the test, man," Sean said. "Nobody's stopping you."

Freddy laughed. "Take the *test*, he says."

"Yeah, take the test."

Freddy started after his nephew.

"Put your money where your damn mouth is," Sean called after him, but Freddy didn't turn around.

Sean shook his head. "We played ball together in high school. Freddy was a helluva hitter. He enlisted too. Good enough guy, but he needs to shut up about the fire department. They think there should be more black guys on the job, they should *take the fucking test*. They talk like there's some secret committee slipping white guys the answers."

Norah didn't much care. "There's a test I think I'll fail."

"What?" Sean said. He turned to look at her. "A driving test? You want to get your license? That's a great idea. My mom's always saying she wished she'd learned to drive."

But then it must have showed on her face, because he said, "What's the matter?"

She shook her head, afraid she might start to cry.

"Your parents said you have to go back? Listen —"

"No, no. I can never go back."

They won't close New York behind me, he'd said.

But Ireland would close behind her.

Helen was living by the calendar, checking off the days until Norah's time in New York was done and she had her apartment to herself again. She barely tolerated Sean's brief visits. Her patience would not expand to include a baby.

Sean, and only Sean, had the power to let Norah drown or save her, though Norah was sure he didn't quite realize this.

"Norah — what the fuck?"

"I think I'm having a baby."

Sean jerked back. Norah forced herself to meet his stunned blue eyes. He had a Hershey bar in his hand and began to methodically break it apart, and the sound was like bones snapping.

"I guess I didn't think it could really happen," Norah said. She ducked her head so her hair would fall over her face and hide the flush spreading over her cheeks and down her neck. Sean had discovered early on that she was a bad liar. When he'd asked if she'd had a boyfriend in Ireland, she'd thought of Hugh and said she didn't. Sean had laid a hand on her reddening cheek and laughed. "Hey, I don't give a fuck. He's there. I'm here."

Norah barely remembered what Hugh looked like. Were Hugh and Sean to stand side by side, she would still be at a loss to describe him, poor Hugh Quinlevan.

"Okay." Sean tossed the Hershey bar down the stoop. "Okay."

Norah stood and ran down the steps to the gate. Sean followed.

She had the gate open. He pushed her hand off it and knocked it shut.

"We'll get married."

Norah started crying.

"I'll ask you the right way," he said. "I was planning to after I got called for the fire department and I knew I could support us. But listen, I'm making decent money at the bar and I can pick up another job somewhere, so what the hell, right? You'll marry me?"

"Yes." Norah nodded, and Sean wrapped his arms around her and she leaned into him and shut her eyes. In her mind, Norah played out the scene sure to happen in the kitchen at home. Her mother leaning one hip into the counter as she held the phone, as if the whole house would collapse if she dared to move. Her father, silent in his seat at the head of the kitchen table, the newspaper set aside as soon as he understood from Ireland's side of the conversation that their second daughter had gone down the same path as their first.

Her father would leave for the pub. Her mother would sink into the couch in front of the television. They would both, at different hours, climb the stairs to the dark hallway where the smell of cooking always lingered, and settle into bed.

Sean stepped back and said, "God, a baby."

"A baby," Norah echoed, her stomach pitching. She hadn't much thought about it as a real, actual child. It was a way to keep Sean. A way to stay.

He'd kissed her first. He took off her clothes, and she let him. She wanted him to. She'd known all the while what would probably happen, and she'd let it happen.

She had, in a way, taken his whole life. Sean didn't realize it. His mother would know.

Norah pressed her forehead into his chest. Sean kissed the top of her head and then spoke against her hair. "It's fine. It'll be good."

April 1983

Norah sat at the kitchen table. All three children were still in bed. Today was Saturday. They'd go back to school on Monday. That would be the start of what everyone was gently calling "getting on with their lives."

She felt sick and hungry at the same time, the way she always did early on. With Maggie, she'd overlooked the nausea and ate what she wanted to, ignoring her new mother-in-law's advice out of spite; Delia had not been happy to have her son's bride move into her house.

Thank God they'd been able to get their own apartment not long after Maggie was born.

Thank God they'd taken the leap before she found out she was pregnant with Aidan, when Maggie was only three months old. Irish twins, Sean said, trying to smile but unable to hide his panic.

If they'd still been at Delia's, they almost certainly would have stayed. As it was, Sean had too much pride to move his family back in with his mother, when he'd just moved them out.

"I suggest you get a second job," Delia had said when they told her.

"I already have," Sean had said, unable to meet her eyes. In fact, he had three jobs. The fire department, bartending at Lehane's and carpentry work thrown his way by an older guy in the firehouse. A lieutenant whose father had worked with Gentleman Jack.

Norah had always preferred to remember the months right after their wedding, before things got very hard. Like the day he graduated from the fire academy, when she'd been so proud to stand next to him, eight months pregnant, still not used to the idea that he was hers to keep. It turned out, the only thing she'd ever come up with for a life's goal was to be Sean's wife, the mother of his children, and it had been enough, most of the time. The days when it wasn't, well, she got through them.

Norah opened the *Daily News*. The story was on page three, with a picture of her and the kids on the steps of the church. The boys were looking straight ahead, as was she, but Maggie had her head turned.

BROOKLYN FIREFIGHTER MOURNED

Firefighter Sean O'Reilly Buried with Full Departmental Honors

Norah shut her eyes and pictured Fireman's Corner in Cross Hill Cemetery. Sean's grave, the first new one dug there since the late 1960s, was allowed because he had family there.

She glanced at the clock. It was going on seven a.m., so it was about one in the afternoon in Ireland. Aoife answered on the third ring.

"Norah, my God, how are you? We're thinking of you here."

Norah said it was still unreal.

"I hope you'll come this summer for a visit." Aoife spoke cautiously.

Norah said, "I'd like to."

An infant. The way they cried. The way you were so tired when you had a new baby, that if you tripped on the sidewalk and fell on your face, you'd only be grateful for the chance to lie down. This time, she would be alone, with no one to spell her.

"Did you ever do more for women's rights?" Norah asked.

"Women's rights?" Aoife's astonishment plain from across the ocean.

"Birth control," Norah said. "The other."

Norah listened to her sister's breathing quicken.

"Birth control is legal here now. You must know that."

"Of course," Norah answered. "The other isn't."

"God, no," Aoife said.

"Do you think it's a terrible thing?" Norah didn't want to use the word "sin." She and Sean took the children to Mass every Sunday, though he had not gone as a child. Had Sean believed in God? It was a question Norah always meant to ask him.

"No," Aoife said slowly. "Sometimes it's the answer. That's terrible, but the thing itself, no."

"Why didn't you, then?"

After a short silence, Aoife said, "That was my first thought. Go to England."

"But why didn't you?"

"We were out at the pub and I got sick on the way home. Peter thought it was drink, like I ever drank that much, and I just said it."

"Peter didn't want —"

"Peter was thrilled. He said we'd get married. I said I didn't want to do that," Aoife said. "He told me he'd get his sister to talk to me. She was married. They had two kids. She'd tell me — I don't know what he thought she'd tell me."

"His sister would have told their mother," Norah said. "And then — the whole of town would have known."

"I thought that's what would happen," Aoife said. "I know it would have. So if I went to England —"

It sounded like she'd moved the receiver away from her mouth.

"Mam and Da," Norah said.

"Destroyed altogether." Her voice was back.

"But you're glad now?"

There was a silence so long that Norah thought they'd been disconnected.

"I'm glad for Noelle. I am."

Norah understood. Noelle was not the sort of child you could look at with regret.

Norah had only met her niece twice. Once when she and Sean visited Ireland when Maggie was a year old, then when they went back for their fifth anniversary. Noelle and Maggie were close enough in age to be compared, and Norah had pitied her daughter. Bright Noelle, who wasn't a bit shy and had the great advantage of being at home besides. Noelle tried hard to get Maggie to play with her, but Maggie often shrank away, burying her face against Norah's leg. She and Sean had more success showing off Aidan, who was handsome and charming and delighted Norah's parents. Their other grandsons lived in England.

After she and Aoife hung up, Norah held the receiver in her hand until it started to buzz. She hung it up and then quickly picked it up again, dialing information. She asked for the number for Planned Parenthood in New York and wrote the number down on the pad by the phone, to call later, or never. The girl on the phone thanked Norah in a voice that was comforting in its blandness. She wasn't judging.

Norah sat at the kitchen table, staring at the newspaper picture of her and the kids on the church steps. She could almost believe they were other people. Then they arrived in the kitchen one by one, looking for breakfast. When the boys were done with their cereal, and left to turn on the television in the living room, Maggie lingered at the table. She was already dressed.

Norah pulled herself to her feet and started the dishes.

"When are we going back to school?"

"You'll go back Monday."

"Are we still going to see Gran and Aunt Eileen?"

"Of course you are. Don't be ridiculous."

"Does our grandfather know?"

"What?" Norah turned from the sink. "Of course he does. I told you, they had a Mass said for your father in Ireland."

"No, the other one. Daddy's father."

"Maggie, the man abandoned his wife and children over thirty years ago. Nobody's told him, far as I know, and what does it matter?"

Norah turned back to the sink, but she was sure the child wasn't through. Indeed, hardly a second passed before the small voice returned.

"Are we going to the picnic?"

Norah turned around again. "What picnic?"

"The company picnic."

Norah answered slowly, "If you and the boys want to, we'll go." She tried to curb her impatience. The Glory Devlins' company picnic was not until August. Right now, she couldn't think past the end of the hour.

"What about the Christmas party?"

"Christ." Norah slammed a bowl into the sink. "You have to stop asking me questions because I don't know. I don't know!"

With a single, stunned look, Maggie slipped off her chair and disappeared upstairs.

Norah started after her and then stopped at the bottom of the steps. She sat down. The uncertainty of what she should do, what she could do, was giving her a pain in her stomach not caused by any baby. She wouldn't get up again until she'd decided.

CHAPTER TWO

Delia Keegan O'Reilly

March 1967

ON ST. PATRICK'S DAY, Delia dressed in a black skirt and a green sweater and went into the city, to the reception at the American Irish Historical Society, a privilege of membership. The same people typically attended from year to year. She had a few acquaintances who went, and after the parade up Fifth Avenue, they would find a bar or restaurant that didn't skew wildly drunk, in order to hold an actual conversation. She generally enjoyed herself, though it was not like the St. Patrick's Days of old when Sean and Eileen were young and she took them to the parade, all three of them skipping school.

In the kitchen, she found Eileen leaning against the sink, spooning cereal out of a bowl. Normally Delia would say, "Sit down, Eileen. You're not at a bus stop," but she didn't want to start the day off with a fight.

"Happy St. Patrick's Day," Delia said, as she started the coffee.

"Yeah," Eileen said and, after a pause, asked, "Is it still March 17 in Vietnam? Or not yet?"

Delia knew that Vietnam was a full twelve hours ahead of the United States. It was nighttime there already, but yes, still St. Patrick's Day.

But she told her daughter, "I have no idea."

"At least he gets to wear green." Eileen put her bowl in the sink.

"That is not funny," Delia said.

"I'm not trying to be funny," Eileen said. "Can I come with you today?"

Delia turned to look at her. "Aren't your friends going to the parade?"

Eileen made a face. "Jackie and Lynn have to go to school. We're meeting up after."

Delia wanted to ask why the girls didn't simply cut class. It was Friday and they were seniors, for God's sake. Perhaps some teacher had decided to be cruel and give a test. She didn't ask. Eileen's grades were good enough. It hardly mattered now anyway. She would be eighteen in a few months, off to Brooklyn College in the fall. It was settled.

"It's not a party, more of a reception. Wine and cheese."

Eileen rolled her eyes. "I just want to watch the parade from someplace warm. It's fucking freezing out."

Cursing, Delia would normally say, makes you sound ignorant. But today she would not lecture.

"You have to dress decently. No jeans," Delia said.

"No way am I wearing a skirt," Eileen said.

The doorbell rang and then the front door opened. Delia and Eileen were silent until Nathaniel came into the kitchen, calling,

"Good morning!"

He stopped when he saw Delia. "So it's the High Holy Day? I forgot."

Nathaniel Kwiatkowski, not much taller than Delia, portly, was an average-looking man who became truly homely when he smiled.

"Coffee?" Delia asked.

He nodded and sat down at the table with a sigh. "What's today then, the sixteenth?"

"It's March *seventeenth*, Nathaniel," Eileen said, laughing. "What are you, Polish?"

"Eileen!" Delia said, but Nathaniel laughed too. He'd come from Poland when he was ten, young enough to learn English without too much trouble, too old to lose his accent entirely.

"Why do the Irish believe they are the center of the universe?" he asked.

"I think it's Americans who believe that," Delia said.

She set a cup of coffee in front of him, black, three sugars, and poured one for herself.

"Yes," Nathaniel said. "But Americans know it and believe the world should too. With the Irish, it's like a secret they're keeping."

Eileen laughed again. "Sean would like that."

"And have either of you heard from our boy lately?" he asked. "He didn't answer my last letter."

"Not for two weeks. But you know Sean, he hates writing letters," Eileen said.

Or he's dead, Delia thought. Or his eyes are gone, or his mind.

Nathaniel sighed. "Letters. A lost art."

"Shouldn't you be at the store?" Delia asked.

It was already nine o'clock. Nathaniel's repair shop was on Flatbush Avenue, near Sterling Place. Most of his business was televisions. In the days of his father, it had been radios, but really, they could fix anything. The sign above the shop said simply, *Four Star Electronics Repair*, a name Nathaniel never liked.

When Nathaniel's father bought the business from his retiring boss, he left it that way, understanding that the family name was too hard to pronounce. When Nathaniel took over, he wanted to add his surname to the sign, but Delia persuaded him not to; he added it to the window as a compromise. The name could be seen that way.

"George is there," Nathaniel said. "I asked him to open."

George was in his twenties, skinny, long-haired, with a touch of genius when it came to repairing anything electronic, almost by instinct, like Nathaniel. He was also lazy and almost certainly not at work yet.

"You *are* going in today?" Delia asked.

"I'll see." Nathaniel gestured to the soda bread on the table. "Is that the magic bread?"

He might have been asking if it was an Agnello's soda bread, but really Nathaniel was telling her not to chide him. Her prayer had been answered, hadn't it?

Delia gave him a half smile, as if to say, Don't forget the price.

"No." Eileen scoffed. "I made that."

Nathaniel tasted it. "Very good."

Delia felt a pang of guilt. He was always finding ways to praise Eileen, and she knew it was to make up for her own bad habit of criticizing her.

"Get dressed if you want to come," Delia told her. "I want to leave in a half hour, no later."

"The parade goes on all day," Eileen grumbled, but she did as Delia asked.

Nathaniel shook his head. "You're making her go with you?"

"She asked to come," Delia said.

Nathaniel raised his eyebrows. "It won't interfere with your day?"

"She'll go off with her friends later. Maybe this is a good chance to talk to her about what she's going to do this summer. She can't quit three jobs like last year. I'm not a bank. She's going to have to work if she wants spending money at school —"

Nathaniel laughed. "Leave her alone. Today at least, leave her alone."

"But she's so — rootless. I asked her what she wanted to major in and she shrugged. She has no goals."

"She's young. She'll get goals later."

"I had goals when I was seventeen," Delia said, and before he could make a sarcastic remark, she beat him to it: "I never reached them, but I had them."

Nathaniel pinched a raisin from the soda bread. "So leave her alone."

"I'll try," she said, and then added impulsively, "Why don't you come with us?"

"I have things to do. You know that. Go and be Irish, heart."

Delia and Eileen got off the subway at Lexington and 79th and walked over to Fifth Avenue, which was jammed with spectators, well bundled against the cold. There were all manner of green scarves, and Aran Islands hats and sweaters. Children were perched on the curb, wrapped in blankets.

The American Irish Historical Society was between 80th and

81st. Eileen grabbed Delia's sleeve so they wouldn't be separated in the throng. Delia noted the heads turning, the smiles for Eileen. That hair. It attracted enough attention the other 364 days of the year. She wore it long, more than halfway down her back, and today she had on a white tam-o'-shanter that Sean had given her for Christmas a couple of years ago, for the express purpose of St. Patrick's Day. It set off the dark auburn beautifully. Auburn, she'd taught Eileen from the start. Never say red.

A pipe band was marching by, and unbidden, the words to the song came into Delia's head:

> *Sad are the homes 'round Garryowen*
> *Since they lost their joy and pride.*
> *And the banshee cry links every vale*
> *Around the Shannon side.*
> *That city of the ancient walls*
> *The broken treaty stone, undying fame*
> *Surrounds your name, Sean South from Garryowen.*

Sean, Sean, Sean.

Whenever she thought of her son, Delia wanted to sit down, hard, wherever she was and call his face to mind, feature by feature. Every night, she fell asleep to the thought, like a drumbeat, that Sean was a gift she was not supposed to have received. And yet she'd already paid for him, hadn't she? The day he was born.

When they reached the AIHS, Eileen stopped and stared up at the building. It was beautiful: narrow and three stories tall, with balconies on the top two floors. The Irish flag and the American flag fluttered in the breeze.

The reception was on the second floor. They walked up the wide staircase side by side.

"This was somebody's house?" Eileen said.

"Once upon a time," Delia said.

"Jesus Christ."

"Dignity, please," Delia said.

Eileen rolled her eyes.

Upstairs, Eileen went immediately to the tall windows that looked out on Fifth Avenue. Delia followed, eager to see Eileen's face when she looked down on the parade for the first time. The balcony was narrow, and not many could step out at a time. Right now it was full, but it was so cold, Delia was sure nobody would be out there long.

"Well, well, Happy St. Patrick's Day."

Delia turned to see Tomás Breen, the novelist. She smiled at him and returned the greeting. He was her age, forty-eight, and also long divorced. When Tomás finally quit drinking, it was too late to save his marriage but, sober, his career had flourished, with two well-received novels.

Delia had first met Tomás at the AIHS two years ago, in October, when he gave a reading. During the Q & A, Delia asked him if he thought his first novel had been denounced by the Church, yet not banned as Kate O'Brien's had been, because he was a man. His answer: probably yes. At the reception following the reading, she'd talked with him and his sister, and they'd gone to dinner twice before Tomás and Fionnula's return to Ireland. Since then, more often than not, when he came to town he'd give her a call.

"Where's Fionnula?" Delia asked.

"Right there." Tomás said.

When they were young, Fionnula dreamed of being a journalist, but there weren't many such opportunities for women, not in Ireland, so she became a librarian. Fionnula edited Tomás's manuscripts. She accompanied him on book tours and to social events, to keep watch over him. Fionnula was shy and it was a trial for her, but for his sake, she came along.

Tomás made gentle fun of his sister but cheerfully admitted that without her, his liver would rise and kill him. She made his work better too. He fell in love with useless paragraphs and found it impossible to let them go, as though they had hearts and he might break them.

She'd never married. Not that she hadn't been asked, Tomás told Delia. There'd been a couple of fellows who weren't afraid of her mind. But she turned them down cold. Their mother had been a beaut. She hadn't known she was expecting twins. It was unlikely she would have, in Ireland in 1918, unless the archangel Gabriel was still in the business of giving unsolicited information to expectant mothers.

Tomás was born first, and nearly died three times in his first half hour. Then his mother had Fionnula, and almost immediately Tomás got better. The priest who'd been called to give him extreme unction had no patience for miracles and their paperwork, but he did testify that as soon as the girl was born, the boy began to breathe normally. Their mother told Fionnula that she was an angel sent to earth to keep Tomás from going to heaven, or some churchy nonsense like that. Like a character from myth, Fionnula had tied her life to his.

Delia looked over and saw Fionnula seated nearby, her hands folded in her lap. She gave her a small wave. Fionnula nodded once. Delia hated to see her sitting there as though she were a secretary of the old order, one who sewed buttons back on cuffs and made dental appointments for her boss. Yet for all that, the Breens' devotion to each other reassured Delia that she'd been right to adopt a child, for Sean's sake.

She and Tomás began a conversation about what they were reading now, and Delia noted the eager and envious people hovering, waiting for the chance to get a word with him.

Eileen drifted over to them. "Nobody's coming in. I don't get it. It's freezing out there."

Delia raised a hand to brush Eileen's hair out of her eyes. Eileen, though, saw the hand and stepped back, just out of reach.

Delia straightened her jacket. "This is my daughter, Eileen. This is Tomás Breen, a friend of mine."

"Your daughter?" Tomás said, his eyebrows raised.

"Can't you tell?" Eileen said.

Delia shot Eileen a warning look. *Don't be rude.*

After all, Tomás had not said what people did all the time. *Oh, yes,*

I see it. Delia honestly didn't know if they were imagining things, or if they were being kind to a girl who would never be as pretty as her mother.

Eileen widened her eyes. *What?*

"Well, good to meet you, Eileen."

"Same here. Where in Ireland are you from?"

"A town in Donegal called Gweedore."

"Oh, north," Eileen said, so clearly disappointed that Tomás looked quizzically at Delia.

"It's not the fictional country of *Northern* Ireland, but it is in the north, yes," he said.

It had occurred to Delia that Eileen might hope to meet someone here. Yet the type of stupid, wild boy Eileen gravitated toward would be in the bars already and vomiting on his shoes before twilight. John Maddox, Bobby Geraldi, Evan (Spark) Lynch, a litany of young men whose foolishness could not be blamed on youth but inherent character flaws. Each was the sort blamed for leading a girl astray. Delia, though, suspected that in most of those cases, the girl was lost, or nearly, to begin with. But with "Oh, north," Delia understood that it wasn't a boy she was after. Eileen was searching for her birth mother.

"My family's from Galway," Eileen said.

"Yes, your mother has told me that."

Delia gripped her glass, certain Eileen's next words would be *Not her.*

"There was a fireman in my father's firehouse whose parents were from Gweedore," Delia said. "He played the button accordion."

"That's right, your father was a fireman. I'd forgotten," Tomás said.

Eileen turned her gaze on Tomás, and then on Delia.

Delia read her thought. Tomás had *forgotten?* How well did they know each other?

Delia imagined her reporting back to Sean. Both he and Eileen surely wondered why the few relationships she'd had over the years went nowhere. Sean, Delia had always suspected, wanted her to re-marry — a fireman, preferably — to prove how little his absent father mattered. Not that Sean ever spoke of Luke. He believed his anger was

a secret. How ashamed and furious he would be if he knew that Delia had been reading the longing on his face throughout his childhood.
He wasn't usually the only fatherless boy — the war — but none of the
others had been abandoned. She'd said it explicitly only once, last year,
when he told her that he was enlisting in the army. Her horror made her
forget herself.

"You don't need to fight a war to prove something to your so-called
father," she'd snapped. "The war he fought had to be fought. This ...
Sean, no. *No.*"

Sean had stalked out of the kitchen.

"Yes, Dad was a fireman. My maternal grandfather too," Delia said, to
get away from her thoughts. "My father was at the Windsor Hotel fire.
It happened on St. Patrick's Day in 1899."

"I've never heard of that." Tomás moved closer.

Delia paused for a moment to gather the facts. As though she were
lecturing her students, she began, "March 17, 1899. The last St. Patrick's
Day of the century. The Windsor Hotel was somewhere along the parade route, I forget exactly where. The Forties, the Fifties, maybe. It
caught fire during the parade. These were the horse-and-wagon days,
and with the parade blocking the whole street, I can only imagine how
long it took for the rigs to get close enough. Anyway, the firemen who
were marching in the parade ran in, dress uniforms and all. My father
was one of them. He was young then, in his early twenties"

Tomás laughed. "Firefighters are our best madmen."

Eileen half smiled. Delia could see her memorizing the remark to include in her next letter to Sean. Would she say "our grandfather" or "your
grandfather"? Eileen had never known either of Delia's parents, with
Jack Keegan dead and Annie-Rose gone long before Sean was born. Did
adopted people consider themselves related to family members they'd
never met, the way blood relatives had to? Delia was ashamed to ask.
She shouldn't think about Eileen as outside their family. She wasn't. She
was *not.*

Delia continued, "A lot of the hotel guests had been watching the
parade from the windows, and when it got too bad inside they started

71

jumping. Of course, this was all right in front of the crowd who were watching the parade. The jumpers landed right in front of them."

"How tall was the building?" Eileen asked. "Where did the fire start, on an upper floor or lower down?"

It occurred to Delia that she was asking the questions that Sean would have.

"My father always said that New York grew *up* too fast. The building was only seven, eight stories. But the ladders the fire department had didn't reach even that high," Delia said. "I forget the total number killed, but the hotel burned to the ground. Birds flying overhead suffocated from the smoke."

"Really?" Eileen said. "Why didn't they just fly higher?"

Tomás laughed. "A practical girl."

"It happened too fast, I guess," Delia said.

Her mother had told her that part. Annie-Rose had been fourteen years old in 1899 and among the spectators. Even with the jumpers and the screaming of those who couldn't bring themselves to jump, with the firemen and the cops fistfighting each other for control of the scene (God, nothing changed, ever) and the chaos caused by a panicked crowd, how like her mother, Delia couldn't help but think, to remember best the suffocated sparrows, falling dead onto Fifth Avenue.

"The monkey was there," Delia said. "One of the companies had a monkey as a mascot, and she rode on the truck. My father used to say the whole company probably had fleas. He didn't like firehouses with exotic pets. Snakes. Parrots. Lizards. He was a dogs-only fireman. I think he said that was a rule at some point in time. Firehouses could have a dog, two cats and birds. No number of birds specified."

"But you just said the company had a monkey," Tomás said.

Delia laughed. "Well, firemen aren't the best at following rules," she said. "At least rules they disagree with."

Tomás shook his head. "Madmen."

"My brother's going to be a fireman," Eileen said, "when he gets back."

Delia knew he'd taken the test, and that by law he wouldn't lose his place on the list because of military service. She could only hope the

city's money troubles would keep him off the job until he was safely settled elsewhere.

A group of four came in off the balcony, exclaiming about the cold.
Eileen dashed out. Coatless, of course. Delia didn't call her back.

"And where *is* your son today? Sean, is it?" Tomás asked.

"Vietnam," Delia said. The very word was bitter in her mouth. "He
enlisted."

Tomás shook his head. "Good God, he shouldn't have done that."

Delia nodded. "He was in college. I asked him to go for two years. I
thought he might study history. He was always interested in the Civil
War. And Irish history."

Yet even as she spoke, Delia knew this alternate Sean, a professor at
some small, prestigious college, or even a high school history teacher
who also coached baseball, existed only in her daydreams. (Would she
wish teaching on him anyway?) Possibly, it was her fault for trying to
counter his fatherlessness by raising him on stories of his great-grandfather and grandfather, and in doing so, teaching him that firemen were
the best kind of men. Hardly an untruth. But there were other professions, less exciting, perhaps, yet honorable. Sean didn't know.

Living right behind the damn firehouse hardly helped. Often over
the years, as the neighborhood got worse, she'd thought of selling the
house and moving someplace where Sean would have met a better class
of boys instead of a crowd whose interests, as far as Delia could tell,
were beer, baseball and girls. Upstate, maybe? Long Island? She'd have
to buy a car. Nathaniel had offered to teach her how to drive. But she
wasn't sure what she'd get for their house, and if it would be enough
to buy a three-bedroom. She wondered sometimes if she should have
adopted a brother for Sean instead. Nathaniel often told her to at least
investigate a move. Yet Delia had never brought herself to go out and
look for some small house, somewhere, whose windows had never trembled at the sound of fire trucks heading out on a run.

Eileen came back inside and rushed over to them. Her cheeks
were red.

"Galway's coming. I'm going to jump in."

"Jump in?" Delia repeated.

"The parade," Eileen said impatiently.

Tomás laughed. "Atta girl."

"I won't be home for dinner. I'll head back to Brooklyn after, to hook up with the girls."

She was backing away.

"Eileen, I don't want you wandering the city for hours by yourself. Not without Sean."

"Mom, come on. It's St. *Patrick's* Day. There's people everywhere."

"Yes, *Irish* people. And we are notoriously well behaved, on this day in particular," Tomás said with a grin.

Eileen returned it. "Yeah, exactly! Bye, Ma."

"Be careful," Delia called after her. She shook her head. "Seventeen. What can I say?"

It was then that Fionnula joined them. "Sorry to break this up, but you should mingle a bit with the masses, Tom."

Tomás sighed. "I may have been happier when I was a has-been."

Fionnula turned a stern look on him. She and her brother had the same face, adjusted for the masculine and feminine. The cheekbones, the chin, the high forehead and dark brows framing their bold eyes.

"If you're happier waking up covered in piss every morning and never writing a word, go right ahead. I won't stop you anymore."

"I didn't wake up in piss *every* morning," he said to Delia.

"I'd believe Fionnula over you any day," Delia said.

Fionnula gestured to a man standing nearby. "You were wondering what the next novel is about? Here, sir, ask him yourself."

Delia shifted, both to make room for the young man who she guessed wanted to be a writer himself, and so she could stand next to Fionnula.

Later, at the hotel, Fionnula was sitting up in the rumpled bed, a pillow behind her, her ankles crossed. She'd put on the bathrobe supplied by the hotel. They were too old, she told Delia, to sit around stark naked.

Fionnula poured herself a fresh glass of wine from the bottle of white they'd bought at the little shop across the street and said, "Your daughter doesn't look a thing like you."

Delia pulled on the other robe. She would have preferred to gather her clothes from the floor, disappear into the bathroom and emerge put back together. But it seemed too prudish. Still, she kept her back to Fionnula as she quickly pulled her underwear on. She was often told that she looked "amazing for her age," which was typically put at younger than forty-eight. It was true enough, she supposed. Nevertheless, her body was soft in a way she couldn't quite get used to.

"Maybe she looks like her father," Delia said.

"There should still be something of you in her. Don't tell me your erstwhile husband had a child with another woman and you raised her."

"Have you started watching soap operas?" Delia sat on the edge of the bed near Fionnula's feet.

"No," Fionnula said. "She's adopted, then?"

"She is, yes." Delia stood and went to the wine.

"Why didn't you ever tell me?"

"I didn't?"

"You know you didn't."

Delia sighed. "We adopted her from Ireland in 1952."

"From Ireland?" Fionnula's voice went up. "Why Ireland?"

"Why not Ireland? Luke was Irish. Born there, I mean. My grandparents were. And the whole process was much quicker."

"I remember the uproar and fuss about the American actress adopting an Irish baby and the Irish embassy issuing a passport for him in a day. The papers — not, mind, the Irish papers — all started asking were Irish children for sale?"

"Joan Russell. That was right *after* I got Eileen." She sipped.

The first time, they'd poured red wine into the plastic hotel cups — like, as Fionnula put it, a couple of aging whores. After that, whenever they met, they bought a set of wine glasses, overpriced in wine shops, of course, but how often did they see each other? Only when Tomás had business in New York. After, they left the washed glasses on the hotel bureaus. Delia liked imagining the array of housekeepers who found them.

Delia sat beside Fionnula and rested her head against the head-board. "I sent the nuns in Ireland a check, and they sent me a toddler."

Fionnula was clearly not surprised. "How do you know your daughter's birth mother is from Galway? Did they tell you that, or —"

"No, no. The home where Eileen was born was in Galway. I thought there was a good chance a pregnant girl might stay fairly nearby. And it made her happy to be from the same county as her brother."

"So she could easily have been from Clare or Roscommon, or —"

"She could be from Donegal. Maybe she's your niece."

Fionnula laughed. "Tomás was never well behaved, but God knows he didn't go 'round Ireland taking advantage of culchie girls."

"Culchie?"

"In America, it might be hick or country bumpkin —"

"I know what culchie means! Why would you say she was one?"

Though Delia tried not to think about the unknown mother, and for the most part had kept too busy to do so, at quiet moments the other woman came into her mind. She'd be taking down a bowl to make oatmeal for breakfast, or laying her book on the nightstand at midnight and reaching to turn out the light, or sitting in her office doing ridiculous paperwork that came with running a school, and she'd pause to consider her daughter's plain face and her teeth before braces and wonder about the girl who'd bequeathed them. How had she stirred the boy to passion? What had made them take the risk? Love, or daring, or boredom? Where had they gone to be together? A car? One of those lush green fields you saw in pictures of Ireland, so undisturbed that you might believe the country was deserted? Or was the girl grabbed off a street and pulled into an alley? Was it an uncle or a cousin? An even closer relative?

"She might not have been," Fionnula said. "Even sophisticates, such as they are by Irish standards, don't have much choice but to go to the nuns." She reached for her cigarettes.

Delia said, "Tomás thinks you don't smoke."

Fionnula smiled as she lit up. "Silly man. Now, I know Sean, you had. He looks like you. Why did you adopt?"

"There were a lot of reasons," Delia said. "I won't bore you with them."

"*Delia*, a lot of questions are asked that have as a matter of course boring answers. Like how was your day? Does this bus go downtown? Are your bunions better? But why did you adopt a child isn't one of them."

"There were complications, with Sean. I didn't want him to be left alone, the way I was."

"I don't know you as well as I should," Fionnula said.

"Oh?" Delia said. "Your twin brother thinks you've devoted your life to him because of your mother calling you his guardian angel."

Fionnula laughed heartily. "My mother was a dozen eggs, all of them cracked."

Delia laughed too, relieved that the conversation had turned away from herself.

"Tomás is talking about moving to New York. Did he tell you that?"

Delia lowered her glass. "No, he didn't."

"He likes it here. Americans fawn over him way more than the Irish."

"Would you come with him?" Delia asked.

"Don't worry. I won't show up at your doorstep in Brooklyn with a suitcase and a sign around my neck saying *Delia's Lover*."

Delia closed her eyes. A lover had soft blond hair and a smile that trembled at the corners.

"What are you thinking?" Fionnula asked. "What are you thinking right now?"

Delia looked into Fionnula's strong, handsome face. "'Peggy Gordon.'"

"The song?" Fionnula asked.

"It's St. Patrick's Day."

"It's Scottish."

Delia smiled. "I know. But you hear it today."

"What line were you thinking of?"

She had a good voice. Her father could sing. Delia sang softly, "*For when I'm drinking, I'm always thinking, and wishing Peggy Gordon was here . . .*"

Fionnula continued, "*I wish I was in some lonesome valley, where womankind could not be found* . . . Wouldn't that be a shame for the likes of you and me."

Delia flinched. Fionnula noticed. She leaned over and put a hand on Delia's cheek, turning Delia to face her. She kissed her.

When they broke apart, Delia asked, "Would you really move to America?"

Fionnula sat back. "And give up my place as the only lesbian in Ireland?"

Delia wondered, as she often did, who had come before, how many, for Fionnula. But such questions, if asked, would then be put to her. She looked up to see Fionnula studying her.

"I miss you when I leave," Fionnula said. "I don't know that you miss me."

Delia leaned over and returned the kiss. "I do."

She felt Fionnula smile and pulled back.

Fionnula touched Delia's cheek. "Well, love, if that's all you have, I'll take it."

Delia covered Fionnula's hand with her own.

April 1941

Delia pressed her hands flat against her desk to keep from drumming her fingers as her students took turns reading aloud from a short story called "The Quiet Witness," a retelling of Our Lady of Fatima from the point of view of a sheep named Argyle. Argyle? Delia thought. In Portugal? The visions had more veracity. Veracity. She loved that word.

She knew that if Blackie Noonan had been in class, before she even said "Begin reading," he would have raised his hand and asked, "What's 'witness'?" She'd explained over and over about learning a word's meaning from the sentence, and still the kid punched the air in a panic. But today nine seats were empty, Blackie's among them.

The Dodgers were playing their season opener against the Giants at two-thirty. The fathers who could afford tickets had brought their sons to Ebbets Field. A few boys had been in class this morning but disappeared after lunch, no doubt to take up positions outside the ballpark, hoping for a homer to sail over the fence. Even in April, the talk was of October and Brooklyn taking the Series after last year's second-place finish.

At lunch, Claire O'Hagan, the school secretary, had said there were more opening day absences than usual this year. It was because of the draft, the first ever in peacetime, instituted by Roosevelt last October. Delia knew her father believed they'd be in the war. Since Hitler invaded Poland in '39, Jack Keegan had been saying that it was only a matter of time. Mayor La Guardia was trying to get a bill passed that would grant firemen exemptions from military service.

Edie Brennan, another student, stuttered over the name "Francisco," and Delia glanced at the clock. It was almost two-twenty. Tomorrow was Holy Thursday, a half day. And then Good Friday, school was closed, of course. Delia didn't care if Jesus never rose again. It was enough that He had died, and on a Friday, so she had three full days off.

When the principal, Sister Francis, asked Delia in her interview why she chose the teaching profession, Delia spoke of a desire to influence children's lives. She was lying. It was her own mind she wanted to shape.

When she was sixteen, she'd discovered Edna St. Vincent Millay. Not in school. They'd never read her in English class. She'd been searching for Robert Frost in the public library, because she had a paper due on him, but instead came across a copy of *A Few Figs from Thistles*, misshelved under its title. She spent much of the next year writing poems, but not one was good enough to let out of her notebook, much less win her a scholarship to college. Vassar was the dream, though she knew she had no chance of talking her father into that. She knew she couldn't demand, because he would dig in. She couldn't cry, because that would be showing weakness. She needed to present the issue practically.

She and her father were at the kitchen table eating the meatloaf and potatoes she'd made for dinner. Her mother was in bed with a headache, she'd said. A covered plate sat in the refrigerator, where it would remain until tomorrow, when Delia would throw it away. As soon as dinner was over, her father would take off for the bar. So Delia waited until they were almost done, because he would be impatient to leave.

While they ate, he read the *Brooklyn Daily Eagle* and she propped her book up behind her plate. This night, she set the book aside and cleared her throat, and he looked up warily.

"College," she said. "I'd like to go."

"College?" her father said. "You're going to that place."

"That place," secretarial school, was his idea, voiced two months ago at the beginning of her senior year of high school. Delia had never agreed to go.

"I'd prefer college." She set down her fork.

"You don't need more school. You need to be able to support yourself."

"I know that. I want to teach."

"Teach? What, kids?"

No, puppies. Delia caught an exasperated sigh in her throat.

"I would like to become an elementary school teacher."

Her father glanced toward the kitchen door, as if hoping her mother might come in and take his side. Though if she were to appear, she would most likely agree with both of them. College might be good. Getting a good job might also be good.

"All three of Bud Mackey's girls went to the secretarial place and they all got decent jobs in the city. You wouldn't believe the money they make. One's with a lawyer, the other's with some big doctor. I forget where the third one is, but Bud says she's going out with a guy who works there. One of the bosses. Bud says he'll retire early and let them support him for a change."

Bud's daughters had been ahead of Delia in school, but she'd known them. All three were pretty and dumb. "Going out with" almost certainly meant "going to bed with." She imagined explaining that to her father, who in spite of his talk of her future after high school believed she knew no more than a twelve-year-old. But derailing the conversation wouldn't help.

"Josephine is going to college upstate. Josephine Cullen, Teddy's daughter. Do you remember her?"

Her father was silent for several minutes, frowning and staring down at his plate. Delia was beginning to think he might not answer.

"Josephine. Little thing. Barely said two words. You in touch with her?" he asked.

Delia shrugged. "She sends me a Christmas card. A letter every now and then."

Her father picked up his fork, then set it down and pointed at her. "Right there, that's the reason. These girls, their husbands get killed and they got nothing. You need to be able to support yourself, kid."

She could have pointed out that fire widows who became fire matrons, like Josephine's mother, were supporting themselves by doing housework at the firehouses. That was their job.

"Well, I'm not about to marry a fireman," she said.

He laughed. "That's right, over my dead body you'll marry a fireman. But you could marry some guy who walks in front of a bus. Same deal."

"So I'll cross blind men off the list too."

He laughed again.

Delia wanted to stomp her foot in frustration. He would tell this story at the bar tonight. *So I tell her, Over my dead body you'll marry a fireman.* The guys would all laugh and agree. No way they'd let their daughters marry firemen. None of them would mean it.

Jack Keegan possibly did.

It had not occurred to Delia before. Maybe he was not just giving a good line. Maybe secretarial school was also about getting her out of Brooklyn and into an office in the city, where she might snag a husband who was on his way up, if not already there.

Delia tried to absorb this idea as he waited expectantly for her next move.

"If the Depression does come back, an office girl has more of a chance of losing her job than a teacher," she said, trying to steady her voice as she used her trump card, which she'd been saving for when he explicitly refused to pay a penny of college tuition.

He sat back, stroking his mustache.

"You've got a school in mind? And don't tell me the place Josephine is going. You're not living away from home."

There was no hint of amusement in his blue eyes.

But Delia had expected that. She explained that Marymount was opening a satellite campus in Manhattan next year. It would be run by the Religious of the Sacred Heart and would be all girls, of course. It was a two-year school. Sister Peter John at school had told her about it and suggested she apply.

Two years was not enough, not nearly, but she would take it. Her father nodded and then glanced at the clock. Delia knew she had reached the limit of his attention.

"We'll talk about it tomorrow."

He stood up and so did she, to begin clearing the table.

At the kitchen door, he turned back. "Teaching? You'd like that?"

Delia was too startled to speak. She wouldn't have guessed he knew anything about her. Sometimes she thought they might have been boarders in the same rooming house.

"I'll like it fine," she'd said, and after a moment in which she thought he might say something else, but didn't, he left to go drink.

What she liked was the idea of being free every July and August, and her workday being done by three every afternoon.

How could she have known that planning lessons for eight-year-olds would require so much thought? Her mind buzzed with children's querulous voices, and her throat ached from suppressed yawns and from repeating "Sit still!" a dozen times an hour.

Delia had not actually believed she would have to teach. She'd believed Marymount would be like boarding a train without knowing where it was headed. But as it turned out, the final destination was the one advertised. No detour. No transfer. No rescue.

Decades from now, what if she was still in front of the classroom, hemmed in by the thumping of the eighth grade above and the yellow floors beneath her, polished in September and scuffed to ruins by December? Turning down guys from the neighborhood who asked her out on dates, waiting for someone better. Constantly reminded of her own years in grammar school, recalling the hostile faces of her own classmates.

When she was in the third grade herself, the mornings her father was home, her mother pulled herself out of bed and made coffee. She might stir oatmeal into boiling water. But if Jack had worked a night tour, he didn't get home until nine o'clock and Annie-Rose stayed asleep. Delia would leave the cold kitchen with her hair combed but loose, moored only by her ears.

Then there was the whole week when Annie-Rose didn't get out of bed at all, and then she was gone. Jack said that she needed a rest.

Sister Regina picked that week to take a stand. "Tell your mother to tie your hair back."

But her classmates knew the gossip the nun had missed.

Your mother's crazy. Your mother's in the nuthouse.

Delia said nothing. She only agreed to give Annie-Rose the nun's message.

Bess Callahan, the matron for her father's firehouse, came over to help with the cooking and the laundry in Annie-Rose's absence. Bess had been widowed two years ago.

Bess laundered Delia's clothes along with the firemen's things, though of course that was not part of her job, leaving Delia to imagine that her school uniforms and nightgowns smelled faintly of smoke. Bess talked about her dead husband as she did the dishes and cleaned the house. George Callahan took her out to Coney Island. The day after the Great Blizzard of '88 was her birthday, and he walked over fifty-foot snowdrifts to see her. George Callahan was the one who started calling her by the nickname Bess.

"You poor thing," she said to Delia once as she settled a clean sheet on the bed.

Delia said, "It's my mother who's sick."

Bess's face went from rabbit to fox. "Self-pity is a sin."

"The boys died," Delia said, repeating what she knew to be the cause, the deaths of her two brothers from the Spanish flu in 1918.

Bess said, "George Callahan jumped out of a building, and he was on fire when he jumped. He fell two stories, but it was the burns that killed him and it took five days. This was on the third day."

She pulled back her white sleeve to reveal a thick scar on her wrist.

"I was at the church lighting a candle for him, and I had to feel a little of what George Callahan was feeling. There isn't anything in the world that hurts like a burn."

Delia thought then, and still did, that Bess was the crazy one. For a long time after Annie-Rose returned, the image came to Delia late at night as she lay in bed listening to her mother pacing the house: Bess Callahan, stoic over a votive, mouth and arm taut as the bright flame licked her white skin.

Delia hadn't thought of Bess much until she began teaching. Bess had remarried, another fireman, of course, and moved out to Queens. Being in the classroom brought back that month Annie-Rose was gone, and the years Delia was tormented over it, saying nothing because there was no defense. It stopped only when her beauty began to outweigh her silence. As young as thirteen years old, she understood why the boys at least began to stammer their taunts when she turned her eyes on them to stare them down.

Delia barely stopped herself from sighing.

Edie Brennan sat huddled at her desk. Henry Carroll stood to take his turn.

"The—"

Henry stared at Delia hopefully. A good teacher would make him sound it out.

"*Vision*," she said.

"—vision was gone," Henry said. "We left the—"

He looked up.

Delia wanted to scream, *Mountain*. Jesus Christ!

When they heard a knock on the classroom door, the children

raised their eyes from their books, grateful for the distraction. As she nodded at Jimmy Valenini to open the door, Delia expected to see a student with a note for her that the children would think was scholarly. It would be from Claire, though. Claire O'Hagan, the school secretary, who was twenty-two, the same age as Delia.

When she first started at the school, Delia wanted to spend her lunch hours reading, but Claire insisted on chatting. Before long, Delia found herself closing her book. She was not particularly interested in the lives of movie stars, but there was something about the way Claire smiled when she told her stories, as if she knew none of it mattered much, that made Delia listen to her. Also there was the frankness with which she spoke of her parents. Her father, she said, lifting her shoulders, was a mean drunk, and her mother was just plain mean.

Delia imagined doing the same: *My mother never got over losing her sons, and my father's entire life is the fire department and the bar.*

What also drew her to Claire were the snide remarks from the one other lay teacher. During Delia's first week, Miss Geoghan whispered to Delia in the teachers' break room that when the O'Hagans moved to Holy Rosary parish two years ago, they claimed to have eleven children. But the youngest O'Hagan had a different look than the rest of the family, with that dark hair when all the rest were blond or redheaded. Claire was *sixteen* when the boy was born. Delia fixed Miss Geoghan with a falsely puzzled stare, trying to goad the old bitch into saying it straight out.

Delia expected the note to be about this weekend. The principal would be furious if she knew Claire was using students to send personal notes, but Claire shrugged and said she'd only yell, and what was yelling?

Probably it would be about the weekend. Claire's boyfriend always had a buddy who needed a date.

But the messenger at the classroom door was Claire herself. She leaned over and whispered in Delia's ear, "Sister Francis wants to see you. I'll watch the class."

Delia pulled back. "Why?" she said without whispering.

The children stopped their perpetual rustling. Claire shrugged but avoided Delia's eyes. Delia was suddenly alert, interested in her day. Sister Francis was certainly sharp enough to sense her apathy. Maybe she was about to be fired. As they changed places, Claire seized her hand and squeezed it.

Delia stepped into the principal's neat office, vowing not to argue for her job or cry. Such was her focus on the nun, who was sitting at her desk with her hands folded, that she didn't at first notice the priest or the fireman, until the fireman spoke.

"Delia."

Delia knew, of course, that there was only one reason for Chief Taulty to be at her school in full dress uniform. He had his white cap under his arm.

Beside the chief stood Petey Halloran, who'd been ordained last year and assigned as a curate to Holy Rosary, so everybody said, because his uncle the bishop pulled strings. What new priest gets assigned to his home parish? He and Delia had been in grammar school together. She still wasn't able to address him as *Father* Halloran. His eyes were wide and frightened.

"What happened?" she asked.

"We caught a job at a typewriter store. Your dad said he wasn't feeling good. We wanted to take him to the hospital but he said he'd go back to the firehouse, get cleaned up —"

"He had a heart attack," Delia said.

"Looks like." Chief Taulty's jaw moved.

Delia inhaled deeply, and when she exhaled, it was as if she were leaving her body.

Sister Francis spoke up. "Miss Keegan, you are of course dismissed for the day, and as long as you need to make the arrangements. We'll have the students pray for him."

"Thank you, Sister," Delia said with effort. As for the "arrangements," she thought, with relief, her father would get a full departmental funeral. She would not need to make many decisions.

"Oh, goddamn it," Delia said. She ignored the nun's reflexive frown. "Where's my mother?"

"The fire department chaplain's with her, and Lieutenant McAleer," Chief Taulty said. "A couple of the wives were heading to your house too."

That part was good. The wives wouldn't be telling her that Captain Keegan had been the best fireman they'd ever known. They'd make coffee and start cleaning the house. Joannie McAleer would slip Annie-Rose a drink, understanding that this was not the time to demand anything new of a person.

"Did he die at the scene or in the hospital?" Delia asked.

"At the scene," Chief Taulty said.

"That's better," Delia said.

June 1941

Without her father, it seemed to Delia that the brownstone grew, the hallways widening, the rooms multiplying then hiding themselves in the daylight. She and her mother were shadows slipping through the space, their feet barely making a sound on the carpeted stairs or the hardwood floors.

Delia wasn't sure what made her get out of bed after midnight. Her mother had always walked the house at night. But in three months of widowhood, there'd been a change in the sound of her steps. Delia imagined Annie-Rose not aimless, but instead purposefully picking up pieces of herself that were scattered through the rooms. Here, beneath the couch. Here, behind the mirror in the hallway. Here, beside the clock with Connemara marble trim that was set to the time in Ireland, an old custom Annie-Rose insisted on following. Midnight in Brooklyn. Six in the morning over there.

Annie-Rose was attending morning Mass every day, something she used to do only intermittently. Delia went down one flight of stairs, pausing on the parlor floor. Through the open pocket door, she peered into the living room, half expecting to see her father in his chair beside the radio, where he'd spent so much of the last year listening to the news about the war in Europe.

When Delia opened the front door and saw her mother sitting on the bottom step of the stoop, her mother turned around.

"It's late," Annie-Rose said, as though she'd come outside and found Delia there. "But I'm glad you're up." She met Delia's eyes.

Delia took a step back.

"Sit for a minute. It's so hot in the house."

Delia obediently stepped outside and chose a step above her mother. Her father would not have been happy to see them both out in their nightgowns.

Delia spied the ring around her mother's thumb, which meant that hidden in the closed palm of her hand was the penal rosary. The penal rosary used to fascinate Delia. When she was very small, her mother had told her how they were invented in Ireland during a time when Catholics could be arrested or even killed for practicing their religion. The penal rosary had only ten beads rather than five decades, plus an Our Father bead and a cross. You slipped the ring over your finger or thumb and tucked the beads up your sleeve, concealing them. To pray the penal rosary, you slipped a bead from your sleeve and into your palm.

"I was supposed to be a nun. Did I ever tell you that?"

"No." Delia curled her toes against the cool step.

"I wanted to go into the cloister but I waited for both my parents to be gone before I entered, because whichever went first, the other would be left alone. My mother said once she thought all the babies had been starved out of her when she was a child."

"Starved — *what?*" Delia said.

"My father said Jack Keegan was fearless in a fire. I saw Jack Keegan and I wanted to marry him. And here we are," Annie-Rose said.

She opened her palm and ran her fingers over the rosary. "You're like him. That's good. I've waited to give you some time. I didn't want to go right away."

"Go *where?* What are you talking about?"

Annie-Rose smiled. "I'm going into the convent."

"The convent?" Delia repeated, as though her mother had said the moon.

"On Cross Hill." She reached over and squeezed Delia's hand.

"For a — retreat?"

Annie-Rose said, "I haven't had a drink since your father died."

Delia snatched her hand back.

"I got a letter from the mother superior today. I wrote to them explaining, and then I went to see them a month ago, and now Mother's written to me. The order will accept me as a novice."

Delia stood up. "I'm going back to bed."

Annie-Rose held up a hand. "Delia, I've been praying for guidance ever since your father died."

"You can't become a nun!"

Annie-Rose only gazed at her, her expression calm, her hands trembling.

"You're married. You had children!"

"You can become a nun if you're a widow. Elizabeth Ann Seton had five children."

"So for years now, you've been waiting for Dad to die?"

Annie-Rose shook her head. "Never! Never. I didn't think Jack would die first. Even with his job, I never once thought he'd be killed."

Delia understood that. She'd never thought so either.

"I've been trying to make sure everything is in order. One of your father's men has a nephew who's a lawyer, and he's been helping me. The house is yours now. I'll leave you the lawyer's name and phone number. Call him if you need help, or any of the firemen. I'm going day after tomorrow."

"The day after — *Mother!* You can't be serious."

"I've been trying to think of a way to tell you. But if you need to get word to me, go to the convent on Cross Hill Avenue. I don't know for sure if I'll be there or upstate. There's another order there, you know. You go where they send you."

"Word to you about what?" Delia said. "If you go in there, you can't leave. Why not find an order that will let you come and go?"

Annie-Rose fingered the rosary. "God has called me to know Him better. To do that, I have to live away from the world. All these years, I thought the boys died to punish me for ignoring the call but now I understand. Mary had to show me a little of her own pain."

Delia stood up.

"Delia, please," Annie-Rose said. "I want to tell you that you should go to college, the one you wanted to go to. Jack was wrong about that. I told him but he didn't listen to me. He never did. Sell the house for the tuition money. You shouldn't be tied to this place."

"The only place I'm going is back to bed." Delia went inside, waiting for her mother to call her back, but she didn't.

In the time remaining, Delia refused to discuss her mother's purported vocation.

Annie-Rose gave up trying to start conversations about it, finally saying that she hoped Delia would understand, in time.

On Saturday night, Annie-Rose insisted on saying goodbye. Delia accepted her mother's tight hug and ignored her tears.

On Sunday morning, Delia woke to find her mother gone, as promised. The penal rosary sat on the kitchen table with a note.

For you, to give to your firstborn daughter.

Delia crumpled the note and tossed it in the garbage. Beside the phone, there was a nail in the wall where a picture had once hung. She took the penal rosary and hung it on the nail.

Then she got ready for ten o'clock Mass, putting on the new blue dress she'd been saving for an occasion that did not seem to be presenting itself. Since she was early, she sat in her father's chair and listened to the silence of the house, the story above her and the story below. At the time she should have left for Mass, Delia slipped off one shoe and then the other.

Eventually, she went to change, but paused at the family pictures that lined the hallway of the parlor floor. She looked at the studio portrait of herself, taken for her confirmation. She'd chosen the name

Rose, for Saint Rose of Lima. Brigid Mary Rose Keegan. Never called anything but Delia. She wore a white dress with a blue sash and stood with one hand resting on the back of a chair. She'd looked often at the picture that hung beside it, a studio portrait of the two boys, taken in 1917, the younger one perched on a stool with the older one standing beside him, his hand on his little brother's shoulder. So often had she looked that it took a moment for her to realize the picture was gone.

Delia gazed at the white space for a few minutes and then went upstairs to her bedroom, where she stepped out of her church dress and left it on the floor. After she changed, she brought her book downstairs and resettled in her father's chair. She left her veil pinned in her hair.

October 1941

When the doorbell rang at nearly eleven o'clock at night, Delia was sure her mother had come back. She had been reading in bed, and she dropped her book and flew down the stairs, nearly tripping at the bottom. When she yanked open the door to see Claire and the child she called her little brother standing on the stoop, Delia was so confused that she actually peered around Claire's shoulder.

"I'm sorry," Claire said.

Claire wasn't wearing a jacket, and the boy had on only a sweater that was too big for him. Delia ushered them inside. Claire came into the hallway shivering, clutching Flynn's hand. Flynn, who Delia suspected was named after Errol Flynn, held a stuffed dog that was missing seams from his smile.

"I had a fight with my mother. She told me to get the f— to get out. I didn't know where else to go. And I brought Flynn because"— Claire stopped —"he's the youngest. The rest of them can take care of themselves."

Flynn was six. The next-oldest O'Hagan was eight. Delia closed the door.

Briskly, she offered her parents' room. It had a double bed. Delia glanced at Flynn, who stared solemnly back at her as though he was delivered to a stranger's house every night when he should have been long asleep.

"Or — there's another bedroom. He can sleep there if you think he won't be scared by himself. It's got a view of the back of the firehouse."

There was a full-size bed that her brothers had shared and a bureau, but no other furniture. Plenty of nights, her mother had slept there.

Claire shook her head. "He's never been alone."

"Okay. But he can always move in there later, if you change your mind."

"Later?"

"You can stay for however long."

Claire pressed her lips to the back of Flynn's hand. "See?" she said to him. "I told you."

Flynn O'Hagan looked up at her, his hazel eyes expressionless, almost.

Claire was steadfast in her refusal to say what prompted her flight from her mother's house. She allowed only that it was worse than the usual. About her boyfriend, Ray Phelan, she said even less. In the first week at Delia's, he'd come by three times, and though Claire would not invite him in, she did consent to talk to him in front of the house. Delia watched from the front window. After Claire sent him away, he stayed on the sidewalk until she shut the front door.

Delia spoke of Flynn delicately, leaving openings for Claire to tell her the truth. Won't your mother come looking for him? Doesn't she want him with her? But Claire said no, her mother was sick to death of kids.

At the start of the second week, Claire went back to get the rest of their clothes when she knew her mother and the other kids were at ten o'clock Mass. Her father would probably be there, but too sick to get out of bed, if he'd made it to the bed.

Flynn stayed with Delia. After saying goodbye to Claire and watching her walk up the block, Delia closed the door and turned to see the boy sitting on the stairs. In the classroom, she had a script to follow. Outside it, she had nothing to say to a child.

Flynn surprised her by pointing at the pictures on the wall.

"Is that your father? Claire said he was a fireman."

Delia moved closer and saw he meant the photograph of her grandfather with his fire company, taken in 1870. The rig was parked in front of the firehouse, the men posed on the horse-drawn fire wagon in their long coats with large buttons. Almost all of them had mustaches. Her grandfather's picture was in a circle in the upper right-hand corner because he was the officer. He must have been about sixty then, she supposed.

"My father *was* a fireman," Delia said, "but that's my grandfather, my mother's father. He was from Ireland." She pointed to her parents' wedding picture. "*That*'s my father there."

Flynn asked, "What was his name?"

"My father was John Keegan. Jack. He once saved a woman from a fire over on State Street. She was already unconscious when he found her at the top of some stairs, and he carried her out. She was having a baby, so —" So she was heavy as hell, she'd been about to say, but cleared her throat. "He got the Bennett Medal for it. That's the highest honor a fireman can receive."

Flynn regarded her shyly. "Did your grandfather save people too?"

Delia knew only one story about him.

"He fought the Brooklyn Theatre fire in 18-something. It started backstage from a lantern and spread very fast. The whole building burned and collapsed. After, some of the brass — the bosses — said that there wasn't anybody inside. My grandfather said that's impossible. Then they looked and found almost two hundred people."

"He saved them *all*?" Flynn asked.

But Delia had meant the dead. The victims had mostly been seated in the balcony and were killed in the stampede for the exit. Burned beyond recognition, many had been buried together in Green-Wood Cemetery.

"Yes," Delia said. "All of them."

"Holy Toledo," Flynn said.

Delia hoped he never heard the truth. There was a good chance he wouldn't; it was one of those forgotten tragedies. She knew of it only because her father had told her the story about her grandfather, and how every year, on the anniversary, he would lay a wreath on the victims' grave.

"Sometimes your mother went with him," Jack had said.

Delia recalled the affection in his voice when he spoke of Paddy, who'd died not long after she was born. As for her father's parents, she only knew that they'd both died when he was a child.

"My grandfather and my dad worked in the firehouse around the corner," she told Flynn. "It was when Brooklyn had its own fire department. You can see above the door it still says BFD, Brooklyn Fire Department. All the fire companies have nicknames. This one is called the Glory Devlins, after my grandfather Patrick Devlin and this other fireman. His name was Jeremiah McGlory."

"That's a funny name."

"He was from Ireland too," Delia said.

"Why's it named after them?"

"I think because they were the first two members of the company. We can go over to the firehouse if you want and take a look around."

Flynn's mouth fell open. "They'd let us in?"

Delia wanted to laugh. Any kid who came to the door would be welcomed. The guys loved to show off the rigs. "Of course," she said. "I know them."

On a Friday night, the last night of October, Ray Phelan came by for the first time in a week. Claire went out to talk to him. Flynn was in the backyard, hoping to find some of the firemen in their own yard. They called the boy Errol.

Flynn reported that "the guys" said he had a future with the Dodgers. He repeated some of the awful things the men said about the Yankees, who'd of course beaten the Dodgers in the "Subway Series" three weeks ago. Delia thought her father would have loved that phrase. Like the firemen, Flynn cursed Mickey Owen, who dropped the third strike that let the Yankees go on to win Game Four. Delia offered to ask the firemen to watch their language around him. Out of respect for Jack Keegan, they might try. But Claire said she didn't care. When he spoke of the firemen, Flynn put together the longest sentences of his life. She'd always worried about him being too quiet.

He knows, Delia thought, that something isn't right.

Delia had a house to herself; the O'Hagans' was overcrowded. Claire's moving in with her would not have raised an eyebrow if she'd come alone. But because of Flynn, Sister Francis had twice questioned Delia about their living arrangements. She wanted to know if Claire's mother had given her permission to take the boy. Delia said she had no idea and stared blankly at the nun. Claire either didn't realize or refused to see that she'd confirmed the rumors about her.

Claire and Ray stood close together as they talked. Or rather, Ray talked and Claire listened with her arms crossed over her chest. When Claire turned to come in, Delia rushed to the couch and sat down. Claire sat on the opposite end with a sigh.

"What'd he want?" Delia asked, though she'd vowed not to.

"He said you could watch Flynn and we could go out."

"Oh," Delia said. "You don't want to?"

Claire shrugged. "I don't feel like it." She stood up and turned on the radio.

Delia was about to ask her what Ray thought of her living here when she was distracted by a commercial ending and a reporter coming on. The USS *Reuben James* had been torpedoed by the Germans early that morning. Most of the crew, over a hundred men, were presumed dead. Claire switched the radio off and sat back down.

"Turn that back on!" Delia said. "We could get in the war over that!"

"Who needs to hear that on Friday night? Anyway, we're not getting in the war." Claire waved a dismissive hand.

"They said the Germans killed a *hundred* of our men, Claire."

Claire chewed her lip. "Ray would have to go."

"So? Is he even still your boyfriend?" Delia asked with more anger than she meant to show.

"Even if he isn't, I don't want him to be killed!" Claire said. "And there's my brothers."

Claire had three brothers of draft age and another who would be soon. In the opinion of the whole parish, all of them were going nowhere fast.

"President Roosevelt might declare war tonight," Delia said. Claire covered her ears with her hands and shook her head.

Delia crossed the room and pulled Claire's hands away from her ears, intending to say, Yes, they all will go, and there's no way all of them will come back.

But Claire's hands were warm and alive against her palms. Delia held them tightly, met Claire's wide eyes, and the words wouldn't come.

Then Flynn dashed in the room, out of breath, and announced that the firemen had gone out on a run, and Delia let go of his mother.

That night, as she did every now and again, Delia opened her nightstand drawer and took out the catalogs she'd been collecting from colleges and universities all over the country. Vermont, Michigan, Pennsylvania, Maine, Oregon, California. She would have to take classes at night and work during the day, but that was fine.

In eleven days she would be twenty-three, almost too old to be sitting in classes with eighteen-year-olds. Maybe already too old. What would she do, exactly, with a four-year degree besides what she was already doing? She could, she supposed, take classes here and there as she liked, but to spend the money on the course fees just because she wanted to?

She tossed the catalogs back in their drawer. It was almost midnight and she was tired. She and Claire had taken Flynn to a Halloween party, thrown by one of the firemen for his sons. Though pleased Flynn was included, Delia realized the real purpose of the invitation. Almost as soon as she, Claire and Flynn arrived, the fireman's wife pulled her younger brother — a fireman, of course — out of a conversation to introduce him to "Jack Keegan's daughter." He was as embarrassed as Delia was and probably would have scuttled away as fast as good manners allowed had Claire not been friendly enough to put him at ease. As they were leaving, it was her number he asked for. Claire declined with a pretty smile.

Tomorrow was November 1, All Saints' Day, and she wanted to go to Mass.

Claire insisted that it wasn't right to be angry at Annie-Rose for devoting the rest of her life to God. The sincerity of Claire's faith surprised Delia. Still, Delia began accompanying her and Flynn to the eleven o'clock Mass at Holy Rosary, the one the O'Hagans didn't go to. After church, the three of them would go to Agnello's, where they'd buy rolls and a sugar doughnut for Flynn, and then walk through Prospect Park, often going to the lake in spite of the cold. Soon the water would freeze over. Delia planned to get Flynn ice skates for Christmas, and she'd say they were from her, not Santa Claus.

Her bedroom door opened with its two-note creak. She sat up.

"Delia, can I sleep here tonight?" Claire hugged the doorframe.

"Why? What's the matter?"

"I had a bad dream . . . It's a little cold in my room. I'm not used to sleeping alone yet. I share with my sisters, and now with Flynn in his own room . . ."

Flynn had been moved to the second bedroom three days ago. Claire and Delia agreed that there was no reason he shouldn't.

Claire half laughed. "Now you know all my secrets. I'm afraid of the dark."

Delia said, "You can sleep here."

For a moment, Delia thought Claire might climb over her, but she walked around the bed, got in and pulled the blanket up to her shoulders. Delia lay on her side, her back to Claire. They remained that way for some time. Delia almost convinced herself that Claire had fallen asleep, though there was no change in her breathing, and she seemed too still.

The sheets rustled as Claire slid closer. Her fingertips stroked Delia's hair.

Delia whispered, "What?"

Claire fit her knees into the backs of Delia's knees.

Delia straightened her legs and then quickly curled them again.

"I'll tell you something I never told anybody." Claire's lips moved lightly against Delia's hair.

"Okay." Delia turned over onto her back, so she could look at Claire.

"I forgot what I was going to say."

Delia laughed, and Claire did too. Then Claire kissed her, and Delia kissed her back. They kissed again, and then for the third time. She put her hand on Delia's stomach.

"Okay," Delia whispered.

At the dinner table, Claire and Delia didn't even let their hands brush each other's when passing the salt or the milk. But Delia asked for things more often than she needed to, for the chance of an accident. The pepper, the butter, the bread. Claire waited almost an hour after their bedtime, which came about three hours after Flynn's, before she went across the hall, always so silently that Delia never heard a single footstep.

Sometimes, in the dark, she touched the scar that bisected Claire's belly, but it made Claire tense up as if it still hurt, and she didn't relax until Delia moved her hand away. Flynn wouldn't turn, so finally they cut her to get him out. Weeks after he was born, her mother made her start school so nobody would suspect. Claire was still walking hunched over, and she had to wear a sweater all day for a couple of weeks in case she started leaking milk. All her classmates wanted to talk about was boys and movie stars.

Flynn's father was a friend of her brothers', two years older than she was. One night he had a party, and she got her brothers to let her go with them. He'd given her beer with whiskey in it. She could tell after she tasted it. She could hardly believe he liked her. They drank the same thing again the afternoon he invited her to his apartment (his father was long gone, and his mother was a nurse who worked the night shift at Kings County). After the first time, Claire figured it hardly mattered if she did it again.

When she told him, he said they'd get married, but a couple of days later, he was gone. His mother said he joined the navy, and it was probably true. He'd been afraid of what her brothers would do to him, and he should have been.

"You never did it with anyone?" Claire asked one night.

"Me?" Delia said, surprised. "No. Only you."

Claire laughed. "But I don't count."

Delia stroked Claire's foot with her foot. She felt Claire smile against her shoulder.

Every day, she and Claire walked home from work together, with Flynn. He was in the first grade, and after the last bell, he joined Delia in her empty classroom until four o'clock. She helped him with his homework and let him write on the blackboard with the colored chalk she saved for holidays. When the three of them turned down her block, Delia found herself looking at each of the houses and saw with relief that hers was no different from any other. Nobody could look at it and say that Delia Keegan had fallen in love with a girl instead of a boy like she was supposed to.

Delia was on the couch reading *The Heart Is a Lonely Hunter*. Claire sat on the floor at her feet going through a stack of albums. Flynn was in the firehouse yard playing ball with the firemen and a couple of their own sons.

Sammy Kaye's Sunday Serenade was on the radio.

"Did your mother like music?" Claire asked.

"My mother?" Delia looked up from her book. "I don't think so. She hardly ever touched the radio. Why do you ask?"

"You never talk about her," Claire said. "I bet she listened to the radio when you were at school."

"I don't think so," Delia said. "My father, though, he had a voice, as they say. At firehouse parties and at weddings and wakes, he was always called on to sing."

"I always liked this one," Claire said. She sang, slightly out of tune, *"Peggy Gordon, you are my darling, come sit you down upon my knee . . .* I had to sing that at our St. Patrick's Day concert when I was in the sixth grade."

"It's not even Irish, you know," Delia said. "That one's Scottish."

"I bet nobody knows that but you." Claire rolled her eyes.

"Did you wear green ribbons in your hair?"

"And a green carnation on my green sweater and a ribbon that said *Erin go Bragh* in gold letters."

"Erin go Bragh. Ireland Forever."

"Is that what that means?"

Delia laughed. "Yes! Didn't you ever ask?"

Claire shook her head. "Why do you know everything?"

But Delia didn't know nearly enough, and this used to matter so much more. Yet since Claire, her plans had grown strangely hazy. She didn't look at her college brochures as often anymore. During the school day when she set the class to do math problems or copy spelling words from the blackboard, Delia tried to envision herself as a student, but instead let her mind wander to the way Claire, after a bath, sat on the bed wrapped in a towel, and how Delia took a comb and gently pulled it through her wet hair, and how Claire did the same for her. Her face grew hot when she thought of the parts of Claire she touched, and how Claire touched her back, and how it felt when she did.

Delia closed her book and grinned. "Knowing *Erin go Bragh* isn't knowing everything."

"Was your mother smart too?"

"No."

"That's mean," Claire said.

Delia shrugged. "She was pretty. How's that?"

"Do you think she's a nun yet?" Claire asked.

"I think it's too soon. Maybe in a year."

"So she might come back?"

"She's not coming back," Delia said. "She might as well be dead."

"You shouldn't talk like that about a woman who's given her life to God."

Delia leaned forward to stroke Claire's fair hair. "Well, I'm an awful person."

Claire tilted her head back, leaning into the caress.

"I told Flynn we'd get a Christmas tree," Delia said. "We always put ours up on Christmas Eve, but he wanted to know if we could get it sooner. I said yes. If we water it plenty, it should be okay."

"Christmas?" Claire said. "Already?"

"It's in two weeks," Delia said, laughing.

Claire sat up and turned around to look at Delia. "I have to tell you something. About Ray."

Delia pulled her hand away. "What about him?"

"He wants to get married."

"So? Tell him no."

Claire got up on her knees. "I said I didn't know if I wanted to marry him, and my mother said I was stupid if I didn't. That was the fight. The night we came here. She said if he was stupid enough to marry me, I should get the ring on my finger and stop giving it away."

"Are you?" Delia asked.

Claire shrugged, and Delia drew in a sharp breath.

"Since us?" she asked.

"No! Not since us. I swear, not since us."

"Your mother can't tell you what to do. You don't even live there anymore! You live here."

"For now."

"For now?" Delia reached for Claire's hand, but Claire pulled back and twisted her fingers together.

"He keeps on asking and I don't know what else to do. If I don't marry him, I mean. We've been going together for over a year."

"You don't have to do anything. We make enough money at school to support Flynn."

Claire looked at her with something like pity. "Oh, God, Delia, how much longer before that old crow fires both of us?"

"Sister Francis doesn't know," Delia said, but she'd secretly thought more than once that if anybody was going to guess about them, it would be that nun.

At school, Delia was careful to frame an excuse for her stops by the office, though the true purpose was to look at Claire for a minute, to watch her glance up and faintly smile, her fingers paused on the typewriter keys, her ankles properly crossed beneath her desk.

"Not — not *that*. She knows about Flynn." Claire was still on her knees. "She's never said so, but she does. She hired me because she felt sorry for me. I wasn't that good a typist then. I never answered phones before. I kept accidentally hanging up on people and she never fired me."

Delia was too surprised to speak. So Claire understood that even the pity of Sister Francis could not withstand her publicly raising Flynn. Because the monsignor would hardly allow it once he caught on. And he would be informed of it by the women of the parish whose own lives had emptied out, with their children grown. They'd decide that since Sister Francis wasn't doing anything about the outrage, they had to. It would be off to the rectory, then, dressed for Mass on a weekday. Soon. Very soon.

Delia reached out a hand. "Let's go. I'll sell this house. We'll go to California, like you said that time, or anywhere we want to. We can say we're sisters."

"Who'd believe that? We don't look anything alike. We have different names." But there was hope in Claire's voice.

"Cousins, then. Or you're a widow and that's why our names are different. Flynn can be yours for real. We'll explain it to him. He's young enough. He'll go along."

"I can't tell him. He'll hate me," Claire said.

"You can't marry Ray," Delia said. You can't leave me too, she thought. "I don't want to."

"Don't."

"I don't want to."

Delia slipped off the couch to kneel in front of Claire. She kissed her fiercely.

"*Don't.*"

Claire pulled back. "My mother will say we're crazy —"

The music on the radio stopped abruptly and an announcer's voice came on. Delia turned to stare at the radio, but Claire kept talking.

"— and then there's my real brothers and sisters. To run off on them —"

"Shut up! Shut up!" Delia dashed across the room and turned up the volume.

Claire also jumped to her feet. "What? What happened?"

The announcer was saying, "*— repeat that. President Roosevelt has announced that the Japanese have attacked Pearl Harbor in Hawaii from the air. This bulletin came to you from the NBC newsroom in New York.*"

"Oh my God," Delia said. "Oh my God."

"What happened? What happened?" Claire looked wildly around the room.

"Japan attacked us." Delia's lips felt numb.

"But what's Pearl Harbor?"

"I don't know! They said it's in Hawaii. The Japanese attacked it." Delia began turning the radio dial.

"Attacked it?"

Delia couldn't find any news. She turned it back to NBC, hoping for an update.

"The whole last year before my father died, he kept saying it was only a matter of time before we were in the war," Delia said. "Mayor La Guardia's been working to get the government to grant military deferments for firemen."

"Why?"

In what turned out to be the last year of his life, her father had spoken of the war often at the dinner table, when in the past the two of them had eaten in near silence, he bent over his newspaper, and she holding her book. She'd listened impatiently, the pull of whatever she was reading stronger than her father's voice, her father's words.

"Dad kept saying New York would be a target and that we'd need real firemen, not some volunteer force they threw together."

"A target?" Claire said. "Us?"

Delia nodded. "The city. Our coastline, I guess."

Claire made a sound in her throat. She ran downstairs to the back door, and Delia heard her shouting, "Flynn! Flynn O'Hagan! Get in here, now. Now!"

Delia couldn't hear his response, but Claire screamed, "Now! Now!"

Hawaii had been attacked from the air. They'd dropped bombs on American soil. Bombs. *America.* Her father said they would. She was suddenly furious at him for dying. Japan would never have attacked America if Jack Keegan were alive. They would not have dared.

For the rest of the afternoon, Delia and Claire and Flynn stayed near the radio.

Two more updates told them that the attack was still under way. An ordinary Sunday morning. A sneak attack on what, they learned, was a military base. Heavy American casualties were expected.

Flynn lay on his stomach beneath the front window, flipping through his baseball cards. "What's 'casualties'?" he asked.

"Don't worry —" Claire began.

"It means a lot of our soldiers are dead," Delia said flatly.

"Delia! He's a kid!"

"He should know. He's *going* to know."

Flynn looked from one to the other before bowing his head over his baseball cards.

The room grew dark, but neither of them moved to turn on a light. Flynn fell asleep on the floor.

Claire whispered, "What happens now?"

"President Roosevelt will declare war on Japan." Delia rubbed her eyes, which felt gritty, as if she'd been awake for days.

"Tomorrow?" Claire asked.

"I think so," Delia said, and then, with more certainty, "Yes. He won't wait. We're already at war."

Delia had paused now and again to wonder why her father had been so worried about the war in Europe. He was not a man with sons. She understood now what she should have all along: he was thinking of the firemen he commanded. All the young men he sent into fire.

Had the mayor succeeded? Delia had no idea. She knew her father had had great faith that he would. The Little Flower was a buff. He understood.

Claire took Delia's hand and laid her head on Delia's shoulder. Delia rested her cheek on Claire's soft hair.

"My mother must be going crazy, worrying about the boys," Claire said. "They're not bums! They just never had a chance to do anything. They'll enlist. I know they will."

Hours later, when they were in bed and the room was dark, Delia whispered, "Don't go."

Claire whispered back, "If you could see your mother, you would. No matter what you say, you would. I'll go by tomorrow, for a little while."

"I can stay with Flynn while you're over there," Delia said.

Claire shook her head, whisking her hair against the pillow. "I'll bring him. Ma'll want to see him. She never hated him or anything. She let me keep him."

"So she could torment you."

"It wasn't like that," Claire said. "Anyway, I have him."

Claire rolled over on her side and Delia followed, wrapping her arm around Claire and sliding down a little so she could rest her forehead against Claire's warm back.

Alone, huddled in her father's chair, Delia listened to President Roosevelt declare war on Japan. Claire and Flynn had left before nine o'clock. Delia had watched from the window as they walked up the block, hand in hand.

The president started speaking at twelve-thirty and was done in five minutes. Delia supposed there was little point in saying much more than that America was in grave danger and was now at war. She wondered if Claire was listening at her family's apartment, surrounded by her brothers and sisters.

According to radio reports, men were overwhelming the recruiting center at the post office on Vesey Street in the city. Women were handing out coffee to them as they waited. Delia considered heading there on the subway. She should do *something*.

At a quarter to one, Delia wrote a note for Claire saying she'd gone for a short walk. Claire said she and Flynn would be home for supper, but if she and her mother got into a fight, she'd surely come back early. She had her own key, of course.

When Delia arrived at the convent, she pushed open the gate before she could second-guess herself. She passed by the statue of Saint Maren. When she was a kid, she'd heard stories in the schoolyard of the saint climbing down from her base and walking the neighborhood at night, offering her outstretched hand to anyone she encountered. Don't touch her hand, ever, it was said. You'll die if you do.

Delia followed the path to the side door. She'd half expected to find a whole line of mothers and red-eyed girls, clutching boxes from Agnello's that held cakes and cookies for the nuns in exchange for prayers to keep their sons and sweethearts safe. But there was no one. Maybe it was too soon. Perhaps none of this would seem real until the men began to leave.

There was a small backyard that ended in a brick wall. Behind it, Delia knew, lay the nuns' fabled garden. Delia turned the knob. The door was unlocked. She stepped into the turn room. The only light was from a lamp that stood on a small table beneath a niche in the wall. In it stood a statue of a female saint robed in red. A sign on the wall read, *In the House of God, talk of Him or do not talk of anything.* The opposite wall was decorated with photographs, some framed, others not. Delia went over and peered at them through the gloom. Some seemed to be fairly recent, but others were far older, daguerreotypes of families, or single men and women in the unsmiling pose of the previous century.

Delia paused. If she'd brought something, she would put it in the revolving cabinet — the turn — and a nun would spin it from her side and retrieve the offering. But she was empty-handed, because she hadn't admitted to herself that she was coming here.

Indeed, she was just about to leave when she heard a scraping sound, and she turned toward a heavy mesh screen in the wall, the size of a window. Behind the screen, a panel opened.

"Good afternoon."

The voice was young. Delia couldn't speak through her disappointment, and her anger at herself for being disappointed.

She finally said, "I didn't bring an offering."

"It's not required." The nun sounded like she might be smiling.

"What's your name?" Delia squinted, but she could see only a shadow behind the screen.

"Sister John," the nun said after a slight hesitation.

Delia wanted the name her parents gave her, but she let it go. "I'm looking for my mother. She might be here."

"There have been a few people here today. I can't say if your mother —"

"Not on my side. On yours."

After a startled silence, Sister John said, "Ah, Miss, I don't think —"

"She entered the convent this summer. She's a widow."

"Oh. Oh, yes."

"You know her?"

"I know *of* her." She stopped. "You can leave a letter. Mother will see that she gets it."

"I need to tell her that the Japanese attacked a place called Pearl Harbor. It's a military base in Hawaii."

"We know. We're praying for the country and the men who were killed."

"How did you find out? Do you have a radio?" Delia pictured the nun looking over her shoulder.

"Father Halloran came by yesterday afternoon to tell us and to ask for our prayers. Monsignor came to say Mass at dawn today, but neither of them have been by since."

Delia understood that they wouldn't, or couldn't, ask the monsignor for an update.

"The president declared war on Japan at twelve-thirty," Delia said. "They think they might hit California next, or even New York."

"We're at war?" Sister John said.

The gentility fell from her consonants. She was from New York.

"Yeah," Delia said, allowing herself the lapse as well. She listened to the nun's quickened breathing.

"You see the pictures on the wall?" Sister John asked. "We're supposed to leave everything in the world behind when we enter, but we're allowed to bring one photograph. Mother doesn't approve, but it's the tradition. We're not allowed to keep them with us, so we hang them out there."

"Do you get to see them when you go out to the garden?"

Again Delia had the sense that the nun was checking that she would not be overheard.

"Out there, where you are, is a public area. We don't go out that way. There's another door, through the kitchen."

"When do you get to see them then?"

"After Mass on the Feast of the Epiphany," Sister John said.

Delia thought of the picture of her brothers. She'd imagined it confiscated, like bootleg liquor, but the mother superior must have told Annie-Rose that she could bring it. One picture.

"Can you — starting from the left, go down five? He's standing by a Ford."

Delia found it easily. The man's face was narrow and, though he was young, he had a receding hairline. Still, there was a certain confidence in the way he leaned against the car door, smiling as if he'd been told he was handsome, and so believed it to be true.

She did not see her brothers. Her mother must have kept it, against the rules.

When Sister John asked Delia if she might, please, put the picture in the turn, Delia had already plucked it from the wall. She placed it on the shelf, its edges curling as though trying to hide itself, and the nun whisked the cabinet around.

"He's my brother," Sister John said. "I'll give it up. I'll confess, but for now . . ."

"Of course," Delia said. January 6 was a month away. Sister John could slip the photo back in place before then.

"God be with you. I'll keep you in my prayers." Sister John closed the screen.

Delia pictured her rushing through halls, climbing stairs, her robe swishing frantically. If the nun had stayed another minute, Delia might have asked her, "Did he leave you? Did it kill you when he did?"

Delia headed home by way of Cross Hill Avenue. She was about to pass the Irishman's monument with barely a glance, as she usually did, but then she stopped. Except for the time her father told her the story behind it when she was a kid, she hardly ever noticed the Celtic cross. Once there had been a garden, but now only some roses grew and a few other flowers left over from the days when it was tended. In December, of course, there was nothing but dead grass. It seemed fitting that the worst day in the history of their country should have come in the winter. It also seemed appropriate that Delia should pay her respects to a dead soldier on this day. The gate was ajar and she went in, wishing she'd brought a wreath.

She traced the intricate Celtic knotwork with her cold hand before sitting on the stone bench nearby. If she'd chosen nursing instead of teaching, she could work in an army hospital. She'd be able to do something to help. As it was, she was useless.

A man paused on the sidewalk, then entered in the same careful way she had herself, stepping past the gate without opening it further. He stood before the cross with his hands clasped behind his back. Delia noted the red yarmulke. She coughed a little, thinking he didn't realize she was there. When he began to speak, it was in a voice so low, she thought at first he was talking to himself.

"I was up the street working in my father's shop."

Delia detected an accent. Russian? Polish?

"This woman brings her radio in all the time, says it's not working. But there's never a thing wrong with it. We can take her money and pretend to fix it, but my father is an honest man. Every time, he tries to show her that she's turned the volume down or she unplugged it by mistake. Maybe it's the cat playing tricks. Who knows? Today my father plugs it in and turns it on and that's how we heard." The man turned around.

"I was with my friend at my house. She's been living with me." Delia hesitated, but this man was obviously not part of the parish. Besides, what did one illegitimate child matter now?

"She and her son. He was outside playing. We were — we were talking. I couldn't believe what I was hearing. I'm glad I didn't have to go to work today. I don't know how I would have stood it."

"Did they give you the day off?"

Delia shook her head. "I teach at a Catholic school. Today is the Feast of the Immaculate Conception. You're supposed to go to Mass." She smiled wryly. "I didn't."

He smiled back. "I said to my father that I can't work today. I have to go for a walk is what I told him. He takes it as another sign of the weakness of young people. But me too, I can't sit still."

Delia hugged her elbows. "The latest I heard was fifteen hundred dead. Civilians were killed too. Families lived there, on the base."

"I heard that they think there are men alive, trapped inside the ships that were sunk."

Delia shuddered. "And it was just a regular Sunday morning. That's what I keep thinking about."

"A man who came into our shop this morning told us that Mayor La Guardia is moving an artillery gun into Prospect Park."

"Oh my God," Delia said. "Why would they drop a bomb on Prospect Park?"

He shook his head. "I guess it's to protect, you know, nearby. I don't think they'd drop a bomb on the park itself, no?"

"If there's an artillery gun in it they might."

He laughed, and she did too. They sat in silence, their breath frosting the air. Delia glanced at him and then away.

"Will you enlist?" she asked.

"I'm going to try, but" — he tapped his chest — "I think probably they won't let me join up. My heart. There's something wrong with the way it beats, the doctor says. Not such a problem in everyday life, but the army, I don't know."

"If I could go and fight, I think I would, I swear to God."

"You know someone who will?" he asked. "A husband, brothers?"

Delia hesitated. "I had two brothers who would be old enough," she said, "but they died a long time ago."

She imagined being able to say to people that she had two brothers off fighting, and she felt a surge of affection for them that she never had before. Certainly, they would have both joined the navy or the marines after high school and then gone on to the FDNY. If they were already firemen today, they'd be reenlisting, no matter what Mayor La Guardia got the government to agree to do. She felt their bravery as almost a palpable thing, as though it existed in place of their ghosts.

"It's the same with me and my brother. I think of him all the time, but it's worse today."

"How did he die?" Delia asked.

He took a step toward her but then hesitated. She slid over to make room for him on the bench. He sat, folded his hands and fixed his eyes on the cross.

"My brother is the baby of the family and I am the oldest. There are three girls in between us. My mother said that of all her children, Mikolaj is the one who loves beauty. She says he liked to look at things, the world around him. The trees, the flowers, the stars. I don't know if he did. She was his mother."

"The Nazis?" Delia didn't mean to interrupt, but she needed to get past the part of the story where the little boy was alive and stargazing and have him be bones in his grave.

The man shook his head. "I don't believe he's dead. I wish I could."

In 1928, he himself was ten years old when the family decided to leave Poland and come to America. The day they were supposed to go, Miko was too sick to travel. Miko, who was five, was placed in the care of an aunt and uncle who were to follow with the boy when he was well. The two families had planned to leave together. But this way, only three fares had to be lost and repurchased, those of Aunt Ewa, Uncle Josef, and the boy, Mikolaj.

"Almost as soon as we got to America, my father wrote to his brother, 'Tell me if my son is still alive. Tell me when you'll bring him . . .'"

There was one brief letter back. The child was still too weak. For months, letter after letter went to Poland, each one more frantic. After a year, his father wrote to the rabbi of their old synagogue, as his mother had been begging him to do. His father had not done so out of fear and maybe shame, since he was the one who had said they couldn't wait for Mikolaj to get well. By then he understood he was not going to hear that his son had died. Perhaps, in some way, he would have preferred it. And indeed the rabbi responded that one morning, the village found that the couple and the child had disappeared.

His parents were not so naïve as to think that the three were on their way to America and the letter with the details of their trip had gotten lost in the mail. Josef and Ewa had a daughter who died as an infant. By 1928, they were in their forties. The nephew put in their arms was young enough to believe any lie about what happened to his first mama and papa, his brother, his pretty sisters.

Had they gone somewhere else in Poland? Or had they decided to slip into America? His mother said that her sister-in-law was a coward and would be afraid of American authorities. For years, she said, Poland! They are still in Poland. Then, the war. She had said it too firmly and too often to take it back: They are in Poland! For three days after the Nazi invasion in '39, she stayed in bed, weeping. When she got up, she would not speak to her husband. She said not a single word to him for three months. Then she did. She told him it was not his fault, but hers. She was the mother. She never should have left her child. But she had, and if he was not dead yet, he would be soon.

His father, though, continued to believe that the boy was still alive.

"I'm with my father. If I can go and fight, I will, so I can look for Miko myself."

Delia asked, "Would you even know him now?"

He smiled. "What would your brothers look like?"

"Tall, like my father, with his hair, the way it waved in the front. It would be very dark brown like his. They had blue eyes. Same as mine."

The man laughed softly. "You see? I will know Mikolaj Kwiatkowski. If not during the war, then when it ends, I will find him. He's eighteen now, a man. He can fight. He can survive."

Delia wanted to believe this. She did.

"What's your name?" she asked.

He put out his hand. "Nathaniel."

Accepting his hand, she said, "Delia."

March 1947

Delia knelt on the welcome mat, though she knew the weave would dig into her bare knees, leaving its pattern. In the winter, wool stockings offered some protection, but it was a bursting spring afternoon and her cotton dress was useless for this.

She spoke into the keyhole, then tried the knob, but Nathaniel never left his door unlocked. "Nathaniel? Please come out? Please come out?"

Behind her, at the bottom of the stairs, Tamar Leventhal hovered. Tamar, who'd called her, saying that Mr. Kwiatkowski had not come down to the shop that morning. And he'd disappeared about three o'clock the day before. Tamar dialed Delia's number, kept on a pad by the phone. Like last time, she heard him walking around but not often, and he wouldn't open the door for her. Tamar, only twenty, was in love with him, a fact Nathaniel politely ignored.

Marry her, Delia said, just as crisply as Nathaniel had told her *not* to marry Luke O'Reilly, two months after Pearl Harbor.

"Be engaged throughout the war, it's just as good," he said. "Then, if he comes back, see if you still like him."

But she'd said they were fated to meet, and Nathaniel sighed.

Luke O'Reilly had known neither Claire nor Ray but attended their hastily arranged wedding reception at Lehane's because he was doing a story for the *Irish Eagle* on wartime nuptials. It was January 10, 1942, and Ray was due to leave for basic training in a week.

Delia bought a new green dress, unsure until she left the house if she would actually go.

Claire's sisters were her bridesmaids.

"But you're my best friend," Claire had said. "I want you to be there."

Delia had hung up the phone and sat on the stairs until the hallway grew dark.

"Come with me?" she'd asked Nathaniel the next day.

"You want to bring a Jew to that wedding?" he said. "You trying to get me killed?"

Delia said she didn't want to go alone. He grew serious and said he would go, for her, but he couldn't. Not on Shabbos.

She did go, of course. Later, she thought it was so she'd know it was real.

Flynn ran up to Ray right before the cake cutting, and Delia, watching from across the room, hoped Ray would be rude to him and that Claire would announce she'd made a mistake and then Delia could take them both home. But Ray touched Flynn's head and leaned over as the boy spoke. "He's a cop, Errol," Delia wanted to shout. "You like firemen."

She'd had two beers, and though she wasn't slurring her words or stumbling, she aimed frequent smiles at no one as she moved through the crowd. A lot of guys from the neighborhood had already enlisted. The rest were about to, having listened to their mothers' pleas to wait until after Christmas. All the girls were hoping they'd be the next bride. Claire, who wore a knee-length white wool dress with green trim at the wrists, gestured to her at one point, but Delia pretended to misunderstand. She gave a short wave back and headed for the bar again.

Luke O'Reilly had dark blond hair, worn so long it nearly touched his collar. He smiled easily at the guests, who spoke quickly with their eyes fixed on his long fingers as he quoted them in his small notebook. When he got to her, leaning against the bar with her glass of beer, he didn't ask her what she thought of the wedding or the war, if she was scared, if she was proud. He said,

"Aren't you beautiful?"

"You're from Ireland?" she said.

"Now how did you know that?"

"Your shoes," she said, and he laughed.

"I'll have to take care of that," he said. "Can't have people knowing I'm Irish."

"Where in Ireland are you from?"

"Sligo," he said.

She laughed, because he had not said Clare.

"Is that the right answer? Do I get a dance?"

Claire was watching, Delia saw. Though Luke's hand on her back felt too heavy, Delia tilted her chin up and smiled as he asked, "Are you a friend of the bride or the groom?"

"The bride is my best friend," Delia said.

Luke, she learned, was twenty-five and had come to New York to work for his uncle, who owned the *Irish Eagle*. Mick O'Reilly, a widower with only a daughter, insisted Luke start out like anyone else, so he'd spent most of a year writing articles about ceili dances and society meetings, until Mick thought he was seasoned enough to cover news stories. After Christmas, Luke planned to start looking for a job at one of the city newspapers. Now, the war. He was going to enlist, of course.

Delia had never met a writer before.

Two weeks later, Luke asked her to marry him, and she said yes. Relax, relax, he'd whisper in her ear, and she tried, gnawing on the inside of her cheek. But she had not conceived before he left for basic training.

Now they were about to celebrate their fifth wedding anniversary, though the marriage felt far newer because Luke had not returned until the summer of 1945. He was easily distracted with bursts of temper. Delia didn't know if the war had changed him or if he'd always been this way. He still spoke of quitting the *Irish Eagle* and becoming a real newspaperman, but as yet he had not looked for a new job.

"Nathaniel? I know you can hear me," Delia said. "Please open the door."

Nathaniel's sisters barely spoke to him anymore. Two had already married into briefer surnames and the third was about to. They were weary of his search for their little brother. Their mother died during the war, and their father right after it ended. Whatever promise Nathaniel, as the son, had made could be put aside. Their village in Poland was annihilated. Nathaniel pointed out that nowhere on the Red Cross lists, or the lists published in Polish and English and German newspapers, did the names Josef, Ewa or Mikolaj Kwiatkowski appear among the refugees, survivors or the known dead.

Nathaniel did find the names of many cousins and neighbors. The rabbi who told his father *they've gone* died at Buchenwald. Nathaniel argued that the Nazis were meticulous monsters. If Miko or Josef or Ewa had been transported to a camp, there would be a record. The sisters said, It's been two years since the war ended. Miko would have surfaced by now.

What's two years after such mayhem? Nathaniel countered. One young man might have been missed by the overworked repatriation people with their pencils and paper who asked the survivors their names and how to spell them.

Nathaniel's sisters didn't understand that letting Nathaniel withdraw from the world didn't work. Left alone, he might disappear into grief, not only for his brother but for every person whose fate he had to contemplate each time he scoured a list and touched his fingertip to a name.

Nathaniel needed to be brought back.

"Natan? You have to open the door," Delia said. "I'm pathetic today."

What if her father, in the year after the deaths of the little boys, had gotten on his knees and called into the keyhole of the room where they died, "Annie-Rose? Annie-Rose?"

Footsteps approached and Delia started to get up, but the door shook as he sat down and leaned against it. Hell, she thought. She glanced at the small bakery box she'd set down beside her when she knelt.

She'd left Luke a note saying she'd gone to Brooklyn to take care of something with her tenants. She didn't take the time to think of what that something might be. He wouldn't be home until late anyway. If by chance he did see it, he would tell her, aggravated, to sell the goddamn house. When he came back from the war, she moved into his one-bedroom apartment in Manhattan, which was not far from his office at the *Irish Eagle*. It was meant to be temporary, but since no baby had yet appeared, there was no reason to move.

Delia rented her house to two firemen and their families. One had the upstairs, one had the downstairs. She saw no reason to hold on to the brownstone, except the thought of her mother, her hair cut short but free from its veil, arriving on the doorstep one day to find that strangers now owned it.

"Do you think my brother is dead?" Nathaniel asked through the door.

Delia jumped as though she'd been kicked.

Nathaniel had never asked her this before. Maybe if Delia finally said yes, he would sit shiva, say Kaddish and then, after some time, make a life for himself. Maybe with Tamar, or maybe a new girl for whom Miko would be simply the younger brother who died in the war, and not the phantom he was to Delia and probably Tamar too.

Nathaniel's sisters believed that if he mourned, it would be done. An illness cured. Delia was less certain. Nathaniel, composed only of grief and no hope. What would become of him?

Nathaniel sometimes followed young men he thought might be his brother, running after them on the sidewalk, approaching them on subway platforms, and in the past year, Delia realized that Miko Kwiatkowski also lived in *her* peripheral vision, the same sun-glare place where her daughter dwelled. The daughter who, so far, Delia had conceived only in her imagination.

Together the black-haired girl and the young man with sad brown eyes stood on the corner waiting for the traffic light to change, or together they walked along the wall surrounding Prospect Park, arms akimbo, or they turned corner after corner ahead of Delia and never did they let her see their faces.

"Do you think Mikolaj is dead?"

"Oh, Nathaniel, how should I know?" Delia said.

"You have an opinion, heart. Tell it to me."

Delia drew in a breath that she thought was for a sigh, but then she heard herself speak.

"I went to a lecture the other night with Luke. He had to cover it for the paper. It was on the famine in Ireland. This is the centennial of the worst year of it, 1847. They called it Black '47. A million died and a million left. My own grandmother, my mother's mother, came to America during that time. I only know her name was Brigid, and she was something like eight, nine years old. I figure the rest of the family died in Ireland or on the ship coming over."

"A famine isn't murder," Nathaniel said.

Delia could have made her case, but Nathaniel hardly cared about laissez faire and the British government. Murder by blight.

Luke hadn't wanted to hear it either. She'd tried to talk to him about it on the way home, saying it was hard to fathom that her grandmother had been a victim. Even though Delia didn't remember her, a grandmother was so close in time. Luke cut her off, telling her that she hadn't fought a war on the same side as England. It didn't matter what the hell they'd done or hadn't done in Ireland a century ago.

"The English were incredible," Luke said. "The men and the women."

The subway clacked and swayed. Their shoulders nearly touched. She felt cold in the middle, as if it had begun to snow inside her.

"I'm not saying it's the same," she said to Nathaniel, tracing the grain of the wood. "But there was mass starvation and disease. The dead were thrown in mass graves too." She stopped. He didn't need that image in his head.

"My point is, there are millions of Irish like my grandmother who probably should not have survived, if you went by statistics and odds. But she did live, and she came here and met Patrick Devlin and married him. When she was about forty, she had a baby. Some people live when they shouldn't."

Delia put her hand against the door where she thought his shoulder was. Nathaniel was quiet for so long that Delia thought she was going to have to try again later, but then he spoke. "So, forty? Maybe there's hope for you."

She grinned. "I'm almost twenty-nine. I can't wait that long. I went to Agnello's today. I did it. I bought a piece of soda bread."

"Ah, the magic bread," Nathaniel said. "Did it work? Are you pregnant yet?"

She laughed. Nathaniel slid back the bolt, and she reached up and opened the door.

Delia pulled herself upright in the hospital bed. She tasted copper, as though not long ago her mouth had been filled with blood. Her tongue hurt. Had she bitten her tongue? She felt like she'd been shipwrecked, waking after dragging herself out of the sea and collapsing on the shore. Her breasts were so sore she was scared to touch them.

Delia lay there, not moving, until the door opened and a nurse poked her head in.

"Well, well. You're rejoining us after all. How do you feel, Mrs. O'Reilly?"

Who? Delia nearly asked. Then she remembered. Luke. Luke O'Reilly.

"The baby? She's okay?" Delia asked. She was hoarse.

"Let me go get the doctor." The nurse vanished.

Delia closed her eyes, and when she opened them again, Dr. Fromson was standing by the bed with a frown that perhaps looked more imposing than it was because he was bald. She could see the wrinkles in his forehead, as deep as if they'd been cut with a chisel. Painfully, she pushed herself up. He congratulated her. She had a son.

Delia asked if he was sure. Throughout the pregnancy, she'd kept a notebook of names. Catherine. Juno. Isolde. Genevieve. Emily. Charlotte. Jane. Maud, as in Gonne, for a middle name. Not Mary, after Luke's mother, whom she'd never met. Not Annie or Rose and never Claire.

Delia felt a sense of loss so strong it made her want to climb out of the bed and go home. She drew the sheet into her fists.

"Your husband seemed happy," Dr. Fromson said.

Maybe it was better. When she told Luke they were having a baby, he'd said, "Well, that's a surprise," then stared out the window for a long moment before turning back to her, a failed smile on his face. Perhaps giving him a son would help make up for not realizing that his proposal had been a wild, romantic gesture and that she should have gently laughed, kissed him once and said, Find me when you come home, soldier. She should have listened to Nathaniel.

Delia asked if the baby was all right. Dr. Fromson said he was fine. Five pounds, three ounces. Small, but not a bad size considering he'd come three weeks before his due date. Delia asked what day it was. The doctor smiled.

November 27. Thanksgiving Day.

"A good way to get out of cooking," he said.

Delia tried to smile. She didn't have the energy to explain that her Irish husband didn't care a bit about Thanksgiving. She'd cooked the first year Luke was back from the war, but the following year, rather than face his pointed indifference, she'd gone to the movies with Nathaniel, though she told Luke she went alone.

"Is my husband here?" Delia asked, glancing at the door, hoping her words might make Luke appear.

"Visiting hours don't begin until eleven o'clock."

"Can I see the baby?"

"When the nurse has a free minute, I'll have her bring him to you."

"I'll just walk to the nursery and see him." Delia threw the blanket off.

Dr. Fromson held up a hand like a crossing guard and said she needed to listen to him.

There had been complications. After the birth she suffered a hemorrhage.

Dr. Fromson looked out the window. Delia looked too. She saw nothing but a brick wall and an expanse of gray sky. Maybe it was going to snow. A white Thanksgiving. That would be nice for the baby. Snow on his first day in the world.

"I'm afraid we had to remove your uterus."

Delia was certain he'd misspoken. He must have put in the word "uterus" instead of something like "socks" or, more likely, "underwear." *Mrs. O'Reilly, we had to remove your underwear.* A hazard of his profession. He probably thought about the uterus all the time, substituting it for different words. Please pass the uterus. I saw the uterus the other day. I've been standing here waiting for the uterus for ten minutes now. What was the plural? Uteri.

"You had to what?"

"Remove your uterus."

"You took out my — my — you took it *out?*"

"To save your life," Dr. Fromson said with sudden spirit. "Unfortunately, you won't have any more children, but you do have your son."

Delia stared down at her blanketed midsection as though she could see what was missing, the way she would an arm or a leg.

She thought stupidly that none of the stories of the soda bread ever mentioned that if you get your miracle, something will be taken from you in return.

May 1951

Delia stood on the sidewalk outside the convent, Nathaniel beside her. Both of them gazed up at the front door through the black metal gate. Somehow it seemed they were the ones in prison. Sean was asleep. Luke said he was too big for the stroller now and wanted her to get rid of it. Delia had so far refused, exactly for days like this when she brought him from the city to Brooklyn. At three years old, he was too heavy for her to carry for any distance. She pushed the stroller gently back and forth, not too worried. A nap after three would mean trouble at bedtime, but it was only one o'clock.

Even though it was a warm spring afternoon, the convent's windows were closed.

"Do you think they see us?" Nathaniel said.

"I don't think they spend a lot of time looking out the windows."

"How do you know?"

"You're right, I don't. Maybe she is looking at us right now. She probably thinks you're my husband."

"And then she's thanking God the baby looks like you."

"He has my eyes," Delia said. "She can't see that from there."

"Your eyes? Your everything," Nathaniel said, laughing.

"His hair is Luke's," Delia said, and looked down at Sean, who slept with his fists clenched as though angry at having to be still.

"Well, yes, that's a surprise," Nathaniel conceded. "When he was really little I would think, Soon he'll be as dark as Delia. But now I'm not so sure. His eyebrows are so light. I think he'll stay blond." He gazed at the sidewalk.

Delia supposed he was thinking of some trait he expected his brother to have, based on the child he'd been. But maybe Miko had grown taller than he ever imagined. Maybe Miko had gone bald.

Nathaniel looked back up at the convent, scanning the windows.

"A boy doesn't have to look like his father. I'd be better off if I didn't," he said.

Delia laughed.

"Does it bother his nibs?"

"I don't think Luke cares," Delia said. *Noticed*, she'd almost said.

"No one in there will think I'm your husband," Nathaniel said. "Nuns are charitable, but not that charitable. Did you think she would break the rules and come and see him?"

Delia stopped pushing the stroller. Nathaniel thought she passed by here only because she hoped that her mother would spy her grandchild and throw open the door. Yet it was also to view what had almost been the scene of a crime, though in the end, Delia had *not* abandoned her infant here.

In those first, confused weeks after Sean was born, she'd plotted to place him in the turn. Dreamed it in the fever of exhaustion. To give him back. The wrong baby. A changeling. The fairies had not even bothered to get the gender right.

For weeks, Delia did not call the baby by his name because she could not readily remember it. John was Luke's father's name as well, and he refused to pass it on. He said maybe Jack Keegan had been a good man, but John O'Reilly was not. Delia chose Sean, the Irish form of John. She thought Luke didn't like it much better, but he was not cruel enough to argue further over the name of the only child she would ever have.

She'd hated Luke during those first months, the way a ghost might hate the living.

He was solicitous and awkwardly kind, as if she were a lunatic handed over to him for safekeeping.

Though he'd always grumbled about Nathaniel before, Luke was only too glad to let him step in. Delia thought she might have died if not for Nathaniel, who, with Tamar gone, either trusted his new, inept employee to watch the store or closed altogether to come into the city as many as three days a week. He brought food and common sense.

Delia tried to explain that her organs were falling into the hole in her middle. First one kidney, then the other; left lung, right lung. Her liver. Somehow she was still living, but one night her heart would tip into the abyss and she would not wake up when the baby began to scream.

Nathaniel explained that this was not happening. She would accept, in time. When she told him the doctor suggested shock treatment, saying it helped when new mothers had these kinds of symptoms, Nathaniel made her switch doctors. Delia might have let them try it. Out of curiosity. To see what happened. The new doctor said that she was a lucky girl to have one baby when some women had none.

When Sean was about three months old, he began to sleep for longer stretches. Waking up became closer to what waking up used to be.

One morning, Delia opened her eyes to see daylight around the edges of the curtain. Babies died in their sleep sometimes. She got out of bed slowly and with her eyes closed made her way to his room across the hall. All the nights he'd woken her she'd done this, led to him by the sound of his crying. Now there was only silence, but she knew well the path between bed and crib. With her eyes still closed, she laid a hand on his chest. Up and down, so gently she could barely feel it.

A fierceness that seemed to be an equal blend of love and terror replaced her indifference. When Sean began to eat solid food, she had to sit on her hands to keep herself from panicking and pulling the food out of his mouth, an act that might well *make* him choke. When he climbed stairs, she stayed right behind him, her arms out, in case he fell backwards. Every kid in the playground was his potential murderer: polio. The fear was punishment, she realized, for being coy with the universe. She'd asked for help from a God she'd barely believed in.

These days, she was trying hard not to hover, to breathe through the acute panic she felt when she lost sight of him for half a second.

"We're growing roots here, heart," Nathaniel said.

"You're right. Enough of this. Where to?"

"Do you walk around the neighborhood until he wakes up, and bring him by the firehouse?"

"No," Delia said.

Nathaniel's eyebrows went up slightly.

"He's old enough now to remember the fuss they'll make over him. Every time we pass by a firehouse he's going to want to go in and jump on the truck."

"Other firemen won't let him?"

"No, they all will. That's the problem."

Nathaniel only clapped his hands together. "To the garden, then."

At Brooklyn Botanic Garden, they settled on a bench beside the Cherry Esplanade, a spot they chose for the wide lane of lawn bordered by cherry trees, the open space ideal for a three-year-old boy who has just woken up. She tried to smooth his sleep-ruffled hair but Sean jerked away and took off running. She jumped up and called to him.

"Sean! Sean! Don't go too far!"

"Where's he going to go?" Nathaniel asked.

"True." Delia sat down.

Sean picked up a stick and began dragging it through the flower petals that covered the grass. Blossoms drifted steadily from the trees like pink snow. It was the first Saturday in May, so the trees were about a week past peak bloom, Nathaniel told her. Every weekend in April, no matter the weather, Nathaniel came to see the cherry trees. Delia knew he also came to scan the crowds who came to see the cherry trees.

He still read the ever-updated Red Cross lists and several Polish newspapers, all the articles, skimming for the name or any stray mention of a young man the age his brother would be. He wrote letters to the American and Polish embassies. He left notes in Polish books in the library at Grand Army Plaza and the big library on Fifth Avenue in the city.

Mikolaj Kwiatkowski, I am here in Brooklyn. Your brother, Nathaniel Kwiatkowski. He left the address and phone number of the store.

Nathaniel had come to believe that his little brother, now a man, would someday find his way to the Brooklyn Botanic Garden. Or the Brooklyn Bridge. Or Prospect Park. Or Central Park. Or the Empire State Building. And he, Nathaniel, would be there when he did. His vigils had no set schedule. When he woke with a feeling. When he had the time.

Delia might have pointed out that maybe Miko had loved beauty before the war but was unable to see it now. He might not be in America. If in America, he might not be in New York. If in New York, he might not be in Brooklyn. But though Nathaniel no longer wore a yarmulke, no longer kept strictly kosher or went to synagogue, he believed he would see his brother again.

Sean scooped up a handful of petals and tried to release them. But they were damp, and Nathaniel laughed at his consternation as he shook his hand wildly to try to get them off. He ran over to Delia and she brushed his palm clean. He ran back to his stick.

"They say the nuns from the cloister come here on days the garden is closed."

Delia laughed. "All of those tales about them escaping. They go to the Green-Wood. They go to the little cemetery, the one where my dad is buried. They go to the movies. But they don't, Nathaniel. They never come out."

"I suppose," he said.

They both watched Sean for a moment, and then Nathaniel asked, "How is his nibs doing at work? Still writing his scintillating stories about the Society of Saint Patrick?"

"The alliteration is a nice touch," Delia said. "His uncle asked again about Luke going over to the business side of the paper, and he said not yet."

Asked again, though Luke's uncle by now certainly realized his nephew had little interest in running a newspaper. During the family dinners Delia was forced to endure every few months, Mick got fairly drunk and told Luke his problem was that he married too young. Got your fire put out early, he said.

"He says he's looking for a new job," Delia said. Without the rental income from her house, they wouldn't be able to pay the bills.

"This is the longest job hunt in history," Nathaniel said.

"Seems so," Delia conceded. "His heart's not in writing anything but letters to England."

"England?" Nathaniel said. "An old friend from Ireland?"

"She's not Irish. At least going by her name, she's not. Charlotte Edgewood. We got a Christmas card last year from her. Luke must have written her back, because every couple of weeks he gets a letter from her. I get the mail, so he knows I see them. He doesn't even bother to have her send them to the office."

Sean ran back and forth, dragging the stick behind him. Delia wanted to get up and snatch it out of his hand. If he fell with it, it could stab him, couldn't it? Through the stomach. Through the eye. She tucked her hands beneath her thighs.

"You don't open these letters?"

Delia glanced at him, and then away from his steady gaze. "God, no. I wouldn't do that."

"Because you don't care enough," Nathaniel said.

"Because tampering with someone's mail is a federal offense."

Nathaniel laughed, and she grinned at him.

"How about while you're here, you go by your house and give your tenants notice? Their leases are up in June, July? Give them until the end of the summer. That's more than enough time."

"More than enough time to toss two families out onto the street."

"When you rent, you go when your landlady says go. The city is no place to raise a boy. The crowds. The noise. The dirt. Brooklyn has all three, but then we have *this*." He waved a hand expansively.

"There's the garden up in the Bronx."

"When do you go up to the Bronx?" He laughed. "Do you ever even make it to Central Park?"

"Hardly ever." Delia hated Manhattan. Or rather, hated living there for all the reasons Nathaniel named. She still felt like a tourist there.

"Get a *get*?" she said.

He'd told her the name for a divorce under Jewish law.

"Get a *get*," he answered.

Delia sighed. She wanted to lay her head on his shoulder and close her eyes for a moment, but she wouldn't do that to him.

Sean was now at the end of the lawn, near the path, rolling down the slight hill and then running back up and doing it again.

"He's going to be filthy. I brought extra pants but no extra shirt. Remember when he was really little and I brought four outfits whenever I left the apartment?"

"You're not even being subtle, the way you're changing the subject. But I'll go along. It's warm out. He won't catch pneumonia. He's a boy.

He doesn't care if he's dirty." Nathaniel smiled indulgently. "I can't believe how tall he's getting."

"All the old ladies on the subway think he's four already. Then they ask me when the next one's coming. What am I waiting for?" Delia said. "I should eat the goddamn soda bread now. Now *that* would be a miracle."

"You have him," Nathaniel said.

"I wanted a big family," she said.

"Please," Nathaniel said. "Maybe you wanted to be a *part* of a big family. You don't want to be the mother of it. Too much time away from your books. You like quiet. I'm glad you have this one, though. That's a good thing."

"Let me show you something." Delia took an *Irish Eagle* article out of her purse and handed it to him. It had been published almost four months ago. Luke hadn't written it.

She watched Nathaniel's face as he read it.

IRISH CHILDREN FIND NEW LIVES IN AMERICA

Accompanying the article was a photograph of four solemn, round-cheeked children standing in a row, right after their arrival at La Guardia Airport, about to meet their new parents. They were all two or three years old, and they'd all been born in the same Irish home for unwed mothers in Mayo, which was run by nuns.

Nathaniel handed it back to her. "Why, heart?"

Delia returned it to her purse. She explained how she kept imagining her and Luke dying. Cancer and a car accident. A fire from which Sean was rescued but she and Luke died. Her mother had been an only child. Her father had been orphaned young, he and his sisters split up after. Jack never saw them again. Perhaps there were cousins, but Delia didn't know their names, much less where to find them. Luke's family in Ireland were out of the question. His two sisters were not married, and were not, according to Luke, the sort to take in an orphaned child.

"You're the only one on earth I'd want to have him. And no court would ever give him to you," Delia said.

A single man. A Jew. A Catholic child. Nathaniel nodded slowly.

Sean would end up in foster care in New York. If he had a brother or sister, then at least he would not be all alone.

"What does Mr. O'Reilly say about this?" Nathaniel asked.

"I was hoping we'd take a trip to Ireland this summer to visit his family, and then we could go to one of the — the places."

"You think he'll see some little cherub and fall in love?"

"Well, it doesn't matter," Delia said. "He won't go. I write to his mother and send pictures of Sean. But I don't think Luke cares if he ever sees them again."

"I know I'm hardly the one to give advice about being practical, but if your husband doesn't want to adopt —"

"I found another home in Galway. I didn't want to go to the one in the article. They're probably being flooded with calls. I wrote a letter and they told me that they needed a letter from my priest. I got Petey — Father Halloran — to write on my behalf."

Nathaniel frowned. "A reference letter?"

"It says Delia and Luke O'Reilly are practicing Catholics."

"Which you are not. Which this priest Halloran knows. Why would he lie for you?" Nathaniel said, and then, "He's in love with you."

"He did have a crush on me when we were kids."

"But even if the Irish don't know New York enough to realize, when the agency comes to inspect your home, aren't they going to find it odd that you take the subway into Brooklyn to go to Mass every Sunday?"

"Nobody's said anything to me about a home visit. As far as I can tell, the nuns decide who gets to adopt. Based on the letter." Delia had to look away from the disbelief, and disapproval, on Nathaniel's face.

"Delia! My God. You've gone ahead and done this already?"

Without telling him first, he meant. She tugged her skirt over her knees. "I just — I don't know. I wanted to."

"One letter from a priest and they send you a baby? You could be a convict or a madwoman. Your husband could be a drunk and a wife beater."

Delia shrugged. "The laws are different in Ireland, that's all. It's much simpler there. That letter from Petey, our baptismal and marriage certificates showing we are Catholic, a letter from a doctor saying we're not 'shirking natural parenthood' — that's obvious — and an affidavit saying we will give the child a Catholic education."

"Are they going to call you every few years to make sure this child is attending Holy Rosary of Saint Sacred Heart?"

"'Holy Rosary of Saint Sacred Heart.' Very good."

Nathaniel was quiet for several minutes. "You gave them money."

Delia hugged herself. "A donation. For airfare and new clothes for her to travel in. For processing the paperwork. They'll issue her a passport to travel on and they'll send her birth certificate and I figure maybe the consent form that the — the birth mother signed. Then we have to adopt her here. It's a formality, from what I understand."

Nathaniel nodded, and silently they watched Sean pick something up off the grass. He grinned and ran toward them, his hands cupped. A rock? A dead bug?

"I hope you find her," Nathaniel said.

Delia reached over and squeezed his hand just as Sean reached them.

January 1952

Delia saved the letter to open after supper. Luke had seen it; she knew he must have. First thing he did when he came home from work was leaf through the mail. She'd left the letter there, distinctive with its air mail stamps. Rossamore Abbey, County Galway, Ireland.

After she'd gotten Sean to bed, which took three stories and four songs, she joined Luke in the living room, where he sat in his armchair reading the newspaper. When she entered, Luke looked up with an expression she often caught on his face, something like surprise and disappointment. Delia retrieved the envelope from the table by the door and sat on the couch. She opened it carefully and pulled out a folded sheet of paper. A black-and-white photograph fell into her lap. She picked it up with a small gasp. A little girl sat on a stone wall, a woman's arm supporting her. Her head was turned slightly, her eyes fixed on the woman. Delia touched her pinkie to the baby's cheek before she leaned over and gave the picture to Luke, who hesitated before he accepted it.

She read aloud:

"Dear Mr. and Mrs. O'Reilly."

She stopped. "E-i-l-i-s?" she asked. "I don't even know how to say that. E-liss? *Eliss* was born on October 2, 1949."

Delia skimmed the letter, looking for the information she cared about most. "Eilis and five other children will leave from Shannon Airport on 20 January and arrive at La Guardia in New York at three in the afternoon. The children will be accompanied by two attendants, who will see each child safely to his or her new parents."

Delia looked up. "We have a daughter. Sean has a sister."

"*January 20?* In two weeks?" Luke said. "This is insane, Delia."

She decided to ignore the mounting panic in his voice.

"Maybe if we adopted here, we'd get an infant, but it would take *years.* A three-year-old is fine. She'll have to adjust, but after a while, she won't remember."

Delia looked down at the picture, at the bare arm around the little girl. It could not be a nun holding her. It might be some kind of attendant, like the one who would be flying with the children, but instinctively Delia knew that it was not. The children at Rossamore stayed with their birth mothers, apparently from birth until the children left the country. The *Irish Eagle* article had had a line she'd chosen not to dwell on: "The children said goodbye to their mothers, and left for America."

"E-liss," Delia said out loud. "E-liss O'Reilly. It's pretty but maybe not for America. Nobody will know how to say it. It says in the letter to let them know if we're going to change it. They'll have the attendant start calling her the new name on the plane. We can pick something close. Elizabeth? Eileen? Ellen?"

Luke folded the *Daily News* and placed it on the small table beside his armchair.

"Delia —"

"We'll have to get a bed for her. A bed or a crib? We can put her in our room at first, and then maybe she and Sean can share. But Luke, we can't stay in this apartment now. It's barely big enough for three of us as it is. A boy and girl can't share a room."

"You have to write to them and tell them we can't take her."

If he had said it loudly, she would have thought it was fear. But he was calm.

"She's on her way," Delia said, as though a baby girl were inside her.

Luke stared at her, then sighed and went to the window and slowly lit a cigarette. He tossed the lighter onto the small side table. She wanted to snap at him not to leave it where Sean could pick it up.

"There's a woman I met during the war. We didn't stay in touch after. There was no reason to."

"The war?" Delia repeated. "The *war?*"

Luke turned around then. He was backlit against the window so she couldn't read his expression.

"This is the woman you write to," Delia said.

"Charlotte, yes," Luke said. His lips moved to smile. Delia watched as he caught himself.

He looked away and then back in her direction. "It's not working for us. I can't spend my whole life doing this. We need to get a divorce."

"Divorce?" Delia said. "We can't *divorce.*"

"We can't stay married," Luke said.

"You couldn't marry her in the church if you got divorced."

"She's not Catholic," Luke said.

"Your family! Your parents, her parents —"

"We don't care if they never speak to us again," Luke said.

For the barest second, Delia admired his refusal to remain unhappy for the rest of his life.

"Why didn't you stay with her right after the war, when you barely knew me? We've been married for nine years. Why wait until we had a child? It wasn't because you were trying to make it work. You're never home. You treat your son like he's a stray dog I took in." Delia covered her mouth with her hand. She'd said it to be as mean as she could, but once the words were out, she saw the truth in them.

Luke shook his head. "I should have left a long time ago. I'm not sorry that we had Sean. I'll never be sorry for him."

He was lying. Delia crossed her arms over her chest. "She was married too? That's why you came home?"

Luke looked at her, startled.

"Oh. Now she's gotten divorced or she's been widowed. She's free. You're going to make yourself free."

"You'll find someone else too. I know you will," Luke said.

Delia held up the letter. "Nobody's going to want me."

"You can find someone who doesn't — who doesn't mind."

At least he didn't suggest outright that she find a nice widower who needed a mother for children already born.

"I'll send you money for Sean."

"Sean and Eilis," Delia corrected.

Luke stood up straight. "Jesus Christ, I told you, you have to write and tell them we can't take her."

Delia had never miscarried. But as she gazed at the rug, she almost expected to see the blood coursing down her legs and spreading over the beige carpet.

"I never meant — when we met, everything that was happening — we got caught up. It's better we fix it now than in another twenty years, when it'll be too late for us to start over." Luke spoke firmly, as though he'd finally found the tone he'd decided on when rehearsing this moment.

Luke disappeared into the bedroom. Delia heard the closet door open. She heard the clatter as he took the suitcase down from the closet shelf and tensed, waiting for Sean to wake up and wander out of his bedroom across the hall, the room that used to be Luke's office, scared and looking for her. But Sean didn't appear.

Drawers opened and closed. Luke's clothes rustled as he packed them. She hadn't moved when Luke came back to the living room holding the suitcase.

"You're leaving for England *tonight*?"

"Not yet, no. I have things to sort out with my uncle first. And we have to start the — the proceedings. I have a lawyer, and you'll need one too. I'll pay the rent for the next three months. A little longer if you need me to."

Delia clutched her letter, wrinkling the paper. Three months? How about forever? She didn't have a job. Then she realized he assumed she would evict her tenants and move back to Brooklyn.

"What on earth are you going to do for a living in England?" Delia asked.

"I'll figure it out," Luke said without meeting her eyes.

So she had money, this woman. "No more writing?" she said.

Luke shrugged. "That wasn't working out, was it? Time to stop kidding myself, about a lot of things."

"Yes, like your wife and son," Delia said. "What the hell am I supposed to tell Sean about where you went? Are you going to write to him? Visit?"

"Tell him the truth," Luke said. "We'll work it all out after I'm settled. He can maybe spend summers with me."

"I'm not sending my son to spend whole summers across the ocean with you and your mistress."

"She's going to be my wife," Luke said, and turned to go.

Delia now understood that in his mind, he'd left a thousand times already. Sean knew, Delia realized. Her baby. He'd already learned not to seek his father's attention. Around Luke, Sean was watchful, quiet. Even as he accepted the vague inquiries — "Were you a good boy today?" — and the distracted pats on the head his father doled out, Sean was waiting for Luke to go away and leave the two of them alone.

Delia called, "Luke? Listen. I won't fight it. I'll sign anything you want."

She'd gotten his attention. He turned around, tense, listening.

"The Irish girl — stay until the adoption is final. Or come back when we have to go to court to finalize it."

The disbelief on his face nearly made her laugh.

"My own son is one thing, but Jesus, I'm not supporting somebody's bastard, Delia."

"Don't call her that!"

"That's what she is! That's why she's up for adoption, isn't it?" Luke said. "What if they find out I've gone and they take her away from you?"

"They won't." Delia was almost sure of it. "I'm not asking you to support her. I'll figure that out. If I don't protest, if I agree to everything, think how much faster you can remarry."

Luke stared at her and then nodded. "Whatever you need me to do, then."

For a long time after he'd gone, Delia stood at the window where Luke, it seemed, had spent most of their marriage. How long before both she and Sean ceased to seem real to him and the guilt eased? The checks from England would stop. Six months? A year? No Catholic school was going to hire a divorced woman, and possibly not a public school either. She might have to say Luke had died.

Delia left the window and went into Sean's room. He was asleep, sprawled across the bed. She gently picked up his foot and measured it against her palm. His toes nearly reached the tips of her fingers. He would be tall, the pediatrician had told her. She wasn't, certainly, and neither was Luke. Good. Far better that Sean was all Keegan and Devlin and barely any O'Reilly.

Delia pulled the blanket over his feet and tucked it around his shoulders. Sean rolled over, and she readjusted for it and moved his stuffed dog closer, so if he woke and looked for it, it would be right there.

Tomorrow she would give her tenants notice. She would give them more than a month to move, perhaps the three months Luke had just promised, though Delia wasn't sure if she could trust him.

Sean would love the bigness of the house. The stairs. He would have a yard to play in. Delia couldn't for a moment imagine a little girl with them, and wondered if it might be better to let her go to parents who would not have to worry about supporting her.

She stroked Sean's hair. If only he had not turned her inside out to get here.

Delia went back to stand at Sean's window. She tried to recall who she'd been on December 6, 1941. What had that girl wanted? Claire.

Claire, who'd moved to Long Island with Ray and their first child after the war. And Flynn too, which meant he'd been told the truth about his parentage. Delia put out a hand as though she might find Claire's shoulder, and cup it.

March 1967

On St. Patrick's night, Delia didn't get home until almost ten o'clock. Fionnula wanted her to stay until morning, but she couldn't do that, of course. There was a Closed sign on the door of Four Star Electronics Repair. She rang the bell. Nathaniel let her in, and she followed him to his cluttered work space in the back of the store. Tamar used to keep everything neat. Tamar, who'd out one day and never returned.

There was a small kitchen off the work room with a table that sat two. Delia took her seat. Her chair had a cushion that Nathaniel had bought for her at a stoop sale. It was green, embossed with white flowers. Nathaniel made two cups of tea and joined her.

"A good day?" Nathaniel asked.

"Overall." Delia tried to smile. "I miss him."

"I do too."

"I pulled a trick on the universe to get him. What if it pays me back with his death over there in that godforsaken jungle?"

"Then we say goodbye."

"I could never say goodbye to my son."

"You will, though. If you know he's gone, you will," Nathaniel said. "And where is our girl? How long did she last at the fancy reception?"

Delia smiled. "Predictable Miss took off after about a half hour. She went and jumped in the parade thinking that her real mother will see her and claim her."

Nathaniel didn't say, as most people would be quick to, that Delia *was* her real mother since she had raised her. He shrugged. "It's human nature to try and solve a mystery."

"It would have been easier on her if she were prettier."

"Because beauty simplifies life? You believe that?"

Delia shook her head. Too tired to pursue this line of thought, too tired to pretend she held her worry for Sean and her worry for Eileen in equal measure, even before Vietnam.

She asked Nathaniel what he had planned for tomorrow. Nathaniel answered that he was going to walk over the Brooklyn Bridge and back again. Then, once back in Brooklyn Heights, he would stroll along the promenade.

"I haven't been down that way in a while," Delia said. "I'll come with you."

"It'll be cold up on the bridge, heart."

"That's all right," Delia said.

"You changed the subject." Nathaniel tapped the table. "Yeats."

Delia recited:

> *Being made beautiful overmuch,*
> *Consider beauty a sufficient end,*
> *Lose natural kindness and maybe*
> *The heart-revealing intimacy*
> *That chooses right, and never find a friend.*

She sighed. "I don't mean that I wish she were a prettier version of herself. I mean it might have been easier if Eileen looked a little like me. Coloring alone would be enough. When we stand next to each other, we look like strangers. She's always been aware of that."

"Beauty!" Nathaniel waved his hand. "What did your pretty face ever get you but your soldier boy who ran off?"

Delia laughed and laughed. He was the one, Nathaniel. He was the one she could not do without.

CHAPTER THREE

Mattie Starwaif Cullen

October 1971

THE CONVICTS BEGAN their songs at dusk. When she was a girl, Mattie walked up the road to stand outside Sing Sing's wall and listen. The voices made her think of the earth, pliable after rain.

Mattie was sitting on the small terrace off her bedroom, which faced the woods behind her house. The air had grown brisk overnight and the leaves blazed. Thirty-seven years had passed since her return to upstate New York. Autumn was the reward for living here. Otherwise, Mattie would never stop missing the city.

Her son lived near his firehouse in Red Hook. Brooklyn's Red Hook, not the Hudson Valley's. Last year, his fool of a wife went off to find herself. He divorced her and got custody of their two boys. Mattie had hoped he might invite her to move in with him, but he was able to arrange his shifts so he had days off at a time. When he had a night tour a babysitter stayed over.

Mattie considered suggesting that she move nearby at least. A small apartment. She'd be clear about that. She didn't want to intrude, but she wouldn't be so far away.

Yet even as she indulged in those moments, she knew it would never be. When there was a daughter, care of the old parents fell to her. Of course, her daughter was Josephine, unmarried. Two years ago, she'd begun yet another career, as a social worker.

Neither of her children would give a thought to her living arrangements unless she broke a hip or had a stroke and was unable to be on her own. At seventy-two, she was not in awe of her age, but the old woman staring out from the mirror with her own blue eyes was a stranger. Away from the mirror, she was only twenty.

Mattie looked at her watch. Michael was always late, unless his destination was on fire. Indeed, it was another ten minutes before she heard his car in the driveway. He entered the house calling to her and, after a moment, knocked on the bedroom door.

"Ma?"

Mattie raised her book so she could pretend that she was not aching to see his face. He hadn't been to visit in a month.

"Come in," she called.

Michael came over and kissed her cheek. "Hey, Mom. Sorry I'm late. Traffic."

"You should allow extra time for it," she said.

He was thirty-nine, which frightened her. Her son, approaching midlife. But still handsome, with only a little white in his dark hair. Michael was a runner and he played softball on the FDNY's team. So many of her friends' sons who were divorced were overweight and bitter.

Michael asked how she was feeling, and she said she was perfectly well. He squeezed her hand and she tried to hold on to it, but he pulled away. He said he was beat. They were doing a crazy number of runs a night. The city was a nightmare. She was lucky to be here.

The boy, Ian, came into the bedroom.

He was eleven. If Mattie squinted, she could be looking at Michael. It made her want to grab the child in a hug, but she knew he would be horrified. "*Zaubermaus,*" she'd sometimes called the baby Ian when nobody could overhear. "Enchanted mouse," an endearment borrowed from her own mother. That was about all the German her mother spoke in front of them, because Mattie's father insisted his sons and daughter speak only English.

Ian carried a composition notebook and a folder under his arm. After he greeted Mattie with a quick kiss, he looked at his father.

"Okay, I'll leave you two alone," Michael said. "You can get started."

Mattie frowned. "Where are you going?"

"I thought I'd go into town, see if I see anybody I know," Michael said.

Mattie had insisted on being "interviewed" in person, not over the phone, because she expected that Michael would stay and listen.

"I'll bring some food back. We'll have a late lunch." He grinned.

Relieved, Mattie smiled at him. Michael didn't hate her.

Ian perched in the wooden chair opposite Mattie and dropped his notebook and folder on the small table that sat between them. Mattie clutched the edges of the book in her lap. Perhaps the phone would have been better.

"Okay, so, I told you this is for school?" Ian said. "We had to pick a family member and write an essay about them."

"Him or her."

Ian squinted. "Huh?"

"Family member is singular. Grammatically, it's 'write an essay about him or her,' which are singular. 'Them' is plural."

"Oh. Okay. So I guess Dad told you, I picked Aunt Josephine's father and how he was killed in a fire."

"Did your teacher say it was all right to choose someone who wasn't related to you?" Mattie asked.

"We weren't allowed to pick our mom or dad or brothers or sisters. Those are the only rules." Ian chewed his lip. "I know I could've picked Grandpa, but he, like, made beer."

Mattie felt a flash of pity for gentle, homely Emmet Brauer, who'd made her smile and even laugh sometimes, though she had not loved him. His death of a stroke seven years ago made her a plain widow, not a fire widow, a term she'd always hated. She did miss Emmet.

If Emmet were here, he would shrug and say that it was impossible to compete with firemen. Still, he would be hurt that his grandson preferred to write about her first husband rather than him.

Ian flipped open his notebook, uncapped his pen and said, "First, about you. You were born in New York City?"

"In 1899, on the Lower East Side."

Kleindeutschland. The Starwaifs were one of the few Catholic families in Little Germany. They'd attended St. Brigid's, with all the Irish. Her father had not cared for the Irish. He thought them shiftless.

"Why'd you leave New York? How old were you?"

"I was six. My father had an offer to manage a cousin's grocery store in Ossining. The cousin had no children."

For three days, Gus Starwaif labored over the letter inquiring about a job. He began it again and again, setting down his pen and tearing the sheet of paper in half.

Ian consulted his notebook. "Okay. So, Aunt Josephine's father was Theodore Cullen, from Brooklyn, New York."

"Theobold," she said. "He was Theobold for Theobold Wolfe Tone, the Irish patriot."

"Theo*bold?*" Ian made a face.

"Didn't you ask Aunt Josephine any questions?"

"I mean, I called her, but she said it'd be better if I talked to you."

Mattie nodded. Josephine didn't want to lie to her nephew. She decided to let Mattie do it. Fair enough.

"Where'd you and Theobold meet?" Ian pronounced the name like he was saying it with his mouth full.

"Teddy." Mattie almost laughed. "We met in Tompkins Square Park in Manhattan. June 15, 1919."

She'd moved back to New York City from Ossining in early 1919, after her father died. She did this in spite of the Spanish flu — that's how eager she was to return to the city. Her mother arranged for Mattie to live with a cousin. Mattie took a job in a factory, sewing collars on shirts. The cousin was indifferent to her, as long as Mattie paid for her board on time and helped with the housework.

But the cousin's husband watched her. Once, when his wife was working an extra shift, he came up behind Mattie while she was washing dishes. He locked an arm around her waist as he put his mouth to her ear and told her no other man was ever going to want her. He put his hand flat on her back. She braced her arms against the sink and shoved backwards. Her strength startled him and he retreated. After that, she made sure never to be alone with him.

"Wow, you remember the date?" Ian wrote it down.

Mattie saw in her mind's eye the fountain in Tompkins Square Park, built as a memorial to the victims of the *Slocum*, and Teddy, tall and slender with his thick hair so bright in the sun, whom she mistook for German. Perhaps a relative or even a survivor. In minutes, Mattie invented for him a whole history of orphanhood by fire or drowning. She'd thought he was near her own age, twenty, but she learned later that he was twenty-nine. Teddy was one of those men who never outgrow boyishness.

"Yes, of course I remember the date," Mattie said.

Ian wrote happily.

June 15. A small prayer service was held by the park's fountain to mark the fifteenth anniversary of the *Slocum* disaster. Mattie suspected many at the service had stopped out of curiosity upon seeing the young minister waiting patiently to begin. His grandmother, he explained, and three of her eight children had been lost. Most of the families of the dead had moved away long ago. The *Slocum* fire marked the end of *Kleindeutschland*.

She let Teddy do what he wanted to prove her cousin's husband wrong. It was a mistake to agree when Teddy, his face stark with fear, said, "I'll marry you, then," with nobility she knew even then he did not possess.

But let the boy think she and Teddy Cullen had been on separate strolls through the park on a summer day.

"Did, uh, Teddy always want to be a fireman?"

Mattie nodded. "His uncle was a fireman."

His uncle had responded to the *Slocum*, and sent Teddy to that memorial service to pay his respects, as he was too sick to go himself.

"His father too, but the father died when Teddy was two or three years old."

"In a fire?" Ian asked.

Drink, Mattie wanted to say, but she thought for a moment. "Tuberculosis. They called it consumption back then. When Teddy was a boy, he used to chase after the firemen when they went out on runs. There were no trucks then, you know. They were horse-drawn wagons until, my God, the 1920s. Those men never wanted to make things easier for themselves."

Ian scribbled and Mattie was pleased. These were the details she could easily give.

"We were married in St. Brigid's the September after we met. September 20, 1919."

"Then, when Aunt Josephine was ten, Teddy died." Ian paused. "And then you stayed in Brooklyn for a while and then married Grandpa and moved here and then Dad was born."

"That is an excellent summary," Mattie said dryly.

Ian smiled. "Thanks. It was 1931 when Teddy died." His voice picked up speed. "An apartment building caught fire because of two boys who were playing with matches."

Mattie pursed her lips. "The father had taken off. The mother was out working."

Ian opened his folder and withdrew a laminated newspaper clipping. He shyly handed it to Mattie.

BROOKLYN FIREMEN KILLED IN TENEMENT BLAZE

It was from the *Irish Eagle*, dated March 2, 1931, the day after the fire.

Mattie had never seen it. She hadn't been reading the papers during those first days.

There was a picture of the scene, a group of firemen standing before the building, staring up at it. Except for the broken windows, it looked undamaged. The firemen were in profile. She saw the nearest one.

"Jack." Mattie didn't mean to speak out loud.

"Who?" Ian asked.

"On the left. Jack Keegan," she said. "Teddy worked with him."

She would leave it at that.

"Maybe I should talk to him?" Ian said.

Mattie looked up from the picture, but the boy's face was innocent.

"Lord, Jackie died in 1941. April."

"*Jackie?*" Ian echoed.

"It's not a girl's name in Ireland," she said. "His parents were from there. Sometimes people called him that."

Mattie held the picture out to him. For God's sake, look at it, she wanted to say. You are a child, but you are not a blind child. Ian accepted the clipping without a glance. But then, the photograph was grainy and Jack was wearing his helmet.

"Him and Teddy were in the same firehouse?"

Mattie nodded. "In Brooklyn. Jack taught Teddy everything about firefighting. Everything the formal training didn't." She hesitated. "Does it say in that article that Teddy saved a boy's life in the fire that killed him?"

"No! He did? How?"

"Check the papers two days after the fire. The reporters would have gotten the details by then."

Ian leaned forward. "But what happened?"

Mattie sighed. Teddy deserved his due.

The firemen were searching for victims. Teddy found a boy in a closet. That was one of the things Jack taught him. Check beneath the windows and in bathtubs for adults, since they try to escape or get to water, but children hide.

Teddy passed the boy out the window to the fireman on the ladder and was about to climb out. Word came up the ladder that the mother was screaming that she had two sons. Teddy went back and never came out. The second floor collapsed.

Ian's eyes were bright. "Oh, wow."

Mattie spoke slowly. "Jack spoke at Teddy's funeral. He said, 'Teddy

145

Cullen was a good fireman.' He was one of the best. Write that in your essay, Mr. Ian Brauer. Write those exact words."

January 1931

Mattie could not touch her bleeding lip because Teddy had her by both arms. She pushed against his chest and he shoved her. Her head cracked against the wall. Pinpricks of white light darted before her eyes. She raised a hand with the thought of catching them in her palm, like snowflakes.

Snow had been falling since early afternoon.

Teddy was saying the usual things. *Bitch, whore, ruined my goddamned life*, but she barely heard the words anymore. She would have the marks of his fingers around her forearms tomorrow, purple blooms that would fade to green and brown. The colors never failed to amaze her, and she often studied her bruises as though they were small bits of art Teddy had gently painted on her arms and thighs and, sometimes, on the smaller and more breakable canvas of her face.

Their upstairs neighbor banged on the floor, aggravated by the noise. Teddy loosened his grip as he turned his anger toward the ceiling, cursing the neighbor. Mattie pushed him again, but this time he nearly fell. She ran for the window and shoved it open. Cold air rushed into the room and she dove onto the fire escape. They were on the fourth floor. Had she chosen one of the other two windows, she probably would have died. Later, she wondered if she was perhaps trying to kill herself. She could have run to the small room where Josephine slept and hidden herself behind the child. He never touched the child.

The metal of the fire escape bit her knees and she pulled herself upright. Her lip throbbed. She turned to see Teddy in the window. His own face was ugly with bruises.

Teddy had not told Mattie what happened. She'd paid the neighbor boy a nickel she could barely spare to tell her. Stevie Crowley was no tattletale but his mother was a widow with a crowd of kids. The boy only gave her bits, enough to earn his money. Stevie told her there was trouble at the Glory Devlins because of the Negro fireman who'd been assigned to the company two months ago.

Mattie knew about that. Even the secrecy of the firehouse couldn't contain the story of how all the Glory Devlins put in for transfers the day the man reported for work. Captain Keegan had refused every single one. Resignations, he said, he would be glad to accept. The man had passed the test. Teddy had told her, bitterly, that Jack figured the nigger would quit in a month anyway. Let it happen natural.

From Stevie, Mattie learned that the newest Glory Devlin was called Micah Barnes. The men threw his bed down in the basement. Three times he brought it back upstairs, and three times they threw it back down. After that, any man who made trouble for him, Micah challenged to a fight in the basement, where, finally, he'd set up his bed.

Mattie was surprised that Jack was letting it go on. Stevie shrugged and said Cap figured better in the firehouse than outside of it.

Teddy's bruises spoke of the man's skill. Mattie saw his face and looked away before a smile could escape.

"Fucking stay out there." Teddy shut the window and locked it. He went and sat down on the sofa, stretched out and pulled a pillow over his eyes to block the light.

For the first few moments, Mattie was at peace, alone in the quiet night. The building next door sometimes seemed close enough to touch, but an alley separated them. At this hour, nearly ten o'clock on a weeknight, and because of the weather, it was empty of drunks and kids up to no good and young couples who somehow thought that it was a private place. The alley was almost pretty in the snow-brightness.

If she'd gone to the nuns to have Josephine, she could have left the baby with them. It was what her mother's cousin flatly advised her to do. But she hadn't.

The blood trickling from Mattie's split lip warmed her chin. As if waking from a dream, she began to shiver. She was dressed, thank the Lord. If she weren't, she'd be blue with cold already.

She shouldn't have started it, but he hadn't come home with his pay. She'd sent Stevie from across the hall to the firehouse to ask where he was. The boy came back and told her that Teddy wasn't there and none of the men would say where he'd gone. Hours later, Teddy had come through the door from wherever he'd gone to drink his horrible illegal beer or whiskey. Before he could hit her, Mattie swung hard with an open hand that left an imprint on his cheek.

"Your daughter is hungry," she said, though she'd given Josephine supper. She was the one who was hungry.

Mattie peered through the window. Probably the idiot meant to pretend to fall asleep but had then really passed out. She wanted to sit down, but soaking herself wouldn't help. She could start screaming. She could bang on the window. Somebody would call the cops. But freezing to death might be better than the shame of the neighbors leaning out their windows to see what was going on.

Mattie looked down, readying herself to climb down the fire escape, measuring the distance she might fall. Then she looked back inside, and there in her white nightgown stood Josephine. She remained at the edge of the living room staring at her father, perhaps wondering if he was still alive.

Mattie crouched at the window, hoping she wouldn't frighten the child too badly. She scooped a fistful of snow off the fire escape and rubbed it on her chin to clean off the blood. She dropped the pink snow and, with her wet fingers, rapped on the glass.

"Josephine? The window! Open the window."

Josephine turned as though half asleep. She was more the size of a child of eight than one who would soon be eleven.

Mattie often chided her over her meals. "Finish what's put in front of you."

Josephine would bow over her plate. The crooked part in her pale hair made Mattie want to rap her on the head with a knuckle or a spoon. She usually held back.

Josephine looked at her father and then back at Mattie, her mouth open wide enough to let a sparrow in. Mattie bit back her impatience. She wondered sometimes if the girl was a simpleton.

"Open the window." She mimed lifting the sash. "Open the window!"

Josephine turned and ran back to the bedroom, where she would probably curl up in her bed and will herself to fall asleep.

Mattie dropped to a crouch. It hurt her ribs, which her husband had punched. But it took a kick to break ribs. A punch, though, if hard enough, did cause babies to drop from wombs.

"Goddamn it! Goddamn stupid girl."

Mattie slammed a numb hand against the glass. She could take off her shoe and break the window. But then the landlord would make them pay for it, and Teddy would be furious. The snow was soaking through her shoes. She would freeze if she didn't move.

She took a cold shot of air and started down the fire escape. The ladder's slips of steps felt no more substantial than pencils. The cold metal burned her palms. At the ladder's end, just before the first story, she jumped before she could think about the height. She landed on her feet and staggered forward but didn't fall. She straightened up proudly.

It took perhaps twenty minutes. She was stumbling by the time she reached the right street. She'd been to the house once, last year, for the daughter's twelfth birthday party. Josephine had been invited, though she and Delia Keegan barely knew each other. Teddy didn't often take his family to firehouse outings. Maybe a son he would have.

During the party, Mattie had kept a jealous eye on Delia Keegan. Delia was quiet and slender, the image of her mother but with her father's sharp blue gaze.

Mattie went to the door beneath the stairs. She used calm, measured knocks, though she knew they might not hear, because she didn't want to pound as if she was being chased. She half hoped Jack would be at work, but she didn't think he would be. He and Teddy generally worked the same shift.

Indeed, Jack opened the door, fully dressed, an unlit cigarette in his hand.

"Holy fucking God." He took her arm and pulled her inside.

He ushered her into the kitchen, where the warmth and the smell of cinnamon almost made her cry. She wanted to sleep. She wondered if his wife could possibly have been baking at this hour.

Jack lowered her gently into a kitchen chair, perhaps sensing she wasn't sure how to bend her knees. He took both her hands in his and rubbed them hard as he studied the injury to her face. His callused palms felt so much like Teddy's, she nearly pulled away.

"Put the kettle on?"

Mattie started to get up, but he put a hand on her shoulder. Only then did she notice Annie-Rose had come into the room. She was also still dressed.

"Kettle?" he said without turning around.

"Tea?" Annie-Rose asked, moving to the stove.

"Tea," he answered.

"Silly question," she said.

Jack gave her a brief smile over his shoulder, which she returned, though he didn't see it. Annie-Rose set the water to boil as Jack bent down to take off Mattie's shoes.

Annie-Rose came to watch. Mattie had never realized how small she was. Maybe not even five feet tall. Mattie felt a familiar surge of envy. She was too tall. She'd always felt her own breasts were too heavy and her hips too wide.

When Jack had her feet bare, Mattie looked up at her and Annie-Rose smiled.

"Oh! Dry socks," she said, and disappeared from the kitchen.

Mattie heard a voice and then Annie-Rose answer. The girl. The voices stopped. Annie-Rose must have sent Delia back to bed.

"Where is he?" Jack asked.

Did beat-up wives arrive on their doorstep once a week? Mattie would have asked but she didn't want to be rude. On the walk over, her mind had flown from one lie to another. She'd gone outside with the trash or to visit a sick neighbor and she'd locked herself out, then she'd slipped and fallen. But there was no coherent reason for walking all the way here.

"He was — asleep on the couch when I left." Her swollen lip made it difficult to talk, as if the words had to climb out of her mouth.

The kettle's whistle turned to a shriek, and Annie-Rose returned carrying a towel and a pair of socks. She handed both to Jack and busied herself making tea.

Mattie took them, as the scrap of pride she had left would not let Jack put the socks on for her. Besides, her hands were warmer now. She could bend her fingers. Her feet were bone white and wrinkled.

"Jesus, Mattie," Jack said suddenly, "where's Josephine?"

"Asleep," she said.

"Asleep?" he repeated. "You'll stay here tonight."

Annie-Rose handed her the mug, nodding.

"I can't leave her alone all night," Mattie said. "Josephine wouldn't open the window."

Annie-Rose and Jack exchanged a look. Jack's mouth thinned even further.

"I want the cops. I want him in jail this time," Mattie said.

Jack sat up straight. "Mattie, come on. He could lose his job."

Mattie raised her eyebrows at him. He wouldn't be fired unless he was convicted and that wouldn't happen unless she testified. She wouldn't go that far, but he might always wonder if next time she would. It wouldn't stop him when he was drunk, but it might when he was mostly sober.

"You have to trust each other on the job. The men hear about this —"

Mattie snorted. Some might think less of him for hitting his wife. Others would say he should have hit her harder. "They would figure it's his business."

Jack frowned. "The decent ones wouldn't, and most of us are decent. My shoes?"

Annie-Rose nodded and left the room again.

"You're not going over there," Mattie said. She sat up straight in a panic.

If she got the police in it, Teddy would spend the night in a cell. But Jack—sending his captain would be a humiliation Teddy might not be able to take. She ran her tongue along her teeth.

Annie-Rose reappeared and Jack took his shoes from her. He put them on and Annie-Rose bent slightly, as though she might kneel and tie them for him, but then stepped back and folded her hands.

"I'll stay at your place for the night. Josephine can't be there alone and I can't bring her here in the middle of the night in this weather."

Mattie looked up at him. She should want to see Josephine, but her lip hurt.

"I'll make up the couch for you, Mattie," Annie-Rose said.

Mattie, of course, had heard the stories about how poor Jack's wife was crazy, but she didn't see it now. Her hands and eyes were calm. She bent over her tea to hide the tears in her eyes at being pitied by a woman who had spent time in a sanatorium. Melancholia, they said.

Jack nodded. "Sleep." He looked at his wife. "Both of you."

Annie-Rose smiled back and lifted her slight shoulders.

"Jack?" Mattie called as he started to leave the room.

Jack turned, his face grim.

"Don't—" She touched the cut in her lip with her tongue. "I don't want *you* to go to jail."

Jack said, very seriously, "I won't kill him."

Annie-Rose followed him out of the room and they stood whispering by the front door.

Mattie leaned forward and saw their silhouettes merge as they kissed. She sat back and stared into her tea.

Annie-Rose came back in. She tucked a lock of hair behind her ear and said, without looking directly at Mattie, that she would get a blanket and pillow for her.

Mattie sipped the tea as Annie-Rose slipped by her with the bedding.

"It's ready," she said shyly. "It's comfortable. I sleep on it sometimes."

"I'm tired." Mattie stood, holding the mug, and headed to the sink, but Annie-Rose took it from her.

"Do you want a nightgown? I have an extra one."

"It would never fit."

"I must have something —"

Mattie shook her head. She couldn't undress. Jack might come back.

When Mattie woke, she knew she'd been asleep for a while, but it was not close to morning. The living room windows were still dark. A light was on in the kitchen. She thought perhaps Jack had returned, but she heard no sound. He wouldn't know how to be quiet. Teddy didn't. Her brothers never had.

She tossed the blanket aside and got up.

Annie-Rose sat alone at the kitchen table, a glass of whiskey before her. Behind her on the counter sat a bottle of Jameson. Mattie didn't know much about Irish whiskey but assumed it was expensive even before Prohibition. She wondered how Jack had managed to get it. But she supposed he had plenty of connections in the fire department. The real question was why Annie-Rose would be drinking it alone in the middle of the night.

Mattie sat and Annie-Rose tilted the glass toward her.

She shook her head. "I never drink."

Annie-Rose took a sip. "They say I shouldn't drink, but I only do on special occasions."

"What's this occasion?"

"You've come to visit."

Mattie didn't know what to say to that, so she said nothing. "Who says you shouldn't drink?"

"Jack. Dr. Neumann. He's Jewish. Jack said I had to go to a Jew. They know what they're talking about, but I'm not so sure this one does." Annie-Rose stood, went to a cabinet and came back with a second glass. Her bare feet made no sound on the floor.

She poured Mattie a small shot and pushed it toward her.

"Take a little."

Mattie sipped and grimaced.

Annie-Rose lifted her glass. "This bottle was my father's. The men gave it to him when he retired from active duty. That would have been

1900. First year of the new century." She smiled. "He kept working for the fire department until he died. In the old days, they used to pour booze down their boots in the winter to keep their feet from freezing. Cheaper stuff, of course. He never drank this. I'm not sure why. Maybe he was saving it for some occasion."

"I didn't know your father was a fireman too," Mattie said.

Annie-Rose's eyes widened slightly, as if there were no other profession. "Oh yes. He came over from Ireland and he used to say he was one of the men who turned the department Irish. It was volunteer in those days, and he was one of the few who got hired when they made the fire department professional and started paying. The city didn't take too many of the fire laddies."

Mattie didn't much care. Fixed in her tired mind was an image of Jack sitting silently in a hard chair from the kitchen, placed with precision in front of the couch, waiting for Teddy to open his eyes.

"In the old country, my father would have picked a husband with a farm, but here it was a man with —" Annie-Rose stopped as if confused. "Jack. It was Jack. A man with fire. You were right to come get him."

"I should have left him out of it. I don't want Jack in trouble if anything happens."

"Jack won't hurt him too bad, not with Emily there."

"Josephine," Mattie corrected.

"Who's Emily?" A small frown creased her brow. She shook her head. "And he's drunk, you said. Jackie won't beat a man who can't hit back."

"Gentleman Jack," Mattie said.

"Gentleman Jack?"

"That's what they call him in the firehouse," Mattie said. "Gentleman Jack."

Annie-Rose laughed. "I never heard that."

Mattie nodded. She understood. Teddy didn't talk about the firehouse much either. "The boy who lives across the hall from us said it once."

"Did he say why?"

"He didn't know. I guess only the firemen know."

"Hmm," Annie-Rose said. She spun her glass twice.

"Jack's a good man," Mattie said bitterly.

Annie-Rose was silent, contemplating her drink. "He is," she finally said. "He always deserved better than me."

"Who deserves anybody?" Mattie said.

Annie-Rose laughed and lifted her glass toward Mattie. Mattie smiled and toasted back.

March 1931

Jack came to tell her. Jack, even though Teddy had transferred out of the Glory Devlins a month ago.

She and Josephine were folding the laundry when Stevie banged on the door to tell them that there was a big fire a couple blocks away. Teddy's company was there.

Mattie and Josephine looked at each other, then Mattie went back to folding clothes. Josephine opened the window and climbed out onto the fire escape. The smell of smoke drifted in. Sirens went wailing up the street. Mattie recalled Teddy's uncle telling stories about the banshee. Americans thought everyone Irish could hear the wail, but that wasn't the way of it. The banshee was attached to certain families, and the Cullens were one of them.

A while later, Stevie came back, panting, to tell them there'd been a collapse. Some firemen were trapped and the rest were digging them out. The Glory Devlins were there too.

By the time the knock came two hours later, Mattie and Josephine were sitting at either end of the couch. Mattie stood up, smoothed her hair and checked that her blouse was tucked into her skirt. Josephine jumped up and seized her elbow. Mattie shook her off, and Josephine sat back down as though she'd been shoved.

Jack stood in the doorway and Monsignor Halloran stood next to him. Mattie stepped aside and let them in. Jack had cleaned himself up and put on his dress uniform, but he reeked of sulfur. His eyes were red, but that might have been from the smoke.

He glanced at Josephine.

"Go ahead," Mattie told him.

Mattie already knew. Stevie would have come with the news of what hospital they'd taken Teddy to if he was only hurt. Yet hearing Jack say the words frightened her. Her hand flew out to the side, searching for something to hold on to.

"Teddy's gone," Jack said quietly. "Him and Jimmy Libretti and Eugene Connelly. Captain Connelly went to see their wives. I said I'd come tell you."

Since Teddy was under Jack only two months ago, Jack no doubt thought he deserved this chore. When Teddy came home and told her that he was being transferred, Mattie thought for a moment that Jack had done it out of revenge for what he'd done to her. When she learned the truth, she berated herself for thinking that firehouse business would have anything to do with a woman.

It seemed that Teddy and three other men went to Jack and told him they could no longer work with Micah Barnes. They wanted out. If he'd asked her, Mattie would have told Teddy what Jack Keegan would do. No matter his feelings about Negro firemen, Jack would not stand for being challenged like that. He granted the transfers. And now Teddy was dead.

"Did you find them?" Mattie asked.

"We got 'em out," Jack said fiercely.

"I'm sorry for your loss, Mrs. Cullen," Monsignor Halloran piped up.

Mattie nodded once. "What happened?" she asked Jack.

"I can talk to you about that later," Jack said. Again he looked at Josephine. Her mouth was open a little but she was otherwise still.

"It's better if she hears it from you," Mattie said without following his glance. He would find better words. She could do that for her daughter at least.

Jack explained that Teddy had saved one boy and then gone back to look for his brother. The floor collapsed. Jimmy and Eugene were one floor below Teddy. All three of them ended up buried.

The priest bowed his head. "Your husband died a hero, Mrs. Cullen."

Mattie stroked her lip. "The one boy Teddy got out. The other?" she asked.

Jack's features contorted. "He wasn't in the building. When the fire started, he got scared and ran out. He came back before we even left the scene. The Firemen's Fund will help you."

Mattie hadn't been thinking about money. Only that Teddy was gone and it was over. A wash of fear replaced the numbness. Where was work to be found these days?

She lifted her chin. "I don't take charity. What will it do for Josephine if I support her on handouts?"

"It'll teach her that the fire department her father gave his life for will take care of you both," Jack said.

Mattie wanted to close her eyes and sit right on the floor. She would never get away.

July 1931

Mattie pulled the sheet taut on the last of the beds. She went downstairs to the kitchen and got her broom and dustpan. Strictly speaking, the outside of the firehouse was not her responsibility, but she liked to keep it looking neat. Children who came by to visit often dropped candy wrappers on the sidewalk. But it seemed to make the men uncomfortable to see her sweeping.

"Hey, Mrs. Cullen, the probie'll do that," one or more of them would say. And the probie would jump to attention, ready to take over. So she'd taken to sweeping when the men were out on a run.

Jack had tried to find her a job at a firehouse in Brooklyn, but no Brooklyn firehouses needed anyone at the moment. Mattie told him not to be ridiculous. If she was going to be a maid, it didn't much matter to her where she was going to be a maid. *Matron*, he'd corrected. Fire matron, that's what they were called.

Jack found her a place in lower Manhattan, not far from Tompkins Square Park. In the few months since she'd begun doing the firehouse's domestic work, cleaning, doing laundry, mending, she'd gotten to know the men and worry for them when the bells rang and they went out — a new feeling. Teddy she'd never worried over. She'd learned to accept the respect the firemen showed her. And somehow, it was respect and not pity, even though her pay came out of their own pockets. She made $13 a week.

Teddy was dead, but sometimes when she heard her upstairs neighbor coming home from work, his feet as heavy on the stairs as Teddy's had been, her heart beat out of time. Josephine didn't miss him, near as Mattie could tell. She'd even stopped hunching her shoulders so much.

Almost possessively, Mattie began sweeping the sidewalk, but stopped when she heard whistling, trying to place the song. It was an Irish tune, she believed. The whistling grew closer and the words flitted just out of range. She waited, the broom still. Emmet Brauer rounded the corner, holding two growlers of beer, though if asked he'd undoubtedly claim they were soda. If the police made him remove the caps, he wouldn't be arrested but he'd lose the growlers, as the cops would take the beer back to the stationhouse and drink it themselves.

Emmet Brauer ran the brewery in Red Hook that his father had started. Emmet had kept it going, barely, since Prohibition, by switching to soda. Beer would be his profession again once the amendment was repealed, supposedly very soon. But the FDNY was his passion.

Emmet set down one of the growlers and took off his hat. His brown hair was thinning. "Good afternoon, Mrs. Cullen," he said shyly. "They're out?"

Mattie nodded. "They've been gone about five minutes."

"Did you hear where the fire is?"

She shook her head. "I didn't."

"Well, I'm sure they won't mind if I get these inside, out of the sun. Then I'll go see if I can find them." Emmet nodded, blushing, and she nodded back, not quite comfortable with reverence.

"Mr. Brauer," she called after him. "The song you were whistling?"

"Oh," he said, embarrassed. "It's an Irish song called 'Carrickfergus.'"

Mattie nodded, but he seemed to feel he had to explain, as though he knew she was repeating his last name in her mind. *Brauer?*

"My mother was from County Cavan," he said. "My full name is Emmet Robert Brauer," he said.

She said, "My husband's given name was Theobold, for Wolfe Tone."

"Oh, I know! Robert Cullen was his uncle. He responded to the *Slocum*."

"The *Slocum*," Mattie repeated.

"The *General Slocum*, a steamboat on a picnic excursion. A fire broke out as the boat was passing Sunken Meadow, near Randall's Island. To this day, it's the greatest loss of life in a single event in New York City history," Emmet said.

"Terrible," Mattie said.

Emmet probably would have kept talking, but Mattie started sweeping again. He put his hat back on, picked up his growlers and disappeared inside the firehouse.

Jack lay still, after. Mattie always kept her blouse on, but unbuttoned. He never asked why, even now when the afternoon gave no breeze, just dead air and the stink of trash from the alley. She and Teddy had never lain together like this. She had never once taken all her clothes off either. He'd never seen her back, unless it was an accidental glimpse as she was getting undressed for bed. But he'd never said.

Though she hardly cared that the bed had been hers and Teddy's, she thought Jack did. He'd never admit that he felt guilty for seeing her, yet she knew he must. He'd never admit that he felt responsible for Teddy's death either. She thought he must, but she couldn't be sure, since she was equally certain that he still believed transferring Teddy and the others was his only choice.

Saturday afternoons when Jack wasn't working, Mattie sent Josephine out and told her to play until it was time for supper. She found out after the third time that Josephine was going to the Keegans'.

Delia Keegan let the younger girl stay with her. Jack began leaving her money to buy them egg creams or tickets to the movies. Mattie ought to have told him not to, but in truth, it didn't hurt Jack much. So many of the men in the firehouse had six, seven or more children. Jack, with only one, was the man they went to when some cash was needed.

Jack's bruises were good bruises and confined to her thighs. The things he did, she had never thought of doing with Teddy. She left her hair down and it nearly reached her waist. She had taken to washing it twice a week. For Teddy, heating the water was too much trouble. She'd worn it twisted and pinned back, out of her face. Cleaner, her hair took on a honey color. She combed it carefully when it was dry, admiring the way it caught the light. There was something to discovering you had a beauty you'd never noticed before, and, as well, noticing it in another.

She liked to simply look at Jack. Teddy had been wiry, strong in that way. Jack was taller and wider across the shoulders. Even at fifty-four, with his dark hair mostly white, and with a nose that had been broken long ago when he'd been thrown from the rig while out on a run, he was the sort of man that women turned to look at on the street.

Between her legs it throbbed a little, but Mattie didn't mind. It was different than with Teddy. Not so much pain as a soreness that was almost pleasant.

Jack was typically quiet after they finished, but today Mattie sensed even more behind his silence. She sat up, pulling the sheet around her. He was staring at the wall, unseeing.

She stroked his chest. "I have no one to tell, you know. The firehouse will never find out."

"I don't care what those guys think," he said.

A lie. Mattie hid her smile. Even his wife and daughter came second to his men.

"What is it, then?" she asked, careful to keep her tone light. From the first afternoon, with Teddy gone only a month, she'd sternly told herself that she'd never be more than the woman he went to. And she would never ask him for more.

"Annie-Rose," Jack said. "She's bad again."

"What's wrong with her?" Mattie asked. Normally, she would never be so forward, but she felt oddly calm, as if she'd been sipping beer.

"Like the last time, a few years ago. She won't get out of bed. She won't talk to us. She doesn't eat. My kid just looks at me like I'm supposed to know what to do."

His voice was flat. Mattie knew Jack had lost two boys. Sometimes Mattie hoped to conceive, though she never had wanted to before. The misses after Josephine had been a relief. But Jack made everything different. She liked the idea of giving him a new son.

Yet what would she do with another child? She could not keep working at her firehouse, or any firehouse. Teddy had been dead for four months, too long to pass the child off as his. She would have to go away.

"She's had it hard," she said, though she thought that Annie-Rose would have done better to accept that terrible things happened.

A minute's silence, then Jack said, "You going to leave?"

"Leave?" Mattie asked.

"Leave the city. Go back to where you're from. I know you've got brothers upstate somewhere. I been wondering why you didn't do that right after."

"I have three brothers," Mattie said.

They had not approved of her marriage to Teddy, or rather, its circumstances. She'd shamed the family after all they were doing to gain respectability in the face of the war, and the bigotry toward anyone with a German accent or surname.

She hadn't spoken to any of them in years, since their mother's funeral. They didn't know she was a widow. Walter inherited the grocery store from their father, and he'd take her in, if for no other reason than his horror at the job she'd chosen. Working as a maid, like an immigrant.

To Jack she simply said, "I *will* support my daughter."

"I should move away," he said. "Get Annie-Rose and Delia out of the city. Go someplace quiet, with fresh air."

"And stop being a fireman?" she said, amused.

"You're allowed out. It's not the goddamned priesthood."

Isn't it? she thought.

"Did you like it where you grew up?" he asked.

"Ossining. It was nice enough," she said.

"Ossining? Yeah? Were you anywhere near the prison?"

"Up the road. The lights in the house blinked when they electrocuted somebody."

Jack laughed. "Jesus Christ."

"My mother made us say a prayer," Mattie said, "for the criminal and the executioner."

"You weren't born up there, right? He said something once —"

He. Teddy.

"No, no. I was born in the city. St. Brigid's parish."

"Why'd you leave?"

Mattie considered the question, asked so casually. Only rarely did anyone ask about her childhood.

"Mattie — what's that short for anyway?" Jack asked.

"Matilda," she answered. "I never liked it."

"That's pretty funny."

"Why is it funny?"

"Theobold Wolfe Tone, his wife was Matilda. Didn't you know that?"

"No," she said. Maybe Teddy had liked the thought of it. He could be stupid like that. Maybe that was why he touched her to begin with.

"Maybe if I were Irish, I would care."

Jack laughed and tightened his arm around her. "Matilda's not so bad. Annie-Rose thought we should name a girl Brigid, after her mother. Said we could call her Delia. That's an Irish nickname for Brigid, you know. But I still wasn't crazy about the idea. When the baby came, Annie-Rose was in no shape to talk about anything, so I just went with it."

Mattie panicked. He would keep talking about his daughter, or go into his own tragedy, or possibly get up to go home.

"Do you remember the *Slocum?*" she asked.

Jack glanced at her, surprised. "Yeah, of course, 1904. I missed it, being in Brooklyn." There was a touch of regret in his voice.

Mattie understood. With over one thousand dead in the fire or drowned in the East River trying to escape the flames, what happened to the steamship was the disaster everybody knew before the *Titanic*. Five hundred more died on the *Titanic*, and besides, that ship's dead were far more glamorous.

"St. Brigid's, that's Little Germany." Jack stared at her. "Jesus, what are you, a survivor?"

Slowly, Mattie sat up and slipped off her blouse. She gathered her hair in one hand and pulled it over her shoulder and then pushed herself off the headboard and lay down on the bed. As Jack watched intently, she turned over on her stomach. The sheet smelled of sweat and the things they had just done. She liked it.

He cursed softly.

"Who'd you lose?" Jack asked.

A good question. Jack was smart enough to know what the number of dead versus the number of survivors meant.

"I had a friend," Mattie said. "She lived upstairs from us. We were five that year. We would tell people we were twins. The Brandts belonged to St. Mark's Lutheran Church. It was St. Mark's that rented the *Slocum* for the picnic. Dora begged her mother to let me come too. Her father told my parents they got an extra ticket from someone who couldn't use it, but I think Mr. Brandt bought it for me. He didn't go. It was a Wednesday. Most of the fathers and husbands had to work."

"Yeah, it was all women and kids," Jack said. "I remember that."

Mattie nodded. "Reverend Haas was there. He survived. His wife and his daughter died. Mrs. Brandt was holding the baby, Gretchen, and Dora was standing by her, and I was standing by Dora. We heard shouts and saw smoke and knew something bad — Mrs. Brandt ran to look for Liese."

"Another sister?"

Mattie nodded. "Liese was sixteen. She was the most beautiful girl in *Kleindeutschland*."

In the years after, Mattie sometimes wished she had a photograph of Liese, just to see her face again, the way one might look at a painting in a museum.

"Almost as soon as we'd boarded, she went off to flirt with this boy she liked," Mattie said. "Liese died with him, I guess. They never found either one of them."

"The mother ran to look for her —"

"Mrs. Brandt screamed at us to wait right there, and we did for a minute but then hundreds of people started running toward us, screaming, and some with their clothes burning, and Dora ran after her mother. She grabbed my hand too and I started to go along with her but then the smoke got very thick and black and you could hear the fire — *you* would know."

"Yeah, I know. It's still scary as hell, and I'm trained for it."

"I took my hand back from Dora. I took my hand back from her. I ran the other way," Mattie said. "I ran the other way. There was someone on fire and my blouse caught —" She closed her eyes.

"Who saved you?"

"The burn, Jackie. You see where it is. I saved myself."

"Hey, Mattie, it was chaos and you were a little kid."

Mattie had gone to confession when she was fifteen and the priest had told her much the same thing. It is normal, sane, to run from a fire, unless you are a fireman. He'd said those very words. In any case, the priest said, a child of five cannot commit a mortal sin. Seven is the age of reason. He'd given her a light penance anyway, a balm to soothe her. That particular rosary remained unsaid.

"Who saved you?" Jack asked.

"A man picked me up and threw me into the water. He was throwing lots of children in," she said. "Some of the mothers screamed that they could not swim . . . burn or drown. Drown or burn. In the water, another man took me and two others and he swam on his back with us holding on. All the way to shore."

"You were conscious?"

"Until we got out of the water. It didn't hurt."

"A burn that deep wouldn't."

Because she'd said so much already, Mattie continued.

It was late in the day, almost night. Mr. Brandt knew his wife was dead. She'd been found with Gretchen in her arms. Mr. Brandt was told by a neighbor that Dora was in the hospital. Mattie didn't know who the neighbor was, but assumed it was a man. The mothers on the block would have known Dora Brandt from Mattie Starwaif. Mattie's father went along, thinking that wherever Dora was, Mattie might be. They eventually found her on her stomach in the oxygen tent. One girl. One daughter for two fathers.

Mattie woke up while they were there. Turning her head to the side, she saw them standing over her. She put up her hand. Her father glanced at Mr. Brandt. Though Mattie wasn't allowed to speak German, in *Kleindeutschland* you heard it everywhere. Her father said to Mr. Brandt, "*Es tut mir leid.*"

I am sorry.

The husbands and fathers made posters, advertising for their missing families. Mr. Brandt did one in English and one in German: *zwei Töchter von Josef Brandt missing, two daughters of Josef Brandt . . .*

"He put them up at all the hospitals and on North Brother Island where the boat finally went ashore. He put one up at Locust Grove where we were going for the picnic. He put one up at the pier where they'd set up a morgue. They put the morgue there because they were pulling so many bodies out of the water, but it was not a good place. So many found they'd lost their wives, all of their children, they threw themselves in the water. They say Germans don't cry?" Mattie said. "They did."

With her eyes closed, Mattie said to Jack, "Mr. Brandt waited for two weeks before he gave up and held the funeral. He had one coffin for Liese and Dora, and he put some things of theirs in it. Dora's doll. Liese's second-best dress. She was wearing her very good one that day."

Jack was silent. Mattie waited.

"What ever happened to him? Josef Brandt."

"I don't know," Mattie said. "He left the neighborhood. A lot of the families moved up to Yorkville. Mr. Brandt was alone, though. I can't imagine there was anything there for him."

"And your family went to Ossining?"

"A new start." Mattie didn't say that her parents had taken her away out of guilt. "They didn't think about the prison until the *Slocum* trials. Then the captain was convicted."

"Yeah, Christ, he did time in Sing Sing, didn't he?"

"Funny, isn't it? Captain Van Schaick became our neighbor. Mama wanted to move again, but we didn't have the money."

Jack shook his head. "Christ."

The captain was the reason Mattie first went to stand outside the prison wall. She was supposed to blame him, but she was not sure she did. He had not conducted fire drills on the ship, but he had not meant to kill anyone, just the way she had not meant to abandon Dora to die alone, frantic to find her mother and baby sister.

After the first time Mattie heard the singing, she began to go every evening in the spring and summer as night came on. She told her mother, but her mother said it couldn't be the convicts. The men inside were not allowed to speak, much less sing. After that, Mattie wondered if the voices were the voices of ghosts.

Jack's finger bumped along her scar. "Does it look very bad?" Mattie asked.

"You never looked? Not once?"

"The doctors said it was better if I didn't and that I was lucky it wasn't on my face or my hands. Mama expected me to be a nun or a schoolteacher because I'd never marry."

But as a child, she'd expected to outgrow the ruin. The taller she got, the smaller the scar would get, until she was a woman and it was no bigger than a nickel.

Sometimes Mattie would run her hand over the rough skin as far as she could reach. It itched, especially in the heat of summer. In the winter it got stiff with the cold and made her think of shirts frozen on a clothesline. That was how it felt.

The one mirror in their house hung on the wall in the hallway. When she was twelve, early one morning when it was just getting light and no one was up yet, she placed a chair in front of the mirror and removed her nightdress. First she studied her breasts, which had begun to grow. She covered them with her hands. She'd turned her back on herself and waited for the courage to look over her shoulder. She didn't, couldn't, just like the day it happened. A coward still. She had not tried since.

"Hell, Mattie, it's not so bad." Jack ran his hand over her skin like he was smoothing a rucked blanket.

After that, Mattie took her blouse off.

Jack brought some kind of sweet lotion for burns and rubbed it on her back. One of the firemen had concocted it during the long hours between runs. Mattie had to laugh. Goddamn firemen and their industriousness.

Jack said it would help make her skin softer, and it did. The itching eased. He didn't let her stay on her back when they were together. He said he didn't mind the way the scar felt. He spoke more about Teddy, as though to talk her into loving him.

"I know you had your problems with him, and he drank more than he should have, but Teddy Cullen was a good fireman," he said once.

Sometimes Jack ate supper with her and Josephine. He would bring meat from the butcher, a cut Mattie couldn't afford herself, and she'd cook it for the three of them.

He tried to talk kindly to Josephine, but she didn't give him more than one-word answers.

Nights, Mattie lay in the center of her bed and thought that what they had was better than a marriage. They didn't have to live with one another. They would not get tired of each other.

She could tolerate her daughter's confused, accusing looks. She could ignore them.

By October, Jack was eating an early supper with them as often as three times a week. One Saturday afternoon when she was cooking *hühnerfrikassee*, with boiled potatoes instead of rice, for Jack, Josephine asked if she should set the table for two or three.

"Three," Mattie said, and Josephine did so listlessly.

When they heard the footsteps pounding on the stairs, Josephine didn't wait for Mattie to tell her to answer the door.

Stevie Crowley was out of breath, his red hair damp with sweat. A fire at the Leonard glove factory went to a third alarm. Captain Keegan was missing. They were searching for him. The boy dashed out. Mattie pulled off her apron and folded it over the chair that she'd come to think of as Jack's. She got her coat out of the closet because the weather had turned cold lately.

"Where are you going?" Josephine cried. "You didn't go when —"

"Shut up," Mattie said.

The block was in chaos, with firemen everywhere and a large milling crowd. Mattie was there only a few minutes when Marco Giancola came over to her.

"It's good you're here," he said. "We're looking for Captain Keegan and Gary Smith. The whole building could go any minute. They're over there." He pointed.

"Who's where?" Mattie asked, confused.

"Annie-Rose and Delia," Marco said. "Gary's wife's not here, far as I know."

Mattie had thought Annie-Rose might be in the hospital again. Jack had not mentioned her name in three visits. But no. Annie-Rose and Delia stood slightly apart from the crowd, or more likely the crowd was standing back out of respect. Annie-Rose wore a gray shawl around her shoulders. Mattie felt a surge of irritation. It was as though she were in a play and had decided the shawl made the best costume for a woman about to learn she was a widow. As though she felt Mattie's stare, Annie-Rose turned and looked directly at her. Delia followed her mother's gaze and took her arm.

Mattie expected them to turn away, but instead Annie-Rose walked toward her, and the girl followed. She waited, refusing to retreat. When Annie-Rose reached Mattie, she turned to face the building. The smoke was thinning.

"They'll find him," Annie-Rose said.

"I know," Mattie said. They wouldn't stop until they did.

"Alive, I mean," Annie-Rose said forcefully. "Jackie isn't dead."

Mattie stared at the wreck of the building. Most of the windows had been blown out or broken. The brick façade was streaked with black.

Annie-Rose turned to Mattie. "Jack said you were on the *Slocum*."

Mattie pulled her coat tightly around herself. "He told you?"

"Was it a secret?" Annie-Rose asked.

"No," Mattie said.

Had he told her about the scar? But then she would know he'd seen it. Had he told her Mattie's story as they ate together at their kitchen table? Or were they in bed? She recalled then what she always tried not to think of. How he and Annie-Rose were with each other the night she turned up on their doorstep.

"You don't have to stay here for our sakes," Annie-Rose said. "You can go home to your daughter."

"Josephine will be fine." Delia sounded angry.

Mattie thought Jack's daughter might be kinder than she looked.

Annie-Rose smiled softly. "Still."

Mattie, and she thought Delia too, waited for Annie-Rose to continue, but she just gazed at the building.

"I'll send Stevie. When they find him," Delia said. She didn't look at Mattie.

"When they get him out, Delia," Annie-Rose said. "Your father isn't dead."

Delia looked hard at her mother, then up at the building.

"Don't bother asking Stevie, Delia. He knows to come and tell us," Mattie said.

Back home, Mattie found Josephine in bed, on top of the covers. Asleep, or pretending to be. Mattie went out on the fire escape. Twilight was beginning to creep over the rooftops before she spotted Stevie sprinting up the block. That he was running and not plodding, watching each foot hit the sidewalk, meant that he was coming to tell her that Jack was alive.

Mattie had lost him. She couldn't say how she knew. But it had to do with the way she was, even in her shock, adjusting to a future without him. Her acceptance of his death lost to his wife's certainty that he had not died.

Mattie let three weeks go by before she went to talk to Emmet at his apartment. His surprise at seeing her did not make him lose his manners. He did not ask why she was there.

He invited her to sit at his kitchen table and offered her the sturdier of the mismatched chairs.

She noted the chairs, and indeed the overall sparseness of the living room, with relief. He did not have a woman. When she told him her idea, he took her hand shyly and said yes, he would help her.

Mattie watched her grandson finish scribbling.

"Teddy Cullen was a good fireman," Ian repeated. "Said Jack Keegan."

Shortly after Michael was born, Mattie told Emmet that she went to him because, yes, she knew he was a good man, but also because of his Irish mother. Emmet laughed and said that if Jack were Italian or Greek, maybe they'd have a problem. Irish, though, could easily pass for German.

Over the years, Mattie wondered if Michael might have asked his half sister for the truth. Josephine almost certainly knew. But the twelve-year age difference meant she and Michael were hardly close. When Josephine left home for good, Michael was a boy of six.

Before her son was born, Mattie would have said it was nonsense, the idea that firefighting was in the blood. True, the department was filled with fathers and sons and sets of brothers and cousins. But didn't the shoemaker's son become a shoemaker?

Michael Brauer was raised upstate. It had been Emmet's idea to move his business there in 1933 when drinking became legal again. Emmet remained a buff, of course. Mattie made one request: "Don't bring it home."

So Emmet never brought "their" son on the business trips that took him into Manhattan and Brooklyn. Michael never visited firehouses with him, never spent hours poring over the collection of newspaper articles, books and photographs about the FDNY.

Perhaps Michael had simply coveted his half sister's father, the dead

hero. Yet. When Michael announced, a week after his college graduation, that he would take the test for the FDNY, Mattie began to believe
that something did pass between fathers and sons. Some innate understanding that it is not every man who can run into fire, and if you can,
then it's your responsibility to make it your life's work.

"Okay, Grandma. I guess I'm finished." Ian closed his notebook. "Um,
thanks."

Mattie nodded once. "You're welcome."

"Is it okay if I go down to the backyard? Into the woods?" Ian
hopped up.

She saw how badly he wanted to get away. He was a boy, after all, and
what was she but white hair, wrinkles and a stern mouth.

"Yes, but don't go far. Your father will be back soon."

In seconds, it seemed, he appeared in the yard below. Mattie watched
Ian take off at a run for the blazing trees. She wanted to call him back.
Wait, Ian Brauer. Wait. She would start the interview over, and this
time begin with the *Slocum*. She would tell the boy what it is like to be
on fire, because he should know. Michael's older boy, Gavin, quiet and
sweet, did not need to know.

Mattie would explain to Ian that it was his grandfather, John Michael Keegan, who taught her the scar. Through his touch, she learned
its breadth and shape and that it was not Dora Brandt in profile, her
mouth arched in a hot scream.

Mattie rose and went to her dresser. In the top drawer, beneath the
small jewelry box that had been her mother's (her mother who had
never touched her again after June 15, 1904; though it hardly seemed
possible, this was what Mattie remembered), Mattie took out the folded
paper, a copy she'd made out of fear she'd lose the original. Her hands
trembled.

In the spring of 1941, an envelope arrived addressed to Matilda Cullen, postmarked Brooklyn, New York. It held Jack's one-page obituary
from the *Irish Eagle*. "Icon of the 'Glory Devlins' Dies." Then, Mattie
assumed that Josephine, away at college, must have sent it. But Mattie

finally admitted to herself that sending the obituary was too bold for Josephine. Now she believed it must have been Annie-Rose. What she could not decide, still, was if it was meant cruelly or in sympathy.

As a buff, Emmet would have heard about Jack's death. No doubt one of his business trips to the city had actually been the funeral. Mattie, in turn, cried only when she had hours alone, so Emmet would not see her swollen eyes. She didn't want him to realize that it was not only grief, but the end of hope. Part of her had always believed Jack would one day find out that he had a living son, and he would come and claim both her and Michael.

Mattie returned to the terrace and sat heavily. Jack had been sixty-five when he died, but in the picture the newspaper had chosen, he was at least ten years younger, not much past the age when she last saw him. Mattie opened her grandson's folder and placed the copy of Jack Keegan's obituary inside.

Jack had asked her once, Who saved you? She'd explained why she'd not burned to death or drowned, but that story wasn't accurate. The answer to Jack's question was *you*. You saved me.

CHAPTER FOUR

Annie-Rose Devlin Keegan

November 1918

WHEN JOHN AND PATRICK DIED, most of me went with them, and that is all that happened.

I knew any boys I had would be born to risk fire, but I never dreamed that it would come from the inside out and while they were still mine far more than Jack's. Their faces were drawn from his, but they had my blue eyes, flecked with green as though someone tossed bits of emerald into the sky.

The boys lay together in their bed. Patrick was three and John was two. I was on my knees beside them when I heard the doctor's slow footsteps climbing the stairs up to us on the third floor of the house that my father bought for me, I'd later realize, certain I'd someday live there with a family of my own.

Without discussion, Jack and I moved in after we married. My parents moved downstairs and we took their bedroom on the third floor. The boys shared the room that had once been mine, the one with the view of the back of the firehouse.

My father built the whatnot that stood in the corner. I used to keep my jewelry box on it, and prayer cards, and switches of palm from Palm Sunday. Now it held the toys Patrick Devlin had built for his grandsons, the wooden trains and fire wagons, blocks with the letters of the alphabet burned into them and a baseball hit into the stands at the old Washington Park on Fifth Avenue, the one that burned when I was five. I never heard the stories of the fires, but my father told the boys, young as they were, on the day he and Jack took them to Ebbets Field, the modern stadium that was made of steel, not wood.

Only the doctor's eyes were visible above his mask. He gazed at the boys, who had been sick since day before yesterday. One hour they'd been running through the house, kept inside because of the influenza epidemic, and the next they were in bed with a fever each. I'd wanted to bring them to Kings County, but Dr. Eymrad said the hospital had no open beds and they were short on nurses and doctors. Nothing could be done for influenza anyway. We had to let it run its course.

My mother sat in a corner of the bedroom. If she wasn't mistaken, or lying, she was seventy-nine years old. The boys were the children my father had been waiting for, but I sometimes wondered if my mother even knew one from the other.

Patrick was silent in his fever, but John spoke, said words that I thought at first were gibberish but then realized were probably Irish. Had she been teaching my boy the old words?

She didn't greet the doctor or so much as turn his way. But from my knees, I put out a hand to him, like a beggar.

Dr. Eymrad said, "The next few days, hours, will be very . . . Maybe it'll be another boy. God bless."

He was gone.

"It's a girl," my mother said.

There had been misses after John, and we'd begun to wonder, me and Jack, if two was all we'd have. But now, heavy as I was, much as the baby punched and kicked, I kept forgetting it.

In the early afternoon, Father Halloran came. The boys were too young to receive the sacrament of extreme unction, so Father blessed them instead. We had our places, my mother in her chair in the corner, my father standing beside her. Jack stood in the doorway. I knelt by the bed on numb legs.

Father Halloran made a hasty sign of the cross over John's forehead and then Patrick's, and said, "May God bless John James Keegan. May God bless Patrick Devlin Keegan."

The priest's hands trembled and he left right after, saying he was sorry but there were four other families in the parish he had to see.

My father and Jack retreated to the kitchen to drink.

A month ago, when it first started, I was horrified enough to read about the Spanish flu in the newspaper, even though Jack told me not to. Fever. Pneumonia. The lungs filled with fluid until the person could no longer draw a breath. A nurse was quoted: "Victims drown from the inside."

It was called the Blue Death.

First it was a tint around their lips. Then the blue spread over their chins and cheeks. I had taken off their nightshirts, soaked with sweat and blood, they were bleeding from their noses and ears, and because they were so hot, I left them uncovered by the sheet. With each sucking breath, the little ribcages appeared.

Patrick was worse. John, content to go, I supposed, was dying more easily. I had two fistfuls of the sheet. I let go and put a hand over Patrick's mouth and nose but then snatched my hand back.

"You should," my mother said.

"God would never forgive me," I said.

"Mary would," she said. "The mother. If someone had come up to her and put a rifle in her hands, don't you think she would have shot her son through the heart as he was up on the cross?"

I covered my ears and told my mother she should leave because she might catch it, even though I knew that influenza wasn't killing the old. My mother said that she'd been dead since she was a child.

John made up songs from things around the room. *Oh bed, oh shoe, oh floor,* and he sang bits of songs that he heard on the radio, in tune. He'd sing, *Ov-er there, ov-er there, 'Cause the Yanks are coming, the Yanks are coming,* and *K-K-Katy, beautiful Katy.* He said if the baby was a girl, we could call her Katy. Jack had laughed. "And if it's a boy, J.J.?" John had no answer.

Jack could sing, but he hardly ever did except for some nights at the bar.

We knew it wouldn't be long, and it wasn't long before Patrick's eyes opened for the first time that day with the effort to breathe and he never closed them. I closed them.

Patrick liked to run halfway up the front stairs and then turn and leap down. Flying, he called it. He liked to climb the ladder in our yard to run to the firehouse. I was always turning to look for him and he was gone. He sat in the driver's seat of the engine and pretended to be speeding to a fire. He shouted, *Clang, clang, clang!*

The Young Devlin, the firemen called him. Offended, I asked Jack if it was some sort of play on "devil," and he laughed and told me that my father was nicknamed the Devlin. Didn't I know that? No. My father never said.

Jack and my father came back upstairs to find the bedroom quiet. Jack shuffled to the bed. He touched John's hand, smoothed Patrick's hair and went to stand at the window. My father came to the bed and drew the blanket over their faces as though they were strangers' children he'd pulled from a fire.

"It's my fault," I said.

"It isn't. You only thought you were praying for them," Jack said.

I didn't know what he meant, and then I remembered how, last week, after the newspapers began calling the outbreak of influenza an epidemic, the women of the parish went to the nuns in the cloister carrying their most carefully baked breads and their sweetest cakes. Some didn't trust their own cooking and scraped the money together to buy something.

The mothers asked the nuns for prayers in exchange for what they brought. Spare my children. Spare them. Spare *us*. As the women left, they paused before the statue of Saint Maren in the front yard. One of them kissed her little stone hand and then the rest followed. Within days, they were kissing hot foreheads.

But I was never there. Saint Maren didn't heal the sick. If you were about to drown or die in a fire, you could call out to her and she might intercede if it was God's will, but sickness she'd never been taught.

I meant that the boys were never supposed to be born at all.

If God calls you and you don't hear, then He can forgive. But if you recognize God's voice, which is not a sound but a feeling, and you know you are supposed to devote your life to Him and you turn away instead, then you are punished for that sin.

"It's my fault," I whispered.

"You don't know who they caught it from," Jack said.

There was something in his tone, some hint of reproach, that made me turn from the boys to look at him.

From you, I thought. From Malbone Street.

Four days ago, on November 1, All Saints' Day, a train on the Brighton line flew off the rails during rush hour as it went into the tunnel at Malbone Street. The Glory Devlins had responded, of course, and my father went too.

Jack said I shouldn't read the papers, not in my condition, but my mother told me to read accounts of the tragedy aloud to her, and I did. At evening rush hour, the train had been packed with people going home from their jobs in the city, and it was traveling way, way too fast for the sharp curve.

There was no official death toll yet. The men they were identifying by their draft cards, but the women were proving more difficult, what with only clothes and jewelry to go by.

That night, a crowd surged outside the tunnel, many terrified because a loved one had not come home, others trying to get a look at the carnage. The rescue workers had trouble fighting their way through. Jack and my father in the middle of it. The corpses, whole or in pieces, were carried out and laid in Ebbets Field, then brought by ambulance to the morgue at Kings County Hospital. When the morgue was filled, and it soon was, the dead were laid down in a laundry room.

My mother solemnly shook her head and I shuddered, even as I couldn't stop wanting more details. Not about the gore, but about the victims. Who weren't us. Not us.

My father, when he arrived home late that night, said wearily that it put him in mind of the theater back in '76. Jack, who came home the next morning, said that it was far, far worse than the Windsor.

The young Italian motorman was a BRT office worker who had hardly any training but was called on to fill in because of the motormen's strike. He'd just recovered from influenza and lost his daughter to it only a week before.

Though I didn't say it out loud — the Malbone wreck — I saw that Jack guessed my thoughts. If it was one of us, then it was you. You, in that swarming crowd. You among the bloody dead. No fire, so no smoke. No smoke, so no mask. *You.*

Jack turned away from me and said to my father, "I'll go and see about arrangements."

I clutched Patrick's arm through the sheet.

"We'll go downstairs," my father said. "Discuss it."

I didn't ask what there was to discuss. As soon as they were gone, I planned to pull back the sheet and look at the boys.

But my mother said we would know soon enough anyway, so he might as well have out with it. My father nodded but still spoke hesitantly. He thought I was delicate. He always had.

"The city won't allow a burial without a death certificate. Because of the flu there are too many dead and too few clerks and doctors to sign them. There aren't enough coffins, or gravediggers. Fewer people have been coming down sick these past two weeks, and so they were starting to catch up. But now, with the Malbone wreck, they're set back again." He shook his head.

"What the hell are you saying, Paddy?" Jack said. His eyes were red, the way they sometimes were when he came home from work.

I didn't wonder if my father was right. Patrick Devlin knew everything that was happening in this city.

My father glanced at the shrouded figures. I followed his gaze and almost screamed, as though I'd just noticed them myself.

"The lads will be in the morgue for days," he said.

"Two little boys?" Jack said. "They'll put them ahead of the — of the line."

My father said quietly, "The Lehanes, did you know they got sick the day of the wreck and died that night? Both of them, and their older girl the next day. There's only the little girl left and the baby born last week. The girl's calling him after Dr. Eymrad. Artie's brother can't deal with that, he's been trying to get them all buried. They'll get to them, he's been told. He's got hold of himself right now, but I don't know how long he'll hold out before he puts the funeral money on some horse."

"Three days ago?" I said faintly.

Neither of them glanced at me.

"You're not saying they're going to start tossing the dead in some potter's field," Jack said.

I touched John's cheek through the sheet. I wanted them all to go away and leave us alone.

My father shook his head. "Last week, I would've said no."

It was my mother's way to listen to the men go back and forth and then say what had to happen. "They need to be waked."

December 31, 1897

On the last night of the City of Brooklyn, I was thirteen years old but already the image of my mother, Bridie Devlin, as if I'd been born from a mirror she gazed in. She poured herself a whiskey and one for me, giving me less than she served herself. A *dropeen*. We would have a wake for Brooklyn, she said, and a wake for our home. We lived in the four rooms on the third floor of the firehouse.

She'd let her sewing fall to the floor as she got up, and I eyed the pile but kept my disapproval to myself. The things should be folded and placed respectfully in the basket that sat between our chairs. She was sewing for the nuns in the cloister. My mother said everybody left apples and cakes galore for intentions, but what the nuns needed were warm socks in the winter and the plain white sheets with which they made up their beds. They needed underthings. I wondered why they couldn't sew, or did they have so much praying to do that they couldn't keep up? She said they wouldn't lift a finger for their own comfort. Once, I repeated what I'd heard about them sleeping not in beds but in coffins, to symbolize that they were dead to the world. Don't be stupid, my mother said.

My mother kicked the white fabric out of her way as she handed me the cup of whiskey, which I accepted with both hands. It was like swallowing a lick of flame. I coughed, and she cocked an eyebrow.

Bridie Devlin came over from Ireland in 1848, when she was about nine years old. The potatoes died. There was nothing to eat. My father, Patrick, didn't come to America until 1862, when he was twenty-five. He said he heard Lincoln was putting on a war, and he thought he'd get in on it. He fought under General Corcoran, the man who refused to march the 69th Regiment in a parade for the Prince of Wales when he visited New York.

My mother and me were alone in the big, warm room, and my father was downstairs in quarters with the other firemen because it was on him to see that there was no trouble. At midnight when the year turned, we would become a *borough* of Greater New York and the Brooklyn Fire Department would cease to exist. Ours along with the departments of Queens and Staten Island and the Bronx were being attached to Manhattan, swallowed up to create one huge fire department.

For over a year now, they'd been organizing, promoting some men, firing and hiring others, by the new training guidelines. The men kept repeating the rumors: Firemen would have to be United States citizens. They would have to be able to read and write in English, even if they'd already been on the job for years. My father would no longer be a district engineer but a chief of battalion. The company numbers were all changing. They had to, so they'd be different from companies in Manhattan and Queens and so on, but the men swore they'd never give up their name, the Glory Devlins.

I understood. The nuns at school told me, "Your name is Anne, like the mother of Our Lady." But I was not Anne, I was Annie-Rose. If I was named for two, and I thought I might have been, I don't know who they were. My mother wouldn't say. The potatoes died. There was nothing to eat.

Annie-Rose. I liked that it was a flower, but even more that it was a verb.

Annie rose. Annie got up. Annie went away.

There'd been talk of renaming our city East New York, but as of that night, it seemed that Brooklyn would stay Brooklyn. My father said he was lucky the new department was keeping him instead of forcing him to retire. My mother said that it was hardly luck. The Fire Department of New York, or whatever the hell they would be calling it, needed him. The men in charge could complain all they wanted about the wild Brooklyn boys and fistfights at fires and drinking too much on duty, but what did they know across the river about our buildings and the way our streets ran, where the trouble happened? Exactly nothing.

Before the Civil War, the fire department had been volunteer, so of course the men all had other jobs. (My father was a carpenter.) A lot of the fire laddies were told to go to hell when the city decided it needed professional firemen who would do nothing but fight fires, but my father was one of those hired on to Brooklyn's paid department in 1865. Now, Consolidation, and he was saved again. Yet officers' families were no longer permitted to live above quarters. All visitors to the firehouse would be required to check in. Women and girls would be forbidden to go past the patrol desk.

"What are we, priests?" my father snapped when he heard this.

But the Fire Department of New York — the *FDNY* — was going to be run like the army, and we were being evicted. We didn't know exactly when, or where we'd go.

So on the last night of the City of Brooklyn, Bridie poured herself a second whiskey and sat again with a sigh. I sipped mine and tried to keep my face from contorting.

Then he was there, Jamesey Walsh, not in the room with us but on the threshold between the big room and the kitchen. He often stayed in doorways, at the tops of stairs. I never saw him, but I knew when he was there. Me, alive thirteen years, and him, dead exactly that long.

"What is it?" Bridie asked.

"Nothing," I said.

"Stop fidgeting, then."

She knew as well as I did that ghosts were real, but if I told her, she would say to stop making myself important. If he was there, he wasn't there for me.

Oh, but he was.

Jamesey Walsh died the night I was born. He didn't leap out a window to get away from a fire. A roof didn't come down on him. A floor didn't buckle and collapse, dropping him into the flames. The rig didn't take a turn too fast, throwing him onto the cobblestones, breaking open his skull. He didn't fall off and then under the rig for the horses to trample. A trolley didn't fail to stop and slam into the engine. None of the usual things.

For a penny, the midwife in the parish, Eliza Brown, would tell the children she delivered about the day they were born. On my tenth birthday, I paid the fee and sat down to listen in the flat she shared with a man she said was her cousin.

December 28, 1884, was a bitter night. Ten days earlier, the men had responded to a fire at St. John's Orphan Asylum. By the time they arrived, the nearer companies had been at work for almost ten minutes. The fire was still out of control.

A nun had fallen from the roof trying to get to the fireman's ladder. The orphan boys of the asylum were freezing in the street, having run or been pulled from the building into the cold. They were dressed at least. Had it been nighttime, it would have been much worse.

For days afterward, firemen went through the debris searching for victims. Jamesey was one of the many who volunteered to do so on their day off. The bodies were in bad, bad shape. Burned. In pieces. The dead had all been patients in the infirmary. The fire started in a room right below it. Because the boys who had been elsewhere had all gotten out, it was decided that the few who remained unaccounted for must have run away.

The funeral was held on December 27. The remains of the twenty-one dead boys fit into three coffins.

For the whole day of the twenty-seventh, Bridie Cavanaugh Devlin labored. She was forty-five and never had a baby before. She had never even miscarried; she said she hadn't.

I wasn't born until close to two a.m., December 28, and at that time, Jamesey Walsh got up out of bed and stumbled toward the firehouse pole, more than half asleep. He fell to the apparatus floor and broke his neck. The company swore to a man that Jamesey had not had much to drink that night. But since St. John's, he'd been having nightmares. They said more than once, he thought he'd heard a cry from the ruins of the building, even though it was clear after the first day that nobody was alive in there. Possibly he heard the infant (me) crying and had turned one urgent sound into another. Eliza told me about the shouts and the sound of running feet and how she thought that the firehouse itself was burning.

From her childbed, my mother sewed Jamesey's mourning ribbons. One was given to the mayor of Brooklyn, one to my father as district engineer, and the third was sent to the Walsh family in County Meath, along with a letter from my mother, dictated to one of the wives, an American girl chosen not only because she could write but also because she was barely twenty, and would have been too scared of my mother to argue with her. Bridie told the Walshes that Jamesey died of injuries suffered while saving the life of a little girl.

He had indeed pulled a child from a tenement two weeks before, and my mother sent the clipping from the newspaper. The article, which appeared the day after the fire, did not give the girl's name. That girl had died of her burns after three days, but Bridie let her live. She wrote that Chief Devlin and his wife had a baby that night. If it had been a boy, she would have been James, but since she was a girl, they'd called her after the child he'd saved. Annie-Rose.

My father was furious when he found out, but Bridie said the mother in Meath would never know the truth. It was better for her to see her son as a hero rather than as a drunk or a fool.

I thought a lot about Jamesey Walsh and me passing by each other as he went out of this world and I came into it. I think we spoke a little. I knew things about him that I couldn't have otherwise. There were two boys in his family, his older brother and himself, at either end of their sisters. He'd wanted the girl his brother married. And his older brother would inherit the farm. Jamesey didn't want his brother to die, but thought if he ever did, he, Jamesey, would wait one year and one day and go home and ask the widow to marry him. He didn't much miss Ireland otherwise, and wouldn't go back but for her.

I was not allowed on the apparatus floor, but sometimes when the company was out, I went outside to look at the plaque they'd put up in memory of James Walsh. I touched the date of his death, my birthday.

Eliza didn't take my penny. She told me to put it in the box in the church for the soul of poor Jamesey Walsh.

I sipped more of the whiskey. I was getting used to the taste. My throat was warm. I turned around again, certain tonight I'd see Jamesey Walsh, but I didn't. He was still there, though, waiting for something.

"Jamesey liked colcannon," my mother said, surprising me.

I thought that unlike me, she could actually see him.

Bridie sipped her whiskey and said, "Maybe I'll make it for them all tomorrow."

The men with mothers or wives or sisters went home for their meals in shifts, but at any given time in our firehouse — in any firehouse, I guess — there were Irish boys who were alone in the city. They hadn't married yet or they were the sort who never would. My mother didn't have to, she had no obligation, but she cooked a meal once a day, and they were grateful. Usually there were between four and six of them. They'd come through the door, ducking their heads as they greeted my mother, who terrified them, and they took their seats at the two tables we pushed together and covered with our second-best cloth. I helped with the cooking, but once, when I picked up a dish to carry it out, Bridie bruised the back of my hand with the spoon she was holding.

"You are not Irish," she said. "You are not a maid."

Often, the men had to get up and go, leaving the food on the table.

They'd come back, sometimes hours later, to finish. My mother always offered to reheat the food, but they'd refuse because the odds were good they'd just have to go again. "Ah, no, no, Mrs. Devlin," said Healy, their spokesman, "you've gone to enough trouble."

"Colcannon?" I asked now.

"Potatoes and cabbage," Bridie answered.

I was disappointed. It sounded pretty in the way the names of Irish towns did. "But —"

"It's all mixed together like."

"Oh," I said. That didn't make it any more interesting. I decided not to ask any more questions. If she did make it, I'd see then.

Then the bells went off and I ran to the front window, dizzy from the whiskey, to watch the company leave. Bannon opened the big doors and leaped on the back of the rig as Flossie and Fancy shot by him, hardly needing to be directed. I once told my friend Mary Clark at school how the number of rings signaled the area where the fire was, and the experienced horses knew where to go without being told, because they counted the rings. She didn't believe me.

I crossed myself. My father told me I'd put a dent in my forehead if I did this every time the company went out on a run. But Bridie, who understood that I was praying for the men of the Glory Devlins, not for whoever they were off to rescue, told me that there was no point in praying for firemen. They'll come back or they won't, and they know it.

"The streets must be icy," I said before she could repeat this. The weather was a mix of rain and snow and fog.

She said nothing in response and I slipped back into my chair, reciting the Hail Mary behind closed lips. The Glory Devlins wouldn't return soon. After they put out the fire, they'd head right to Halloran's up the street. Firemen were allowed to go into any saloon they wanted while on duty as long as they didn't sit down to drink. Halloran had installed an alarm gong on the wall behind the bar so the men would know if they had a run.

My father had already warned the men that Consolidation was going to change this.

My mother looked toward the window as though considering the night. Then she turned and stared into our contained fire. I expected her to pick up the discarded sewing, but she didn't.

Instead, she told me that there was a storm on the day she was born. The wind was such that it seemed that the mountain itself might be swept into the sea.

"The mountain?" I repeated, and she said what sounded like "sleeve" and then the boy's name Kieran. Sleevekieran.

I repeated it madly to myself so I could find it on a map later, to see that it was a place in the world. The potatoes died. There was nothing to eat.

Bridie went on talking. The day was January 6, 1839, and it was said that a war was fought between the English faeries and the Irish faeries and the Irish won. That was how she knew it was a story, the Irish winning. But of course there was no war, only the worst storm to hit Ireland in centuries.

I held my whiskey, now warm from my hand, and wondered if I was dreaming. Bridie hardly ever talked of Ireland, but when she did, she used half sentences with so many possible endings that I could never guess them all.

"The sixth of January," I said, to keep her talking. "The Feast of the Epiphany?"

She said it was that, yes, but also the day for women to rest after all the work of the Christmas holidays. "*Nollaig na mBan*," Bridie said.

That was Irish, the old language. Bridie claimed to have forgotten all but a few words, but she and my father spoke it in the night. It had a peculiar sound, like a talking song, and moved so quickly I could never tell the end of one word from the beginning of the next. I supposed most of the time she held the words somewhere inside her, perhaps in her womb, which had produced only me, but too late for her to ever be happy. The potatoes died. There was nothing to eat.

Bridie bent over and picked up her sewing. I sat miserably, trying to think of a way to lead her back to the story.

Before I could, we heard a knock on our apartment door. It might be one of the neighborhood boys, to report that something had happened at the fire, but the Mulgren brothers or the O'Leary boy would have run up the stairs like a lunatic. Whoever was out there had arrived soundlessly.

"Is it the living or the dead?" Bridie called, as she always did to a knock on the door.

"The man in between."

"Ah." My mother nodded at me to answer the door. I opened it. Jarlath Reliable, the coffin maker, was the man my father used to work for.

Within a year of coming to America, my father was referred to Jarlath for work, as one Galway man to another. At first my father made deliveries, himself and his partner carrying coffins through the streets to the homes of the dead. Later, he assisted with the coffin making. My father told stories of setting coffins down in the street and running to an alarm. His partner was a fireman too. Jeremiah McGlory, from Donegal. The coffins were always there when he and Jeremiah went back for them, often set carefully aside, off the sidewalk. A coffin was a thing of bad luck, and that kept some thieves away, but it was a time when anything that could be stolen and sold would be. But Jarlath was a man respected and, even more so, feared.

Reliable wasn't his real name, of course. When Jarlath came over, he tried to find work but nobody would hire him. When Jarlath asked one man why this was, the man, a foreman at some factory, told him the Irish were not reliable. When he learned what it meant, he made it his name. Jarlath had started as an apprentice to a cabinetmaker who also built coffins, typical back then. He soon took over all the coffin making and eventually opened his own shop.

His wife, an Italian with a name I loved to say aloud, *Paola*, had died giving birth to their daughters. They were sixteen now. From the time they were young, the twins worked with him in the shop. The parish said, Girls doing work like that! He'll never get them married. I doubted Jarlath cared about his daughters finding husbands.

Jarlath only ever moved his narrow lips in the direction of a smile, and he did so now. His pale blue eyes seemed to haunt his narrow face.

"Annie-Rose," he said, "I know Paddy's not here because I passed the lads on the way, but your mother?"

I stepped aside so he could come in. He might think her sewing was for him. He paid her to make shrouds, but she didn't charge when it was a child or the victim of a fire. I helped with the hemming, but I had clumsy hands. My attention wandered. I pricked my fingertips and they bled.

Jarlath charged the rich a lot of money and used it to bury the poor. Many well-off or outright wealthy came from Manhattan to Jarlath's small shop. Some had parents or grandparents from Ireland. Others, according to my father, didn't know why they wanted the coffins except that they cost a lot and had a memorable name. Coffins weren't made by furniture makers anymore but by machines in factories, and then the undertakers bought them. Not Jarlath. He was not an undertaker and never had been.

Jarlath accepted the whiskey my mother offered him.

Bridie said, "You shouldn't be out in this."

The firelight smoothed her wrinkles, did away with the shadows beneath her eyes. Bridie lost ten years in the firelight. She offered him my seat. I hovered, waiting to be sent from the room. He did look tired, but no more than usual. After he sipped his whiskey, he said,

"Your one is dying."

"Is she?" Bridie asked. "Are you going?"

"I'll be in after, to bring her out."

Bridie nodded and frowned at the same time. "When?"

"Tonight, maybe tomorrow, not much longer than that, from what Una told me." Jarlath sighed and stood. "I'll wait downstairs for Paddy. We'll have a drink for the end of Brooklyn." He paused. "You should bring your girl."

My mother turned in her chair to study me. I remained still through her inspection. Whatever she was looking for in me, she found, because on that, the last night of the City of Brooklyn, we went out in the rain and wind to the cloister on Cross Hill Avenue.

Some houses were dark, but in others the bright windows told of people waiting for the new year. I walked beside my mother, trying to match her step for step. The convent was a ten-minute walk from the firehouse. Though I wanted to ask questions, I said nothing. The reward for my silence came when we were almost there. I had walked by the convent hundreds of times, but I had never gone inside to ask for an intention. The women of the parish did that.

We came to the black gate. A statue of Saint Maren stood in the front yard. She wore a long robe with a shawl around her shoulders. She gripped the shawl with one hand and a rosary was draped over her fingers. The other hand was extended, palm up, as if she was about to accept a small gift.

My mother didn't stop at the gate as I thought she would, and I had to run a bit to catch up to her. She went down the street that ended at the cemetery and then stopped at the gardener's door, built into the stone wall. She put her hand in her pocket and it emerged with a key, startling me. The door opened soundlessly.

The garden, in hibernation. I wanted to walk along the pathways, bare now but surely in every other season hemmed by flowers. In a set of three evergreens that formed a half circle, I saw a small crèche. Mary and Joseph and the Christ child, the shepherds, awaiting the wise men who would arrive in five days' time.

I followed my mother to a back door and she produced another, more delicate key. She fitted it into the lock and I seized her sleeve with both my freezing hands.

"We can't go in!" I said.

"I lived here," she said.

She shook me off and unlocked the door, the click as loud as a shout. My mother stopped and I stood beside her. The room was a kitchen. There was a long table in the middle of the room but no chairs. Several covered dishes sat on it, and the room smelled of fresh bread.

The fireplace was dark and there was a stove in one corner with a small pile of wood beside it. It was also not lit and the room was cold.

"We came in through the door in the wall. The sisters hadn't been here long yet. It was April or May. The garden was still wild."

"You came *here*," I said.

Bridie presented me with her profile. "What do you know about them?"

"They're a contemplative order," I said, as though I were being quizzed at school. "After they take their final vows, they leave the world behind."

We were taught the story at school.

In 1840, one of the nuns of the order traveled to the United States and founded a convent in upstate New York. Then, 1845, in Ireland. The potatoes died. There was nothing to eat. The starving Irish began staggering over the ocean. The sisters in Ireland and in New York agreed to break cloister. The Irish nuns went into the workhouses, what Americans would call poorhouses, and collected orphaned children. The New York nuns retrieved the children from the docks, often taking others who had not been orphans when they'd left Ireland, but were by the time they arrived in America. The intention had been to bring them out of close, dirty Brooklyn to the fresh air of the convent upstate, but the poor health of the children made traveling impossible. A benefactor working in America for famine relief in Ireland loaned his house to the nuns, he said, for "the duration of the crisis."

After the blight disappeared, the sisters returned to seclusion. Their benefactor had gone to help in Canada, where ships were also landing from Ireland, and there he'd died. The nuns tried, it was said, to find his grave, but never could. He left the house to the Catholic Church. And so the nuns from upstate who'd come to Brooklyn stayed there. By the end of the Civil War, the Irish orphans were grown and gone.

I looked at my mother keenly. "You were one of the orphans? You lived here?"

"For seven years," she said. "Seven."

Bridie was silent for so long I didn't think she was going to continue.

"I learned English," she said.

"And then?" I was brave to ask.

"They sent me into service."

Domestic service, she meant.

"Mr. Reliable was one of them too, wasn't he?"

Bridie glanced at me and said, as though she thought I knew all this already, "Jarlath and myself came over on the same ship."

Bridie walked across the room and I followed. She slid open a panel door and then we were in a short hallway. A stairway curved to the second floor. A crucifix hung on the wall and candles flickered in wall sconces. The air smelled of wax and incense.

She gestured to a set of double doors at the end of the hallway.

"That's the chapel. Two of them will be in there saying the rosary. The rest will be up at midnight."

"For the new year?" I asked.

"They get up every night at fifteen minutes before midnight. Starting at twelve, they pray the Sorrowful Mysteries. Then they go back to bed until sunrise."

Bridie began to move toward the stairs. The chapel door opened and we turned. A nun with a black veil over her face closed the door and came toward us. I stepped closer to my mother, but without touching her.

"Una."

"You shouldn't call me that," the nun said mildly.

Bridie said to me, "It's what we called her before she lost her head and joined them."

I flinched. A nun receives a new name upon entering. She cuts her hair and becomes a bride of Christ.

"You know my name," she said.

"I do," Bridie said. "I don't know why you're walking around like that in the middle of the night."

The nun touched the veil and turned to me. "We wear this when greeting outsiders. Usually it's only through the screen. We thought you'd come."

"I'm an outsider now, then?" my mother said.

"You're not a nun. And neither is your daughter. This is your daughter? She must be," the nun said.

"Annie-Rose," Bridie said ungraciously. "Annie-Rose, this is *Sister Joseph*."

"Thank you," Sister Joseph said, and then, to me, "I knew your mother before. So she feels like she can talk to me any way she likes."

Bridie laughed. "There is no before."

Sister Joseph touched the rosary hanging from her waist.

"Has your one been asking for me?" Bridie asked.

"She was, day before yesterday. She hasn't spoken much since. She'll go home tonight."

"All the way to Roscommon?" my mother asked.

"To the Lord." Sister Joseph lowered her head for a moment.

"I'll go then, and make my peace," Bridie said.

"I hope — is that why you've come, Brigid?"

Even through the veil, I could sense the nun studying my mother's face.

"It is," Bridie said.

I could see that she was lying, and I believed Sister Joseph did too. She briefly lowered her head again.

"We're going." Bridie turned toward the staircase.

"I'm afraid Annie will have to wait in the turn room."

"Annie-Rose."

"Annie-*Rose*."

They stared at each other for a moment.

"Go with Una," Bridie said to me. "I won't be long."

I wanted to run after her but I followed the nun instead. We went back down the hall, passed the kitchen, and came to another door. Sister Joseph opened it and we were in the turn room, where people came in from the outside. Candles burned here too. The floor was uncarpeted and empty of furniture except for a church's pew against one wall.

The turn was built into the wall opposite the door that led to the outside. To the left of the turn was a prie-dieu set in front of a heavy screen, the kind confessionals had. From behind the screen the nuns greeted their visitors. Was this how Jarlath knew the nun was dying? Because he'd come and brought them something? I couldn't quite picture it.

Sister Joseph gestured to the church pew. I sat, unbuttoning my coat and straightening my skirt. I tried to smooth my hair, which was loose from its braid because of the wind.

Sister Joseph folded her hands at her waist. Then she sighed and lifted the veil. I flinched and then blushed at the small smile of amusement on her plain face.

I wanted to know if she was committing a sin by letting me see her, and I wanted to tell her that I was not worth it.

"I knew your mother would come tonight. She has a sharp tongue but a kind heart."

"Yes," I said doubtfully.

Sister Joseph touched the rosary beads at her waist. "Coming here was hardest on those who still had some family left. I didn't." She crossed herself.

"Coming here?"

"When we came over, from Ireland."

My hand wavered as I wondered if I should cross myself too, for whomever she was thinking of.

"She never told me," I said.

"She wouldn't have," Sister Joseph said.

"Why didn't — if there was somebody left, why didn't they come too?"

"The workhouses." A shudder went through her. "The sisters in Ireland had to choose the ones they thought had the best chance to make it to America." She paused. "A lot of them didn't anyway. Your mother had a sister left. The nuns chose not to bring her. She died in the workhouse."

"My mother never told me," I said, and wondered why she, Sister Joseph, would. The thought must have been on my face, because she smiled sadly.

"Imagine, Annie-Rose, if no one spoke about what Christ suffered."

I tried to take that in, but couldn't. My mother was hardly Christ. "But — ?"

"Nobody would pray for Him."

I thought about it: if those who'd watched Jesus die on the cross had simply gone home. The crowd and the soldiers and Pontius Pilate himself and Simon who helped carry the cross and Veronica who wiped Christ's face, all of them not talking, as though it were a secret, then all of them, over the years, dying in the ways that people die, of old age and accidents and diseases, so one day nobody on earth knew about the crown of thorns, or the nails driven into His hands and feet, or the sword that pierced His side, or the wound Doubting Thomas put his hand into.

I folded my hands but I was too shy to pray in front of a nun. "Was her name Annie? Or Rose?"

Sister Joseph tilted her head to the side, as if I'd asked a very strange question. "Your mother never said her name. And I never saw her. She was in the room with the sick." Sister Joseph looked at me with pity. "And now I have to go back to the chapel," she said. "I've left Sister James on her own too long. It's our job to wake the others for midnight prayers."

"Are you the one who stays up every night?" I asked.

"No, each of the sisters takes her turn."

"Do you know it's New Year's Eve?"

"Yes. We do keep a calendar."

"Did my mother like it here?" I asked.

"That is something you'd have to ask her."

"Where did she go?" I meant after she left here, but Sister Joseph misunderstood.

"To Sister Benedict's cell. The sister who is watching over her would have left when your mother went in. Even the ones who weren't here in the '40s would know that she must be one of the girls. Up the stairs, the fourth door along the hallway."

I waited until I was sure Sister Joseph had time to make her way back. Still, I was relieved when I got to the chapel and saw the doors shut.

I had cat's feet. It was dark the night my mother first came here. From the edge of my eye, I saw the hollowed children climbing the steps beside me, dying with every step. They'd always be hungry. One of them was Bridie Cavanaugh. It's not only the dead who have ghosts. The children disappeared as I reached the top of the stairs. They were back at the bottom, starting the climb again.

The fourth door was open slightly and it was the only one with a light on. Behind each of the five closed doors — I counted quickly — lay a sleeping nun.

I went into the room and my eyes jumped to the still figure on the bed. Shadows fell over her wasted face. She wore a white nightgown and was covered with a sheet. Her hands were folded at her waist and I could see that she held a rosary, though most of it was hidden in the cup of her hands.

Bridie was sitting in a chair beside the bed. She beckoned me closer.

"Una went back to the chapel, then?"

I nodded.

"And you came up here on your own?"

I nodded again. I didn't say that *Sister Joseph* had all but given me permission.

Indeed, my bare answer pleased her. "Good girl," she whispered. "Shut the door."

I did, and then she had me stand at the foot of the narrow bed.

"Sister Benedict was the one in charge of us when we first got here." Bridie leaned over. "*A mhúinteoir Béarla?* I have all my words in order."

The three of us breathed.

Then Bridie spoke to me. "Not many of us brought anything from home, not many had anything left, but the ones who did, the things we had, she took away. She told us we were starting new lives. You're to speak English or you're not to speak. *An mhúinteoir Béarla.*"

Bridie knelt, and I was relieved because I thought she was going to say a prayer for the safe passage of the nun's soul into heaven, but instead she reached underneath the bed and drew out a tin, the sort that held sugar or flour.

"They're supposed to own nothing, but they don't always." Bridie paused in removing the lid and said, "You'll do well to remember that."

She must have seen the confusion on my face because she added, "The clergy don't always follow their vows to the letter."

I didn't believe her.

Bridie set the lid aside and reached in. First she drew out a folded piece of paper and handed it to me. "Tell me what it says."

I slowly unfolded the brittle paper. I had to hold it close to my face to read the small print in the candlelight.

At the top of the page it said, "*Newry Telegraph*, December 23, 1845."

I whispered, "'To the Farmers and Peasantry of Ireland: Directions for making wholesome food from diseased potatoes. First, grate down the potato by means of a grater, which may be made from a piece of sheet iron ... or a better machine may be had for four or five shillings ...'"

Around the middle — the fourth or fifth step — she interrupted and said, "Go to the end."

Relieved, I jumped to the final two sentences: "'This meal will serve very well for making both broth and soup, and for mixing it with oatmeal to make bread. In this way almost every potato can be made into wholesome food.'"

I held it out, hoping she wouldn't tell me to put it in my pocket. But she returned it to the tin. Next was a handkerchief edged with two rows of Irish lace, clusters of flowers and vines. It was stained and stiff and the lace had torn in places.

My mother tried to smooth it on her knee. "That's seawater did that."

Ruined as it was, I could see how beautiful it must have been.

"I suppose they thought they'd sell it when they got to America." Bridie turned it over and pointed to a particular stain. "Green, you see?"

I peered closer, but in the dim light I saw a dark stain of no color.

"She took it from her mother's pocket and tried to wipe the grass from her mother's mouth and then she put it in her own pocket and kept walking."

Bridie put the handkerchief back. "She never got better. She died here on the third floor, where we slept."

Bridie looked up at the ceiling and I did too.

She put her hand back in the tin and pulled out what looked like rosary beads, but smaller, with a ring on one end and a crucifix on the other.

She held it up and I moved closer. The rosary was just a single decade and the beads were made of wood. My mother slipped the ring over her index finger and deftly tucked the beads up her sleeve.

"To pray in secret. From the days when you could be killed for going to Mass."

With her thumb, Bridie slipped the rosary, bead by bead, into her palm.

"Do that ten times and you'll have said a whole rosary. *An paidrin beag*," she said. "The little rosary."

It was the only time my mother spoke her language and then told me what she said.

"If she'd tossed it away or buried it in the garden. But she kept it." Bridie opened her hand to let me see *an paidrin beag*.

This had belonged to her. She didn't have to tell me.

Bridie turned back to the nun and began to sing in a whisper.

Sister Benedict's eyelids flickered. I sensed that up and down the hallway, each nun was either lying still in her narrow bed or propped up on one elbow, but all had an ear turned to the sound. As quietly as she sang, they heard her. Those who'd been here a very long time might know the voice. Perhaps those sisters were wondering if Bridie Cavanaugh had finally come to take revenge on them all for saving her life.

After getting the rosary back, my mother grew quieter. I saw my father look at her with concern, but I don't think he ever asked her what was wrong. Consolidation had him busy. We didn't see him for days at a time. A month after New Year's, on February 1, the Feast of Saint Brigid, we moved into the brownstone behind the firehouse. The third floor was ours, and my father intended to buy the house when the old lady who owned it died. She'd already agreed. Her only son, against her advice, ran off and married a wreck of a girl, and his mother answered back by selling his inheritance.

Though I thought often of the peace of the cloister and the peace on Sister Joseph's face, something missing entirely from my mother, the night Sister Benedict died was not the night I heard the call.

March 17, 1899, the last St. Patrick's Day of the century, was a beautiful day, until the fire.

Mary Clark and I were fourteen. We stood shoulder to shoulder in the crowd lining Fifth Avenue. Her older brothers had ridden with us on the trolley over the Brooklyn Bridge. They were twenty and seventeen and supposed to be our chaperones for the day, but after they secured us a spot in front of the Windsor Hotel and told us to stay put, they left with the promise that they'd be back in three hours. Mary said they went off to drink. They might be back or we might be going home by ourselves.

We wore green ribbons in our hair and Mary had a green bow around her waist.

On my blouse I had a sprig of fresh shamrock with a green ribbon that said *Erin go Bragh* in gold letters. A pipe and drum band passed by playing "The Wearing of the Green."

The windows of the Windsor Hotel framed the guests who were watching the parade.

They were smiling and pointing, as though they were on a ship leaving port. On one of the higher floors a woman held a baby wrapped in a white blanket. She made its little hand wave to the assembly of firemen in their finery.

My father was marching in the Brooklyn parade. He didn't see the point of my going all the way across the river for a St. Patrick's Day parade, but my mother said I should get out of Brooklyn once in a while. Mary thought she saw her uncle and began hopping up and down, calling to him.

There was one long scream first, and then in the next second, a dozen. Our heads all turned, the entire crowd at once, to see black smoke pouring from the hotel windows. The firemen in the parade were already running toward the hotel.

I opened my mouth but nothing came out. Mary seized my arm,

breathing in gasps. Men and woman started streaming out of the building, and those higher up threw fire ropes out the windows and climbed down, some of them holding children.

The police shouted at the crowd to move back. The cops tried to stop the firemen from running in. The firemen shoved back and threw punches.

The hotel guests began to jump. The *thump, thump, thump* of bodies hitting the sidewalk sounded like the drum in the pipe band. Birds dropped from the cloud of smoke, and this was as frightening as the fire. To see a bird stop in flight, and fall.

One shriek rose above the other screams. I looked away from the sky and back at the blazing hotel. I sighed and clapped my hands once as a white bird flew from a high window. Then I saw the flutter was not wings but a blanket falling away. The mother leaped from the ledge after the baby.

In the newspaper the next day, they would be listed as "unknown woman, unknown child." Why, the newspaper reporter asked, had the mother not jumped with her child in her arms? They might have died together. My father said in disgust that clearly she hoped that if the child were released alone, someone below would catch him. But I believe she thought her child would become a bird. She hadn't known the sparrows were dying too.

St. Patrick's night, kneeling at my bedroom window, I looked out at the firehouse. A light was on in the kitchen. Someone was always awake. Tonight many of the men would be up, talking about the Windsor, discussing the collapse, the search for the bodies that would start again at dawn, the luck of the men who'd gotten to fight the fire.

I said the rosary and then stayed on my knees. The nuns at school spoke of a God who never stopped plotting ways to catch us sinning and to punish us for those sins. According to them, we were always disgracing Christ, who'd died for us. For my father, God was like fire. He rarely spoke about his job at home, but once he said that fire has a mind but no eyes or ears. It kills blindly. My mother's God was indifferent to everyone, except for the Irish, whom He hated.

But that St. Patrick's night, I understood what none of them did. God was the baby, saved from one death and handed another. But God was also the baby in flight, the moment when it was not child but bird, not falling but flying. That was God. Everything beautiful, everything sad.

By telling me what the words *an paidrin beag* meant, my mother handed me her legacy of suffering. She knew, I was sure, that Sister Joseph had told me about her sister, a girl with a grave across the ocean. She gave me her dreams. The workhouse and the ship coming over and the first years in the convent. My father too, though not on purpose. I thought of what he must have seen in the war, and what he must have seen fighting fires in New York but never spoke of. Except for the Brooklyn Theatre Fire. Every year on December 5, he took me with him to lay a wreath on the grave in the Green-Wood where the 103 victims who could not be identified are buried together. The monument was erected by the City of Brooklyn. I could close my eyes and smell the smoke and feel the panic set in. Jamesey Walsh finding in the fire the organs of the dead boys. I confessed to the priest once, and he sighed and told me to put my mind to other things.

I thought of the peace in Sister Joseph's face. I wanted to spend my days alone, in prayer. I didn't know what else to do with the weight my parents bequeathed me. The weight of hunger and fire.

Because entering the cloister would mean never seeing my parents again, I would not go until they were both gone.

After I left school at sixteen, I took a job in the post office, in the dead letter office. I liked the work, solving mysteries, always the chance to reunite people. Misspelling was often the reason for a letter gone awry, and so the solution was a matter of deduction based on the first letter of the name and the house or building number. But other times, a street name might be written beautifully but there would be nothing by that name in any borough directory. I would bring it to my father and he would tell me that the street had been renamed, or no longer existed.

In September 1913, a memorial was being dedicated to the firefighters of New York City on Riverside Drive in Manhattan. Firemen from all over the country came to New York for the days of events that preceded the dedication ceremony, like the baseball game between the police and fire departments at Ebbets Field.

My father asked me to accompany the niece of a fireman at the Glory Devlins who was visiting from out of town and wanted to go to the ceremony. She was nineteen years old. Her aunt didn't care for crowds. My father would be attending with the other brass.

I was not happy about giving up a Saturday, my day off from work, and also felt a flush of shame. Spinster escort. I couldn't think of why a girl her age would want to go to something like that, a parade of firemen and fire equipment and then a lot of speeches. She must have been short on excitement. When I saw her — Elizabeth, her name was — dressed in what was clearly her best, with a ribbon in her hair she kept fussing with, I realized she was hoping a fireman would take notice of her. I kept my sigh to myself.

We took the trolley into the city and found our way to the grandstand.

I hadn't expected to be moved by the ceremony, or the sight of firemen from all over the country assembled in uniform, or the speech of the son of Isidor Straus, who'd done so much to raise money so that the monument could be built, and who had died last year on the *Titanic*, along with his wife.

It was such a windy afternoon that firemen had to climb on top of the monument and hold down the American flags covering it.

For the unveiling, four girls, about eleven, twelve years old, stepped forward. The daughters of firemen killed in the line of duty. I was startled. *Daughters?*

The girls tugged the flags, and the men on top of the monument stood. The crowd, as one, took a breath, I think, at the sight of the four firemen in silhouette against the sky.

My father opened our house that evening. It was like him to skip the official reception and host his own party. Elizabeth found other girls her age, as relieved to be free of me as I was to be released from duty.

I could have hidden in my room, but the noise would have made trying to read or sleep pointless. One of the Glory Devlins, Bill Hegarty, and his brothers (his actual brothers) were Irish musicians, and they set up in a corner of the kitchen.

I went out to the backyard where it was quieter, though there were many people outside as well, smoking, drinking, talking, enjoying the warm evening. Summer was not entirely behind us yet.

I headed to the far corner, near the fence that separated our yard from the firehouse. If you stepped behind the tree there, you could not be seen from the house.

When I saw a man standing near the tree, smoking, it was too late to retreat without looking like a child running away. He was tall, with dark hair and a full mustache, indistinguishable from more than half the men filling our house, but still, I was sure I'd never seen him before. He greeted me, and I nodded.

"Nice night," he said.

"Yes," I said, stuttering slightly, which embarrassed me. "Especially after all the rain yesterday."

"You're Paddy's daughter?"

I nodded.

"He gave you a name?"

"My mother did. It's Annie-Rose."

"That's very pretty," he said. "Jack Keegan."

My hand twitched at my side, uncertain whether I should offer my hand to shake, but then he didn't offer his. I tugged at my skirt, then smoothed it. A silence fell. I looked around the yard, and every time I looked back at Jack Keegan his eyes were on me.

"You work in Brooklyn?" I said, desperate to fill the silence. We'd established that the weather was good. I couldn't plead a chill with any dignity. My shyness was already amusing him.

"Yeah."

"Well," I said, "I should get back inside."

"Someone waiting for you?"

"No," I answered. "It's just — late."

He smiled. "You're not sleeping with that racket. Stay. Enjoy it with me."

The Hegartys were playing a reel. Flustered, I looked past him, then down at the ground.

"I'm going to be twenty-nine," I said.

I looked younger, to the point where I wasn't believed sometimes when I gave my age.

"Tomorrow?" Jack laughed.

I felt my face get hot. "No. December."

"I've been told I was born in August."

It was an invitation to ask what he meant. Told by whom? What had happened to his mother? I wanted to know, and at the same time understood that he was teasing me. The whole conversation, in fact, was occurring, I guessed, only because he'd been drinking (though he wasn't drunk) and he was a bit bored. He wore no wedding ring. There were probably a lot of girls here seeking his attention.

"I'm going to be a nun," I said instead. "I'm going to enter the cloister."

I had never said it out loud before. There was something childish about my words, and it scared me. Jack Keegan noticed, I think.

"What are you waiting for?" he asked.

"I have to wait until my parents are gone," I said.

He frowned thoughtfully. "Most parents are happy when a girl's got a vocation."

"They only have me."

"You haven't told them?"

I shook my head.

"Don't. Paddy will live forever out of spite."

At that, I laughed. I couldn't help it. "You know him, then?"

"He once tried to recruit me." Jack nodded in the direction of the firehouse.

"What did you do to get his attention?" I asked.

"Maybe ten years ago, I got into some trouble at a fire. Not *in* the fire," he said with a quick grin. "At the scene. The Lyons school?"

It took me a moment, but then I did remember it. The school was for Irish girls sixteen and older, and it was not run by the Church, which many did not care for. The students lived in. The temperature the night of the fire was below zero, and the firemen banged on the door of the closest house so the girls and their teachers could get inside and stay warm. The owner refused to let them in. Some of the firemen took exception. Another neighbor did open her home, and after the fire was out, some of the firemen returned to the first house.

"It was in the papers," I said. "A fireman punched the man who owned the house when he came running out to see who was smashing all his windows."

"That is what happened." Jack grinned. "This gentleman went over to Paddy and told him he wanted the fireman who hit him to go to jail. Paddy told him all he had to do was identify the guilty party. He had seven of us line up, and Paddy said, 'Which one struck you, sir?'"

"And he couldn't say." I smiled wryly.

"Didn't even try."

Seven mustached firemen, soot-streaked and probably still helmeted. Of course he couldn't say.

"Why didn't you come to the Glory Devlins?" I asked.

"I wasn't sure if there was room enough for both of us in one firehouse."

I stared at him. "That's bold."

Jack smiled.

"You were one of the men on top of the monument today?" I asked.

He'd been about to smoke but instead lowered the cigarette. "Yeah. How did you know? Did your father tell you that?"

My father once said there were some firemen who simply wanted in on the action, wherever, whatever it was. Jack Keegan seemed the type.

"No. It was just a guess," I said. I was never *bold*.

"A guess," he repeated.

Jack's expression changed from the one of mild amusement he'd been wearing since we began talking to a frankly appraising stare. I'd surprised him. He pinched the end of his cigarette, extinguishing it.

A slow air was coming from our kitchen. I turned to look, as if I might see the notes drifting out the open window.

"Those are the Irish pipes," Jack said. "Bagpipes are Scottish."

"Well," I said, backing away. "I, ah . . . Enjoy the rest of the night." I turned and hurried across the yard.

"Annie-Rose!" Jack called.

He caught up to me and took my elbow. Last week, I'd stopped at Agnello's to buy bread for my mother, and the clerk's fingers had brushed mine as he handed me the package. I'd nearly grabbed his hand, just to hold it.

The palm of Jack's hand was warm. The palm of Jack's hand was the whole world.

When there is something to be done, there is a fireman who can do it. Whether it's building a new staircase in your house, shingling a roof, helping you move, shoveling your walkway after a snowstorm, illegally burying two little boys who died of influenza — look to a firehouse, any firehouse, in any borough of New York City.

Two of them came quietly into the bedroom carrying the coffin between them. If my father could have handled it alone, he would have, I knew. I never thought of him as old, but he was old that night. There were things he couldn't ask of Jack, the father.

Patrick Devlin knew no fireman would refuse another fireman who asked for help, not for his own sake or for the sake of his wife and children.

And so Chief Devlin went to Ryan and McGinty. Both were past fifty. One was a widower with no children, and the other was a bachelor. Their mothers had been gone a long time. My father sent them to Reliable's, where Frances and Lucy were working their hands raw to keep up with demand, but they hardly could. Their coffins were built to order, with a few kept above ground as samples of their work and quick sales for the few who wouldn't, or couldn't, wait. They'd learned the craft from their father, Jarlath, gone for years now, and kept his way of doing business.

The Reliable daughters gave Ryan and McGinty the only completed coffin they had left. It was shaped in the Irish style, with a Celtic cross engraved on the lid. Too small for a grown man but bigger than a typical child's coffin, it may have been for a child about to be no longer a child. Or a small woman. Both boys would fit in it. I would fit in it. Jack would not fit in it.

Ryan and McGinty set the coffin down in the middle of the room. Jack pulled me to my feet, away from the bed, hard enough to bruise my arms. My legs couldn't hold me, and he guided me into the chair that had been set by the sickbed, the one I'd given up for kneeling.

Bridie came into it then. The men retreated to drink in the kitchen, and she washed the boys with a white cloth dampened in water she'd heated on the stove. I was grateful. She could have used cold water. She touched the cloth to their cheeks and foreheads and noses. Nothing took the blue away. She washed the runnel of dried blood that left a trail from their ears down their necks and the one from their noses to their mouths. She ran the cloth over their hands and turned their hands over to stroke their palms, one by one by one by one. Down their legs and over the bottoms of their feet. She sent me to fetch a comb and the sewing basket. I brought them both back, and without a word to me, she took the scissors and snipped locks of their hair, tying Patrick's with green thread and John's with blue.

"J.J., blue. Paddy, green. Remember that," she said.

Then she combed their hair, though she didn't lift their heads from the pillow to get the back. Patrick's hair always got so tangled. He was a restless sleeper. Bridie told me to pick what I wanted them to be wearing. I chose their Easter suits, which they'd worn when we had their photograph taken at the studio on Fulton Street this summer, a present for my father's birthday. They'd been about to outgrow them.

"There," I said, fastening buttons and straightening collars after Bridie had dressed them. "There."

Bridie called for the men.

Jack lifted them into the coffin. He laid them carefully beside each other. I put in a whistle for John, and for Patrick, one of his fire wagons. For them both, I put the rosary I'd gotten as a gift for my first communion. A full rosary. I entwined it in one hand each, binding them to each other.

The baby never stopped moving. I shoved at her, anchored when I wanted to be light, so I could follow the boys.

My mother took the comb to me and untangled the nest of my hair. I looked at it spread over my shoulders. There were gray strands. I didn't put it up and she didn't make me. She only pinned a black veil in my hair.

The half-moon night was the kind often found at the end of October, fresh and starry, threaded with both autumn and winter. Jack, my father, Ryan and McGinty carried the coffin on their shoulders. My mother and I followed.

At nearly eleven o'clock, the streets were empty. A neighbor might see and tell the police, since it was illegal what we were about to do. Nobody would, my mother said. If there was any danger at all, it was that others might ask the firemen to do the same for their children.

The procession stopped at the door in the cloister's garden wall. My mother went ahead with the key and unlocked the door. As the men carried the coffin past her, she said something I couldn't hear. They went ahead down a stone path. We followed. The air smelled of smoke. Our feet rustled the leaves littering the path. By the evergreens, where the crèche had been when I was here as a girl, they set the coffin down on four chairs that must have come from the firehouse. The men moved away and Jack came to stand beside me. He took my arm and I leaned into him, wanting him to take the weight of the baby from me.

On the way, Bridie had told me that hours ago, four younger firemen had been let in with the key by my father and they'd set to work digging. Two dug and then two relieved them and so on. They'd been asked to finish in three hours, and they had. The grave was near the stone wall beside the rosebushes, which were bare but for ladders of thorns.

Annie rose. Annie got up. Annie went away.

The four set their shovels down and came toward us. My father put up his hand and stepped forward. His quiet tone carried. He told them that he was grateful, he would always be, but they shouldn't come closer. The men retreated back to the stone wall to watch from there, their heads respectfully bowed.

We all turned at the sound of rustling leaves. They came through the dark in their black clothes and veiled faces. Around their waists they wore rosaries whose silver crucifixes shot slips of moonlight. Six nuns stopped behind us. They tucked their arms up their billowing sleeves and also bowed their heads.

My mother lifted the lid of the coffin and beckoned to my father. He stepped up and laid a hand on one chest and then on the other, as if to make sure the boys' hearts weren't beating. Then Jack touched their hands and their cheeks and then backed away, his breathing shallow. My mother stepped up and gazed for a moment and she looked at me.

I moved forward and studied their faces, so still, already unfamiliar. They lay on the small pillow, ear to ear, their faces turned up to the sky. The last the sky would see of them.

I smoothed their fine brown hair and kissed John's forehead and kissed Patrick's forehead. The baby bumped the coffin.

I retreated to Jack, who took my hand, and my mother stepped up again, to close the lid.

I thought. But then she began to sing in Irish, the first language, the lost language.

For the first time upon hearing it, I didn't let my greedy ears try to separate one word from another, to sort the vowels from the conso-nants, to find the beginnings and know the endings. I listened not for her secrets, but only the sound, the raw edges and soft centers.

The keen finished, Bridie gently closed the coffin lid.

Six days later, my water broke in the middle of the night. Jack was at work and my parents were one floor below. The pain presented itself, a river in which I could drown myself.

I pressed my face into my pillow for hours, until my throat ached from turning screams into whimpers. My mother appeared at the foot of the bed. Not herself as she was, an old woman, but a young one. She told me without speaking that she would give me the chance to die. But my daughter would follow. Bridie vanished. I rode out the next pain. When it had faded, I climbed out of the bed, made my way out of the room into the hallway and called for my mother.

CHAPTER FIVE

Maggie O'Reilly

MAGGIE TIPS HER FACE to the gray sky. Mist touches her forehead, her cheeks. A soft rain, the Irish would say. That is, rain that seems to fall both up and down at once.

She is on the cobblestone path to the building that houses the humanities. Lysaght Hall, with its stone façade covered in red ivy, its steep staircases and random alcoves, suits their department of literature professors and writers. They joke about being in exile at the very northern edge of campus, but the truth is they like being outsiders. This part of campus doesn't get many passersby.

Though Maggie doesn't mind the rain, she has been in Ireland for a little more than a year and has become enough of a local to enjoy winning one against the weather. She rushes inside and is already halfway up the stairs before the heavy door slams behind her.

She is relieved to find her office empty. She and the adjunct professor with whom she shares the space keep to opposite schedules, as the office is too small for both of them to comfortably use at the same time. The day they met, Cillian told her he was far more musician than teacher, but as far as jobs go, he's had worse. She told him she was one of those

people who choose to teach because they can't do . . . *fill in the blank.*
He'd laughed.

Maggie sets her bookbag on the desk and goes to the window. The
rain is falling harder now, but she can sense it more than she can see it.
She touches her hair and finds it is not a bit damp. She has it pulled
back in a low ponytail today because she has a class at noon and has
the idea that putting it up helps distinguish her from her students.

The clouds are so low over Slievekeeran, the mountain that lies four
miles outside the village, that she can imagine climbing straight from
its summit into the sky. Later in the morning it will surely clear, and
then this afternoon, rain again. She loves the way Ireland lights its
days, takes the light back, returns it.

Her office hours are from ten to eleven, but she is not expecting any
students to appear this morning. Michaelmas term is just two weeks
old. The first paper, due in a week, is the short one whose sole purpose
is to shake the summer cobwebs out of eighteen- and nineteen-year-
old brains. Her students are almost exclusively undergraduates, many
of them taking literature classes only because they have to. The next
paper, a longer one, will likely see pre–due date visits, because the class
will have learned how she grades and that, yes, grammar counts.

Maggie turns her computer on, and as it boots up, she puts her
glasses on and sips her coffee. This morning's line in the bakery turned
her ten-minute walk to campus into a twenty-minute commute, but
Murt's coffee is strong and she got out of bed still tired. Yet she needs
to get some real work done. She is determined to use every block of
free time to make progress on her dissertation. The start of September
has brought a sense of urgency. She finished her own course work in
the spring. This semester and next are about teaching and, even more
so, about writing.

If all goes well and her dissertation is accepted, by the start of next
summer she will have her postgraduate degree. Soon enough, she will
have to decide whether to look for a job in Ireland or go back to the
States.

Before settling down to work, Maggie skims her email. Rote stuff

— except that her standing four o'clock meeting with Dr. McAlary has been canceled. He canceled last week too.

Dr. McAlary is the head of the English Department and her dissertation adviser. If you were casting an Irish literature professor in an American film, he would be as blue-eyed and as clever as Rory McAlary. He would be named Rory McAlary. During Maggie's first semester, she was his teaching assistant, grading his papers, sitting in on his classes, occasionally handling part of a lecture. She ignored his practice of not letting students call her by her first name but adopted his policy of calling on the reluctant. Often, he told her, that student's opinion will be far more interesting than that of the girl in the front row with her hand up. Not to be sexist, he'd said with a grin, but it's always a girl. Maggie believes it's more likely that the guy with his hand up is not seen as a pest.

Rory is forty-three, Dublin born. He lived in New York for a time in his twenties but returned to Ireland for his then girlfriend, now wife, who grew up in Ivehusheen. Her uncle, in fact, owns the town bakery.

Maggie sometimes thinks about Rory drinking in Hell's Kitchen on weekday afternoons after the day's construction job ended. He was, he said, typically on a barstool by three-thirty. She would have been eight, nine years old, in her plaid skirt and knee socks, walking home from school to her family in its first configuration of five. Father, mother, herself, two younger brothers.

Maggie gets up and goes back to the window. An Outlook calendar cancellation. She wonders if he will sneak a call this evening from his backyard when he goes outside for a cigarette.

When she hears hesitant footsteps in the hallway, Maggie half hopes they will disappear, and in fact they stop in midstride. Cillian has told her the campus is haunted, built as it was on the grounds of a workhouse. Kilmaren College's main administration building was once the intake building where the destitute Irish who'd come to live there were processed before being sent to dormitories segregated by gender and age. Lysaght Hall is the former fever hospital. The chapel is where the mortuary once stood. The garden was planted over the cemetery, where the dead were buried in mass graves during the famine, when the workhouse was overrun with the sick and the starving.

Right now the garden's black gate stands open, though it isn't supposed to be for another two hours. The college's security staff locks the gate every afternoon, but by morning it is often found this way.

The footsteps start again, and in a moment an American girl who took Maggie's class in *Dubliners* over the summer peeks in.

Amy O'Connor is smart, though she tends to pause while giving her opinion, waiting for approval before continuing. Maggie has learned not to rush a silence.

"Hi? Um, Maggie?" she says. "I wanted to talk to you, if you have a minute."

"Come in." Maggie smiles and gestures to the chair in front of her desk.

Maggie is probably supposed to favor the girls who arrive at Kilmaren already bookish, but it's the ones like Amy who interest her more. These are the girls who likely daydreamed through their high school English classes, and who would never have spoken to *her* if they'd been classmates.

Amy sits and crosses her legs, pulling her skirt over her knees.

"I already talked to Dr. McAlary a little while ago. It's about me maybe doing my master's here." She offers a nervous smile.

"Okay." Maggie hides her surprise. She thought Amy was going to ask for late admittance into one of the classes Maggie is currently teaching. She folds her hands on her desk. "Dr. McAlary gave you the basics?"

"Sure. How to apply and the courses you have to take, all of that. He said I should talk to you to get the real story since you're in the program."

Maggie smiles. "He wants me to tell you how much hard work is involved. See if I can scare you off."

Amy laughs and sits back, relaxing.

"When will you get your BA?" Maggie asks.

"I'm a junior now, so a year from this May," Amy says. "I know that's a long time, but I'm a communications major, so since I'm switching to English, I've got some catching up to do."

"What you take here will count toward that." She speaks briefly about the application requirements and deadlines.

"Have you told your parents that you're thinking of grad school?"

"Not yet," Amy says. "They're coming to visit in a couple of weeks, from Oregon. I'm sure once they see Ireland, they'll get why I want to stay."

"Well, good. I've yet to get my mother to pay a visit, and New York is much closer."

Amy laughs. "You're from New York? Somebody said that."

Maggie has wondered how much speculation goes on about her personal life among her female students. Quite a bit, she thinks. She is herself both professor and student, older than they are but not by much. She's an age they want to be. Because she is unmarried but still under thirty, she gets to be independent, not lonely.

Amy is looking past Maggie, scanning the bookcase, which Maggie notes with approval. A real reader will always look first to the bookcase, no matter what room she is in.

"Is that your daughter?" Amy asks.

Maggie doesn't turn to see the picture Amy is pointing at. It's in a frame on top of the bookcase. Rose, a year old, at her first Glory Devlins Christmas party, wearing a red velvet dress with a matching bow in her black curls, smiling on Santa's lap.

"That's my little sister," Maggie says. "She's seventeen and a senior in high school. But I like to remember the time before she learned to talk."

The second configuration of five: Mother, herself, two younger brothers, baby sister.

Rose is the reason Maggie was up late last night. She called at a decent hour New York time, seven o'clock at night, but, as ever, failed to remember that it was midnight in Ireland.

Rose is still angry that she didn't get to visit Ireland this August, though their mother had only promised to think about it. In the end, Norah decided she could not miss work. In a phone call she had no time for, Maggie listened to her mother explain, and instead of pointing out that she and Marian owned Irish Dreams and didn't need permission to take time off, Maggie said it was a shame that August was such a bad month. Then she hung up.

Last night, Rose announced her plan to come by herself over Christmas break. Aidan told her no way in hell was he letting her fly by herself, and Rose pointed out that she will be eighteen by then.

Maggie listened to Rose's account of the fight, relieved that she was an ocean removed from it. If Aidan was so worried, Rose said dismissively, then he should come with her. Maggie knows he won't. Visiting her is not a priority for either of her brothers, but in Brendan's case it's because of his recent move to L.A. He is broke, since he had to buy a car, and right now he's working as a bartender.

Maggie does hope Rose visits, but at the same time, she knows what it will be like afterward. Though only in Galway for a week, Rose will become a character in the lives of all those she meets. How is Rose, Maggie will forever be asked by professors and other postgrads, shopkeepers, by all the regulars at Derrane's.

Rory McAlary has called Maggie beautiful. She isn't, but it was nice to hear. He won't say it again if he meets Rose. Nobody who has seen her sister would say it about them both.

"I couldn't shut up either when I was seventeen," Amy says, laughing. Then she shifts in her seat. "Will you be a professor here when you graduate? I'm just wondering if you'd even be here if I get in."

"That I can't say." Maggie explains about the need to be flexible in this field, and how you often have to go where a job opens up.

She is not going to say that there is at least a possibility of a position at Kilmaren. Rory has explained that the college did not generally hire their own postgraduate students right away. They didn't want the programs being seen as a fast track to professorship. But he's suggested that they might make an exception for her. As an alumna of the MA program and an American, Maggie would be an asset with regard to attracting international students. And Kilmaren, which touts the benefits of studying in the Irish countryside, near the mountains and not far from the sea, is working hard to compete with cities like Galway proper and Dublin for study-abroad students.

Maggie has already proved popular. Her classes have all filled. It is partly word of mouth, but Maggie believes her name also attracts those students randomly thumbing through the course catalog for a class. They might find her bio in the back with its small black-and-white picture, which she admits is flattering, and read that she is from New York.

She never says Brooklyn.

As she was writing up the dry paragraph detailing her education, she typed "M-a-g" and then, without planning it, her finger came down on the "d." Magdalena O'Reilly was certainly a more intriguing woman than Maggie-presumed-to-be-Margaret. If you threw a stone into a crowd in Ireland, you'd hit a Margaret O'Reilly. If you threw two stones, you'd hit two. Magdalena O'Reilly sounds like a woman with a past.

Which she is. And her present is nearly as convoluted.

She accepted Rory's invitation to give her a lift home from an evening on-campus event and reception. She usually walked home. But it was a cold night in early February, a month into the semester. Her friendship with Cillian had begun to tip into flirtation, not only in the ten minutes or so they saw each other as she was arriving at their office and he was leaving, but in the evenings too, at Derrane's, the pub where the professors and grad students gathered. He played in the weekly *seisiúns* there, and joined the group when the music was done for the night.

She had even mentioned him to her cousin — offhandedly, she thought, but email didn't dull Noelle's instincts.

How are things progressing with the fiddler?

Maggie hadn't mentioned his name. Noelle asked a few times before Maggie finally answered.

Re: the fiddler. Nice guy. Cute. Shared office. Could get awkward.

Noelle responded with a phone call Maggie didn't return, and then, in an email:

> If you sleep with him and break up, draw a line in chalk
> down the center and tell him you'll kill him if he puts a toe
> over it.
> P.S. Stop being an ass.

Maggie laughed but had not taken her cousin's advice. She climbed in Rory's car that night, aware that he was going to make a pass at her, and that she would let him.

But Rory let her kiss him first, which she realized later was probably so he could say he did not start things, if he was ever asked. She began showing up late to her office hours to avoid Cillian, who retreated to a politeness so casual that Maggie decided she must have misread his attraction to the woman he thought she was. Later, though, she wondered if he was simply not interested in competing with Rory. She is not naïve enough to think the relationship is a secret.

She could easily see them, if they'd been schoolboys together: Rory assuming he was greatly and constantly envied; Cillian humoring him, aware without conceit that he had more depth, and that he would almost certainly win a fistfight as well.

Maggie has assumed from the first that the affair would come to its natural end when she graduated. But possibly she'd convinced Rory too well of her own maturity, and perhaps he thought she wouldn't care if he both dumped her and hired her.

"I hope you're still here if I get in," Amy says.

"One thing to consider, Amy, is that it's never a bad idea to take some time after college before applying to grad school."

"That's what you did?" Amy doesn't sound pleased.

"I was twenty-six when I applied."

It's probably a typical age to head to grad school, and Maggie knows she is making it sound intentional, a timely college graduation followed by either an unsatisfying first career or a free-spirit stretch. She is not going to volunteer that she only got the last six credits for her BA so she could apply to Kilmaren.

"You didn't always want to be a college professor?"

"My grandmother was an elementary school teacher. When I started college, I thought that's what I'd do."

"What made you change your mind?"

"Dealing with my sister," Maggie says.

Amy laughs.

"I am serious, in a way," Maggie says. "As I got older, I realized there was more to teaching than getting to write on the blackboard. Keeping their attention is half the job. Those who can do it, like my grandmother, thank God for them."

"What made you figure, hey, so I'll be a professor instead? For me, I've always liked to read, but only what I wanted to, not what I had to for school. Then I took your class, and you know so much, and you really seem to love it."

Maggie knows Amy wants to hear something that resonates. She wants to believe her new career goal is real.

"Love of literature," Maggie says. "I like discussing books, and thinking about the decisions the writer made, and discovering why he or she turned the story this way or that. The best books, the best stories, it doesn't matter if you already know the ending. No matter how many times I read 'Eveline,' I always hope she gets away. She never will. But I always think, this time, she'll get on the boat. Why doesn't she?"

"Well, I think —"

Amy starts to speak but Maggie laughs.

"I'm not asking. This isn't a pop quiz."

Maggie reaches into her desk and takes out a brochure advertising the program and hands it to Amy. She tells her to read it through and stop by or email if she has any questions.

After Amy leaves, Maggie returns to the window. She tugs on it, even though she knows it is painted shut.

Love of literature.

Hypocrite, Maggie tells herself. She knows that motives don't have to be so pure. You can want to be a college professor because it's a job you can do, but also because you like being on a college campus every day. You like the energy and restlessness and being around incarnations of yourself when you were at your own best.

Unlike the writing faculty, Maggie doesn't have access to the inner lives of her students. She knows that tragedy doesn't necessarily mark you. But her students are young enough to believe in their own lives. They are certain that mistakes, even the worst ones, can be undone, and that there is a thin boundary between their dreams for their lives and their lives as they will be lived.

"Mrs. O'Reilly?"

Maggie turns to see Mrs. Sheehan, the department secretary, filling the doorway, her arms crossed over her imposing chest.

Maggie presses her hand against the center pane of the window, trying to hide how startled she is. Mrs. Sheehan wears thick rubber-soled shoes, like a nun or a nurse. She has been the English Department's secretary for more than twenty years, though it's rumored she is an original inmate of the workhouse. Which closed in 1870.

Ms. O'Reilly, Maggie almost snaps.

But Mrs. Sheehan would have been the one to process Maggie's application to the program, which had her date of birth on it. Maggie O'Reilly is twenty-eight; Maggie O'Reilly should be married.

She peers at Maggie over the top of her bifocals. "A girl came to see you this morning before you were in, and I didn't know what to tell her, about whether or not you'd be showing yourself today."

Her tone suggests Maggie has missed an appointment with the Pope.

"Dr. McAlary was here, so I asked him to speak with her."

Now Mrs. Sheehan sounds as though the maid didn't show up, forcing the Pope to mop the floor himself.

"She came back and I spoke with her," Maggie says. "It's fine."

"Dr. McAlary left for his class, but you can be sure and let him know when you see him. He was concerned that there might be some kind of problem."

"I have no problems whatsoever."

"You'll have to tell him then, at your four o'clock meeting."

"That's been canceled, so he'll have to be concerned until tomorrow," Maggie says.

"Again?" Mrs. Sheehan says.

"Dr. McAlary had to take one of his kids to something," Maggie says. "New school year. New schedules. They're still working it out."

This is probably exactly what he will say when he calls. Maggie tugs on the window again.

"That's been painted shut since the week after paint was invented," Mrs. Sheehan says.

"I know that. I've called maintenance twice to come fix it. It's a fire hazard. This is the only window in the room. You're supposed to have two means of egress. If the door is ever blocked—"

Mrs. Sheehan almost certainly knows that at these weekly meetings, Dr. McAlary and Teaching Assistant O'Reilly don't wear their clothes. Yet Rory puts the meetings on his calendar, as if they will be discussing the progress she's making on her dissertation. It amazes Maggie how a man as intelligent as Rory can be so unaware of his own reputation.

She thinks that's why she started sleeping with him: to find out. She said as much to her cousin in an email. Noelle wrote back:

> You're not the sort to go with a schmuck. His wife is the attraction. You don't want to be with anyone who might expect you to stick around.

After college, Noelle moved to New York to study acting. The joke in their family is how Maggie and Noelle have switched places. Maggie knows her aunt Aoife does not find anything amusing about her daughter living in New York. Ever since Noelle left, Aoife has believed she would tire of the apartment in Queens that she shares with two other Irish girls and return to Ballyineen. But Noelle now works as a fundraiser for a nonprofit theater in the city. It was her idea that Rose apply to a performing arts high school for her junior and senior years. She was the one who told Brendan to stop moaning about wanting to be an actor and do something about it. His little sister was already out-pacing him. Guiltily, Maggie knew she'd probably have left him alone, bartending at Lehane's, hooking up with a different girl every weekend, playing ball in the bar league as he laughed at Aidan's attempts to get him to take the test for the fire department.

Maggie replied:

> Since you're saying schmuck, do I have to start saying eejit?

Rory is not a schmuck. Either she'd described him badly or Noelle is misunderstanding the word. Rory is funny and charming and smart. He is a liar, but not a loser.

Maggie pushes at the window again. "I just want some goddamn fresh air."

Mrs. Sheehan turns to go, then pauses. "You should know, Mrs. O'Reilly, that this is the time of year when Dr. McAlary starts cancel-ing meetings. The new crop of postgrads coming in. The new teaching assistants to train. There's lots of extra work."

It is about two o'clock when Maggie arrives back at Lysaght Hall. She'd taken her cell phone out of her bag to see if Rory left her a voicemail, and she'd forgotten it on her desk. She will grab it and go back to her apartment. This afternoon will be spent writing, not moping.

She hears Irish music and stops for a moment, dismayed. Cillian is at the window, chipping away with a screwdriver.

He turns when she comes in. "Mrs. Sheehan gave me the business. I tried to explain that I don't work in maintenance, but she seems to think I should have seen to this some time ago."

Maggie sighs. "I was complaining about it earlier. It's not your prob-lem. Really, just leave it."

"She scares the snot out of me," Cillian says. "Reminds me of my grandmother, tell you the truth. She said you deserved some fresh air. And I'm sure that's true."

He goes back to chipping at the window. Maggie drops her eyes and scoops her phone off the desk.

"Well, I'm heading out."

"Surely. It's Tuesday. We're at Derrane's tonight. You should come by."

"Maybe. I'll see. I've vowed to spend all my spare time writing this semester." Maggie smiles and shrugs to signal her regret.

The music cuts off so abruptly both she and Cillian look at the radio in confusion.

A grave voice explains that they have an update on the situation in New York.

"Situation?" Maggie says.

He shakes his head. "I'd just turned it on —"

Cillian leans closer on one side of the desk and Maggie leans in from the other.

The newscaster announces that it was indeed a plane that hit one of the twin towers of the World Trade Center complex and not an internal explosion. Eyewitness accounts from lower Manhattan report seeing it fly into the building. Continued updates as the situation unfolds.

The music comes back on.

"Jesus," Maggie says, "the pilot must have been unconscious. Or maybe there's heavy fog? I wonder if it's on the news — the news here. Not that it matters, since I don't even have a television. My brother is going to be furious."

"The one who's the fireman?"

"Aidan just got transferred to Brooklyn," Maggie says. "He used to be in midtown, and his old company is probably responding. He's going to be pissed he's missing this."

Maggie hopes Aidan's at least working today and is in some way involved. His goal is to join a rescue company. Rescue companies are responsible for getting to firemen in trouble at the scene. Elite units, they're officially called. Cowboys, unofficially. He needs more experience, more action, before he can try for it. He figured being in Brooklyn would help.

She flashed on her grandmother's anger when Eileen requested her transfer to the Glory Devlins. But Eileen had pointed out that having a brother and sister in the FDNY was rare enough. The odds of both of them dying out of the same firehouse had to be astronomical. Fucking astronomical, actually, was how she'd put it.

Maggie says goodbye again. She is about to leave when the music stops and the newscaster returns. His tone has lost its measured gravity. He is speaking rapidly, like a boy telling a story he is sure won't be believed.

Maggie steps closer to the radio. Cillian goes still, the screwdriver clutched in his hand.

A second plane has hit the other tower.

The newscaster says there is a tremendous emergency response under way in Manhattan. The number is impossible to know at this point, but loss of life is expected to be considerable, given that thousands of people work in the World Trade Center.

Maggie is not sure if she is the one who reached out to clutch Cillian's arm, or if Cillian grabbed hers. But it hurts, and it is what keeps her standing.

An hour and a half later, alone in Cillian's apartment, where she asked to go for the sake of his television, they have watched one tower and then the other fall.

Maggie has still not reached anyone in her family. She has spoken to her aunt Aoife, who was barely coherent as she said that Noelle had a meeting this week in one of the towers with a man who wanted to donate a lot of money to the theater. Aoife could not recall what day. Maggie tried to assure her that she can't reach Noelle because cell phone service is messed up. She has dialed Irish Dreams and gotten no answer. Her mother's house and her grandmother's. Aidan. Eileen. Even Nathaniel. If not for the pictures on the news, Maggie would think a nuclear bomb hit the city and that there was no one at all left in New York.

Maggie finally gets hold of Brendan, in California. He hasn't reached their mother either but thinks she must be trying to get to Rose. Maggie was about to ask Brendan if he knew whether Aidan or Eileen was working, but he cut her off. His friends decided to drive back to New York. Planes might not fly for weeks. He promises to call if he hears anything, and hangs up, leaving her shouting his name into the phone.

Maggie has not thought of Rose's high school in Manhattan. She can't recall where the school is exactly, except that Rose has a view of the Brooklyn Bridge.

Maggie's phone keeps ringing, but it's the Irish. Friends and co-workers.

"Kids wouldn't have been in there, right?" Maggie says. "No school is going to schedule a class trip for so early. What time is it there?"

She is the one who should know. But numbers are a muddle in her head.

"You're six behind. It's, ah, was about nine-thirty there," Cillian says. "Yeah, that's too early for kids. You'd never get them organized on time."

Organized. Maggie seizes on the word. "Yes! They'd never get organized this early."

"Are you thinking of your sister?"

"No. Not my sister."

She reaches for her can of Guinness. They are on their second. He has turned away the friends and family members who have come knocking on his door, trying to get him to go to the pub with them to watch the news.

"There's a little girl," Maggie says. She feels both rooted to Cillian's couch and untethered, like she might float to the ceiling if she kicked off her shoes.

"She turned nine on August 27."

This girl was born with blue eyes, she explains, and they have probably stayed blue, though possibly they might be green.

Cillian is sitting on the couch, one cushion away.

"What's her name?" he asks.

"I don't know her name."

"But she's your —"

"Daughter," Maggie says.

November 1991

"I think I'm going to go with you tonight," Maggie said.

Maggie had never bothered with the Gradys' Friday-after-Thanksgiving party when she was in high school, though the Gradys lived four houses away and, if she opened her bedroom window and looked, she could see people in the yard, their frozen breath and cigarette smoke indistinguishable.

Not my scene, she'd say, rolling her eyes. I have a working brain.

Yeah, right, Aidan would respond, smirking in a way that infuriated her.

There was beer at the party, lots of it, but still their mother always let Aidan go because Grace and her husband were home to supervise. It was Grace's way of keeping her sons close on the biggest drinking night of the year after St. Patrick's Day and New Year's.

Maggie and Aidan were clearing the table. Rose and Brendan, who were supposed to do it, had disappeared because their mother wasn't there to enforce the rule. Even though Irish Dreams had been closed today, she'd gone in to check the messages at four o'clock. At six, Maggie decided to make dinner. Now they were done and Norah still wasn't back. Some crisis, Maggie supposed. A couple got bumped from the honeymoon suite. Some group complaining that the package tour they'd chosen did not, in fact, show them the "real" Ireland. Some *thing*. Maggie understood, or tried to, that since her mother and Marian had bought the business, both were nervous about continuing its success. They'd been running it for years, really, and were now free to make changes without even pseudo-permission from Sullivan Jr., as both her mother and Marian called him, who had never been interested in taking over for his father.

"Yeah? You're cool now that you're in college?" Aidan said.

Maggie grinned. "Yes. It only took two months of getting out of here."

Aidan snorted and dumped Rose's leftover turkey in the garbage. She hadn't touched it. In a half hour, Maggie figured, she'd be asking for a hot dog. Rose would soon be eight, but she was still as picky as she'd been at three. Brendan's plate was so clean, Maggie could have put it right back in the cabinet.

After a slight hesitation, Maggie asked, "The party is happening, right?"

Grace Grady had died of cancer in February, near Valentine's Day, which Maggie remembered because Rose's construction-paper hearts had been Scotch-taped to every window in the house the night they went to the wake. The three Grady boys, Kevin, Brian and Danny, stood beside their father in a row, unfamiliar in their jackets and ties.

"Of course they're having it." Aidan leaned against the counter beside her. "Kev won't come because his wife won't let him, but Brian'll get the beer. Danny will definitely be there."

He gave her a stagy nudge with his elbow.

She shoved him. "*That* was done this summer."

He laughed. "I'm leaving around nine to go pick up Jen."

"You don't have a car. You going to give her a piggyback ride to the party?"

"Shut up."

Maggie knew Jen from the neighborhood but hadn't met her, since Aidan began going out with her only a couple of weeks ago. Maggie still got a small thrill to think of life at home going on without her. Though she was surprised that Aidan wanted to be tied down during his senior year of high school. It had been the opposite for the girls, she recalled. From the start of the school year, her classmates had been anxious to have boyfriends lined up for the prom.

"I'll leave with you," Maggie said. "If Mom's back, I mean."

"If she's not, maybe we bring the kids with us."

Maggie laughed.

Brendan had probably already tried beer. Rose would no doubt hop up on a table and sing. She'd have the crowd bowing to her. Rose O'Reilly, a name that sounded like a song itself.

Their grandmother had already said more than once that she should have voice lessons. Maggie figured a couple more months of their mother ignoring this suggestion — because it was one more thing to research, to pay for, to coordinate the to-and-from — before Delia would take care of it herself.

Norah arrived home at close to seven, apologizing, and then aggravating Maggie by asking if she'd fed Brendan and Rose.

Maggie didn't look back at the house as she and Aidan left, but she knew Rose was at the front window, peeking from behind the curtain.

"We'll take them somewhere tomorrow," Maggie said, and Aidan agreed.

Every light in the Gradys' house was on. Maggie went inside alone, shrugging off her coat. She scanned the room and saw a lot of people she'd gone to grammar school with and a few girls whom she'd been in high school with. They looked younger, with calmer makeup; that is, no dark lip liner and pale lipstick, or mascara that left each eyelash distinct from the other.

Maggie and her two friends from honors English had been, she thought, part chameleon. When they walked the hallways between classes, their skin turned the institutional-green shade of the walls, rendering them invisible, neither part of the crowd nor singled out for ridicule. Yet invisibility also forced Maggie to listen to endless conversations about their boyfriends, blow jobs and love. She always wished to interrupt and say, "Oh, please. In five years you won't remember his name."

It amused her to see how, in the six months since high school graduation, those girls had grown to look more like her.

Nearly everyone held a red plastic cup. Maggie heard talk of a keg in the dining room and pushed her way through the crowd, nodding at a few people who said hello to her. The Gradys' house was exactly like theirs but they had a dining room table in their front room. At her own house, it was a loveseat and a bookcase and was her favorite place to read.

Indeed, a quarter keg sat on the dining room table. There was a group of guys standing around it, older, almost certainly friends of Brian's. Neither he nor Danny had thought to cover the table with a cloth.

Maggie took a cup from the side table, where she noticed a pile of un-opened mail that had grown so high it had tilted, sending the envelopes in a slide. The sight stirred a memory of how things that should have been easy were simply not. One afternoon that first summer after the fire, Maggie had spent an hour helping Eileen open their mail and put-ting all the bills in a single pile. From now on, Eileen told her, collect the mail and set aside every envelope with a window.

Maggie turned to the keg, desperate to lose the edge of self-con-sciousness.

"— seriously, he fucking showed up." Brian came into the room, talk-ing over his shoulder to a guy behind him. "Maggie! Hey!"

He pulled her into a hug. She was too startled to hug back.

Brian sometimes played ball with her brothers, and when his mother babysat for Rose, he'd play with her, but Maggie he'd never paid much at-tention to. Over the summer, when she and Danny had been going out, she hadn't seen Brian that much. He went out to bars and he could get Danny in, but nothing could be done for her: she didn't have a fake ID.

"We haven't seen you lately. Where you been?" Brian said.

"Prison," she said. "My mom finally posted bail last night."

Brian laughed. "Nah, you're at school, right? Dan said you got a full ride. Where are you?"

Maggie nodded. "Gilbride College. It's in the Hudson Valley, about two hours from here."

She had wanted badly to go out of state, even though her mother didn't like the idea.

Maggie found a surprising ally in her grandmother, who agreed that if you were going to go away to school, you should go far. Massachu-setts, Vermont, Maine. Then Joe Paladino let her mother know about the scholarship for children of deceased firefighters, police officers and EMTs. A full ride indeed, but only at a CUNY or SUNY school.

After she won it, Maggie tried to find a reason to turn it down. The experience of living in a new state was more important. Maybe there was someone with a more recent loss or someone whose mother was dead too. But her grandmother turned back into her practical self. There are three more behind you, Delia told Maggie, and unless you're planning on studying law or medicine, you should be cautious about student loans. Well, she was not going to study law or medicine. She intended to major in education, with a minor in English.

"Hey, come with me." Brian turned to his friends. "Be right back. This is my brother's girlfriend."

Touching her lightly on the shoulder, Brian led her out of the dining room. Maggie followed him through the crowd, noting the number of girls who turned to look at him. It had been like that with Danny too.

As they entered the kitchen, Maggie said, "I'm not Danny's girl-friend."

"If he had half a brain you would be."

Maggie didn't know what to say to that.

Brian opened the refrigerator and Maggie peeked in. There must have been a dozen six-packs.

"Oh my God, Brian."

"The secret stash." He grinned. "It's a beautiful thing. Take anything you want."

She chose a Budweiser. He opened the beer for her and handed it back and then took one for himself.

"Aidan's here, right? Let him know too."

"He's on his way," Maggie said, and then, trying for nonchalance, "Where's Danny?"

"Upstairs." Brian rolled his eyes.

"Why? What's the matter?"

"Who the hell knows? He's been talking some shit about not going back to school. After I moved out to Bay Ridge, he got some crazy idea that Dad shouldn't be alone here. But first Dad told him he'd break both his legs and then he said Danny had to stay at least one semester, because that what he's paid up to. Go on up. Give him this." He opened the beer he'd taken for himself and handed it to her.

"Drag him down here." He grinned. "Or don't."

"Very funny," she called as she left the room. In the living room, she skirted the crowd and headed for the stairs in the corner.

The silence of the second floor struck her. She wondered how long it would be before couples began migrating to the bedrooms. Surely nobody would go near the master bedroom. At least nobody who'd known Grace, the mom who was so cool that everybody had called her Mrs. Grady as a mark of respect. Maggie felt a twinge of anxiety and then reminded herself it was not her problem if the house got trashed.

She paused in the hallway to gulp half the beer. She and Danny had first gotten together at his high school graduation party this past June. Maggie understood, even if Danny didn't, that he stayed by her side that night because when she saw him, she had not asked, How are you *doing?* How's your father *doing?* How are your brothers *doing?*

Throughout the summer, they'd never used the words "boyfriend" and "girlfriend." Both of them were aware that they were due to separate in September, she to go upstate and Danny to go to his college outside Boston, Kevin's alma mater.

Danny's bedroom door was partially open. Maggie peeked in. They'd spent plenty of days this summer in the twin bed on the right, the one that had been Brian's. Danny lay on his own bed with his arm tenting his eyes. Two beer bottles sat on his nightstand.

Maggie knocked with one knuckle.

"*What?*" Danny didn't move.

She pushed open the door. "It's me."

Maggie had forgotten — or had let herself forget — how much she simply liked looking at him. All three of the Gradys had black hair and their mother's green eyes, but Danny was the one not just good-looking but handsome.

"Maggie! Hey!" Danny jumped up off the bed and, as his brother had done, pulled her into a hug.

When they separated, she couldn't quite meet his eyes. She knew if she glanced in the mirror on his bureau, she would see a flush over her face and neck.

"Uh, from Brian," she said, and thrust the beer at him.

"I've got a full one." Danny took the beer and set it on the night-stand beside the others.

"Here, sit down." He picked up a pile of clothes from the bed and tossed it on the floor.

Danny leaned back against the headboard and she perched on the edge of the bed. She resisted the urge to stroke his feet.

"How've you been? You like school?"

"I love it," Maggie said.

If she'd had more than half a beer in her, she might have made a fool of herself by blurting out how she felt when she walked up the wooded slope that led to the library, a stone building that made her think of a castle. After the fall colors began to appear, she'd sometimes walk to class wondering if she was in a dream. She formed new friendships quickly, starting with her roommate, who spoke Spanish fluently and planned to go into the Peace Corps. She suggested Maggie think about it too. Even though she couldn't see herself in the Peace Corps, Maggie found that she liked imagining different scenarios for her future, ones that she had never before considered.

"That's great, Mag," Danny said. "I'm glad to hear it."

"Brian said something about you wanting to come home."

Danny pushed a hand through his hair, making it stand on end. Maggie drank from her beer, to keep herself from straightening it. He needed a haircut.

"Fucking Brian," Danny said. "I don't know. My dad's here all by himself now. I don't know what he's doing when he's not working."

Your dad, Maggie thought, went to work on Thanksgiving night, the first one without your mother.

"And my roommate's an asshole. I thought Brian was a slob. The classes are not all that different than high school. Dad says I have to at least stick it out until the end of the semester."

"You'll probably like it better once baseball starts," Maggie said. "Stay for a year. If you still hate it in May, don't go back in September."

"That seems like a long fucking time."

Not to Maggie it didn't. She was already considering the cost of a summer class and dorm room for six weeks. She thought she might be able to get a summer job on campus.

"Do you miss home?" he asked.

Maggie looked at him, surprised that he'd come so close to guessing her thoughts.

"Not too much, no," she said slowly. "It's nice, being on my own."

At Gilbride, nobody knew that her given name was Magdalena. Nobody knew how her father had died, or when. The lack of curiosity had startled her the first few times she encountered it. The rote nods told her that it was not just manners keeping the questions at bay. Maggie understood soon enough. An eighteen-year-old might have lost her father to a heart attack or a stroke. A man in his sixties. Too young, but no epic tragedy. Eventually, Maggie figured she would tell, but it was nice to be free of the story for a time.

"Maybe I should come visit you some weekend," Danny said.

"Uh, maybe." She finished off the beer.

Danny sat up straighter. "You seeing someone?"

"I've hooked up a few times, but no, I'm not really dating anybody. Dating's not a big thing at my school."

"Hooked up?" Danny stared at her.

Maggie put her empty beer bottle next to his. She picked up the one Brian had given her for Danny and drank from it.

"Yes, in college the boys actually like me," she said. "Surprised?"

"No." He grinned. "I'm the last person who would be surprised. I've missed you, Mag."

He snagged the belt loop of her jeans and pulled her closer.

Laughing, she put her hand over his. "Let's go downstairs for a while."

He let go of her and sat back.

"This party is Brian's thing." Danny shook his head. "He set up a fucking keg on the dining room table."

"I saw it."

"I know my mom let us drink, but everybody respected that you weren't coming here to get piss-drunk. If Bri gets arrested for giving alcohol to minors, he can forget the fire department. You can't get on with a felony on your record."

Maggie wasn't sure it was a felony, but she was silent as Danny drained his beer.

The words would be easy to say. Come visit. Take the train up on Friday and stay until Sunday.

But it was far too soon. Maggie had imagined her and Danny living separate lives for all of college, maybe a bit beyond. She would be teaching in Manhattan, and maybe living there too, in the Village. They'd see each other at Brendan's high school graduation, or Aidan's wedding, or even on an April 5, at her father's memorial Mass.

In July, they'd run into Amred Lehane at the FDNY vs. NYPD baseball game. He smiled and said they were a good match, as though they were a royal couple in an arranged marriage.

"Whack job," Maggie said after Amred left. Danny laughed and said he was harmless.

Danny snagged her belt loop again. "I really have missed you. The girls at my school are stupid."

Maggie pushed his hand away but then leaned over to untie her shoes. She kicked them off and closed the door. She climbed into the bed beside Danny, and he put his arm around her. She leaned into him, his solidity.

January 1992

For as long as Maggie could remember, her family and the Gradys kept the keys to each other's houses.

At close to one o'clock, Maggie quietly let herself into Danny's house. His father's car had been in the driveway all day yesterday, but today it had been gone since she first looked, at about ten a.m. He had to be at work. She took off her snowy boots and hung up her jacket on the coat rack beside Danny's.

She called to him.

"Mag?" he called back from upstairs, surprised. "Come up."

As she walked into his room, Danny picked up a pile of shirts from a laundry basket and tossed them into a suitcase that was open on the floor. It was the last Thursday of winter break. She planned to take the Metro North back to Gilbride College on Sunday, and he was catching Amtrak to Boston. Monday morning, she was scheduled to be in American History I, and in the afternoon, English Literature II.

"You're packing already?" she said.

"Change of plans. Brian's going to drive me back. We figure we'll go up early Saturday, hang out Saturday night, and he'll drive home Sunday. Unless he's too hung over," Danny said, laughing. "Then it'll be Monday morning."

Maggie stared at him. She'd waited too long to pull him to the place where she had been for almost a month. The room began to tip, as though they were at sea. She lay down on the bed. He leaned over her and they kissed.

Then he went back to tossing shirts into his suitcase. "I know it's a day earlier than I said. But you'll come up. I'll be down to see you."

Was that even right geographically? Maggie wondered. Who was up and who was down?

"I only hope the weather's okay by Saturday."

"Snow is general all over Brooklyn," Maggie said.

"Huh?" Danny said.

Maggie might have laughed. "It's from a story."

"I can finish this later," Danny said, kicking his suitcase. He stretched out next to her and she shifted to make more room for him.

"Our old sled is still in the basement. We should take the kids sledding on Monument Hill. That's where we always went."

Monument Hill in Prospect Park. Schools were closed. Rose and

Brendan would love to go sledding with Danny. Maggie turned to look out the window again. She could barely see the house next door.

Danny tugged on a lock of her hair. "Mag? Sledding?"

Maggie sat up and leaned back on her elbows. "I'm pregnant."

Danny bolted out of the bed. Before she even turned to meet his eyes, Maggie felt guilty for not being able to spare him.

He asked if she was sure, three times, and she told him that she was, without relating the story of the first pregnancy test, bought with snowman gift tags and wrapping paper, or the two others, purchased at different drugstores. It made handling the money difficult all three times, because she'd kept her gloves on to hide her bare ring finger.

Danny slowly sat down on Brian's bed. "What do you want to do?"

She guessed that he was hoping to hear a simple request: half the money. If he had reservations, he could file them away inside the simple truth, that it was her body.

Maggie moved so she was opposite him, their knees nearly touching. Folding her hands in her lap, she killed his hope of a quick and secret resolution. It was 1991 — no, it was 1992 — and she didn't care what other women did. But she kept hearing this voice, like from the bottom of a well. She wished she did not.

"How long have you known?"

"Since New Year's Eve."

He leaned closer, as though he wasn't sure he'd heard her correctly.

"Maggie, Jesus. How could you not have told me sooner? You shouldn't have been going through this alone."

But she'd been praying that there was a God, and that He was both cruel enough and kind enough for this to be a warning. Next time, children, be careful! But wishing for a miscarriage was probably like standing outside in a thunderstorm and hoping that a bolt of lightning finds the crown of *your* head.

"It was already going to be a pretty bad Christmas for you guys."

Danny started to speak and then stopped. He dabbed one eye and then the other with the back of his wrist. "What are we going to do?"

Maggie told him exactly what they were going to do. The other A-word. Adoption.

For a week, Maggie hadn't been able to button her jeans. According to one of her books, she was showing right on time. According to another, she should have been good for at least another two weeks since it was a first pregnancy.

Maggie's mind kept darting to twins, or a very big baby that would require a C-section, or that she was giving in too much to the constant hunger that had replaced the nausea. Their refrigerator was full of the snacks that went into Brendan's and Rose's school lunches.

Today was March 29. April would be month five. Upon waking, she'd intended to go to Macy's at the Fulton Mall and buy a couple of pairs of jeans. Though she flinched at the thought of shopping in the maternity section, sweatpants were not an option either. She was not going to spend the next few months wearing, essentially, pajamas.

But by the time she was dressed, she was already wondering how long it would be before she could go back to bed.

Maggie went into the kitchen, where she found the Sunday *New York Times* on the table, fresh from the stoop. Delia was separating the paper into sections and greeted Maggie briefly. Delia began with the front-page news, moved on to Arts & Leisure and then Metro, followed by the Book Review.

Maggie poured herself some orange juice and sat at the table. Delia was already reading. Maggie started with the weddings.

The summaries of couples were short-short stories, each ending on the happiest day.

Maggie looked up from the paper and watched her grandmother sip her coffee. "I would kill for a cup."

"A little bit of coffee won't cause permanent damage," Delia said.

For the first three months, Maggie felt only a low-grade queasiness, like motion sickness, as though the earth had picked up speed. She glanced at the inert faces of the other passengers on the F train but only the teenage Orthodox girls in their long skirts and long sleeves ever turned her way, curiously scanning her up and down. But they'd always done that. It was not like they could tell.

The morning her pants didn't button, she'd gone downstairs to the kitchen, where Norah had been both getting ready to leave for work and packing a bag for Rose, who would be spending the afternoon and then the night with the McAleers from around the corner, who had two daughters close to her age.

Maggie had lifted her shirt. "Look! Is it too soon?"

Her mother glanced at Maggie and then away.

"Too soon or not, you'd better go shopping," she said, and called for Rose to pack her toothbrush in her backpack.

When her sister and brothers were home from school, Maggie had been doing her crying in the bathroom with the water running. But it was Saturday morning, and Aidan was in there shaving. Brendan was pounding on the door, yelling at him to hurry up, but no doubt only trying to make Aidan cut himself. Soon Aidan would fling the door open and Brendan would take off running, Aidan in pursuit.

Maggie escaped to her grandmother's. When Delia came home from the early movie with Nathaniel, she found Maggie in the bedroom that had been her father's, curled up on the bed.

Delia fetched a box of tissues and sat at the desk. When Maggie stopped crying, Delia stood, told her to get some sleep and said that she could stay as long as she liked. Her grandmother may have meant she could spend the afternoon, or she may have meant move in. Maggie didn't ask for clarification. She simply didn't go back home.

Most of her father's things had been packed away a long time ago. Delia wasn't the kind to keep a shrine. There were three baseball trophies, and one for basketball. There was a framed photograph of him and her aunt Eileen on the day Eileen arrived in America. The two of them were sitting on the stoop. He was smiling. Aunt Eileen was not. She stared solemnly at the camera.

Maggie felt a slight flutter, infinitesimal, like when someone wiggles their fingers to tickle but doesn't actually touch you. According to her books, it might be the baby moving. Or it might not. She considered asking her grandmother when she'd first felt a kick but rejected this idea.

Asking her grandmother about pregnancy was akin to asking her about hardware stores. Maggie only knew that after her father was born, Delia could not have more children. Maggie's doctor suggested she find out what happened, though it was unlikely to be anything genetic. Maggie hadn't yet worked up the nerve.

Maggie and Delia read in the silent kitchen. Nelson-Newman both loved miniature golf. They were married in Montauk and were hyphenating their name. *Please.* They were totally destined for a murder-suicide at their house in the Hamptons. The only question was which one would pull the trigger.

Maggie shifted the pile of newspaper and a green masthead caught her eye. She unearthed the *Irish Eagle*. The address label read *Nathaniel Kwiatkowski.*

"Nathaniel reads the *Irish Eagle?*" Maggie asked.

Delia sighed. "A long time ago, I mentioned that there are Holocaust survivors in Ireland. Not many, but a few."

Maggie blinked. "Oh. The brother."

"The brother," Delia said. "Nathaniel added the *Irish Eagle* to his reading list. He gave this issue to me because there's an obituary in there of a writer I used to like. Tomás Breen. He wrote his last novel in about 1985. After that, he started drinking again and never wrote another."

After skimming the article, Maggie said, "They think there may be an unpublished novel? That's interesting. His sister won't say one way or the other."

"She'll never let it go if it's subpar, no matter how much money she's offered," Delia said without looking up.

The phone rang. Delia got up to answer it.

"Oh, Daniel. Hello."

Maggie shook her head. Delia said, "Yes, she's here. Just a minute."

Maggie shoved back her chair and glared at her grandmother as she crossed the room to take the phone. Delia started to leave the kitchen.

"You don't have to. This won't take long," Maggie said to her, and then, into the phone,

"Hey."

"Hey? What the hell is going on? You move out of your house and don't tell me?"

"It's a couple blocks away. I didn't leave the state."

"Everything okay?" Danny asked.

Over the phone she sensed his frustration and the deep effort to be patient.

No, she wanted to say. Clearly everything was not okay, and would not be okay until the end of August. Instead, she said, "It's just quieter here. I don't have to share a room with an eight-year-old."

That was good: blame Rose, who'd taken to climbing into Maggie's bed early in the morning and pressing against "the baby."

"What time is the Mass next Sunday?"

"I imagine all the Masses are at their usual times," she said.

"Come on, Maggie. My dad mentioned it. He's off, so he's going. He told me to ask you what time."

"The ten o'clock," she said.

This year, the ninth anniversary, was a Sunday, so the ten o'clock would be her father's memorial Mass. Maybe if it were winter and she could keep her coat on, she would go.

The guys still at the Glory Devlins knew, but the others who'd retired, transferred or got promoted out of the firehouse would find out that morning. Some men would pay a visit to the firehouse first and hear about it there, and others would go straight to the church and be filled in before Mass. Guys she hadn't seen since she was a kid, and their wives, would greet her heartily. They'd say, "Hey, sweetheart!" but be thinking, Poor Norah. Poor Grace, God rest her.

Maybe she could get Noelle to go to the Mass as her stand-in. They were the kind of first cousins who could pass for siblings. Noelle had arrived in New York last September to attend NYU for a year.

"Maggie? Are you still there?" Danny asked. "I'm coming over."

"I'm working. I have a paper due this week."

"Can I come by in a couple hours, then?"

She gave in. "Yes, okay."

Danny hung up right away, before she could change her mind.

Maggie looked at her grandmother. "I'm not going to the Mass."

"That's your prerogative," Delia said. "But I will tell you that Daniel has the right to make decisions about what happens to his child."

"The decision has already been made by both of us."

"You might feel differently when he's born. If you do, we will —"

"I'm not going to change my mind!" Maggie said. "I have a life to live."

"All I'm saying is that giving up a baby might be more difficult than you seem to be anticipating."

Maggie still had the phone in her hand. She turned her back to hang it up and saw the rosary, which had hung on the nail beside the phone for as long as she could remember.

She'd never touched it before, but now she plucked it from the nail. "Why don't you ever use this keychain? Because it's rosary beads?"

"It's not a keychain. And be careful, it's old." Delia held up a hand.

Maggie had intended only to change the subject, but her grandmother's protectiveness piqued her interest.

"What is it, then? How old?"

"It's called a penal rosary. Have you ever heard of that?"

Maggie shook her head.

Delia explained as if she were lecturing a student, perhaps also relieved to be talking about something else. When the Penal Laws were passed by the British government in the 1700s, it became illegal for the Irish to speak their language, have Gaelic names, practice their religion, own property and so on.

"The penal rosary was invented so the Irish could pray in secret. You put the ring on your finger and pray on each bead, like a regular rosary. You slip them into your palm. It's tricky to do. It takes practice."

Maggie found it odd: Delia never went to church on Sundays, and though she used to go to Mass with them on Christmas Eve, she hadn't since before the fire. It was hard to imagine her saying any kind of rosary, much less one that required practice. Delia would, however, go to the memorial Mass, Nathaniel beside her.

Maggie held up the penal rosary. "So this is from Ireland, back then?"

"Lord, it's not that old," Delia said. "It belonged to my mother. I don't know where she got it. Some religious goods store, I guess. Maybe one of those Irish gift shops that sell squares of peat."

Maggie slipped the ring on her index finger. She was wearing short sleeves, so she gathered the beads in her palm. "You'd think a rosary would be the one thing you'd take if you were going into a convent."

Delia laughed. "I used to think the same thing. My mother wanted me to have it for some reason. She told me to give it to my firstborn daughter." She shook her head.

"Really? Will you give it to Aunt Eileen?"

"I hardly think Eileen would be interested."

"Maybe Quinnie will want it," Maggie said doubtfully. Her cousin was only two.

"You're my oldest granddaughter," Delia said. "When I die, you are welcome to it. For now, put it back, please."

Maggie hung the rosary back on its nail.

The phone rang again. Maggie stepped aside. "I'm not here if that's Danny."

Delia sighed and answered the phone. "Oh, Norah, yes."

Maggie sat down and went back to reading the *Times*. After which she would get to work, because she really did have a paper due. *Due.* She tried to imagine that the word had meaning only in its college context, but pushed the thought away.

Maggie had formulated her plan before she'd even told Danny. She would take the spring semester off and wait out the pregnancy in Brooklyn. Her due date was August 21. College resumed on September 8, the Tuesday after Labor Day. Credit-wise she'd still be a freshman, but she'd take courses over next winter break and next summer too. Start next fall a full-fledged sophomore. Go abroad for her junior year.

Then her grandmother suggested she take classes at Brooklyn College, ones whose credits would transfer. Maggie couldn't believe it hadn't occurred to her. She'd lose less time than she'd thought. At first she figured she'd get math and science out of the way, but Delia told her to pick something she could focus on easily. Again, sound advice. Maggie had chosen two literature courses.

Delia hung up. "It seems your mother's going to be stuck at work for a bit. She asked if you could pick up Rose and bring her over to Brendan's baseball practice."

But Maggie did not want to sit with the parents of Brendan's teammates and whoever else might stop and watch the boys play. There had been an article about her scholarship in Holy Rosary's newsletter last summer, and in the *Irish Eagle*. Though her family was hardly going around announcing the news, the neighborhood knew why she'd come home. She didn't need stares and cheery inquiries about how she was doing.

"Maybe instead, you can —"

"I don't think so, madam. You may be pregnant, but I'm old."

"You're not that old."

"You're not that pregnant."

"Very funny," Maggie said. And it was, sort of.

Maggie arrived at Irish Dreams to see her mother slam the phone down and spin her chair to talk to Marian, who was standing nearby, clutching a coffee mug with both hands.

"Double-booked, that's what they're saying. I'm telling them I've got a group of ten coming in next week, and where am I supposed to put them? And they're saying sorry, it was a clerical error!" Norah pushed a hand through her hair.

"I know you don't want to, but we'll have to split them up between the two B&Bs," Marian said.

"If they were a younger bunch, I'd say fair enough, but these are God's classmates, Marian. Five couples who've been married nearly half a century. They don't want to talk to each other. The men want to drink with the men, and the ladies want to gossip with the ladies about whichever one of them just got up to go to the loo. Maybe we can send the husbands to Farraher's and the wives to Coyne's."

"Can we do that?"

Norah laughed. "If only it were that easy."

Maggie grinned as well. She loved Marian. Eileen once said if someone told her it was raining cats and dogs, Marian would get an umbrella and a can of cat food and head outside.

Marian said, "I thought you were serious."

"I'm desperate, that's what I am," Norah said.

Maggie cleared her throat.

"Maggie!" Rose called from her perch on the edge of their mother's desk. "There's a group of old people with no place to sleep in Wicklow."

"Tragic," Maggie said.

"Not tragic," Norah said, "but certainly a problem, as they've paid us a lot of money to make sure their trip goes smoothly."

"Maggie, hi," Marian said. "How are you feeling?"

"Better these days. Okay. Tired."

Rose jumped down from the desk and threw her arms around Maggie. Then she lifted Maggie's shirt.

"Look, Marian, she can't button her pants anymore."

"Rose!" Norah said. "You do not do that in public. Don't do that anywhere!"

But Maggie, who had grown resigned in the past week, thought it was funny. Or at least her mother's horror was funny. She straightened her shirt. "Who's here but us?"

"Did you notice, Marian?" Rose asked.

"I did. Right when she walked in."

"Did you really?" Maggie asked. "I know from the side, but I thought —"

"All right then," Norah said. "I am sorry to do this to you, Maggie, but I've got to sort this out. This group is scheduled to fly out in two days. Wicklow is their second stop."

"Well, *then*." Maggie unclipped Rose's pink barrette, smoothed her hair and refastened it. "Time to go."

At Rose's request, they took the route to their grandmother's that led them by the firehouse.

Rose paused before the two memorial plaques hung side by side to the right of the apparatus doors, which were open.

DEDICATED TO THE MEMORY OF
FIREFIGHTER JAMES WALSH
BORN IN IRELAND FEBRUARY 1861
DIED DECEMBER 28, 1884

Rose touched the letters of his date of death. She paid no attention to the plaque beside it, unveiled in a ceremony on a rainy April morning when she was less than a year old.

DEDICATED TO THE MEMORY OF
LIEUTENANT SEAN PATRICK O'REILLY
WHO DIED IN THE PERFORMANCE OF HIS DUTY
NOVEMBER 27, 1947 – APRIL 5, 1983

Rose peered inside and waved.

Maggie looked. "Who're you waving to?"

"The fireman," Rose said.

"Nobody's there."

"He's right there." She pointed, bouncing on the balls of her feet.

Rose had long insisted that there was a ghost in the firehouse. A fireman in "oldie" clothes. It was easy to dismiss it by saying she'd heard the story of James Walsh from Brendan once too often, but Maggie remembered her going on about it when she was as young as three. Once, when Maggie asked him, Brendan said scornfully that he wouldn't have told Rose any ghost stories when she was that little; Aidan would have killed him. Maggie had it backwards. Rose told Brendan about the fireman, and he told her about James Walsh.

Maggie didn't even pretend to look. "Okay, whatever you say," she said, waiting for Rose to sulk, the way she did whenever she sensed she was being humored. Rose wasn't easy to fool. But then she also had a short attention span. She put a hand on Maggie's belly. Maggie resisted the urge to push her hand away.

"Will the baby's last name be O'Reilly or Grady?" she asked.

"Rosie, you know the baby isn't coming home with me."

"But why not?" she asked, as she had been since Maggie first explained it to her.

Because of you, Maggie thought. And Bren. Because if I didn't know what it was like to have an infant in the house, maybe I'd be dumb enough to think I could do it.

"Because I have to finish college. I can't take care of him now."

"I'm her aunt, though?" Rose asked.

"I guess you will be. Technically." Maggie hadn't thought about that. Her mother's grandchild. Her grandmother's great-grandchild. Eileen's great-niece or -nephew. Cousin to Quinn. Uncle Aidan. Uncle Brendan. Aunt Rose.

"Hey, girls."

Joe Paladino was standing just inside the doorway. He held up a hand and Rose slapped her hand against his in a noiseless high-five. Nine years ago, he and her father had studied for the lieutenant's test together. But when it came time to take the exam alone, after Sean's death, Joe decided not to. He did take it eventually, and just last month got promoted off the list.

When Maggie remarked that it was about time, Aidan told her Joe had put it off because the promotion to officer would have meant being transferred out of the firehouse and away from them. Still, Maggie had said. Still.

"How are you doing?" he asked Maggie, not quite meeting her eyes.

"Oh, never better."

"She's having the baby in August," Rose volunteered.

He grinned at Rose. "Isabel was born in February, but her middle name is May."

Rose laughed. "Does Christopher have a middle name?" she asked.

"Robin," Joe said, and Rose laughed again.

Actually, it was Sean, Maggie knew. Christopher Sean Paladino was born a year after Rose.

The bells went off.

"Outta the driveway, girls," Joe called over his shoulder.

Maggie put a hand on Rose's shoulder and guided her back several steps. The guys waved as they took off. Rose waved back.

"Can we go to the park?" she asked when they were gone.

Maggie hesitated. "How about a nap?"

"You and me? In Daddy's room?" Rose said.

Funny she called him that when she hadn't even known him. "Sure."

Maggie guessed it was almost noon.

Maggie was sitting up in bed, the doorstop that was *The Norton Anthology of English Literature* open on a pillow she'd put on her lap. She had a lot of reading to do for class, and usually she'd break it up over a couple of days, but she'd decided instead to save it all for tomorrow, April 5, which she planned to spend at the library. Her family would be descending on her grandmother's house after the Mass, and so Maggie intended not to be home until late afternoon.

There came a soft knock at the door. Maggie sat up and straightened her shirt before she called, "Come in."

The door opened and her grandmother stepped in. She was wearing a jacket.

"I thought you might like to come with me to Nathaniel's."

"Uh, is he sick or something?" Maggie asked. Why her presence would be needed she couldn't guess.

"No," Delia said. "Tonight, at sunset, it will be April 5 by Jewish law. If you want to come, get your shoes on and let's go."

Maggie had no idea what Jewish law had to do with April 5, but she got out of bed.

Nathaniel lived above Four Star Electronics Repair. The store was closed, but Delia surprised Maggie by producing a key and opening the door. They walked through the dark shop to a set of stairs in the back and climbed up one flight. Maggie waited to see if her grandmother would come up with another key, but she rang the apartment's doorbell. Nathaniel answered right away and smiled when he saw Maggie.

"Good," he said.

As Maggie stepped inside, she peeked into the front room. She knew it used to be his sisters' bedroom back when Nathaniel's whole family had lived here, but it was now where Nathaniel kept his files. The products of his search for his brother were meticulously organized in boxes and on the shelves he'd installed around the room.

Maggie and Delia followed Nathaniel to the small kitchen.

To Maggie he said, "Should I ask how you're feeling, or are you tired of that question?"

"Tired of that question," Maggie said.

"So I won't ask."

Nathaniel opened a cabinet and took out a small candle in a green-tinted glass. "So, had you ever heard of Yahrzeit before today?"

"I've never heard of it at all," Maggie said.

"You didn't explain to her?" Nathaniel said to Delia.

"I figured you would do a better job," she said.

Nathaniel sighed. "'Yahrzeit' is Yiddish and it means a year's time. You light the Yahrzeit candle on the anniversary of the death and let it burn for twenty-four hours. Usually you go by the date of the death according to the Hebrew calendar, but we don't use that. We don't need two April 5s."

He smiled sadly at Delia. The corners of her mouth lifted in return.

"We do mark the day as you should according to Jewish law, from sundown the day before to sunset on the day. Tomorrow, your Mass, but tonight, this."

"I'm not going to the Mass," Maggie said.

"They aren't going to judge you, you know," Delia said. "Nobody's going to say your mother did a bad job by herself. In fact, somebody will probably offer to build you a cradle. Somebody else will say to call when it's time to take you to the hospital, since your mother doesn't have a car. You know how they are."

Maggie did indeed know. "Well, I don't need a cradle."

And were that widely known, Maggie thought, somebody probably would offer to keep the baby.

Hey, me and my wife will take him. The kids'll double up. We'll get bunk beds. I'll build 'em myself.

"So, good." Nathaniel closed the cabinet. "If you're not going tomorrow, all the better you're here tonight."

He went over to the narrow kitchen window and pulled the shade. Holding up the candle, he said, "The window is a prettier place for a candle to burn for a day, but out of consideration for Lieutenant O'Reilly, who would no doubt be telling us how dangerous that is —"

Delia laughed.

"— we do this." Nathaniel set the candle in the sink.

He opened a drawer and took out a book of matches, which he handed to Delia.

She stepped up, struck the match and brought the flame to the candle. The wick jumped to life.

Nathaniel said, "For our Sean. Son, husband, father, friend, soon-to-be grandfather — "

Delia made a small noise. Maggie crossed her hands over the baby.

"— who died in the service of his city."

Delia drew in a breath, about to speak.

Maggie expected her grandmother to recite a poem. Yeats, maybe. Instead, Delia said, "I miss him."

After Maggie blew out the candles on the Entenmann's devil's food cake and put aside the piece given to her, she went out to her grandmother's backyard. It was June 20. Yesterday Aidan turned eighteen, and tomorrow Maggie would turn nineteen. Rose loved celebrating the day her brother and sister were the same age.

When Eileen came over with her daughter, and bearing a gift, it became annoyingly like a party. Then Noelle showed up, all the way from Queens.

Aidan wasn't any more interested in cake than Maggie was. He'd gone out with his friends last night and was still hung over. He stepped back after the candles were lit.

"Go ahead." He waved a hand. "You need a wish way more than me."

If Rose and Quinn (and their grandmother) hadn't been present, Maggie would have told him to go fuck himself.

Alone in the waning light, Maggie lowered herself into a wrought-iron chair nobody ever used.

Almost immediately, she heard the back door open and was ready to snap that she needed a damn minute to herself. But then she saw it was Eileen, not her mother.

Eileen pulled up the matching chair, which had been tipped over on its side, and set it down next to her. She wore shorts and a *Fidney* sweatshirt with the words in bold white on the back: *Keep Back 200 Feet.* She stretched out her legs. Maggie stared enviously. Her aunt was the fittest person she knew. She'd once run the New York City Marathon, and planned to again this year, now that Quinn was two.

"Sorry about all this," Eileen said. "I should've known it wasn't your idea. I don't know what your mother was thinking, letting Rose do this."

"Nineteen! Something to celebrate," Maggie said. "At least, if you're not pregnant."

"Norah told me you're still considering a closed adoption."

Just jump right in, Maggie thought. "I've already told you, we're not considering it. That's what we're going to do." She thought it was stupid to give your child away and then get letters from him, as if he were away at camp.

"Closed," Maggie added, "but the agency we went to lets you leave word that you want to be contacted once he's eighteen. They have this book that you can look at, of parents. I'm thinking we should pick somebody out of state."

"I was born in Ireland, and I still stared at the woman in Macy's and the woman on the bus and the substitute teacher. Me and your dad used to do it at the St. Patrick's Day parade. We'd look for women with red hair and jab each other and say, Maybe her? Maybe her?" Eileen said. "I think you get my drift."

"No. What is your *drift?*"

Unfazed, her aunt said, "The adoptive parents can tell him he was born in Timbuktu and he's probably still going to keep an eye out for possible birth mothers."

Maggie listened with growing unease. "I guess he'll have to deal with it then. All kids deal with stuff."

"You're not too much younger than your mother was when she had you," Eileen said.

"So? Mom wasn't going to do anything else with her life."

"Maggie, for God's sake," Eileen snapped.

"Mom's said herself if she hadn't met Daddy, she would have ended up back in Ballyineen, stocking soup cans in her father's grocery store."

Eileen was silent for so long that Maggie began to relax, and then her aunt said, "Don't do it."

Maggie stared at her. Eileen was studying her hands.

"You can't be sorry Gran adopted you."

Eileen took too long to answer. "Up until your dad died, I was satisfied with my family."

Before Maggie could answer, Eileen tried a grin. "Hey, this is not something for you to be worrying about on top of everything else."

"Are you looking for your birth mother?" Maggie had never dared ask.

Eileen hesitated. "I've written to the place where I was born a few times. The nuns who write back say the records are sealed. When me and Madd went to Ireland we looked." She paused. "We wanted to see if we could find out anything before we had a baby. They told me in person what they said in letters."

"Quinnie's fine," Maggie said.

"She's fine so far, and yeah, so am I. But does heart disease run in the family, or diabetes? Madd's got a huge family, so we thought if there were genetic diseases, they would have cropped up. Stupid logic, but it made us feel better."

John Maddox, the fifth of six kids, the only boy. Spoiled rotten, he liked to joke. Maggie knew her grandmother certainly agreed. He was the last male of his family line, and Delia once said that was a good thing.

"Our agency gives medical records to the adoptive parents," Maggie said. "It's not the Dark Ages anymore."

"Well, the way it was done from Ireland was pretty dodgy. The nuns falsified birth records, gave the birth mothers fake names. They've made it impossible for mothers and kids to find each other."

The baby began to kick hard. Logically, Maggie knew that it was because her aunt's voice went up. A fetus could hear in the womb. But she pressed his foot as if to reassure him.

"That was Ireland in the fifties! Again, nothing to do with me."

"You're right. I know," Eileen said. "I've never been in your position. I get that. But I will tell you, I couldn't have taken care of a baby when I was your age. I wasn't sure I could do it at forty. But you . . ."

"Me, what?" Maggie said.

"You're a lot more together than I was. I know after your dad died, your mom probably leaned on you a little too hard. Me and Delia could've done a better job picking up the slack. Both of us were gone in our heads most of that first year. Raising a baby would be hard, and I'm not saying it wouldn't be, but I think you'd be okay."

"If all that is true, then don't I deserve a break? Shouldn't I be back at school with nothing to worry about but my grades?"

"Yeah, no doubt. But you know what?" Eileen pointed at Maggie's belly. "That's a baby, and it's yours."

Maggie tried to summon her best sarcastic tone. No kidding! She shook her head instead.

"But my best advice, if you do go through with this?" Eileen paused. "Make it a private adoption, so that you and Danny can make some of the rules. Tell the adoptive parents that you'd like their contact information, a phone number or an address, and they can have yours. Now. Not in eighteen years. If something happens and you need to get in touch, you can."

They were quiet, letting the dark fall between them. The back door opened and Noelle stuck her head out.

"Eileen? Your kid's got to pee and she won't let anybody else help her. She actually said no to Delia, which I have to admit impressed the hell out of me."

Eileen sighed and went in. Noelle came out and took Eileen's seat.

"I heard what your auntie said."

"Eavesdropping?"

Noelle laughed. "Just not deaf. Don't let her put her crap on you. You're doing the right thing. It's what I'd do."

Maggie glanced at her to see if Noelle was humoring her, but she could read nothing patronizing in her cousin's expression.

"Did you not think it could ever happen, or were you both just drunk?"

"Excuse me?"

"Well, you're the last girl I'd ever have thought this would happen to," Noelle said, and then added, "That Danny's gorgeous, though. I'd jump on him in a minute."

"I didn't jump on him." Maggie wanted to be mad but she felt something akin to satisfaction. She had at least surprised everyone.

"Did you know that it was my mother who was supposed to come to New York to live with the old auntie?"

"No," Maggie said. "With my mother?"

"Instead of, more like," Noelle said. "Granny said my mother was all set to go but she got married instead. Because she was up the pole. With me. That's what Granny meant but she wouldn't say it. She told me this sad story the day before I left. Her way of warning me. She got the wrong granddaughter, didn't she?" Noelle laughed.

"Yes, apparently."

"Ah, lighten up," Noelle said. "It'll be over with soon and you'll be back at school."

Maggie felt her spirits lift. Noelle, at least, understood that she just wanted to be done with it. She still remembered how it had been on the trip to Galway they'd taken when Rose was a baby. They'd stayed for most of the summer. She and Noelle had grown close, to the point where the townspeople began to tease them by calling out their mothers' names as they rode by on their bikes. Maggie had not wanted to go home.

Noelle reached over and put a hand on Maggie's belly.

"I can't believe how much bigger you got in two weeks."

"God knows what I'm going to look like after," Maggie said.

"You're going to look like your mother," Noelle said. "She's had four kids and she's grand."

Noelle started to sit back, but Maggie took her hand and moved it to where the baby's feet were. She pressed down, releasing a flurry of kicks.

"Does it hurt?"

"No," Maggie said. "It's impossible to describe. It feels like a baby kicking and nothing else."

"And you're really not finding out? I couldn't stand not knowing what it is."

"I enjoy surprises."

"I'll be there with you, if you want," Noelle said, withdrawing. "In the room, when you're having him. Or her. Your gran's too proper. Eileen, not after this stunt tonight. Your mam, well, you may need to remind her that you're having a baby."

"She doesn't like talking about it."

"More like blind denial. Before, asking you to get the plates. God, look at you."

"What's really funny is that it's *my* birthday."

Noelle started laughing and Maggie did too. It felt strange.

When they'd gone quiet, Noelle asked softly, "What does she say, your mam, about the adoption?"

"That I should do what I think is best. And she'll support me."

"That's it?" Noelle said. "Nothing about, ah, if you were to change your mind?"

"Mom knows my mind is made up," Maggie said. "Danny wants to be in the delivery room too."

"And well he should be. There'll be room for both of us. Women bring in their whole family and the postman besides these days. But listen, don't let him talk you into doing something stupid like getting married. My parents haven't slept in the same room in years."

"Neither have mine," Maggie said.

Noelle put her head back and laughed. "Very good."

Maggie was sitting up in bed, watching Aidan install the air conditioner she finally requested after surviving June and July with just a fan. Her grandmother never had air conditioning anywhere in the house, and Maggie didn't want to bother her about it. But this past week, she caved and asked if it would be okay. Sleeping was difficult enough now. The heat was making it impossible. Her grandmother said that was fine, adding that she should have asked sooner.

It was delivered late yesterday, but Aidan said he was going to a Mets game and had to get going. Delia made him promise to do it tomorrow. He'd banged on Maggie's door at eight-thirty.

Maggie called for him to come in, and he opened the door so hard it slammed against the wall. The baby stretched and kicked.

"You woke him up," she said.

He glanced at her and then looked away, a flush creeping over his neck.

He had been angry ever since she told him. Aidan told her that their father would be furious about her giving his first grandchild away. He wouldn't have let her do it.

She didn't know where Aidan's certainty came from. Long ago, she'd lost her father's reactions to her life, except in the vaguest sense: happy, sad, angry. Maybe he would not want his grandchild living with strangers; maybe he would want his daughter to reclaim her college scholarship, deferred for a semester, and go away to school again.

For Aidan, Maggie thought, it was a matter of math. In his mind, the baby would make them a family of six, as they should have been. But it didn't compute. The baby made seven. Their family was always going to be one number off.

After Maggie skipped the memorial Mass, Aidan stopped speaking to her, except when necessary.

When he was nearly finished putting in the air conditioner, she spoke: "Gran didn't mean literally first thing in the morning."

"I'm going to church. At St. Brendan's."

She laughed. "What the hell for?"

Aidan looked at her, hard. "It's August 2. The anniversary of Waldbaum's."

"You're going because you think Dad would?" Maggie said.

"He never missed it."

Sure, in the five years longer he'd lived. The news stories about their father had all mentioned Waldbaum's. As in, "And this August will mark the fifth anniversary of the Waldbaum's fire in which six firemen were killed . . . the most ever in Brooklyn at a single fire . . ."

"That's why you woke me up at the crack of dawn? Waldbaum's?"

"It's almost nine o'clock," Aidan said.

"I'm sorry, but I'm kind of nine months pregnant."

"Yeah, no kidding," Aidan said. "You wanted an air conditioner, now you got it."

He left, slamming the door.

Late that afternoon, when she heard the knock on the bedroom door, Maggie assumed it was her grandmother.

"Come in," she called.

Danny opened the door. "Hey."

He closed the door and kicked off his flip-flops. He was holding a rolled-up newspaper, which he tossed on the desk.

He moved the pillow from behind her back and fit himself in the bed behind her. At least this bed was a full. Her parents had lived here when they were first married.

Maggie lay back down. He pushed her shirt up and put his hand on the side of her belly, and together they watched the baby shift beneath her skin.

Maggie was nearly asleep when Danny spoke.

"My brothers came and talked to me again yesterday. They're still not happy about this, and my dad's still not saying anything except, You're responsible for this, you take care of it. He said if Sean O were alive, he'd kick your ass and I'd let him."

"Well, Sean O is not alive, is he?" Maggie said. "And Aidan's not going to do it."

Danny half laughed. "Lucky for me you don't have any big brothers."

"Even if Aidan were older, he wouldn't bother. He likes you way better than he likes me. I think he's pissed at me for screwing up your baseball career."

Unlike her, Danny had simply dropped out of college. He'd taken a job with Brian's construction crew. Though Maggie had told him he should go back to school, he said no way was he going to leave her alone in Brooklyn.

"Yeah, sure, if not for the baby, I'd have ended up playing first base for the Mets," Danny said.

Maggie smiled.

"Listen, my brothers. Kev wanted to take him, but my sister-in-law said no way. Conor's almost two, and they want another one soon."

"It's not a good idea anyway," Maggie said quietly. "Would Kevin and Nicole say they're his parents? Then someday he finds out that his uncle is his father?"

"It doesn't matter anyway. I told you, Nicole said no." He paused. "Brian did say that maybe him and me can get an apartment together. He's got a roommate now, so we'd have to get our own place."

"What about school?"

"I can go around here or in the city. I might not even fucking bother if you didn't need college credits to get on the job. Brian figures once he's on, he can arrange his tours around whatever my schedule is and babysit —"

"It wouldn't be babysitting! It's forever. What if Brian meets a girl and wants to get married? And you're working nights and sometimes working twenty-four, all on your own with a kid? Or would Brian's wife move in with all three of you?"

"Maggie, listen to me for a minute, will you? I told him I wouldn't lock him in like that. But I figured I should tell you —"

"In case I did think it was a good idea?"

"I guess so," Danny said. "I don't know what to fucking think anymore."

"We need to choose," Maggie said.

They had narrowed the decision down to three couples from the book at the adoption agency. It worried Maggie that no matter how many times she read their profiles, it was like trying to picture what cartoon characters would look like as real people.

Maggie outlined her belly with her hands. "Soon. Look at me."

Danny kissed her shoulder. "I'm looking."

They lay in silence. Only the baby's constant shifting kept Maggie from falling asleep. After one particularly hard jab, Maggie flinched and opened her eyes.

"The couple with the cats?" she said.

"I hate cats. When I'm on the job, if there's one stuck up a tree, I'm fucking leaving it there. And forget the two with the poodle. I'd never get my kid a poodle."

Maggie pushed herself up on one elbow. "We aren't choosing understudies."

Danny got up, then set the desk chair beside the bed and sat. "I want to meet the people we give our baby to. I want them to have our names and addresses so they can find us if they have to. When the baby's eighteen, they can give him our names, or their lawyer can."

"My aunt talked to you, didn't she?" Maggie said coldly.

"Eileen's adopted. She knows what the fuck she's talking about," Danny said.

He took the newspaper from the desk, unfolded it and held it up for Maggie to see that it was the *Irish Eagle*.

"You want to call people from an ad in a newspaper?"

He shook the paper. "They're Irish."

"You want him with Irish parents?"

"Irish, Irish American, yeah," Danny said defiantly. "If he finds us someday, I want to have something in common with him. This way we'll have something to talk about besides, Hey, how's your life been since we gave you away?"

Maggie looked down at the newspaper. There was an ad for Irish Dreams on the same page. Wasn't that funny.

"Let me see it."

Danny pointed to the middle ad. Maggie read it:

An Irish-Italian couple promises a life filled with
unconditional love, joy, and financial security.
Large extended family. Please call Charlie and Laurel.
1-888-491-4139.

"Irish-Italian. My mom was half Italian. I want to call them," Danny said.

Maggie felt she should be angry, but instead she was relieved.

Charlie and Laurel. Irish and Italian. Maybe Danny was right. It was a point of reference. A context. And she had already set one big rule: No couples who already had biological children. Even if they were adopting because they had all boys and wanted a girl, or the other way around.

Danny had not been pleased. He definitely did not want the baby to be an only child. If this was the condition he wanted to set, then it was okay, because Maggie owed him. She said that other adopted children would be fine, or the intention to adopt again, and Danny eventually agreed.

"Okay," Maggie said. "Understudies it is, then."

Two weeks later, she and Danny sat together in Buckley's restaurant on Avenue R in Flatbush. Danny had raised his eyebrows when she chose the place, but Maggie didn't want to stay in their neighborhood. Danny borrowed Brian's car, to spare her the subway and a bus in the ninety-degree heat.

Within ten minutes of their arrival, Maggie and Danny were seated in the booth Maggie chose deliberately, the one in the corner right out-side the big room with the fireplace. It had been Maggie's idea to meet the McKennas for dessert. She didn't want to be trapped for an entire meal if they turned out to be awful. Danny agreed.

"You think of everything," he said.

"No, I don't. Obviously," she said.

The McKennas weren't going to be awful. Maggie could see that as they trailed the hostess through the restaurant.

Charlie McKenna was, Maggie saw at once, the Italian half of the couple. His brown eyes were warm, and he'd taken her hands in both of his when he introduced himself and his wife. He looked to be in his late thirties. Laurel was probably about the same age, with the kind of leanness Maggie associated with runners like Eileen. Maggie had no-ticed the heads turning as Laurel passed through the bar. Her dark brown hair was pulled back in a low ponytail.

They discussed traffic, the drive. The waitress took their order and left with a smile. Maggie wondered what she thought was going on. The McKennas were too young to be a set of in-laws and too old to be friends of hers and Danny's.

Laurel Rourke-McKenna spoke into the silence. "First of all, thank you for answering our ad and for being willing to meet with us."

Both she and Danny nodded.

"Just quickly, about us," Charlie said. "I'm a lawyer. I do a little bit of everything but a lot of clients are small businesses. Contracts, employer-employee issues, that kind of thing. I enjoy it, boring as it sounds. Laurel's the one with the big job."

Laurel shot him a frown.

"I'm with a firm in the city that specializes in real estate," she said. "Which in other cities might not be too exciting, but in New York it is." She smiled hard. "It's not too big a job, though. Not too big to be a good mother."

Maggie nodded politely. The waitress set down coffee cups and a tall glass of decaf iced tea for Maggie. They waited until she came back with the coffeepot and went slowly around the table.

"Are you going to keep working, then?" Maggie asked when the waitress had gone.

Danny shifted in his seat. Both McKennas sat up a little straighter. Charlie leaned slightly toward Laurel but she didn't glance his way.

"Yes," Laurel said. "But my firm is generous with maternity leave."

"Laurel's on track to making partner. The first woman. They're not going to want to lose her," Charlie said.

Laurel quickly brushed his hand.

Maggie read the gesture to mean, Be quiet, stop making it sound like I'll never be home. "With their maternity leave, there's no difference between adopting and having a baby?" Maggie asked.

"No, that's illegal," Laurel said. "When you adopt, it's the same as if you gave birth."

Maggie had the urge to lift up her shirt and say to Ms. Rourke-hyphen-McKenna, "Oh yeah?"

"How come you're adopting?" Danny said.

Maggie admired his bluntness.

"With regard to biological children," Charlie said, "it hasn't worked out for us."

Laurel stirred her coffee and looked at Maggie.

"We started trying almost four years ago. At this point, we feel we've exhausted our medical options," Laurel said.

Danny cleared his throat. "Are you are planning on adopting again? I know you said so on the phone, but I'm the youngest of three and Maggie's the oldest of four. Brothers and sisters are important to us."

"Yes, absolutely. Siblings are definitely something I want for my child," Laurel said.

"My parents have been married for almost forty years. I have two older sisters, and they both have kids, so there are lots of cousins," Charlie said. "But we do intend to adopt again. At least once, but ideally, we've always said three children. We live in the city right now, but we plan to move to Long Island once we start a family. We both grew up there."

Maggie asked where they met, and Charlie explained about a lecture called "Women in Law, from the Mid-1950s Through the Present" and how he and his friend were the only two men in the audience. After the lecture, Laurel approached him, curious as to why he'd attended. The answer? To score points with a professor on the panel.

Maggie was disappointed. Too dry to make the *New York Times* Weddings section.

"So, what do your parents do?" Charlie asked.

"Our fathers are both firemen," Maggie said quickly, before Danny could correctively put her father in the past tense.

"My mom stayed home with me and my brothers. She died of cancer a year ago," Danny said. He glanced at her. But she would not add that her father was also dead. She did not want them branded as screwed-up teenagers.

"I'm sorry to hear that," Charlie said. Laurel nodded.

"You've had a lot to deal with," Laurel said.

Danny shrugged. Maggie touched her foot to his. See? Pity.

"And your mom?" Laurel asked Maggie.

Maggie liked that she was tactful enough not to dwell on Danny's mother.

"She co-owns a travel agency that does trips to Ireland. She was born in Galway."

Charlie offered Monaghan, on his father's side. Laurel had Mayo.

"We've been talking about taking a trip to Ireland and Italy," Charlie said.

Laurel glanced at him. "But everything is on hold these days," she said.

Maggie guessed Laurel meant they were waiting to see what happened with their ad. She was curious about how many answers they'd gotten, and of that number how many were promising. Not many, Maggie sensed. There was something running between the McKennas, some tension that wasn't only nerves.

"How would this work, if we decided that we want you to adopt the baby?" she asked.

Danny glanced at her, startled at the direct question. But this wasn't the adoption agency, with its rules and contracts and "decision counseling," which she and Danny hadn't done because they'd never actually chosen adoptive parents.

Laurel folded her hands on the table. Charlie said, speaking carefully though his voice shook, "We'll have our lawyer draw up the papers for you to sign after the baby's born. You should also have an attorney look them over. We would like to offer to pay for that. We can recommend someone who's well versed in adoption law, but feel free to choose your own lawyer if you're more comfortable with that. We'll absolutely still cover the cost. There's a medical questionnaire we would ask you to fill out. Just basic information."

Danny nodded, and Maggie could tell he liked the offer to pick their own lawyer.

"As far as contact . . . ," Laurel ventured.

"This is not the sort of thing where you're there in the delivery room," Maggie said.

"Really? We'd thought we'd videotape it," Laurel said.

Danny sat back in his chair, and Charlie said, "Laurel, hey."

But Maggie laughed. Laurel grinned at her.

"We mostly want some way to reach you," Danny said. "Like if something medical did come up that we thought you should know about." Danny glanced at Maggie. "We wouldn't expect to meet until he's eighteen and can decide for himself if he wants to. Maybe we could get pictures every now and then."

This time Maggie stepped on his foot. They had never talked about pictures.

"That's very mature of both of you, I must say," Charlie said.

"Brave," Laurel said.

Maggie nodded. Oh, the bravest. It's in the blood.

"If you ever needed to contact us, you could do it through our lawyer's firm. Even if our guy someday moves on or the office physically moves, they'll have the information. Does that sound good?"

"I think so." Danny looked at Maggie. Now he put his foot over hers.

"We have to talk this over alone," Maggie said firmly.

Charlie grimaced and Laurel pressed her lips together.

"Before we make a final decision," Danny said.

The word "final" seemed to comfort them. They both managed smiles and murmured quick agreement.

Danny said that they'd give them a call tomorrow. Maggie was annoyed about the secure deadline, but she knew he was right. They had to settle this.

Charlie asked them both about college and what they were studying. Maggie excused herself to go to the bathroom while Danny answered.

She was washing her hands when Laurel came in.

"I'm not cornering you," Laurel said. "I just wanted to talk to you alone for a minute. This is the only place to do it.

"First of all, Maggie, whatever you decide to do, thank you for talking with us."

Her sincerity made Maggie uncomfortable. She liked the Laurel of the videotape remark.

"We're just trying to figure out what's best," Maggie said.

"I was thirty-four when we decided to get pregnant. Your fertility isn't supposed to fall off a cliff until you're thirty-five." Laurel blew out a hard breath. "I'm not sorry I became a lawyer. With regard to my job and my hours, I feel like we were skirting the issue. Charlie's paranoid about it, with the birth mothers. But I'm well established now. Once we have a baby, I'm going to take some time off."

"Oh, well —"

"Not forever. I will go back to work. I've always planned to open my own practice." Laurel smiled ruefully. "Charlie doesn't like me to talk about this. To be blunt, I make more money. The law isn't Charlie's passion. His grandfather, his mom's dad, owned a family restaurant and that's what Charlie grew up wanting to do. But his father didn't approve. Charlie figured he would practice law, save money and then, for a second career — well, I'm getting off track here. My point is that Charlie thinks the birth mothers will worry about our financial stability if I say I'm quitting my job and that his goal is to open a restaurant someday. Just so you know, we have enough. Plenty," Laurel said.

"We're savers. We're prepared to start a college fund the day the baby comes home."

"That's good," Maggie managed to say.

"I want to be a mother very, very much."

Maggie nodded. "I'll think about that. About everything."

"Thank you," Laurel said. "Thank you."

By the time Danny helped her out of the car, Maggie wanted nothing more than a nap, such as naps were these days. What she really wanted was to wake up alone in her body. For the past month, she'd been convinced she'd go early — this couldn't possibly drag on for weeks and weeks. The doctor shook her head when Maggie mentioned this. All women said that. It was August 17. Her due date was still four days away. First babies were usually late.

Danny said he'd call her later and they would talk. He had to return Brian's car and take the subway back from Bay Ridge. It was not until he'd pulled away that Maggie realized he'd inadvertently dropped her at her own house, not her grandmother's, and she hadn't noticed either.

It was almost three o'clock and probably still ninety degrees. If she tried to walk to Delia's house, Maggie figured, she would go down on the sidewalk. Somebody would call an ambulance. The Glory Devlins would respond too.

She went inside. The house was marginally cooler. A fan hummed near an open window. The living room was cluttered with Brendan's and Rose's things. Housekeeping had never interested her mother much, even before she was working. Rose's library books were scattered all over the coffee table. She always chose five, six books at a time and then never read any of them. Maggie stacked them neatly. She picked up an open bag of pretzels and rolled it closed. A pair of Brendan's sneakers were in the middle of the rug, as though he'd just stepped out of them and kept going. She couldn't bend over, but she kicked them beneath the table, one enormous shoe at a time.

She was about to collect two dirty glasses, one that had been drained of orange juice and one that had a puddle of chocolate milk on the bottom, when she heard laughter from the kitchen. Aidan? she thought. The baby began kicking hard enough to make her skin ripple, probably a reaction to her own quickening heartbeat. She stood still for several seconds before slowly heading into the kitchen. Brendan was standing at the table, leaning over the newspaper.

He looked up and his grin changed to an expression of alarm.

"You okay?"

"It's just — it's hot," she said.

Brendan grabbed a chair and brought it to her. Even as she sat down, harder than she'd intended to, she was impressed that he'd thought of it.

"When did you get taller than me?" She smiled weakly, realizing that the answer was this summer. He was almost fourteen.

"Should I get Mom? She's in the basement doing the laundry."

Maggie lifted her hair off her neck and shook her head. Monday was her mother's day off. If she'd remembered that, she probably would have tried walking to their grandmother's, and right now she'd be prostrate on the sidewalk.

"Get me some water?"

Brendan ran to the sink and filled a glass. He brought it to her, then went back to the freezer and got an ice cube.

"No practice today?" she asked, to distract him.

"Canceled because of the heat," he said in disgust.

He played soccer in Holy Rosary's summer league. Maggie was ashamed because she had no idea what position.

"Where's Rosie?"

"Bowling with the McAleers."

"Bowling. Of course."

Maggie pressed the glass to her cheek. Brendan shifted from foot to foot.

"I shouldn't get Mom?"

"No, no. I feel better."

She was about to tell him that he didn't have to stay with her, when he said, hesitantly, "It's going to be soon, right?"

"What gave it away?"

Brendan didn't smile. His blue eyes were troubled. He sat back down in his chair.

"End of this week," Maggie said. "I hope."

Again he hesitated. "Aidan says it's wrong to give the baby up."

Maggie drew in a deep breath, the kind that was supposed to ease labor, or so she read.

"Aidan is not the one who will be giving up his whole future. Aidan is not the one who would have to be raised by a mother who gave up her whole future."

"He says you'll change your mind when you have him," Brendan nearly whispered.

He looked like he might cry.

If Aidan had been in the room, Maggie might have slapped him across the face, such was the flash of her anger.

"And live where?"

Brendan looked puzzled, then said, "Here."

"This is Mom's house, not mine," Maggie said. "I can't just crash in on her with a baby. She's already spent years and years supporting us on her own. Now I hand her another kid to take care of? It doesn't work that way."

"You'd be the one taking care of him. And you could get a job too."

"And then who would watch the baby? What about college?" Maggie said. "I've thought this through. Don't ever think I haven't, Bren."

He was silent, his eyes on the floor. "You're going to do it?"

"Yes."

"Will it be the people you met today?"

Was it wrong, she thought, to hand your baby over to a couple you met once in Buckley's?

"I think so. Me and Danny have to finish talking about it."

"What if you and Danny got married?"

Danny hasn't asked, Maggie nearly said. But she only shook her head. "We're not ready for that either."

Brendan pushed himself into a slouch. Maggie finished the water and dumped the ice cube into her palm. She wanted to drop it down her shirt, but settled for rubbing it along her forehead.

"What were you laughing at when I came in?" she asked.

"Huh? Oh, *The Far Side*."

Maggie dropped her hand. The ice cube began to burn her palm. "You sounded like Dad."

"What?"

"*Dad*. Daddy. You laugh just like him. Has anybody ever told you that?"

"No." Brendan sat up straight. "I do? Really?"

Nobody had noticed, Maggie supposed. In the context of their father's death, it was Rose everybody thought of first, the child he never got to see. Then Aidan, the firstborn son. Then Brendan, who was the athlete his father had been. Then herself. Possibly.

"You do," Maggie told him.

Maggie woke up to see her mother folding the laundry. The clothes were in four neat piles on the couch.

"Well, hello," Norah said.

"What time is it?" Maggie had no maternity clothes here, so she'd taken a pair of scissors and hacked her jeans into shorts. Then she'd gone into the living room and settled in her father's easy chair, figuring it might be easier to sleep half sitting up. She'd positioned the fan so it would blow right on her.

"Almost six."

That was nearly two hours without jerking awake like she was in a car that slammed to a stop. But she had to pee, and badly.

When she got back to the living room, she returned to the chair. "That's the best sleep I've had in two months," Maggie said.

"The heat's been awful."

"Yes, that's the reason. The heat."

Norah shook out a shirt of Brendan's. "I'm ordering pizza if you want to stay for dinner. I don't want to turn the oven on."

"That'll give me really bad heartburn."

"Up to you."

Norah's hands didn't stop moving. Shake, fold, place on proper pile.

"Not sleeping has more to do with being nine months pregnant than it being the dead of summer," Maggie said.

Norah held up a shirt of Brendan's and examined it, frowning. "I think your brother eats buttons, I swear to God."

"Our meeting went well," Maggie said.

Her mother placed the shirt on Brendan's pile. She didn't turn around. "Did it?"

Maggie nodded. "They're lawyers. They make really good money. Right now they're in the city but they're going to move to Long Island. Maybe they'll have a pool. God, that would be nice, especially since he'll have a summer birthday."

Norah picked up Rose's school blouse. "As people, you liked them?"

"Sure," Maggie said. "They're nice. They really, really want a baby. I think they'll be good parents." She traced figure eights on her belly.

"What do they look like?"

"He's one of those guys who was probably really cute when he was younger and now he's okay-looking. But she's pretty, really pretty."

If anything happens to him, Maggie thought, she'll be fine.

"Danny wants me to ask Madd to check them out."

"Oh, Maggie, I would leave John Maddox out of the equation."

"I never got everybody's problem with him. He's funny and he's a good dad."

Their father had been gone more than a year before he and Eileen got married. Madd wasn't a stand-in-dad kind of uncle, but he'd taken them to Shea Stadium and out to Coney Island a few times. He didn't come to a lot of their family occasions because Delia didn't like him, and it was mutual. When Maggie was a freshman in high school, Madd and Eileen separated for a time, so the family didn't see him at all for several months. But he was crazy about Quinn. Nobody could deny that.

"Your father used to say he would've made a good cop or a good criminal," Norah said. "It could have gone either way."

"Well, he picked cop, so Danny figures if there's anything to find out, he can do it. We should at least see if they've ever been arrested."

Norah sighed. "Well, I can't tell you what to do anymore, can I?"

Maggie watched her hands whisk Rose's blouse into a neat square. "What would you have done if Dad hadn't asked you to marry him?"

"What are you talking about?"

"I can count, Ma. I know when you were married and I know when I was born."

Norah turned, clutching a blue pillowcase. "My God, you're not getting married?"

"No!" Maggie said. "Absolutely not."

"Good. Don't pile one mistake on top of another." She snapped the pillowcase.

"Like you did, you mean?"

The pillowcase was folded and set down in its place before Norah spoke.

"Me and your father were a couple, not just fooling around. If we hadn't married sooner, we would have later." Her voice was tight, quavering.

"Great. Now I'm a slut," Maggie said.

Norah turned to fully face her.

"You are going to listen to me very carefully. It is one hundred degrees in here. I have to finish all of this and then drag your sister home from the McAleers after a fifteen-minute argument about why she can't spend the night there for the third time this week just because she doesn't like sleeping in a room by herself. I haven't got the patience to chat about things that happened twenty years ago."

"Nineteen," Maggie said. "The month I was at college, she had our room to herself. But anyway, I'm really sorry my getting knocked up has upset Rose."

"*Magdalena*. I understand that you're not feeling well, so I'm going to let that pass, but from now until you have that baby, you might consider counting to ten before you speak." Norah turned her back.

Maggie pushed herself up and onto her hip, then lowered herself onto her side and closed her eyes. She was seven pounds of baby and twenty pounds of cruel words. She knew what her mother deserved and what she did not. Still, an apology wouldn't come.

She knew, as well, that it was wrong to change the story, to cancel her parents' wedding and replace it with an adoption. Erase her brothers and her sister. Yet it was too intriguing a thought — her father, her mother and herself in the same world but set in different orbits. What they all might have been spared. Each other, how it ended.

The nurse kept telling her to push. Bear down. Maggie tried, but she was numb below the waist and this whole thing had been going on since yesterday, and it was getting dark again.

The nurse had rolled in a full-length mirror because she said it would help.

"Aim for the mirror," she said.

Maggie was afraid to look. But Danny's attention was fixed on the mirror as though it were a movie screen. Noelle, on her other side, lowered her voice to be heard above the nurse, who clearly believed that being tough was going to produce results.

"Just two or three more," Noelle said.

"Two or three?" Maggie said.

"Don't talk, push!" the nurse said.

"You get to sleep when you're done," Noelle whispered.

Maggie pushed again and then again and then a third time. The doctor, who was standing by Maggie's feet as if she were waiting for a bus, suddenly tensed.

A fourth push, and in spite of the numbness, Maggie felt the moment of separation. She sensed the emptiness. She saw a small purple body cupped in the doctor's hands. "It's a girl!"

The doctor put the screaming baby on Maggie's stomach. Maggie's arms, of their own accord, reached for the infant as though the baby were perched on the edge of a cliff.

"Born at 7:07 on August 27. Lucky!" one of the nurses called out cheerfully.

"A girl." Danny touched the baby's arm and pulled his hand back. Her eyes were shut tight. The wailing seemed bigger than her whole body.

"She's so little," Noelle said. "I can't believe how little she is."

The nurse lifted her from Maggie's arms.

"Wait." Maggie tried to sit up. She and Danny had elected to see the baby after the birth. The hospital staff were supposed to know that.

Noelle put a hand on Maggie's shoulder. "She's cold. They're wrapping her up is all."

Maggie sat back.

"A girl. I can't believe it. A girl," Danny said. "I didn't think — Maggie? Are you all right?"

"Yes. No. I think so." Her whole body was shaking. She couldn't feel her legs.

Danny cast a frightened glance at the doctor, who didn't look up. A nurse slid the mirror away. Then another nurse walked toward them with the baby, now quiet and wrapped in a blanket. She wore a snug white cap.

Maggie's arms automatically formed a cradle and the nurse laid the baby in it.

"Seven pounds, eight ounces. Another seven. Perfect."

Danny moved the blanket to better see her face. Her eyes were open.

"Hey, you," he said. "Look at you." Danny put his finger on her cheek. She turned to the touch.

Maggie couldn't stop staring. She tucked the baby closer. Yesterday she would have said that all infants looked alike, but this baby, her baby, looked familiar. She picked up the tiny hand and cupped it in her palm.

"She has your eyes," Danny said.

"All infants have blue eyes," Maggie said. "Don't they? Is that true?"

Maggie was curled up on her bed. Her breasts hurt so much, just moving was excruciating. Her grandmother's house was quiet, and Maggie was glad she had not gone back to her own house after her release from the hospital as Norah had expected her to.

She didn't answer the knock on the door, but Delia came in anyway, carrying a plate with lettuce on it.

Maggie blinked at her. "You made me a salad?"

"Cold cabbage leaves. It helps."

"I think I should feed her a little. I'm sure if I called them, they'd let me come over."

In the five days since she'd given birth, Maggie had not been able to say their names out loud.

Delia closed her eyes for a moment. "I don't think you'll be allowed to do that," she finally said. "Feeding her might help the pain, but it would only make you produce more milk."

She set the plate down on the nightstand and left. Maggie steeled herself to sit up. She took the cabbage leaves off the plate and tucked them up her shirt.

Gently, she lay back down. When her grandmother came back a little while later, Maggie managed a grimace.

"Better?" Delia said.

"A little. Why cabbage leaves?"

"Cold anything would probably help, but the cabbage leaves are supposed to dry up the milk."

"That's crazy. Who told you that?"

"I had a friend." Delia paused. "She had a baby outside of marriage and she had to pretend he was her little brother —"

"Are you kidding?"

"This was in the late 1930s," Delia said. "She went back to high school right after he was born. This old aunt of hers told her about cabbage leaves. I imagine it was usually done when a baby didn't live."

Maggie found it difficult to imagine her grandmother having a real friend besides Nathaniel, but her mind was too full to pursue this line of thought.

On the Saturday before Labor Day, Noelle came by. The baby was ten days old. She would still have her little bit of umbilical cord.

Delia seemed relieved to see her and left them alone in front of the television. Noelle sat down.

"You look good," she said.

"I look fat," Maggie answered.

"Five or six months instead of nine," Noelle said. "It'll go away."

"I was never going to make it back to school this fall," Maggie said.

"No, not with that due date."

"I wish somebody had told me."

"Aidan never thought you were going to give the baby up. Your grandmother never says anything unless she's asked, far as I can tell. Eileen, the same as your brother. Aunt Norah thought you'd be on the train, still bleeding."

"But you knew."

"It's what you needed to believe to get through it."

"I don't know what to do now," Maggie said. "Tell me what to do."

"Get your school to defer your scholarship another semester. If they refuse, threaten to sue for pregnancy discrimination, or whatever it's called. Take another class at Brooklyn College. It's only the seventh. There's got to be late registration. Borrow the money from Delia if you have to. She'll give it to you. Then sign up for classes at your college over the winter break. You'll go back when mostly everyone is gone, and you can get adjusted again and start full time in the spring. How's that?"

Maggie nodded listlessly. "That sounds like a plan."

But she still hadn't found out about Brooklyn College by Saturday, September 28, when Danny called to see how she was doing. He'd come home for the weekend. During the pregnancy, his brothers had persuaded him to apply to a few schools closer than Boston, and Maggie told him they were right. Now he was at Stony Brook. *Long Island.*

Maggie suggested that he come by. He said he would, but he couldn't stay long. His nephew's birthday party was in the afternoon, and he hadn't gotten a gift yet.

Maggie dressed more carefully than she usually bothered to these days. She wore her maternity jeans and a green shirt that Brendan had outgrown a year ago. If anybody saw her and they didn't know about the baby, they'd think she'd fallen victim to the freshman fifteen.

Though it was a rainy day, Maggie suggested they go for a walk. She needed air. She needed exercise.

Danny came by her grandmother's house and she went outside to meet him. He wore a Mets cap in lieu of an umbrella. Maggie wore her blue jacket with the hood.

"Hey," he said.

"Hi."

The baby had turned a month old yesterday. The umbilical cord was almost certainly gone by now. Maggie wondered what Laurel had done with it. Did you just toss something like that in the trash like an egg-shell, or was it something you saved like a lock of hair? Maggie hadn't read the postpartum chapters of her books.

Maggie started walking and Danny fell in beside her, letting her take the lead. They walked up Cross Hill Avenue, and when they passed the Celtic cross, she led him to the convent. They stood on the sidewalk outside the gate. The three-story building was in need of repair. Shingles were missing from the roof, and the paint on the door was peeling.

"I should tell my dad about the roof. It's probably leaking," Danny said. "He'll get some of the guys to fix it. I guess you'd ask Father Halloran to talk to the sisters. Or you could go into that little room where you ask for prayers."

Maggie looked up at him. "You've done it?"

"Me? No. My mom, when she got sick. My dad was pissed. I guess he didn't want her hoping for a miracle or something."

They continued walking in silence. Danny said nothing when they arrived at Cross Hill Cemetery, and nothing still when she led him through the gate and to Fireman's Corner and her father's grave. Maggie squatted to clean off the stone, which had muddy, wet leaves stuck to it. She wished she'd thought to bring paper towels.

She traced his name with her finger. If the baby had been a boy, she would have named him Sean Patrick.

"What are we doing here?" Danny asked.

Maggie stood up. "Let's go get her."

Danny shook his head. "The McKennas will be good parents."

"She won't even remember them. A month is nothing."

"Not to the McKennas."

"Who cares? We'll take our baby back, they'll adopt somebody else's and decide it was meant to be."

"It's done."

"It isn't." Maggie took his hand. "There's a reason the law gives birth mothers time to change their minds. We've only got two weeks left. We have to do it now."

"The night she was born, Brian told me to stake my claim. He said you can't give your daughter away. He said we could name her Grace Elizabeth, after Mom. I told him no."

"I like Grace. But her middle name is from my family." Maggie walked over to the statue of the fireman holding the child and touched the name engraved on the monument. Patrick Devlin, her great-great-grandfather.

"Grace Devlin Grady. That's pretty," Maggie said. "But then I thought it should be my grandmother's maiden name. So it's Grace Keegan Grady."

"That's not her name."

"That's what I put on her birth certificate."

"Maggie, what are you talking about? The McKennas are the ones who named her."

In the hospital, the day after the baby was born, the McKennas arrived to take her, sharing constant, uncertain glances. Maggie asked for the baby's name. They exchanged a quick look of utter relief and then, as Charlie swallowed again and again, trying to speak, Laurel answered casually, "We haven't decided yet, believe it or not. We were afraid we'd jinx ourselves."

Maggie did not believe it.

She explained to Danny that adoptees have two birth certificates. The original one has the birth parents' names on it, and it gets sealed, locked away in some building in lower Manhattan. The adopted person is never allowed to see it, ever — at least in New York that's the law. The other one is the amended birth certificate, and that has the adoptive parents on it and whatever name they pick.

As the baby's mother, Maggie got to fill out the birth certificate. She could have simply put down "Baby Girl Grady," since it was never going to be used, but she didn't. She put "Grace Keegan Grady" on it.

"So she's all set. She has a name and it's legal because there hasn't been any adoption."

"Maggie, no. That's not her name. That'll never be her name. Please stop it."

"If she were your son and not your daughter, would you go after her?" Maggie asked.

She expected him to get mad, but Danny only hunched his shoulders.

"No. The second I saw her, I forgot about a boy," he said. "But the whole time you were pregnant, yeah, I was picturing me and Bri in some kind of bachelor pad with a little boy running around. There we are, just the guys. And then, there she was, and all I could think was how would I raise a girl? How could I raise any kid? I can't support her. I can't give her anything. It's just fucked up."

It never occurred to Maggie that Danny might refuse. She'd assumed he was waiting for her to call it, like shooting off a starting pistol.

"We have a problem, Danny," Maggie said. "The problem is that I had a baby. This is a very big problem."

"Let her go."

"It's a bad thing to give away your baby. I know this, because I did it."

"I did it too, and I don't think it's wrong. Before she was born, I wasn't sure, but now I am. She deserves better than you and me. Everything you were saying the whole time is right."

"I'm not always right."

"You are, Mag. Being right is your thing."

"Fine. Then I'm right about this."

"You're upset, that's all. My sister-in-law told me that she hoped your mother was keeping an eye on you for postpartum depression."

"My mother! Please. My mother, who didn't once tell me that I could bring the baby home if I wanted to."

"Because we told everybody that we were giving her up at the same time we told them you were pregnant. Case closed."

"Mom asked if I was sure, but she didn't once say I could live with her if I wasn't."

"She's not a mind reader, Mag," Danny said.

"She was afraid I would say yes."

Danny shoved his hands in his pockets. "Maybe."

"Your mother wouldn't have been afraid to ask."

"Yeah." Danny stared off into the trees. "I think about that all the time. She wouldn't have let us do it."

Before the baby was born, if he'd said such a thing, Maggie would have been furious. Yet she knew there was truth to it. Grace would have supported whatever decision they made, but she would have offered other solutions. She guessed that Grace would have volunteered to watch the baby while she and Danny attended college and worked whatever jobs they could get around their class schedules.

"Mom wasn't a widow, working and raising kids by herself," Danny said. "We're not being fair."

"I know," Maggie said, and she meant it.

But Grace was dead; her own mother could have asked.

Maggie unzipped her jacket and, as much as it hurt, squeezed her right breast, just hard enough to dampen the front of her shirt.

"Maggie, Jesus Christ." Danny snatched her hand away and yanked her jacket shut.

"I only did it at first because it hurt so bad I thought if I pumped a little bit, just to relieve some of the pressure . . . but then I started thinking. And then I kept going so I'd be ready for her, when she comes back."

Danny glanced down at her father's grave, as though hoping Sean O'Reilly might be able to help.

"We'll just go get her," Maggie said. "My grandmother's got the whole brownstone to herself. I think we can bring her there."

There were tears in Danny's eyes. "We'll see her again."

Maggie wrapped her arms around herself. She wanted the baby back because she couldn't stop thinking of that small face, and how her eyes opened suddenly and briefly before shutting tight again, the little moving mouth, the tiny fingers curled around her own index finger.

Surely it was the same for Danny, but he was willing to live around the chasm of her absence, hard as it was, for the baby's sake. She, Maggie, only wanted the longing to stop. Even without a daughter to parent, he was the better parent.

"What if she doesn't come looking for us?"

"She will," Danny said.

"And if she never does?"

Danny exhaled again. "Then we miss her! We miss her for the rest of our stupid fucking lives!"

"Here's the thing. This is going to sound crazy, but I'm not crazy." Maggie stepped closer to him. "I knew I'd have the baby, and she'd be gone. But it's like I thought I was giving her to my father, not some couple from Long Island. But it turns out I gave my baby to some couple from Long Island."

Danny glanced around the cemetery. But there was no one to help him. Maggie looked down at her father's name.

"I don't know what you mean."

"I don't mean anything." She didn't know how else to explain.

Her father, who had been alone so long, was still alone because she had given birth not to an imaginary child but to a living daughter, who, like the rest of the family, was beyond his reach.

September 14, 2001

The gathering in the garden is just beginning as Maggie arrives. The service has been timed for shortly before twilight, and though it's open to the public, the garden is too small to accommodate all who have come. The crowd numbers far more than the Kilmaren community and the townspeople from Ivehusheen.

Ireland has declared Friday, September 14, a national day of mourning. The Irish government shut down its offices, and schools closed for the day. In Dublin, people waited for hours in front of the American embassy to sign a book of condolence that would be sent to New York and Washington. The Dublin Fire Brigade visited the embassy in a show of solidarity with the FDNY.

When Maggie tells the story of September 12, how she got out of bed and turned the television on, she says she stared at it in disbelief. But she leaves it at that, because the truth sounds like something a novice screenwriter would imagine for the daughter of a fireman who has grown up knowing that the Worst Day in the history of the FDNY was in 1966, at the 23rd Street Fire. Twelve men were killed. The Worst Day.

She was standing well beyond the border of the carpet as the anchorman gave the number of New York City police officers and Port Authority officers unaccounted for, but Maggie barely listened. She was waiting.

"— and as many as three hundred firefighters are dead or missing."

Maggie dropped as if she'd been hit in the back of the knees with a baseball bat.

Since the afternoon of the twelfth, Maggie has been at her grandparents' house in Ballyineen, where she went to be with them while waiting for flights to the United States to resume. Cathal, her mother's brother, flew over from England, and Maggie was grateful the job of trying to comfort the Mulryans was not left to her. She has barely visited them during her time in Ireland, impatient with their shyness around her, too immersed in her own life to try to remedy it. Later, she'd always told herself. Later she'd plan a long visit.

The only phone calls she answered were from her family. It was nearly three p.m. on the fourteenth before she sat on the narrow bed that had once been her mother's and listened to her voicemails. Message after message from friends and even students, telling her how sorry they were and letting her know about the commemoration in the garden.

Go, her uncle told her. See your friends. There's nothing you can do here.

There is a crowd gathered outside the garden wall, huddled in small groups. Many are holding candles. Without hesitating, Maggie heads for the open garden gate. People glance at her and then step aside to let her pass. Whispers rise and fall her in her wake. She remembers well the privilege of loss. It is easy to assume again.

The group of traditional musicians who play at Derrane's are assembled at the far end of the garden. Maggie keeps walking until she is near the front. There are no seats except for the performers. This event was put together hastily.

She deliberately stands off to the side, and it is understood that she wants to be left alone. She sees Rory McAlary with his wife and sons. Because he is her boss, more or less, Maggie had emailed him to let him know that she was going home as soon as she could get a flight. She could not say for sure when she would be back.

Maggie nods and Rory nods back. His wife has a hand on each boy's shoulder, and that's when Maggie realizes that the wife knows. She looks away, too tired to be ashamed, or possibly not ashamed.

The musicians, the regulars from the Derrane's *seisiúns* — the bodhran player, the uillean piper, a tin-whistle player — are seated in a semicircle in front of a cluster of moonflower vines. Without prelude, they begin to play. Cillian is on the fiddle.

Cillian says the titles of the tunes in a low voice in Irish and English before they begin each one. They are playing traditional Irish songs only, with Irish language lyrics, as if to please not the dead in the city across the sea, but the dead whose bones lay beneath them.

"Dóchas Linn Naomh Pádraig."
"Caoineadh Cú Chulainn."
"Caoineadh na dTrí Mhuire."

As Cillian says the last one, a girl moves forward from the crowd and stands to his left. He nods. The musicians relax above their instruments. She begins to sing *sean-nós*. Literally, old mouth. Unaccompanied.

Maggie knows what the title of this song means, "Lament of the

Three Marys," but she doesn't know the lyrics in Irish or English, so she cannot follow the path of the song, only listen, and it is beautiful to hear, the way the garden is beautiful to see.

She is afraid to turn around, afraid she will see that the famine dead have come to stand and listen among the living.

Maggie isn't sleeping when he comes to her apartment at midnight. She lets him in and leads him into the living room. They kiss once, then again.

Maggie lifts her shirt, just enough to show her stomach.

Cillian shakes his head. He doesn't understand.

"Nothing," she says.

It is possible to die in a fire and it is possible to have a baby without being marked. She is like her father in his coffin. She pulls her shirt down.

The first night of the wake, as they went into the room, her mother told her and Aidan not to be scared. He looked like he was sleeping. But her father slept on his stomach, often with a pillow over his head, a firehouse habit from trying to block out the sound of the other men's snoring. In the coffin he lay on his back, in uniform. There were rosary beads entwined in his hands. A firefighter stood at either end of the casket, staring fixedly ahead, an honor guard. The men switched every hour, the whole two days and nights of the wake. There was a kneeler in front of the coffin, and she and Aidan sank in perfect unity. They landed together and their shoulders bumped. Aidan tried to get up right away, but she pulled him back down because she was trying to be proper and say the Hail Mary but the words kept breaking apart in her throat.

Maggie does not call Daniel James John Grady on their daughter's birthday anymore. They have nothing to say to each other. This past August 27, and the one before it, she hiked up Slievekeeran and spent the afternoon wandering the deserted famine village on the side of the mountain. For the first few years after, Maggie was grateful. She could undress for a man without having to explain. But for a long time now she has wished for a C-section scar or stretch marks. Something to see in the mirror. Something to touch.

"The picture in your office?" Cillian says.

Maggie explains that it *is* her sister, but the question is the reason the photo is there. She likes to hear it. Each time she's asked, she comes close to saying yes, just so she can. Is that your daughter?

"Did I tell you that my father died?"

"You've never mentioned your father to me."

"He drowned in a burning building."

Maggie has never been able to resolve that paradox — fire, smoke, water — even though the story is simple enough. When she was sixteen, she went to the big library at Grand Army Plaza in Park Slope and read the archived newspaper stories on microfiche. There was an explosion, a collapse, he got trapped in a basement that filled with water, and he ran out of air before the firemen could reach him.

Maggie thinks for a moment how strange they must look, she and Cillian, standing in front of each other in the center of the room. She sees that he also realizes that they cannot move until she is done.

"My mother was ashamed when I got pregnant," Maggie says. "Then I thought she was embarrassed about what the neighbors were saying, and she was, but now I see that she thinks she failed my father. It didn't occur to me then, but it should have."

She tells Cillian that when she couldn't be around her mother anymore, because of how she turned away from even the most offhand comments about the pregnancy, her grandmother gave her a place to go.

Stay, she'd told her. Six years later, Delia was the one who said, It's time to go.

She's not coming back. Not anytime soon, and maybe never.

Delia handed her a college brochure that had on its cover a photo of a stone building covered in red ivy. Lysaght Hall, Kilmaren College, in the town of Ivehusheen, County Galway.

Delia's own grandmother Brigid only ever mentioned one place in Ireland, and that was Slievekeeran. *Sliabh-na-caorthann*, Mountain of the Rowan. Maggie has not yet taken the time to look for written records. But in the way you simply understand some things, she knows that this place is where the story begins.

Cillian steps forward and runs his hands lightly up and down her arms.

"I don't want to be inside," she tells him.

It's chilly, so she grabs a jacket. Cillian pulls the blanket off her bed.

Once outside, he takes her hand and instead of following the road to campus, he leads her into the woods, down the path that ends at the garden. The gate stands open, though everyone has gone home.

Maggie drags her feet, but Cillian tugs her hand and they enter *an Gairdín Cuimhneacháin*, as it's officially called. The Garden of Remembrance grows over an acre of graves. Maggie and Cillian lie down near the roses. Their petals are closed, at peace, blind to the dead.

December 1984

Maggie scanned the Christmas tree for Irish Santa.

Last night, when they were putting up the tree, she'd been hunting for it in the jumble of ornaments in one box when Brendan scooped it out of another. If she'd snatched it back, her mother would have said, He's six! So Maggie had to let him put the ornament somewhere near the bottom, on the side of the tree that faced the living room.

Brendan and Aidan were watching *The A-Team*. Aidan taped every single episode. Maggie hated it, but at least it was keeping the boys busy while she fixed the tree. The Glory Devlins company Christmas party would start in a half hour.

Last year, a week before Rose was born, their mother said they'd get an artificial tree because it was easier. When Aidan had mentioned this on one of his visits to the firehouse, the next day Joe Paladino and Mickey Carson came over with a real tree and put it up for them. They'd done it this year too; today, when she and Aidan got home from school, the tree was up in the living room, perfectly straight in its stand, the lights on, the boxes of ornaments from the attic in a stack nearby.

Maggie spotted Irish Santa, in his green coat and hat with the shamrock on it, and rescued him from the low branch where Brendan had stuck him. She settled him in his proper place, near the top and on the side of the tree that faced the window.

"Maggie!" her mother called.

Maggie flicked a red bell with her finger, but neither of her brothers took his eyes off the television.

She arrived in her bedroom doorway and saw that her mother had been attempting to get Rose into a pair of white tights. Rose was lying on Maggie's bed, kicking her legs and giggling. Maggie folded her arms across her chest as her mother said, "Will you get these on her, please? I've got to check in at the office before we go."

She was off for the Christmas party, though she usually had to work Saturdays because she was still new at Irish Dreams. She'd started in September. Before trying to put together a résumé, since she'd never in her life had one, she'd called Marian Clark and asked if the agency needed anyone to answer its phones. Marian had become the manager when Norah's own aunt Helen died.

Marian suggested Norah start as a travel agent. After the holidays, Irish Dreams would be hiring another agent, someone who didn't mind working weekends. Until then, Maggie and Aidan and Brendan and Rose spent Saturday afternoons at their grandmother's. If Aunt Eileen was free, she came to their house, which was not nearly often enough, because she bartended on her days off from the firehouse.

Her mother handed Maggie the tights, looking her up and down.

"That's what you're wearing, then?"

Maggie had on jeans and her blue shirt with the buttons on the cuffs.

"You can make me go, but you can't make me get dressed up."

"There'll be boys there, you know," Norah said.

Maggie made a face, and her mother laughed.

"Try and get that little bow in her hair? It's on the dresser. Work your magic."

She left the room. Rose was bouncing on the bed. Maggie had the urge to sit on her to keep her still. But Rose would think that was great fun.

"Rose! Time to get dressed now."

She took hold of Rose's ankle.

Maggie got the tights and dress on Rose with minimal squirming. It drove her mother a little crazy how Rose obeyed her. Not all the time, but better than with anybody else. Aidan thought of himself as the one who took care of her. What he did was play with her.

Rose's new dress had a satiny top and a red velvet skirt. She would wear it for her birthday too. In five days, she'd turn one.

Maggie thought about carrying Rose down the hall, to show off that she'd gotten her ready in less than ten minutes. But her mother would be sitting at the rolltop desk in the corner of her bedroom, if not on the phone then writing in her notebook, which was always on the desk, a square of green in the middle of papers and Irish magazines and Irish newspapers, things her mother read to keep up with the news back home and to get ideas for Irish Dreams. Her father used to sit at the desk to pay the bills and to study for the lieutenant's exam.

Instead, Maggie took Rose downstairs. Rose toddled over to the couch, and Aidan pulled her into his lap.

The Christmas party was held in the basement of Holy Rosary Church. The basement door was at the back of the church, and they went in, her mother nodding at the guy manning the table where the company T-shirts and hats were for sale. Maggie didn't know him. She guessed he was a probie.

Each long table was covered with either a red or a green tablecloth. Grace Grady was sitting at a table with a wife Maggie didn't know. Grace beckoned them over, and a few other people called out greetings as they crossed the room. Norah smiled and waved back, Rose on her hip. When they reached the table, Grace said,

"Norah! You'd remember! I was trying to tell Mary about . . ."

Maggie looked around. She saw Danny Grady with a group of boys across the room, but she didn't see his brothers. Of course, one was in high school and the other was in college, way too old to bother with this.

Her mother lowered Rose to the floor and started taking off her coat.

"I do remember that! It was at the picnic a couple of years ago."

Coat off, Brendan took off at a run for the stage in the front of the room. A chair was already set up for Santa Claus, who wouldn't be arriving until three o'clock.

Rose took a few steps after Brendan. Aidan caught up and took her hand.

"She walks really well," Mary Paladino said, surprised.

"She's been on her feet for more than a month, but it's only this past week she's added a bit of speed," Norah said.

"She looks like Delia," Grace said.

"She does, doesn't she? I told Delia that when Rose was born, and she says to me that babies looked alike until they were six months old. I said, Oh, really? But now I get to be right about one thing for the rest of my life."

They all laughed. Maggie checked their faces for pity but found none. It was as if her father was in the group at the bar, or in the kitchen helping with the food, or had slipped out to the store to pick up more beer.

My father's dead, you know, she wanted to remind them.

Maggie left the table. She heard her mother's voice, though not her words. The others all laughed again. Isabel Paladino and two other girls, the Donnelly sisters, were playing with Rose and glancing at Aidan, who was standing nearby with a few other boys.

Maggie heard somebody come up behind her and turned to see Danny Grady, looking past her.

"Hey, Roses. That's a pretty dress."

Rose reached for him, and he picked her up.

Maggie loved the days they went to the Gradys' after school, because Grace took over Rose and she didn't have to do a thing. That was Mondays, Tuesdays and Wednesdays. Thursdays and Fridays, they went to their grandmother's.

Grace would hold Rose up to her husband. "Don't you want to try for one of these?"

He'd actually smile and take the baby from Grace. Last week, he'd plunked her on top of the refrigerator. She kicked her heels and laughed.

Maggie stayed as close as she could, petrified, ready to catch her if she pitched forward.

Danny put Rose up on the stage, which was only as high as Danny's knee. He took both her hands and swung her in the air. She squealed when she landed with a soft thump.

Aidan laughed. "You're gonna have to do that a thousand times now."

Danny shrugged and put her back on the stage for another turn.

Again. And then again. Aidan liked Danny and didn't mind sharing Rose with him. They were on Holy Rosary's baseball team together. He talked about Danny's brothers all the time too. Brian got a motorcycle. Kevin's dating some girl two years older than him. Maybe Aidan wished he was a Grady. Maggie didn't blame him.

Maggie left, weaving through the crowd. It was like being in a forest, a forest of firemen. She scanned the room as she walked, pretending to look for Brendan but really listening to the snatches of conversation for Sean, O'Reilly, Sean O. She didn't hear the name.

"— Pillar of Fire Church. Can't beat that."

"There was debris from one end of Sterling to the other —"

Her mother was up getting food, probably for Brendan. Maggie snatched her coat from where she left it on the back of a chair and started crossing the room. Nobody asked where she was going.

Outside, free, Maggie began walking, already scripting her mother's reaction when she couldn't find her. First annoyance: "Well, she can't have gone far!" And then, her accent thickening once she discovered that Maggie had not gone to Delia's or even Nathaniel's: "Where is she?"

In less than ten minutes, Maggie arrived at the cloister. Only after she'd stopped in front of the black gate did she admit to herself that the convent had been her destination.

If Annie-Rose was still alive, she would be turning one hundred in two weeks. She had been Maggie's favorite of her dead relatives, before her father went and joined them. A wedding picture of Annie-Rose and Jack Keegan hung in the hallway of her grandmother's house.

Maggie liked to look at the bride with the dark hair and light eyes who was not smiling, even though the sad things were still to come.

Rose would have been named Sean if she'd been a boy, of course. Their mother said that the three of them could come up with a girl's name. Murdoch was Brendan's choice, and they were all polite about it. Aidan chose Daisy, as in *The Dukes of Hazzard*. Maggie had often wished her father had chosen Annie-Rose for her, but when she offered it to the baby, her grandmother spoke up from her seat by the window of the hospital room and said, "That I couldn't abide. Please, one or the other."

Annie-Rose. She would have left the name behind when she went into the convent. Maggie wanted to bring it back from the place of lost things.

Maggie pushed open the gate and looked up at the convent, which was bare of Christmas decorations. Curtains covered each window. She stepped into the front yard, stopping before the statue of Saint Maren. Maggie had tried to find her in a few different books, but there was never more than a brief paragraph. Saint Maren founded a contemplative order in Galway in 17-something. She was given as the patron of those in danger of fire or drowning, of bakers, knitters and bell makers. It was like the church had a list of professions in need, and whatever saint was next on the list got assigned them. Maggie knew the wives at the firehouse considered Maren their saint, but that was made up, and maybe even a joke.

Maggie stared up at the statue's blank eyes. She put her hand toward the saint's outstretched hand and then pulled back.

Where were you? she thought.

Maggie walked away, afraid to look behind her, afraid the statue would have jumped down to follow her, trying to apologize, and perhaps explain.

Too soon, Maggie was back, across the street from the church, standing in front of Lehane's.

A fire truck was parked in front of the church, and there were a few kids waiting for a turn to climb in. Brendan wasn't among them. Nobody noticed her.

The October day Brendan was born, her father picked her up from kindergarten and brought her to Lehane's after telling her the news. Maggie and Aidan had woken that morning to find their grandmother in the kitchen, which meant scrambled eggs instead of Frosted Flakes. Maggie and Aidan had looked at each other desperately, but they'd known better than to object.

Eileen was working. Back then, bartending had still been her main job. Without her father even asking, she poured him a beer and got Maggie a Coke.

Maggie sat on the barstool beside her father's. If she sat up very straight, she could see her reflection in the mirror above the liquor bottles.

"So, Magee, you happy about your new baby brother?" her father asked.

"No," she'd said.

"Oh well, back to the drawing board, then," he'd said, putting his hand on her head, knocking her headband askew.

"What's he weigh? Eight pounds? I'd give Norah at least a couple of days," Eileen said, and the two of them laughed.

Maggie had straightened her headband. She climbed down from her barstool and stood next to his. He leaned over and pulled her up into his lap with one arm. She couldn't recall what T-shirt he'd been wearing, but except for when he dressed up, he nearly always wore a T-shirt with writing on it. Maggie thought she'd probably learned to read from her father's shirts. F-D-N-Y, the letters she knew before A-B-C-D.

T-u-r-k-e-y T-r-o-t. K-n-i-g-h-t-s o-f C-o-l-u-m-b-u-s. B-r-o-o-k-l-y-n I-r-i-s-h.

Now Maggie pushed open the door to the bar and went inside. Her aunt Eileen told them yesterday that she was working at Lehane's in the afternoon, more as a favor to Lizzie, since there would be no tips on a Saturday afternoon so soon before Christmas.

Maggie was not sure how often Eileen worked at the bar since she'd left the neighborhood to take an apartment on Carroll Street. She lived on the top floor of a brownstone. When Maggie and Aidan rode their bikes over to see her, they would take the Carroll Street Bridge, though Eileen always told them that one of these days it was going to collapse and drop them right into the Gowanus Canal. Take 3rd or Union Street instead. But they liked the Carroll Street Bridge best, and not only because it was the shortest route. It didn't look like it belonged in Brooklyn, somehow, in spite of its obvious disrepair. Maggie thought the cobblestones made it look like it belonged in some other city, maybe in Ireland. She and Aidan would get off their bikes, stand on the bridge's walkway and stare into the canal.

Some days — only some — the water bubbled as though boiling, and if the stench wasn't too bad, Maggie and Aidan imagined that a creature of some kind might burst through the water's oily surface. Maggie pictured the Loch Ness monster, but Aidan said it would be something deformed, two-headed, like from radiation.

Maggie looked behind the bar but her aunt was not there, only the Lehanes. Amred was reading and Lizzie was knitting. Maggie turned to leave.

"Sit." Amred gestured to a barstool.

Maggie crossed the room, climbed up on the barstool and wrapped her feet around its legs.

"Hi there. Would you like a soda? Black cherry?" Lizzie kept knitting as she spoke. She wore her gray hair back in two barrettes, one blue, one green.

Who offered black cherry first? Maggie thought. Cans of black cherry were always the last in the cooler at the company picnic.

"Coke, maybe?"

"Oh, sure." Lizzie sounded surprised.

Lizzie, Maggie had always heard, originally intended to become a librarian. The bar had belonged to the uncle who'd raised her and Amred, and when he died, near the end of the Depression, Lizzie took over, although women weren't allowed to drink in Lehane's in those days. Right after Pearl Harbor, Lizzie opened the bar for wartime wedding receptions, which were often planned only a couple of weeks ahead, if that. Delia, Maggie knew, had been one such bride.

There were two old men at the bar, sitting opposite each other, both reading the newspaper. Neither looked up.

"On the lam from the Christmas party?" Amred asked.

Maggie nodded. "Aunt Eileen said she was working here today."

"She said she'll be in tomorrow," Amred said.

"We'll see," Lizzie added, setting a Coke in front of Maggie in a pint glass.

"How is the baby? She has a birthday soon, am I right?" Amred asked.

"December 20," Maggie said.

Amred put his book down without marking his place. "Do you know what tomorrow is, Maggie O'Reilly?"

"It's nothing. Sunday," Maggie said.

"Sunday, December 16," Amred said. "But not nothing. It's the twenty-fourth anniversary of the Park Slope plane crash."

Maggie blinked. "A Christmas tree seller on the ground was killed?"

"Yes!" Amred said. "I knew Sean would have told you."

Sean. To hear his name spoken without a pause either before or after it. *Sean.*

Amred leaned over and pulled a knapsack into his lap from which he withdrew a red folder. He set the folder on the bar and opened it.

He turned the folder around so it was facing Maggie.

"This is Sterling Street." He tapped the picture. "They think the pilot was trying to land in Prospect Park, or possibly the Botanic Garden. It nearly hit the school, St. Augustine's, and then crashed into the church and a row of buildings."

Maggie leaned closer. She knew the street. Nathaniel's store was up the block, on Flatbush Avenue. The photograph was black and white. The tail of an airplane was sticking up at a slight angle, the word UNITED clearly visible. Amred flipped to the next picture, a shot of a group of firemen standing on the wreckage.

"The caretaker of the church was killed. It was actually two guys selling Christmas trees. Between the six folks on the ground, this plane and the one it collided with that went down over Staten Island, 134 people were killed."

In the next picture, two firemen were carrying a covered stretcher between them.

He flipped the photo gently and pushed the one beneath it closer to Maggie.

"This," Amred said. "This."

It was a shot of the crowd, but Amred had focused the camera on her father and Eileen, who were standing with a group of other kids. They were beside each other, shoulders nearly touching, their gazes fixed on the disaster before them.

"What year was this?" Maggie asked.

"1984 minus 24," Amred said.

"I can't do math in my head," Maggie said.

"1960," Lizzie answered. Her hands went still, though she didn't look up from her work.

"John Kennedy had been elected a month earlier. It was like we'd found a king. We all thought he'd be president forever. That's why they killed him."

Maggie looked up at the picture of JFK, tucked into the mirror behind the bar. Who's "they"? she wanted to ask, but Amred was tapping the picture.

"Sean had just turned thirteen," he said. "It was a Friday. Fog and snow. A miserable morning. That's John Maddox next to Sean. The girl on his other side is Judy Lister. She moved out of New York after her mom and dad passed. She was named Judy for Saint Jude."

"Patron saint of lost causes," Maggie said.

"Funny, since Judy herself was something of a lost cause."

"Amred," Lizzie said, a mild warning in her tone.

Amred continued. "Behind Eileen is Ally Coen. He died in Vietnam."

"That's a boy," Maggie said. He was taller and stockier than her father, with dark hair falling into his eyes. His hands were jammed in his pockets.

"Short for Alistair," Amred said. "His mom was British. He was a quiet kid, Ally. Didn't have a lot of friends, never said boo. If you handed him a ball, you know, stuck it in his palm and wrapped his fingers around it, he'd drop it. Not too bright either. But, *hell*, could Ally hit. Coach put him in right field and had Sean cover, best he could. Sean played center and he was fast. Senior year, the last game against St. Phineas, this big kid whacks the stuffing out of the ball and Sean takes off. It was boiling hot, more August than May. And that's why the ball starts to drop. Not a breath of air. Sean gets under it. He goes into a slide and Ally doesn't have the wits to get out of the way. He takes Ally down. We thought he was out cold but it was just shock. Sean holds up the glove. He's got the ball. We won the game. Coach takes Ally aside after and tells him to stay the hell out of Sean's way. The two of them could've been hurt bad."

Hearing about the past was like visiting some other place, Maggie thought. The place where her father now lived.

"It was Ally getting killed that got Sean to drop out of college."

"Mom said he dropped out to go into the army," Maggie said.

Amred nodded. "Yeah, yeah, after Ally got killed."

"Sean told you that?" Lizzie asked.

"Didn't have to. Day of Ally's funeral, all the boys came in here after and Sean said he wished he'd shattered Ally's leg that day."

Maggie searched her memory for the name Ally Coen, but she knew she wouldn't find it.

"Nothing's that simple, Amred," Lizzie said.

"No, Elizabeth, some things are," he answered.

Lizzie shook her head. But Maggie agreed with Amred.

Surely when Amred showed this picture to others, he pointed out her father, giving his name and his fate in one short sentence, as though reading the last line in a book.

"When Sean got back from Vietnam, he tried to get a cab at the airport and the driver refused to take him," Amred said.

"He didn't want to drive to Brooklyn?" Maggie asked.

Amred laughed and Lizzie smiled.

"Yeah, maybe it had nothing to do with politics. The guy just figured, I'm not driving into that shithole."

"Cabs don't want to come here because they have to drive back alone," Lizzie said. "If you're going to the city from Brooklyn, you're tak-ing the train."

"Joke, joke," Amred said.

"Did he get another cab?" Maggie asked.

"Nah. He caught the train back. See, Sean grabbed the guy and pulled him halfway through the window. Airport security came running over. He's lucky he wasn't arrested."

Maggie could picture it. Easily. His temper. The thing they didn't talk about and probably never would again. It had surfaced mostly with her mother, when they were trying to get out of the house and she couldn't find her keys, or Brendan needed something for the car ride. Or when the house got too messy.

"Jesus Christ," he would shout. "Let's go."

"Jesus Christ! Look at this place. What do you do all day?"

And her mother, pressing her lips together but saying nothing in her own defense.

He'd yell at Maggie and Aidan, less often but just as loudly: "How many times have I told you —"

They knew to scuttle away. Brendan, too, had already understood. It was like the way a thunderstorm turned the night instantly fierce. Mag-gie wondered sometimes if her father even remembered afterward.

He'd fought with Eileen over the fire department. The only person Maggie had never seen him get mad at was Delia.

Lizzie leaned forward. "Santa must be coming."

Maggie looked. Across the street, kids were pouring out of the church basement and gathering on the sidewalk.

She left the bar, after trying to explain that she could get money from her mother to pay for the soda, and being waved off. The fire truck was just turning the corner, siren chirping, Santa perched on top, waving.

Maggie, waiting for the light to change, expected to hear a shout. "There she is!"

But nobody looked in her direction. Every pair of eyes was fixed on the truck.

She crossed the street and spotted Brendan with a bunch of boys his age near the front. She went over to zip up his coat. He shoved her hand away but she succeeded. Then she saw Aidan near the back, holding Rose's hand.

She stopped beside them. "Where's Mom?"

Aidan looked at her like she'd asked a really dumb question. "Inside."

"I was just gone forever."

"Huh?" Aidan glanced at her and then down at Rose, who was tugging on his hand. Aidan picked her up. She craned her neck.

"Hey, Aidan, you want me to put her on my shoulders?"

Maggie turned. Brian Grady was behind them with Danny.

"I've got her." Aidan hoisted her higher. Brian frowned, then reached forward and grabbed the two boys who were standing in front of them.

"You two, outta the way," Brian said. He tugged on the collars of the boys' coats.

The boys, who were about twelve years old, scowled as they turned, but when they saw who it was, they jumped aside. Then other kids followed suit, backing away, jabbing the kids in front of them, until Aidan was able to move right up to the truck, Rose still on his hip. Maggie moved next to him, ready to catch her if Aidan happened to let her slip.

Danny stepped up so he was beside her as Santa jumped off the fire truck into the swarm of kids.

"That's Kev," he whispered, nodding at Santa.

"My father did it once, when I was a baby," Maggie said.

"Oh, yeah?" Danny said. "That's cool."

Kevin was bellowing "Merry Christmas" and the kids were trailing behind him. Maggie shoved her hands in her pockets and followed the crowd inside.

Nobody would want to hear what she was thinking. Not her mother or her grandmother or her aunt. She missed the wild days. The lawless months right after the fire were a better match for what had happened to them.

For the first two weeks after the funeral, the wives had come to their house and cooked, cleaned and did the laundry. Poor Norah, they whispered in the kitchen.

They brought dinners in Tupperware or covered dishes and made Maggie watch where they stowed them in the refrigerator. Chicken. Lasagna. Baked ziti. It should go in the oven for this long. Turn the oven to this many degrees. Leave the cover on or take the cover off. Here is the extra sauce. Heat it separate on top of the stove. Heat, don't boil!

Can you do that?

Yes, Maggie said. Yes.

The times their mother was in bed, hunched into a question mark, Maggie set up snack tables in the living room in front of the television and put the food, right out of the refrigerator, on three plates. Then the three of them just ate Breyers Neapolitan ice cream out of the carton anyway, the boys competing for chocolate, Maggie preferring vanilla, all three of them turning to strawberry only when they had to. Their mother was sick all the time, and for a while Maggie and Aidan thought it was because of the fire.

The meals stopped coming because their mother told the wives, Thank you, but we're fine. We have to get back to normal. We have to be alone in the house. About a week after she said that, Aidan, peering in the refrigerator, said, "We're running out of rations."

Eileen brought the two of them to Key Food. "Get whatever you guys think you need."

Aidan tossed in a package of Oreos. Maggie put in Vienna Fingers. Eileen said nothing. Later, they unpacked the grocery bags together, laughing. Reese's peanut butter cups. Hershey bars. Cap'n Crunch. Entenmann's chocolate doughnuts.

"Dad would kill her," Aidan said, and Maggie agreed.

Their grandmother had forgotten their names, and possibly how to speak altogether.

When Norah began cooking again, it was deep into summer, and you could tell she was having a baby. She made the meals they'd always had when their father worked a night tour. That is, hot dogs, grilled cheese sandwiches, English muffin pizzas with French fries or Tater Tots. For a long time, dinner tasted like he would be home in the morning.

Then, strangely, not long after Rose was born, when their mother was even more tired, she began baking chicken and making meatloaf, dumping frozen peas or corn niblets into pots of boiling water, adding dashes of salt. She set Maggie to work peeling potatoes, and boiled or mashed them herself. She made them sit at the kitchen table and poured glasses of milk. Even though they were drinking milk every night again, they never ran out. They had full plates of food but no father. Soon, a highchair was in his place at the table.

Back inside the church basement, Maggie sat at the table by herself. Her brothers were sitting with all the other kids on the floor, waiting for Santa to pick up their gifts and call their names. Brendan could go up by himself. Aidan would take Rose. She had a present too. It was in front of her, still wrapped. A book, Maggie could tell.

She also could not explain, not to anyone, that time had grown confusing. The summer after her father died, she sometimes woke up on Saturday mornings certain she heard him whistling in the backyard. She ran to the mirror to see how old she was.

Rose's name was called, and Aidan picked her up and set her on Santa's lap. Their mother stepped forward with the camera. She would be the only mother to do so. The Christmas music got suddenly loud. Maggie knew that the men who'd tried to save her father were present. She tried to tell by their faces which ones had been working that day, but they looked very much the same, serious and angry, as they watched Rose get her present.

Aidan lifted her down and then hoisted her up again. She looked huge in his arms. Maggie felt every fireman in the room shift toward them. But Rose was content. Rose didn't know any better. Aidan lowered her to the floor and she started picking at the wrapping paper. For the past month, Maggie had heard people say again and again that it didn't seem possible that Rose could be turning one already.

Rose and the fire were separate events entirely, yet sometimes Rose appeared in Maggie's memories of the months right after the fire. The baby's nighttime crying was all of their crying. It confused Maggie, how her father had died and then Rose had come, as though one could not be here with the other.

CHAPTER SIX

Eileen O'Reilly Maddox

September 11, 2001

THE MOON WAS EDGELESS, with air like fog but a fog just solid enough to breathe. The moon was on fire. The moon was filled with firefighters wandering its rocky surface. Eileen knocked herself in the head a few times to make sure her helmet was still in place. She'd lost it briefly in the dark. A man handed her a bottle of water. She rinsed out her mouth and splashed some of the water in her burning eyes.

She was off the rocks and in a street — what she thought was a street. There were more people. A lot of them, in this uniform or that, were simply standing still, staring.

A hand seized her by the forearm. Hard enough to hurt through her turnout coat. She looked to her left and saw Thomas Grady. He was gray from head to toe.

He put his face close to hers. "Lieutenant!"

Eileen blinked hard. "What?"

"Get in the ambulance. They'll take you to the hospital."

Eileen jerked her arm back. "I've gotta find my guys."

"You're not gonna find them if you're blind. You need your eyes rinsed out and you need that cut looked at. Four, five stitches, I figure."

She'd been aware of the pain in her head but had been afraid to touch it, and then she forgot about it.

"We were starting the climb," Eileen said, and as she spoke she was remembering. Words, her own voice, making it real. "The windows blew out —"

"That was the first tower going down. Listen —"

"I don't know if they got out before it fell."

Chief Grady took her arm again and dragged her to the ambulance. She tried to pull away from him but his grip was too tight.

"There's no time —"

"The second tower went down almost an hour ago."

She stopped struggling and stared at him.

He let go of her and an EMT, built like a football player, leaned out of the ambulance and hauled her inside.

Chief Grady said, "Make sure they check her for a concussion. I'd love to fill your bus, but I say get these two out of here now."

Eileen sat hard on the stretcher beside a young fireman — a kid — whose hand was wrapped in a filthy, bloody cloth.

"He just did the same thing to me," he said.

The EMT started to pull the doors shut.

"Wait a minute!" Chief Grady shouted. "Eileen!"

The EMT opened the doors and Eileen leaned forward.

"You seen any of my boys?" he called.

She shook her head. Chief Grady pivoted and walked off.

The EMT slammed the doors again and banged on the roof. The ambulance started moving.

The kid said, "Father Judge got killed."

She and the kid, whose name was Ray, ended up in the empty ER together on adjoining stretchers. They didn't pull the curtain between them.

Eileen refused to put on a hospital gown. "I'm going right back," she told a nurse. "You've got ten minutes to do what you've got to do."

Ray refused too.

She did let the nurse put in an IV, to rehydrate.

Eileen's phone had a signal here, and she called Madd's cell. Since he left her a little over a year ago, she'd spoken to him only when absolutely necessary, preferring email to the sound of his voice. No answer. Then his house phone. Half hysterical, his girlfriend told her that Madd had headed in after the first tower went down. She *had* reached him after the second collapse; he was alive. Eileen said to let him know Quinn would be at her mother's.

Then Eileen called Delia and got her answering machine. Frustrated, she left instructions: Get Quinn from school and bring her to the house. Keep her with you. Madd is okay. I don't know when I'll be back.

Eileen called the school. The secretary was crying so hard she could barely get the name of the school out. Then the principal was on the line. Crisp, authoritative, calm.

"Delia picked Quinn up about ten minutes ago," Sister Ann Marie said.

"How is she?"

"Calm, with effort. Delia told her that she was sure you would call as soon as you could. I" — the nun's voice broke — "we'll be praying for all of you."

Eileen hung up, grateful that'd she'd been adopted by a woman with a level head.

She tried Norah. No answer. Irish Dreams. No answer. Aidan, Eileen knew, was not working until later in the week. He was down Breezy Point doing carpentry work. His friend owned the business.

Eileen had no doubt Aidan had jumped in his car the second the first tower was hit, but no way would he have gotten to his firehouse in Brooklyn to get his gear, and then into the city, before the buildings fell.

An older woman wearing a badge that said VOLUNTEER brought her and Ray bottles of water and granola bars. Eileen opened the water and drank half of it. She stuck the food in her back pocket.

One nurse flushed her eyes out and another did Ray's. They got a doctor each too.

"Do you know what hit you?" Eileen's doctor asked.

"A big building," she answered.

The doctor wanted her to have a CAT scan. She told him she was fine; she'd been dehydrated. Now that she knew her daughter was being taken care of, her impatience to start searching was becoming unbearable.

Ray's doctor stitched up his hand and told him to use it as little as possible. He said he'd do his best.

Eileen's forehead was stitched by a plastic surgeon who'd been at his apartment on the Upper East Side and rushed downtown to volunteer. The hospital cleared the ER, ready for the waves of the injured.

"Nobody's coming," he said.

"Nobody will be," Eileen said, "until we start pulling the survivors out."

He paused in his work, and then resumed silently. When he was done, he stepped back, satisfied.

"You won't even have much of a scar."

"Do I look like a fucking beauty queen?" she said.

"You look perfect," he said.

Eileen jumped off the gurney.

"You're going back, right?" she said to Ray.

"Jesus yeah," Ray said. "My mom says my dad was at MetroTech when he heard, and he ran in over the bridge. He's got to be looking for me."

To earn a ride back, she and Ray helped a couple of EMTs finish piling supplies into ambulances: bandages, antiseptic, masks, rubber gloves, syringes, IV bags. Then they jumped in, along with the woman who'd given them the water.

Eileen's cell phone rang. It took her a minute to get to it.

Norah's accent always thickened when she was angry or upset, and now Eileen could barely understand her. She finally realized Norah was saying over and over, "Are firemen dead? Are firemen dead?"

Eileen got her to slow down and then learned that Aidan had worked last night after all. He'd made a mutual with somebody who needed Saturday off. He never said no to overtime. His company had been sent after the first tower was hit, and before the second. He'd gone in with the day tour even though he was off duty.

The thought Eileen had been pushing away came at her like the black cloud had. Hundreds would have been climbing toward the fire.

Are firemen dead?

Hundreds.

Hundreds of firefighters are dead.

Eileen wasn't sure if she said this to Norah, or if it was her silence that told, but Norah wailed.

Norah, who'd only looked at her in bewilderment when Eileen told her that Sean was gone. Eileen jerked the phone away from her ear. Ray and the volunteer stared at it.

"Aunt Eileen? Aunt Eileen?"

Eileen put the phone back to her ear. "Rose? Rosie?"

"Aidan's not dead," Rose said calmly.

"He was still at the firehouse when they got called. His lieutenant wouldn't let him go, because he was off duty, but Aidan jumped on when the guy wasn't looking. He rode like that into the city, hanging on to the back of the truck. Him and some other guy."

"Jesus Christ!" Eileen said.

"They got jammed in traffic and he jumped off and came to my school. He, like, blew by Orlando, the security guard. But who's going to stop Aidan, right? He gets the secretary to look up my schedule and he found me in my classroom and pulled me out. We stopped in the principal's office and she told him they were trying to decide whether or not to evacuate, what was safer, do they wait for the parents and all. I guess some channels were saying something exploded in the first building and hit the second one. Aidan's all, 'It was another plane, the city's under attack, and get the fuck out of here.' Kids were starting to leave anyway. Aidan told me to go home. Walk over the bridge. Don't get on the subway. We left, and then coming up the block was Justin."

"Who the hell is Justin?"

"Nathaniel's nephew Justin! He goes to Stuyvesant. He hadn't gotten to school yet. He got off the subway and heard people on the street talking. He was coming to look for me. Aidan tells him to stay with me or he'll feed him his own nose."

Right, Justin. Eileen had met him plenty of times. A shy, brilliant boy who'd been in love with Rose since they were thirteen. Rose was polite about it.

"You listened to Aidan and just got out of there?"

"Yes!" Rose said.

As though she always did what Aidan, what anybody, told her to.

"Justin was all, 'I need my nose.' He's here with us now. So is Nathaniel."

Eileen touched the bandage on her forehead. "This was before they went down?"

"Yes," Rose said. "Me and Justin were on the bridge when the first one fell. Then we watched the other go down from the promenade."

The promenade in Brooklyn Heights, from which Manhattan looked close enough to touch. Eileen gripped the phone so hard her hand hurt, picturing the two teenagers beside each other. Tall, gangly Justin, and Rose, who barely reached his shoulder. She tried to work out the timeline. If Aidan pulled her out of school right after the second plane hit, and they watched the first tower go down from the bridge, then Rose was not accounting for a hell of a lot of time. She and Justin had probably gone to get a closer look. Or Rose had, and Justin followed. And Justin, who had his uncle's common sense in abundance, got her to get the hell out of there.

It also meant that Aidan was only blocks away on foot before the first collapse. He'd been there. Eileen bent at the waist.

Norah came back on the line. "Find him, Eileen. You have to find him. Find him!"

She was gone again, and Rose was back.

"Aidan's not dead. I promise, he's not," she said. "It's Noelle who's dead." Rose's voice broke.

Eileen's head ached. Refusing any pain medication may have been a mistake. She tried to think. Noelle worked for some Irish theater. Eileen had no idea where it was.

"She had a meeting with a guy, a banker or something, who was thinking of giving them a big donation. She wanted him to come see the theater and all but he was too busy, so he set up a breakfast meeting with her. He worked in one of the towers. Declan can't get her on her cell and keeps calling here. Aunt Aoife too."

Declan, Noelle's fiancé.

"Cell phones are fucked up, Rosie. She probably can't get through. Tell your mother to call the hospitals."

Even as she said it, she knew Norah would not be able to do it. She thought of the echoing ER they'd just left.

"Never mind your mother. Gran is on her way there with Quinn. Tell her to do it. Tell her to answer the phone whenever it rings. Can you do that for me?"

"I saw her on the bridge," Rose whispered. "For a second. She appeared and then disappeared. They do that."

"Who does that?"

"The dead."

"For fuck's sake, don't say that to her mother. Or your mother."

"Yeah, Maggie told me that too."

"You talked to Maggie? She's okay?" Eileen asked, though Maggie was more than safely out of it, in Galway.

"I told her to come home! Brendan's driving back from L.A. with a bunch of friends from the movie he was in. Did Mom tell you that he got a part? He has some lines. It's going to take him days to get here. Mom's freaking out. 'I want Maggie! She has to come home!' I can't — I can't —" Rose started crying.

"Rose, listen, sit tight. Tell your mother I'm on my way back down there to look for Aidan."

After Eileen hung up, the volunteer pulled rosary beads out of her pocket.

"The Sorrowful Mysteries. We're going to skip right to that today."

She began to recite the Our Father. Ray, beside Eileen, moved his lips to the prayers.

Eileen leaned her head back and closed her eyes.

Firefighters stretched in lines, passing buckets from hand to hand. They lifted chunks of concrete. They shouted names and company numbers. They climbed the piles of debris and jumped down into voids that were clearly unstable enough to collapse at any time.

They shouted:

"Hello! Hello! F-D-N-Y!"

"If you can hear me, say something!"

"Hello! Hello!"

Eileen found Aidan's company mustering in front of their smashed rig. They had not seen any of the men who'd left the firehouse this morning. They were organizing a search. She found the Glory Devlins, grouped together doing the same thing. They had not found anybody either, or the rig. None of them were guys whom Eileen had been with this morning. None had been in the collapses. Eileen was the first one they'd found who had been there. The captain bombarded her with questions. Where had they been sent? Whom had she been with? What equipment did they have?

"Now we at least know where they were," Nevins said. "North Tower."

"Yeah? And where was it?" Petrie said.

He was the biggest wiseass in the firehouse, a hard honor to win, but now he was serious. This morning, where had that 110-story-tall building been standing?

Eileen and the other Glory Devlins began walking. She scanned the landscape constantly for her nephew and asked every firefighter in shouting distance if they'd seen him. Aidan O'Reilly? There were a lot of body parts, some so gray they were almost indistinguishable from debris. A glint of light caught a silver ring, and they paused to look at a hand that had only the ring finger and thumb.

"What are they doing about this?" Rogers asked. "On the way down here, I saw half a leg on the roof of a car."

Nobody knew. They left it.

"Aidan O'Reilly, you seen him?"

Finally, a lieutenant who'd been in the academy with Sean paused and frowned. "Yeah, I might of. Over that way." He pointed.

"When?" Eileen asked. "Where?"

He shrugged. "I guess an hour ago. He was walking that way."

The relief made her actually grin. "You see him again, tell him his aunt is looking for him and that he'd better call his mother."

The lieutenant responded with a ghost of a smile. "Will do."

She considered trying to find a radio or leaving the site to find a phone but decided she'd wait until she'd seen Aidan herself before letting Norah know he was okay.

Eileen stayed with the Glory Devlins. Near their best estimate of where the North Tower had been, they spread out, calling, digging and climbing small mountains of debris that shifted beneath them. They ducked under steel beams so scalding hot they would burn flesh to the bone if touched. They had no tools. The tools were with the guys who were missing, or in the rig, and they had no idea where that might be either.

A man came by passing out white paper masks. Eileen took one and put it in her pocket. They might come across a survivor who needed it.

Her phone had no service. Aidan, she figured, had sought out a landline somewhere by now. He'd know better than most what his mother was going through.

Late in the afternoon, a shout went up that 7 World Trade was going down. Everybody on the wreckage ran for it. Eileen and a group of other firefighters stopped on a street corner and stood beside a fire truck. Nobody spoke. On any other day, a forty-seven-story building's collapse would be a huge job.

Once the building was down, they had to wait for the all-clear before climbing back on the debris. The firefighters she was with sat on the curb. Eileen started wandering, up one block and down another. She didn't bother looking at the street signs to see where she was.

She saw a deli and tried the door. It was open, and empty. There was an inch of ash on the floor. A cup of coffee and a doughnut sat on the counter, also covered in ash. She walked to the back. The stockroom, and yes, a black wall phone.

She dialed Norah's number. It was almost six o'clock.

Delia answered on the first ring.

"Eileen! Where are you? Are you all right?"

"I'm down here. I'm fine," she said. "Aidan? He called, right? And Norah's niece?"

Delia's silence answered the question.

Eileen didn't try to find her men. She circled the site, asking every single firefighter she passed if they'd seen Aidan O'Reilly. Tall, light brown hair. Blue eyes. She got nos and head shakes. For the totally blank looks, she added, "Sean O'Reilly's son." The younger guys said, "Who?" But if the firefighter was older, he said no, he had not seen Sean's son.

There were a lot of men looking for their sons. There were sons looking for their dads. Guys looking for their brothers, brothers-in-law, nephews and cousins.

They (whoever "they" was; no one knew who, as in what city agency, was running the operation) brought in big lights, like from a movie set, which made jagged shadows creep up the edges of the debris. Beyond the lights, it was dark.

Eileen decided to find out who was in charge of figuring out who was dead, who was missing, who was alive, and see if Aidan was on an official list.

The wreckage was beginning to rise and fall in front of her eyes. All day, she had eaten only the granola bars given to her by the woman in the hospital. When she came upon another bucket brigade, she gave them a wide berth, not wanting to be called on to relieve somebody.

A firefighter turned and looked at her, then abruptly walked away. She saw the back of his turnout coat. O'REILLY. He disappeared down a slope.

The bucket brigade knitted itself together, simply closing the space where he had been standing.

Eileen broke into a run, tripping over rocks and God knows what else. She passed the line of working firefighters and stopped. He was less than a foot away, sitting on a slab of concrete, his back to her.

"Sean!" she called. "*Sean!*"

He turned. "What?"

Norah. Eileen would not, after all, have to crush the same person twice. She tried to control her breathing as she approached him. He put his back to her again as she neared.

She stopped beside him. "You're okay?"

Aidan looked up at her bleakly.

"Where's your helmet?" she asked.

"I lost it in the second collapse. Is Rose dead?"

"Rose? No," Eileen said. "She's been home since this afternoon."

The relief on his face made him look like a child.

"I went to her school and pulled her out. I told her to go straight home."

"Which is what she did," Eileen said.

He stared at her as though trying to see if she was lying. "She never listens to me."

"Yeah, well, Nathaniel's Justin does."

"I got down here and they told me at the command center that the guys had been sent into Tower Two, so I went to find them. There were all these people coming down from the upper floors. Burned. Bleeding. An EMT who didn't have a stretcher or anything asked me to carry a woman out. The building went down when I was on my way back. After that, all I could think was what if Rose ignored me and came down here for a better look? I kept trying to imagine telling Mom that I sent my little sister out into a terrorist attack."

"You didn't know the buildings were going to fall."

"I should have left her in school, safe with her teachers," Aidan said.

Yes, that was exactly what he should have done. But there was no point in saying it.

"What the fuck do you think your mother was thinking all day with no word from *you?*" It came out angrier than she'd meant it to.

"Early on, I tried to call," he said defensively. "Nobody's phone was working. Then I found our guys who just got here. We started digging. Six guys are missing. Six! We still haven't found them."

"Ours either," Eileen said.

He gazed around the site and said, "They're dead, aren't they?"

"Yeah."

"All of them."

"All of them, yeah."

Aidan leaned forward, hands on his knees. Eileen remembered Noelle. But she didn't want to tell him when they were standing on the debris. When they were on the ground, she'd let him know that his cousin was missing.

"Up. Let's go."

"I'm not going home yet."

"You think I am?" Eileen said. "We have to find somebody with a working phone or somebody who can radio either your firehouse or mine. Get someone to call your mother."

Aidan nodded and got to his feet. They began to walk.

Eileen never mentioned how she called him by his father's name. He never mentioned that he answered.

December 1960

Eileen and Sean stood on the corner of Flatbush Avenue and Sterling Place in the crowd of onlookers. The tail of the plane was sticking up at an angle. UNITED, it said. The street was filled with debris from both the destroyed plane and the buildings it hit on the way down.

The freezing air smelled of smoke.

Eileen thought the street looked like pictures of London during World War II in her history textbook. Sean bounced on the balls of his feet. Eileen knew how badly he wanted to get closer, but the street was blocked off. They'd all heard the roar of the plane's descent.

Eileen's class had been doing math. Sean had been studying geography. Sean told her he'd just been asked to name the capital of Alaska when they heard the terrific roar from the sky. His teacher, a nun, had screamed, "Under your desks!" Eileen's teacher, who was not a nun, covered her ears and ran to the window. Then, not long after, sirens started wailing. Fire trucks. Ambulances. On and on. Within the hour, the principal announced over the loudspeaker that a plane had crashed in Park Slope. She asked them to say a prayer for the passengers.

Some mothers had come to school to take their kids home. Eileen knew their mother, as a teacher herself, would not be able to. Her work-day didn't end at three p.m. During the Christmas season, she worked Mondays, Wednesdays and Fridays, from four to eight, at the A&S on Fulton Street. Today was Friday. Eileen and Sean were supposed to go straight home, keep the doors locked, not answer the doorbell. They were supposed to call Nathaniel at the store if they needed anything while she was gone. In an emergency, dial 911. Do not call the firehouse directly. They might not be in.

The empty house never bothered Sean. Eileen, though, fifteen minutes before their mother was expected home, began sneaking peeks out the window when Sean wasn't looking. She would not have been able to explain to him the enormity of her relief when she spied the slender figure coming slowly up the block.

But today, when they met by the schoolyard gate at three, Sean said he was going to get a look at the crash. Their neighborhood was between Park Slope and Windsor Terrace. No way the Glory Devlins hadn't responded. She could come with him or go home. She said she'd go with him, and he grinned.

They stood at the front of a small crowd, mostly other kids, some from this neighborhood and a few from Holy Rosary, who'd also walked or biked over.

Eileen held her coat collar closed with one gloved hand because she'd forgotten her scarf. The other hand was in her pocket. It had snowed this morning, enough to dust the ground. Nathaniel's store, right across the street, was closed, so they couldn't go in there to warm up. Eileen supposed this was one of those days when Nathaniel didn't go to work. Usually he was open until six o'clock.

"The fires are out," Sean said. "The smoke's white. If it were black, that'd be bad."

"There are body parts all over the street."

Eileen turned to see John Maddox push past Ally Coen to stand behind her and Sean.

Ally regained his balance and stepped farther back. John was Sean's age, thirteen, but they weren't in the same class. He called Eileen Howdy Doody because of her red hair. Sean had fought him more than once. John always lost, but he was so dumb that he never seemed to remember this. Or so dumb that he thought he'd win the next one.

Sean was always so pleased with himself for having defended her that she never told him she didn't much care what the boys said about her. The boys would pick on you and the next minute let you play ball with them. The girls smiled when they said cruel things and they never turned kind.

You're from Ireland, right? How come you don't have a brogue? Where are your real parents? Are you an orphan? Is your hair the reason for your temper?

Temper. They were only repeating what the teacher said.

"Eileen O'Reilly, you have to learn to control your temper!" she'd shout when Eileen whirled around to shove a girl who pulled her hair.

She hated the girls. They were the reason for the "outbursts," as the principal called them.

Two weeks ago, she had been shoved on the stairs by a girl from another class. She had turned, snatched the books out of the girl's arms and tossed them over the banister.

Eileen had been suspended for three days. Her mother told her that when she felt herself getting angry she should count to ten. By the time she reached ten, she would be calmer. Eileen tried to explain that when she got mad, there was no time to count. For three days, she sat with Nathaniel in his store, listening to his stories of Poland before the war. He spoke of his teenage sisters, who were so pretty, boys waited outside their house to see them. He spoke of his little brother, who learned the names of flowers and trees from a book and had Nathaniel take him on walks to look for them in life, refusing to listen when Nathaniel tried to explain that he was searching for things that didn't grow in their village or anywhere in Poland. Eventually, Nathaniel kept quiet and let Miko search.

Sean looked at John, and Eileen could see him fighting the urge to shove him for shoving Ally, and the need to hear what he had to say.

"Body parts — who told you that?" Sean asked.

"My dad was there this morning," John said. "There were shoes with feet in them. He almost puked."

Eileen knew that John's father was a cop. Probably he wasn't lying.

Sean turned and looked back at the scene. He'd forgotten his hat, and his ears were bright red. Her neck, his ears. She hoped their mother didn't find out about the scarf and the hat. Their mother was always saying they couldn't afford pneumonia.

Eileen hunched her shoulders. So many firemen were walking around the wreckage that it looked like they were the only ones there, though she knew there were still cops working, because of all the police cars parked on Flatbush.

"The Glory Devlins are there too," Sean said.

"Oh yeah?" John said. "And which one of them's your real father?"

Eileen flinched. She would never ask Sean, but she thought he probably did wish one of them was his dad. O'Brien and McAleer were his two favorites. Both of them were married, though, with kids older and younger than Sean. The guys who were still single were too much younger than his mother, who had turned forty-two in November.

Neither could recall when Delia first told them about Luke and how he left. They'd always known the story. Luke O'Reilly met a lady in England during the war and decided, after he'd been back in America a few years, that he would be happier with her. It was that simple, and they weren't to make more of it and they weren't to listen to the neighbors' gossip. He was never coming back. Sean and Eileen were not to talk about the English lady.

When Sean was first due to start at Holy Rosary, their mother had said she and Sean's father were separated. Unsatisfied with this answer,

Sister Mary Alice, the principal, went to the monsignor. He had told the nun to let it be. Yet if talk of a divorce got around, parish gossip would force him to kick both children out of Holy Rosary. Then they'd have to go to public school. Eileen knew her mother didn't care if they had religion as a subject, like math or English. She just thought Catholic school would keep them both out of trouble. But Sean had a theory about Luke. Maybe he was Eileen's father too. Maybe he'd been a spy during the war and the Germans were still after him. He met the Englishwoman and the two of them had Eileen and then had to go on the run, so they sent her to America to be Sean's sister. Eileen didn't want the Englishwoman to be her real mother but she liked the idea of being Luke's daughter, because that made her and Sean blood relatives.

Lately Sean had stopped telling the stories. Eileen tried to reignite his interest. Maybe the Englishwoman was a spy too. But Sean would shrug like it was a game he'd grown bored of playing.

Sean grabbed Eileen's sleeve. "Come on. We can see better from over there."

John didn't follow them. Eileen had been hoping to go home. It was cold and would soon be getting dark. She stood shivering beside Sean, watching as two firemen carried a stretcher covered with a green blanket out of the middle of the street.

Sean nudged her. "That's a dead body."

Eileen turned away quickly and saw Amred Lehane standing behind a barricade, taking a picture. She tugged on Sean's sleeve and pointed.

Sean looked, then called, "Amred! Hey!"

Amred lowered his camera and dropped the strap around his neck. As he walked over to them, he took a loose cigarette out of his pocket and lit it. He extinguished the match between his fingertips and dropped it on the wet ground.

"Whatta you hear?" Sean asked.

"Bad business," Amred said. "This plane collided with another that crashed out on Staten Island."

"That's true?" Sean said. "All day we were hearing different stuff.

The teachers wouldn't tell us anything except to pray for the boy who survived." He pointed down the block. "Did anybody survive on the other plane?"

Eileen waited hopefully. The boy who lived was eleven years old. They'd taken him to Methodist Hospital. Her class, and she guessed all of the classes at school, had prayed for him and were told to do so again when they said their bedtime prayers. She and Sean didn't say bedtime prayers, but tonight, Eileen might. The boy was burned. Burns, Sean had told her on their walk over, burns were bad. If you got burned deep enough, it didn't hurt, but that meant real trouble. Your nerve endings were all dead.

Amred shook his head as he exhaled a stream of smoke. "No. They were all killed. But they got lucky — it went down in a field. Here, there are people missing from the neighborhood. They don't got a number yet, or they're not telling. I talked to Tommy Galton. He said two guys who were selling Christmas trees on the sidewalk are gone. Nobody in the apartment buildings so far."

"Are they sure?" Sean asked.

"I don't know. That's the cops' job. They're talking to the residents, making sure nobody was caught in one of the fires. The caretaker of the church is dead. They know he was in there. Pillar of Fire Church. How about that?"

"How many companies responded?" Sean asked.

"No numbers yet. Mayor Wagner will be talking to the newspapers again tomorrow morning. Probably Commissioner Cavanagh too. It went to five alarms. They're saying a hundred, two hundred off-duty firemen came in on their own. Heard and ran in. I'm thinking this is the biggest thing in Brooklyn since the theater fire in 1876."

"Yeah? Wow." Sean nodded, his eye fixed on the scene. "When did you get here?"

"About twenty minutes after it happened." Amred patted his camera.

"Were there body parts on the street?"

Amred dropped his cigarette on the sidewalk and ground it out. "Yeah. Everywhere. I don't take pictures of that stuff. I'm no ghoul."

Eileen scanned the scene. What used to be the plane now looked like chunks of garbage all over the street. It wasn't good enough. She wished she'd been suspended from school this morning. She and Nathaniel would have heard the plane's engine roaring, and they'd have run out of his store in time to see the plane hit the church and the church burst into flames. She wished she could have watched the whole thing, from its start to the terrible end. She didn't want to see the deaths. She was no ghoul either. It was instead a need to know exactly how such a thing unfolded. Eileen wanted to be the plane itself and the boy who lived.

"I wasn't asking that. Somebody said it. I was seeing if it was true," Sean said.

"It's true," Amred said. "The guys're not stopping because of the dark. They're bringing in lights."

"But they don't think there's a chance anybody's alive?"

"There can't be," Eileen said.

"You don't know —" Sean started to say, but Amred shook his head. "Eileen's right. They're staying for the dead."

Then Amred said he was going to try to sneak into one of the nearby buildings to get some shots from the roof. He put his finger to his lips and slipped away.

The gray sky was getting darker. Eileen had given up holding her coat closed in favor of keeping both her hands in her pockets.

"Sean?"

"Huh?" He looked at her.

"Mom's going to be home soon."

"Yeah, yeah, I know. Let's go. We can come back tomorrow." He stopped. "Hey, I bet the Christmas party gets canceled."

"You think so?" Eileen asked.

The Glory Devlins company party was tomorrow afternoon. They were always invited. The last two years, Delia had sent them by themselves.

"The guys will probably all be here."

"Well, maybe next Saturday."

"That's Christmas Eve, dummy." Sean stopped walking. "Wait! That's Hugh."

Eileen saw the fireman coming toward them. Hugh McAleer.

"You two! Your mother's looking for you," Hugh called as he got close. Hugh had six kids, mostly boys, and one was in Sean's class. The McAleers' house was one of the places Sean went without her.

"Mom's at work," Sean said.

"She didn't go in," Hugh said. "The girls are at your house, mobilizing."

"Mobilizing?" Eileen repeated. "The girls," she knew, meant the wives of the firehouse.

Hugh looked at her and his face lost the mad look. "Getting stuff together for the families who live here. Clothes, shoes." He nodded over his shoulder. "Maureen and her just came down here with some of the stuff, and your mom asked me to look for you. They're at the church on St. Johns."

He recited directions: Go down Flatbush to Eighth Avenue. Make a right onto St. Johns Place. Walk all the way down the block. The church was on the corner.

"Get your tails over there," he said.

"How'd she know we were here?" Sean asked.

"You kidding? Your mom's no dummy," Hugh said. "And Sean, listen, you should know better than to bring your little sister here. Something like this. Got it? Go on, go."

Sean's face was already raw from the cold, but even in the falling darkness, Eileen saw his color deepen. He hunched his shoulders and began walking so fast she had to nearly run to keep up.

Sean wiped his eyes on the cuff of his coat. Eileen looked away so he wouldn't know that she'd seen him. She waited until they'd turned onto Eighth Avenue.

"What does he know!" Eileen said. "I'm not some little kid."

"I know. But if I do come down here tomorrow, maybe you shouldn't come with me," he said.

Eileen stopped short but Sean kept walking. He noticed but pretended not to.

She ran a few steps to catch up and shoved him from behind. He stumbled and turned.

"I'll wear a disguise," she said. "I'll hide my hair under a hat."

Sean gave her an appraising look. "That could work."

December 1960 was already a month the guys would be talking about for ages.

Three days after the planes crashed in Park Slope and Staten Island, killing everybody on both planes — even the little boy who initially survived, plus six people on the ground — an aircraft carrier caught fire in the Brooklyn Navy Yard, two miles from the Park Slope crash. All the same companies responded.

The ship also caught fire in the morning, but there was no announcement over the loudspeaker at school. Some kids who went home for lunch brought the news back. Marian Clark, who was in Eileen's class, told her. Marian was the other girl nobody much liked, and she thought it made her and Eileen friends. Eileen ran to find Sean, who never stayed with her in the schoolyard. Marian followed. She found him in a cluster of boys. They already knew. Disappointed, she turned and walked away. Marian, with a last look at Sean, did the same.

After school, Eileen anxiously waited for him at the schoolyard gate. When Sean arrived, he told her that right before the final bell rang, he'd been called to the principal's office. Their mother was on the phone. She told him that the ship was still burning. He was not to go down there. A street corner was one thing, but the navy yard was another. He would not get close. If he didn't listen, she would no longer let them stay alone after school. She'd send them to Nathaniel's store, or she would make them come to work with her and sit on folding chairs behind the cash register.

"Do you think she means it?" Eileen said.

"Yeah, I'm pretty sure," Sean said. "Amred's probably there. He'll show us the pictures later."

They entered the silent house and changed out of their uniforms.

They were supposed to do their homework before watching television, but they never did.

Sean was restless, pacing the house. There was no news on. Eileen thought of the radio. Their mother listened to music when she was cooking, but they never touched it. Sean turned the dial until he found the news, and before long they learned that the aircraft carrier, the USS *Constellation*, had been under construction. The fire was still raging.

"The dog!" Sean said. "The guys have been gone since this morning."

Both of them put their coats on and went into the kitchen.

On a nail near the phone hung the short string of rosary beads and the key to the backdoor of the firehouse, left over from the days of Jack Keegan. Sean took the key and led the way to the backyard. He went up the ladder first. Eileen waited until he was over the fence before she went. The ladder wasn't the sturdiest. Sean unlocked the backdoor and they stepped into the kitchen.

Eileen told him to go back and wipe his shoes on the mat. The guys would murder them if they tracked mud all over the place. A call had interrupted breakfast. Plates of congealed eggs sat on the table. Eileen checked the stove. They'd remembered to turn the burner off, which was good. One time they went out and forgot. Luckily, it was a false alarm and they were back in ten minutes, but a pot had been scorched black. They sent the probie to borrow one from Delia. She told them to keep it. And to be more careful.

Sean was calling, "Burney! Hey, Burney!"

The dog came trotting into the room, wagging his tail. Sean knelt to pet him. Burney was a brown mutt sprinkled randomly with white, as though he'd walked beneath dripping paint. Fur was beginning to grow over the spot on his back where he'd been burned. He and his owner had been rescued from an apartment fire. Unable to care for the injured dog, the owner abandoned him at the vet's. One of the guys called to check on him and was told that since there was no one to pay the bills, he'd probably have to be put down. The Glory Devlins took up a collection, and when the vet released the dog, they brought him back to the firehouse.

Sean gave Burney a pat and opened the backdoor and let him out.

A minute or two later, he came back in wagging his tail, and Eileen gave him a treat. She also filled his water and food dishes. Sean left the kitchen, and when Eileen was done, she found him on the apparatus floor. The dog trotted beside her. The apparatus floor always looked huge without the rigs. He was up front near the housewatch, reading the riding list written on the blackboard to see who was on today.

On the far wall were the hooks for the turnout coats. When the guys were in and the coats were hung up and the boots placed neatly beneath them, it reminded Eileen of the coatroom at school. Sean ran up the spiral staircase and in a moment appeared in the pole hole. "Hey!"

Eileen and Burney looked up.

"I'm Joe Walsh!"

He slid down, landed on his feet and dropped to the ground. "Splat!"

"It's James, dummy," Eileen said as he got to his feet, laughing.

"Whatever. Come on."

Sean ran for the stairs, and she and Burney followed. On the second floor, they went down the uncarpeted hallway, bypassing the office, which was in the tower, and the bunkroom with its rows of neatly made beds, to the narrow set of stairs that led to the third floor. The four rooms there were used for storage. There'd been some talk of turning them into a rec room, but nothing had been done about it.

The heavy air smelled of dust. Sean started poking in some of the boxes. They mostly held old logbooks, which were kept by the housewatch and listed every alarm, every firehouse visitor. Sean liked to read them.

Eileen went to the front window to gaze out over the gray rooftops of the neighborhood.

"I wonder if the guys would mind if I moved up here."

Eileen stared at him. "Now?"

"Not now, stupid. When I can live wherever I want. If I'm a fireman here, then I can just walk downstairs to work."

He tugged a cardboard box from against the wall into the middle of the room and pulled out one of the old logbooks. He knelt and began to leaf through it, reading a line out loud here and there.

The handwriting was faded and spidery. He liked the boring entries even more than the entries about the runs the company went on, which detailed the kind of fire, the address and how long it took to put out.

"'Firefighter Carroll returned from breakfast,'" he read aloud. "'Visitor for Firefighter McDonnell.' It's dumb that it doesn't say who the visitor was."

Eileen envied how he would someday have two places to live, his house and the firehouse. They heard a sound on the stairs. She turned quickly and so did Sean.

"Who—"

He put a finger to his lips and, as quietly as he could, went to the door and peered down the stairs.

"There's nobody there," he said. "We'd have heard the guys come in."

"It must have been Burney," she said.

"That dog can't move that fast," Sean said.

They stared at each other for a moment. James Walsh was said to haunt the firehouse.

"Boo!" Eileen whispered, and Sean laughed.

April 1967

Eileen focused on getting up the stoop. She put one foot carefully in front of the other. The peppermint was losing its freshness. Halfway up the steps, it began to burn. She imagined a little smoking hole in the center of her tongue and spit the candy out. It landed in the neighbors' front yard. The Smyths didn't live there anymore. They'd left Brooklyn for Long Island.

The house was being rented now. There were three apartments, one for each floor.

One of the new people would find the half-sucked peppermint tomorrow. That made her laugh as she stumbled up the next step, cracking her knee. She hissed through the pain. They'd sat on Jackie's stoop, opening beer after beer. Jackie's mother had a couple with them and then went up to bed. She always said it was better than them drinking in Prospect Park. Now, with less than a month to go before high school graduation, most of the girls were already eighteen anyway. Only Eileen and Terry Lynch were still seventeen, because of their October birthdays.

Eileen reached the top step, turned and stared down. It had to be after midnight, but the neighborhood was never really quiet. Music was playing from somewhere. From another house she could hear shouting.

The hall light had been left on for her. Eileen kicked off her shoes and went into the living room. She knocked the lamp over. Pulling it by the cord like she was reeling in a fishing line, she set it right and turned it on.

Then her mother appeared in the doorway.

Eileen smoothed her hair. "Hey. Were you waiting up for me?"

"Yes," Delia said, but the slight hesitation before she answered told Eileen she was lying.

It was Sean she was waiting for.

"Right." Eileen turned her back, but she stumbled and pitched against the couch. She sat down, hoping it looked like that's what she'd been aiming to do.

"Why do you do this to yourself?" Delia said. "It's Thursday night and you can barely walk."

"Thursday night!" Eileen said. "Okay, I'll only get smashed on the weekends from now on. And I'm fine." Her stomach started to quiver.

"You're about to pass out."

"I'm *about* to go to sleep," Eileen said. "If you'd let me."

"Fine. Go to bed. We can talk about it tomorrow."

"I'm graduating high school in two weeks. You can't tell me what to do. Anyway, you never could."

Delia, who'd been about to leave the room, turned back, her face stony. "I absolutely can tell you to stop making a fool of yourself. You're smarter than this."

"Nope! I'm not." Eileen stretched out on the couch. The room began to tip.

If he were here, Sean would have jumped in, pointing out that he was usually around anyway. Nothing would happen to her.

"The blind leading the blind," Delia might say, but not in anger. She didn't care how much Sean drank.

When they were alone, though, Sean would tell her the same things that Delia said: You've gotta knock it off. Some guy's gonna think . . . stay away from those jerks . . . those guys are going nowhere . . . I'm not always gonna be there to drag you home before some shit happens.

But where was Sean?

Vietnam.

Eileen woke in the middle of the night. Mostly sober. Terrified, not sure where she was. It was still dark and she was covered by a blanket. When she sat up, she almost puked into her lap. Her foot hit something. A pot, the big one they used to make spaghetti. Dropping to her knees, she brought up a torrent of beer. There was a glass of water on the coffee table. Eileen rinsed her mouth and spit it into the pot.

She left the pot where it was, unable to deal with it. With the blanket wrapped around her shoulders, she walked up the stairs. The door to Sean's room was shut. No light was on. Eileen went down the hall and peeked in her mother's room. The bed was rumpled but empty. Eileen often heard her walking around at night these days. Usually when it had been a couple of weeks since they'd had a letter.

Eileen hated to remember the look on her face last year when Sean told her he was enlisting. Delia had saved enough to pay for two years of college for both of them, just the tuition. Dorm fees were out of reach.

She stared at Sean and got out only one word: Why?

Sean said he could be drafted until he was twenty-six. Why sit in a classroom for two years of school, then get sent to Nam right as he was ready to start some kind of life? Might as well get killed first.

"Nathaniel can possibly help pay tuition for two more years of school, so you'd be safe for four years." Delia was clenching her fists so hard her knuckles were white.

Of course, if Sean were an only child, Delia wouldn't have to split her money.

"No way in hell am I taking money from Nathaniel to get out of going to war," Sean said.

"World War Two was a war." Delia lost her pleading tone and was now angry. "America was attacked and we fought back. This? What is *this*? Sean . . . no. *No.*"

"I'm no coward," Sean said.

"You don't need to prove anything to a man who abandoned you," Delia said.

Sean looked fiercely at her for a long moment, then turned and left the room.

Eileen knew, and she knew their mother certainly did, when Sean set his jaw like that the conversation was finished.

Eileen tried to talk him out of it too, but only when they were alone, because she would never take their mother's side against him. He could have her college money. She was too dumb for school anyway. But he refused, adding that their mother wouldn't let her do that.

"Wanna bet?" Eileen said.

Now Eileen went back down the hall and hesitated outside Sean's door. Behind it, no doubt, Delia was sitting in the dark beside the bed. Eileen didn't dare open the door or knock. She went to her own room and crawled into bed.

After school on Friday, Eileen went straight to the convent. It always looked deserted. When they were kids, she and Sean wondered if there was really anybody in there. Maybe it was a hideout for a gang; maybe Sean's grandmother hadn't become a nun but had just run off.

Eileen pushed open the heavy gate and shut it carefully behind her, trying not to make a sound. She was lucky that she never blacked out. Some of her friends had sex without remembering a thing. She, at least, remembered everything, if hazily.

She put her white box, neatly tied with red string, in the turn with a note that said, *Please let me not be pg.*

Please turn back time so that on St. Patrick's Day she never left her mother's side at the boring reception at the American Irish Historical Society to jump in the parade. Never went to a bar afterward with all the old people and married couples she'd marched with. Never left them for the backroom where a group of four Irish guys were hanging out, celebrating their first New York St. Patrick's Day. Never went to another bar with them, and then another. Never did shots of some kind of whiskey. Never went back to the dingy apartment in the Village that smelled like old socks and worse. Never woke up in a bed naked, facing a pale, freckled back. Never crawled around a sticky floor, snatching up her clothes and putting them on in the dark. Never snuck out without saying Hey, what's your name? Never got back to Brooklyn believing it was the middle of the night, to find it was only eleven-thirty and her mother wasn't even worried yet.

Most girls would probably cross their fingers out of superstition but not real fear, not until they were later than two days. But Eileen existed because of a girl it had happened to.

When she reached the gate, she heard the front door open, and she turned away as though she'd been caught burglarizing the place.

A girl came out the front door and paused at the top of the steps. Her brown hair was pulled back in a barrette, and her round face was solemn. She wore a plaid skirt, though not a school uniform, and a blue blouse that was untucked a little in the back. She had on a pair of red-rimmed glasses.

Her attempt at being daring? At fashion?

Eileen hadn't seen Marian Clark much in the past few years, since they'd gone to different high schools. She looked the same, as if she hadn't grown up, only taller.

"Hi, Eileen," Marian said.

Eileen asked, "What the hell are you doing inside the convent?"

"I work here. Reading and sorting the mail. Wrapping up the soda bread. That kind of thing."

"They pay you?"

"The nuns don't. The diocese does," Marian said. "How are you?"

How is Sean, she meant. Eileen always made fun of the girls who fawned over Sean, and Sean would laugh. Except for Marian. Leave her alone, he'd say with a half smile. Maybe it was that Marian didn't wear lipstick. She didn't laugh loudly with her friends and touch her hair when Sean passed by. She didn't try. But Marian hoped, and it was obvious. Sean felt sorry for her.

"Fine," Eileen said.

"Everything okay?"

Eileen left without answering her.

The cookies not only worked, they gave Eileen an idea. A solution to the problem she'd only been able to focus on once she knew she wasn't pregnant.

One of the older women she'd marched with in the parade was from Sligo. She and Eileen were at the bar together.

"I'm Irish too," Eileen said, and the woman, whose name Eileen couldn't remember, said cheerfully, "All Americans think they're Irish."

Eileen explained that she actually was. She'd been born in a place called Rossamore Abbey in Galway. She was going to call the home there and ask for the name of her birth mother. Tomorrow. Maybe even tonight.

The woman had gestured for Eileen to come closer. The bar was noisy.

"They won't tell you a thing over the phone," she said. "They'll say the records are sealed and hang up on you. But I'll tell you this. Write them a letter. Do a little bit of begging. Send them money. I don't mean a twenty-dollar bill either."

Eileen took a long swallow of beer. "How much money?"

"As much as you can spare," the woman said.

It was on Easter Sunday, which Eileen spent with her mother and Nathaniel, all of them trying not to look at Sean's empty chair, that she thought of Marian, opening the nuns' mail.

The following Saturday, she took a chance and knocked on the convent door. Indeed, Marian answered.

"Don't ask me why your prayer wasn't answered," she said. "I'm sorry you're pregnant."

"I don't know why —"

"That's what girls come here for." Marian shrugged. "What are you going to do?"

"I'm not pregnant," Eileen said impatiently. "It worked."

Marian's mouth dropped open. "Oh. That's unusual."

"Listen, I've written a letter to Ireland, and I asked them to send their response to me here at the convent," Eileen said. "I haven't mailed it yet. I wanted to ask you first."

"You can't get mail to your house? Is it a man you're writing to?"

"No," Eileen said, annoyed, though she knew that was a logical guess. She'd tried to think of a lie, but only the truth made sense. The letter was to the home in Ireland where she'd been born, asking for the name of her birth mother. Her mother — Delia — would recognize the return address. Eileen did not want her to know. As for a post office box, she'd never used one before. It seemed too easy for a letter to be put in the wrong one. In exchange, Eileen would give Marian an address where she could write to Sean. Nobody else had it.

Marian studied the tips of her shoes. When she looked up, her face was pink.

Eileen wanted to laugh. Had she actually thought her feelings were a secret?

"I would do it for nothing, Eileen," she said. "Everybody should know who their mother is."

"I knew you would," Eileen said. "This isn't a bribe. It's a thank-you."

By the end of May, Eileen no longer stopped by the convent on Saturdays to see if the letter had arrived. She was weary of Marian's small head shake and pitying stare. She lay awake at night wondering if her letter had even made it to Ireland, or if it had been stolen by somebody who figured out there was money in it. Unsure of how dollars-to-pounds worked, or if an American check would be any good, she'd sent cash. Stupid, she told herself over and over. If they cashed a check, she would have at least known.

One rainy Saturday in June, she and her mother were eating dinner, mostly in silence, when the doorbell rang. Eileen set down her fork. Delia, her face stark, got up without a word and went to the door. Eileen spit a mouthful of meatloaf into a napkin, unable to swallow.

Her mother returned to the kitchen, Marian behind her.

"You can leave the dishes, Eileen. I'll get them."

Wordlessly, Eileen led Marian upstairs to her bedroom and shut the door. Marian reached into her purse and pulled out a cream-colored envelope.

Eileen took it and sat down on her bed. Not Sean, she was still thinking. Not Sean.

"I should've probably called, but —" Marian said.

"What did you tell my mother?" Eileen asked. She looked down at the envelope.

My mother.

"I said I was visiting a friend nearby and thought I'd stop in and say hi."

Eileen supposed it hardly mattered. Marian could have told her the truth and Delia would not have registered it, too relieved that it was not army officers with a telegram.

"I'll go," Marian said.

"No, stay for a few minutes at least. She'll think you came here to sell me pot or something."

Marian laughed.

"Might as well get this the fuck over with."

Eileen hastily opened the envelope, ripping it, and pulled out a single sheet of paper.

Dear Miss O'Reilly,

Thank you for your inquiry, but I am unable to answer your question.

Adoption records are sealed. What we offer the girls who come to Rossamore is assurance that their children will be sent to good homes, and that their own privacy will be protected. To give you her name would be a violation of that promise, and the law.

I understand your curiosity, and though I was not here at the time you were born, I spoke with a sister who does remember your birth mother. You can be assured that she was from a good family who were much pained by the circumstances she found herself in. They were grateful to resolve the situation through her term at Rossamore so that she could then go on with her life, which, from what I understand, she has done.

Thank you for the photograph you sent. It is indeed gratifying to learn that one of our children has grown up so well in America. Sister Bartholomew said she would have known you anywhere.

With regards to your generous donation, we thank you sincerely. Know that it will go a long way in providing for children who are in our care, as you once were.

Yours in Christ,
Sister Francis

Marian was standing against the wall. Eileen handed the letter to her. Marian read it, glancing up at Eileen twice, and handed it back.

"Um, how much money did you give them?"

"Two hundred fifty dollars," Eileen said.

"God, Eileen. Where did you get that kind of money?"

"Fifty was mine, saved up from work. The rest I borrowed." Eileen tossed the letter on the desk.

"From Sean?" Marian asked.

Eileen hesitated, then nodded.

Sean had kept the money from his job bartending at Lehane's in a fireproof box on his closet shelf, so if he ever felt like taking off, he could just go. The day before he left for basic training, Sean told her he was going to buy a motorcycle when he came back. Then he'd ride it all the way to California.

Eileen lay back on her bed. "You can go now, Marian. I won't be bothering you anymore."

———

September 16, 2001

In the center of the Brooklyn Bridge, where the pedestrian walkway widened to a platform, the five of them stopped. Norah's sister broke away and walked to the railing, and Norah moved up close behind her. Eileen and her nieces stayed back.

Maggie and her aunt arrived from Ireland this morning. At first the plan was for Aoife to visit the Pile. Norah had asked Aidan to escort them, but he refused. It was his job to find Noelle and all those like her. Eileen cautioned Norah not to argue with him. He did not need another reason to be angry right now. She offered to go in his place.

He'd been working the Pile all day and into the night, only to head back again early the next morning, ignoring his mother's pleas to take a day off and get some rest.

Eileen was also staying until after dark, but now, after a week, it was clear that nobody else was coming out alive. Quinn had been going to Norah's after school and staying for dinner. Rose's school was still closed, with no indication of when it would reopen.

Like her nephew, like all firefighters, Eileen would leave the Pile only reluctantly. The Pile was the real world. Wide awake, eating or reading the list of missing firefighters or looking at your kid, an image of it jumped in front of your eyes. Better to be on it, digging, than to be surprised by it.

In the car on the way in, Aoife changed her mind. She didn't want to see it. Maggie quietly suggested they go up on the bridge.

Eileen had not seen Maggie since she left for Ireland.

She looked younger than when she left. Partly it was her hair, which she'd let grow way past her shoulders. She was too thin, and she was quiet. Eileen hoped that a year in Ireland had given her a way forward, but she could not read her niece's silence. It might be shock and grief, or it might be the same stillness from after the baby, at first constant and then not, but never gone. Because of her own daughter, Eileen recognized it for what it was. Watchfulness. That particular way mothers have of being busy, getting done what they need to get done, while listening, always listening for a call or cry.

Maggie and Rose stood together watching their mother and aunt.

There were a few people on the bridge taking pictures of the city. Several glanced at Aoife and backed away, lowering their cameras and bowing their heads. They nodded respectfully at Eileen too, though she was sure they were mistaking her for a paramedic.

Aoife stared across the water. Norah stayed close behind her, as though she were afraid Aoife might jump. The two were only a year apart, but today the age difference looked as great as the one between Maggie and Rose. Maybe getting closer would help Aoife believe. Eileen had been noticing that with the victims' family members. With nothing to bury, their loved ones seemed to have gone to a place from which they could perhaps return. But seeing the destruction outside, beyond television, was making it real.

Still, a lot of fire families vowed to hold off on the funeral. When a firefighter was found, if he couldn't be identified by sight, then he could by the name on his turnout coat, or if there wasn't one, the company was often revealed by his helmet or his radio or a scatter of nearby tools. In that case, the man's company was summoned to bring him out. With the civilians, it was much more difficult.

Eileen felt a tug and turned to see Maggie with a fistful of her sleeve.

"I've been too scared to ask this, and because nobody's said, I think it can't be good. By the numbers alone, I think it can't be good," she said. "Danny?"

"He's alive," Rose said.

Maggie inhaled and then breathed a long sigh.

Relief, Eileen knew, that she wouldn't have to break that news someday.

"But —" Rose looked at Eileen.

"What?" Maggie asked.

Eileen answered, "Both his brothers are missing."

Aoife turned from the railing. "Could you see them from here?"

Norah nodded, and Maggie said "Yes," almost inaudibly. Rose pressed her face into Maggie's shoulder. Maggie kissed the top of her head.

Before last week, if Eileen had overheard a tourist ask such a thing, she would have laughed. From this distance, with the violence not apparent, it was as if the towers simply vanished in some peculiar magic trick, leaving nothing behind but the quiet drift of smoke rising from the skyline.

Eileen found herself in charge of welcoming the family members of the men they'd lost.

In the two weeks or so right after, they came to the firehouse to wait for news. Now, in October, the visits were tours. The wives and old-enough kids and the parents and siblings wanted to see his locker, and sit in his chair at the kitchen table and on his bed. They asked exhausting questions.

How did he spend his downtime? What's your favorite story about him? When did you last see him? How much did he know? Was he scared? Did he mention me? Is there a letter for us in his locker?

Mrs. Jimenez came to the firehouse alone. Eileen told her that Alex liked to work out in the weight room in the basement. He liked to shoot hoops in the yard. As the probie, he had to do the dishes, and he stacked them in the drain with crazy precision. Somebody had joked that he must be a mama's boy, and he'd said, "That's right," without embarrassment.

"Show me the yard?" Mrs. Jimenez asked.

She and Eileen walked from the apparatus floor into the kitchen. Silence fell and the guys jumped up. They'd been reading some of the letters the firehouse received from all over the country. There were a bunch of teddy bears on the table too. None of them could figure out why the hell so many people decided to send teddy bears. Petrie had put himself in charge of snipping off the bears' red-white-and-blue ribbons to make them less September 11–ish, so they could bring just a regular fucking teddy bear home to their kids.

Mrs. Jimenez stood in the yard in silence, her head down.

Eileen waited, her hands in her pockets.

The Friday after the attacks, Eileen had visited Mrs. Jimenez and told her the details of the morning. They were in the North Tower, just starting the climb, when the other tower fell, though they didn't know that then. She told how she'd searched for Alex, but didn't mention that she'd screamed his name, like she was his mother and not his lieutenant.

Alex! Alex! Alex!

"I told him to take the test," Mrs. Jimenez said, clutching a fistful of tissues. "He said, 'Oh, Mommy, that's for the Irish. They don't let anybody else on.' I said, 'Who ever told you that anyone is better than you?'"

"He was a good firefighter," Eileen said. One of the best ways to keep from crying was to look directly into the sun. The pain confused the eyes.

Her probie. Her responsibility. He'd been beside her one minute and so completely gone the next that they'd yet to find him.

"Ma'am? Can I show you something out front?" Eileen asked.

There was no driveway, so they went back through the kitchen. The guys jumped to attention again. Chris Jones and Tim Cassidy were out front, straightening up the shrine of candles, thank-you cards, flowers.

"Beat it, guys," Eileen said.

With nods to Mrs. Jimenez, they disappeared inside.

Two memorial plaques were set on the brick wall of the firehouse, side by side. There would be seven more. When that would happen, where they would go, Eileen couldn't yet say.

James Walsh, December 28, 1884. Sean Patrick O'Reilly, April 5, 1983.

Eileen touched Sean's name.

"This is my brother," she said. "And for a long time, I thought it was my fault."

Eileen liked the fact that Mrs. Jimenez didn't say, "No, no, that can't possibly be true."

She did say, "Why?"

"In 1966, Sean went to Nam. He wanted to buy a motorcycle when he got back. Take off across the country. He had a little over two hundred dollars saved up from bartending. Some girl once told him he should be an actor."

Eileen paused. *Sean.* She missed the way he'd laughed at his own

333

jokes, making others laugh ahead of the punch line. She missed the expression on Delia's face when he walked into a room. She missed how he'd looked at his kids. How he'd bent closer to Norah when she spoke and how he rested a hand on her back when he stepped close to her. She recalled Sean as he'd been when he left for basic training, tall and handsome, with a peace in his blue eyes he'd never have again.

Mrs. Jimenez was waiting.

"While he was over there, I stole his money. Not for anything illegal. Just stupidity. Think of it like somebody who gives money to a TV preacher."

Mrs. Jimenez nodded, though she frowned, puzzled.

"Sean came home late in 1970. I told him what I'd done. He was pissed, yeah, but more — tired." Eileen sighed. "He'd taken the test for the fire department before he enlisted. When he got home, instead of buying a motorcycle and taking off, he took his old job bartending to make back the money. I was working in the bar too and handing all my tips over to him. He met a girl there one night. An Irish girl. They got married. Right before their first baby was born, he went on the job."

"I think I see," Mrs. Jimenez said.

"Without what I did, he wouldn't have met Norah. He might have been gone from New York when he got called for the fire department. Maybe he would've made a life somewhere else." Eileen touched the date of his death. "On April 5, 1983, Sean might not have been a fireman with a wife and three kids. Soon to be four."

"You going to tell me that it gets easier with time?" Mrs. Jimenez asked.

Eileen shook her head. "The rest of the world will say you're not responsible for Alex being at the World Trade on September 11. They'd say it's crazy, there were a thousand other things that had to happen to bring him to *that* place *then*. But we know it's not crazy. My point here, what I want to say, ma'am, is that you can learn to live with it. It's hard. But you can. I have."

Mrs. Jimenez studied the plaque for a long time.

"Thank you, Lieutenant," she finally said. "Please keep looking for him."

An hour after Mrs. Jimenez left, as Eileen and the captain on duty were in the office talking logistics having to do with the next day's funerals, one of the guys came in and told her Norah was out back.

Eileen went outside, where Norah was sitting on the bench, her face tilted up to the sun. The bench was a post-9/11 thing, for the families.

"It's a beautiful day," Norah said.

Eileen had lately become aware of how she'd avoided close consideration of Norah over the years. Norah, alone in the living room after the kids went to bed. Norah, putting the Christmas presents under the tree alone. Filling Easter baskets by herself. Norah, on a date, smiling and nodding as the guy spoke, surely, every second, comparing him to Sean. Now the widows were passing her number around like it was a hotline. Now Norah's house always smelled of strong coffee, in case of drop-ins. These aren't the times for tea, she'd said.

"You all right?"

"Just getting old," Norah said. "But I shouldn't be complaining about that, should I? I told the girl you sent by yesterday that Maggie would go to her house to help sort her bills and things. I came by to get her address from you. I forgot to ask."

"Maggie? You've pulled her into this?" Eileen was surprised.

"They're getting checks in the mail and they're not cashing them, out of guilt. Thousands of dollars, Eileen, sitting in drawers. I've told them to take every penny that'll let them spend time with their kids. Maggie's going to help organize all of it. She'll go to the bank and deposit the money and help them with the paperwork. The department's trying, but they're overwhelmed. There are men whose ex-wives are still named as their beneficiaries, and men who got married but their parents are still on there and not the wife. There are girls who were only engaged, so they can't be considered next of kin. There are girlfriends of married guys who are turning up too." She shrugged. "That's not for Maggie to sort out, of course."

Eileen knew some of the paperwork mess. She could not even begin to get into that.

"She's not going back to Ireland?"

"Not yet. They're holding her job for her. She said the school will pay the rent on her flat. With Noelle being one of the Irish citizens killed, they want to do something. I suppose she'll go back for the next term. She hasn't said. She's not all right, none of us are, but it's because of Noelle. I think going away has helped her move on from the other."

Your grandchild? Eileen almost said, but that would have been cruel. She remembered the day Norah called her at the firehouse and asked her to come over when she got off in the morning. They'd had a rough night, in and out. Eileen found Norah sitting at the kitchen table, and when she asked her, impatiently, what was wrong, Norah said that Maggie wasn't going back to school. She began crying so hard that it took Eileen several minutes to understand the reason why.

There had been tears for Sean, quiet crying at the wake and funeral. Norah must have gone wild at some point, more than once, but Eileen had never seen it.

"I expected Noelle to help her more, after, you know." Norah sighed. "But she was a girl herself and she had her own life. I think Maggie scared her, the way she was, after."

Eileen recalled, too, how Noelle visited often at first, then less and less.

"But she tried at least," Norah said. "I didn't do anything but wait for Maggie to bite my head off about something. I would have been very glad for it."

Eileen thought all of them were confused by a Maggie who didn't know what she wanted. She took college classes, stopped. Worked mindless jobs. Quit. Back to Brooklyn College. Norah was right. They all just waited for the old Maggie to reappear and she never had.

"But Maggie's here, isn't she? All my sister can talk about is how she never once came to visit her daughter in New York. Never got to know her life here."

Aoife was living with Norah, in Aidan's old room. She'd set a deadline of Noelle's birthday; if she was not accounted for by then, they would have a funeral.

Eileen nodded. "How is she?"

"Not good," Norah said. "She never will be again."

"And your parents?" Eileen asked.

"My brother Cathal's still with them. Noelle was the one grandchild brought up in Ireland, you know. I'll go over whenever Aoife goes back, for the funeral, but I can't be away from here too long." She shook her head.

"Do you think it really helps, them talking to you?" Eileen asked.

"I don't know about the talking, but I think it helps seeing someone so long past it. They're looking at me and seeing that a kind of moving on does happen."

"I guess that makes sense."

"You know what a lot of them ask that I didn't think they would so soon?"

Eileen shook her head.

"They want to know why I haven't remarried."

"What do you tell them?"

"I was busy with four kids. I had to find a job once I was able to, after Rose. It was a lot to juggle. One day you wake up and you're fifty-two years old," Norah said. She touched her necklace with its gold replica of Sean's badge.

"What's the truth?" Eileen asked.

"I thought he'd come back," Norah said. "Sean. Until September, I thought so."

It was close to midnight, and Eileen was alone in the firehouse kitchen, a strange feeling after two months of constant activity. But with operations at the site officially scaled back, though not as much as Mayor Giuliani wanted, things were quieting down.

Eileen still didn't agree with reducing the number of firefighters working the recovery, but at the same time, it would probably be a good thing for a lot of them to step into some kind of regular life again. Like Aidan, now that they knew he wouldn't be going to jail.

Two days ago, the city had announced that charges would not be pressed against the firefighters from the protest who were arrested at Ground Zero after scuffling with the cops when the cops refused to let them onto the Pile. Eileen had been at the protest but she lost sight of Aidan despite her efforts to keep tabs on him. At least he wasn't the one who'd punched a cop. That guy was still in a lot of trouble.

She wondered about Brendan too. Far fewer volunteers were going to be needed, and he might find himself at loose ends. He'd been down at the site constantly since the day after his return from L.A., volunteering with the Salvation Army or the Red Cross, Eileen wasn't sure. He'd been wearing an FDNY sweatshirt and cap, both of which had belonged to Sean. Firefighters, of course, recognized them as the real deal, not tourist crap.

From the start, guys sought out Brendan when they needed something like a new pair of gloves or more eye drops. Brendan, a natural leader of his teammates but at the same time not exactly given to thinking about other people, put his charm to good use, quickly getting what was needed. Not from the city, but from businesses eager to help.

Brendan was still wearing the hat and the sweatshirt, since the weather had not gotten cold even though it was the middle of November. Eileen was beginning to wonder if it was going to stay balmy autumn forever. Thanksgiving was next week, for God's sake.

Brendan hadn't mentioned going back to California, but Eileen supposed he would after Noelle was found, or once her parents went ahead with a funeral.

She and some of the guys were in the food tent one day where Brendan was working, and one of them said something about "your nephew and his harem," and another said, "I bet that kid's getting laid."

There was some truth to it. Brendan had a crew of girls around him, eagerly doing whatever he asked. Put out some more bread? Can you run and get more forks? Eileen was sure they were out-of-towners, probably members of a church who had organized a group to volunteer for a month. New York girls would've said, "What, are your legs broken?"

But then again, maybe not. This was the new New York.

Eileen protested that this was her nephew and to shut the fuck up. The guys laughed. She pretended not to remember that a couple of guys in the group were among those who'd given her the silent treatment when she was detailed to their firehouses years ago. She and a few of the other women who'd been on the job a long time joked about it when they ran into each other on the Pile. Post–September 11 memory loss.

When she heard the knock at the backdoor, Eileen thought Rose had probably climbed the ladder in the yard to come look for Aidan.

A couple of weeks ago, his captain declared that off-duty firefighters could no longer stay at the firehouse. Everybody had to go home. Aidan had taken to coming by the Glory Devlins instead. He'd broken up with the girl he'd been dating since the summer after she gave an interview to the *Daily News* in which she called herself "a New York City firefighter's girlfriend." Rose said he was better off, since the girl was an idiot anyway.

Aidan wasn't sleeping in the bunkroom but on the third floor in the old apartment. There were still piles of sleeping bags up there from the first month, when the firehouse was crowded with not only their own people but the firefighters from Long Island who'd come to cover for them and the out-of-state people who'd arrived to volunteer.

Eileen opened the door to see Maggie, wearing pajama pants and a black coat. She stepped aside to let her in.

"I couldn't sleep," Maggie said. "I tried working on my dissertation, but I can't focus." She looked around. "I haven't been in here since I was a kid. It hasn't changed."

"Martha Stewart's coming next week to take a look, see what she can do." Eileen sat down at the table.

"That's a joke, right?"

Eileen laughed; she couldn't help it. "Yeah, that's a joke."

"Well, with all the free stuff the firehouses are being offered, I thought maybe somebody . . . Anyway, that was stupid. Aidan said he had the chance to go to Bermuda. I wish he'd gone." She chewed on her lip.

No way in hell would Aidan have left New York right now. She wouldn't either.

"You never came by after your dad died?" Eileen asked.

Maggie shook her head.

"How come?"

"Nobody asked me."

Eileen sat back. "Maybe your engraved invitation got lost in the mail."

She kept her tone light, but Maggie was too smart not to catch what Eileen was thinking. Not now.

They still hadn't found their guys, though three of Aidan's had been brought out.

"It doesn't matter," Maggie said softly.

"So, you like it in Ireland?" Eileen asked.

Maggie smiled. "I do. Once I get my degree, I have to decide if I should come back here and look for a job or stay there."

"Have you, uh, met anyone?" Eileen asked.

She was no good at girl talk. Eileen was still ashamed of the flash of dismay she'd felt when she heard, It's a girl! But her daughter had been a tomboy and was now growing into a genuine athlete. With a more even temperament than either of her parents, she had the potential to do really well in her favorite sport. Quinnie was a runner. She was patient, steady. If she reminded Eileen of anyone, it was, ironically, Delia.

"I have been seeing someone," Maggie said.

Eileen raised her eyebrows. Norah didn't know. She would have been too thrilled not to share that news.

"Is it serious?"

"He's married," Maggie said. "And he's not leaving his wife. Nor would I want him to."

"Jesus, Maggie," Eileen said. So much for the idea that Maggie was doing well now.

"But I sort of got together with someone on September 11," Maggie said. "Someone I knew, before. We happened to be together when it came on the news."

Eileen had heard stories like that down on the Pile — or rather, the Pit, as it was now being called. So-and-so is hooking up with so-and-so. Starting a relationship in the middle of a crisis was not the best idea, Eileen knew. She'd hooked up with Madd weeks after Sean died, when she was still playing Sean's death in a loop in her mind. Sean radioing for help as he ran out of air and the basement filled with water.

"You can't be dating the September 11 guy," Eileen said. "You left a few days later."

Maggie shrugged. "I guess we'll see when I get back."

Eileen nodded. She was thinking, It's late. What do you want?

Maggie pressed her hands against the table. "Do you think Aidan will be all right?"

"Eventually," Eileen said. "They found his buddy. The one he jumped on the truck with that morning."

"That was his idea, you know."

"He didn't tell me that."

"I guessed," Maggie said. "He's still beating himself up over Rose too."

"He needs time."

"He's drinking too much."

"A lot of guys are, Maggie. I don't know what to tell you. You must know as well as I do that you're not getting his ass to a therapist."

"I know," Maggie said. "Mom suggested it. He almost took her head off."

"Let him do his job. Later, when we've gotten back everybody we can get, you can try and talk him down, if you're still here."

"If," Maggie said. She nodded.

"Are we done?" Eileen rubbed her forehead. The stitches were long gone, but the spot ached when she was tired.

"No," Maggie said. "I have to ask you something. I didn't actually come here to talk about Aidan. I've been meaning to, yes, but that's not why I climbed a ladder in the dark."

Eileen waited.

"You've never found your birth mother?" Maggie asked. "I remember what you said about adoptions from Ireland being dodgy. That's how you put it. But there are reunion stories too. I've read them online."

Eileen shook her head. "It's been a long time since I've tried. The place where I was born won't give it up. The records are sealed. One nun told me she's never come looking for me, and maybe that's a lie but I have no idea. I will be happy to go into more detail, Maggie, but not now. There are nine kids from this firehouse alone who lost their dads."

"A lot of them have been to my mother's house. I've met them. I *was* them," Maggie said defensively. "One more question?"

Eileen sighed and nodded.

"If your birth mother suddenly contacted you when you were a kid, what do you think your reaction would have been?"

Eileen wanted to put her head down on the table. She took a deep breath instead.

"Adoptees fantasize about meeting their birth parents. I did. They're famous, they're royalty. They left us with our adoptive parents only for safekeeping until they could make it back. She's somebody you know already. She had a very, very good reason for giving you away, a better reason than being a kid herself. Something you can't even imagine." Eileen paused. "But if she had called up out of the blue, I probably would have been pretty confused. I would have been scared of being taken back to Ireland, away from my brother and my mother."

"You and Gran don't exactly get along."

Eileen controlled her temper with great effort. In the months after the baby was born and gone, and Maggie was walking around with shadowed eyes and looking past anybody who spoke to her, like somebody who was actually caring for an infant, Eileen had wanted nothing more than to yell in her drawn face, "What the hell did you think was going to happen?"

"That doesn't mean I wanted to trade her for a stranger with red hair."

Eileen paused again, trying for a calm, neutral voice.

"I'm guessing where this is going, and let me just say, Maggie, I don't think the parents are going to say, Sure, because of September 11, it's fine to barge into our lives."

Maggie reached into her jacket pocket and pulled out a folded newspaper clipping.

"This is from the *Irish Eagle*, an article called 'Those We Lost in the Irish-American Community.'"

"Noelle?" Eileen unfolded it.

Her eyes immediately went to the color picture in the center of the page of a very pretty woman with wavy brown hair. She was leaning against a fence, a green landscape behind her, unmistakably Ireland.

"I give up. Who is she?" Eileen asked.

"Her mother," Maggie said. "She worked in a law firm in the South Tower. They haven't found her, but they had the funeral last week."

Eileen was about to ask if Maggie was sure, but she recalled that she and Danny had met the adoptive parents.

"God, no," Eileen said. But three thousand people were dead. Why not the baby's adoptive mother?

"What's her name?"

"Me and Danny called her Grace."

"This child's parents didn't name her after Danny's dead mother, Maggie."

Maggie looked at her strangely, as though she'd made an inappropriate joke.

"Her name is Kaitlyn Rourke-McKenna. A friend is quoted as saying the family had recently gotten back from a vacation to Ireland."

Eileen repeated the name to herself. Sean's granddaughter. She could not grasp it. When she thought of Sean, she preferred to think of the boy who still had years and years to live.

"My daughter was there, in the same country, and I didn't even know it."

"Why would you? You haven't had any contact —"

Maggie shook her head once. "I feel like I should have known she was nearby."

Eileen had nothing to say to that. "Does Danny know?"

"No. He's got seven fatherless nephews to take care of. I thought I would talk to you first and then —"

"You want me to give you permission to . . . what? Call her up?"

Maggie met her eyes. "Yes, Aunt Eileen. Yes. *That* is why I'm climbing ladders in the dark."

She was quite serious. Eileen's first thought was to remind Maggie that she had rejected her adoptee expertise nine years ago and then to say that it was too damn late.

"What if, after your father died, some man rang you up and said, 'It's sad that Sean O'Reilly got killed, but it's okay now because I'm stepping up'?"

"Isn't that what the firemen did?"

Eileen shook her head. "It's not the same thing, and you know it. *Don't.*"

Maggie said, "When I was pregnant with her, you told me she'd be looking for me everywhere."

"What if she doesn't know she's adopted?"

Maggie looked so stricken, it was clear this never entered her head. "She's an only child."

"So is my kid. So are a lot of people," Eileen said. "Her father just lost his wife. I sure as hell don't think he's going to let you contact his daughter. You must realize that."

"What if he's glad that there's somebody with a connection to her who knows what she's going through?"

"Maybe he would be," Eileen admitted. "The mother died with co-workers?"

"There were sixteen others from her firm."

"She probably had friends in the group, and some probably had kids. I think it's way more likely that her father would be afraid of losing his daughter, too, and he'd never let you near her."

"I'm not talking about trying for custody!" Maggie said. "I'm talking about letting her know that I've been where she is."

"She's traumatized as hell. Then she meets you and finds out that her two uncles and a cousin also died on 9/11? How does a kid process that?"

"They said they were going to adopt again," Maggie said bitterly. "That was a lie. She's all alone."

"Maybe they tried and it didn't work out," Eileen said.

"I don't think so," Maggie said. "She told me she was quitting the big job to open her own law firm, and she obviously never did."

Eileen shrugged. "She chose her career over more kids. I've heard a million times that I'm a bad mother, if not in those exact words, because I have a dangerous job. You know how many times the guys hear it? Zero. I waited to have a baby until it was too late to try for another, and my husband left me for it. There you go."

Maggie reached across the table and took the clipping back. She smoothed a hand over the picture. "I just wish she weren't alone."

"She's got her father."

"She needs a mother too."

"Her mother got killed," Eileen said.

Maggie crossed her arms over her chest. "You were the one who told me to keep her."

"I said then you should keep your baby," Eileen said. "I'm saying now, you don't barge into the life of a nine-year-old. It's too late."

"I'm her mother too."

"Listen to me." Eileen leaned forward. "You are not her mother. You're an idea in her head, if she even knows you exist at all. She is not ready for you to be real."

"But I am real."

"I'm sorry you have to live with this kind of regret, but you don't get to give away your kid and then, when it suits *you*, walk back in."

Maggie flinched, then rested her arms on the table and laid her head down.

Eileen stood and got a box of tissues from the counter. The only thing to do was wait it out. Nobody stuck his head in the door to see what was going on. Things were that fucked up these days. A woman sobbing in the kitchen late at night was not unusual.

Maggie wasn't being quiet about it either.

After several minutes, she raised her head and wiped her eyes. She got up to throw the tissue away. Eileen thought Maggie was going to leave, but she sat back down.

"I told Danny it was my mother's fault, because she never said I could bring her home."

"Yeah? You don't get to blame your mother or Delia or me or anybody else for your decision."

"I don't anymore," Maggie said. "I gave my daughter away to pick up my life where it left off."

"And then didn't," Eileen said.

"I wasn't ready to be a mother at nineteen," Maggie said. "But I *was* a mother at nineteen. That's what I didn't understand until after I handed her off. You were right."

"Fine. Nine years ago I was right," Eileen said. "You gave her away for *your* reasons, but you need to stay away from her for *her* reasons. Her mother is dead. That is more than enough to deal with for now."

Maggie smoothed the newspaper again. "How long do I wait?"

"The technical answer is, you wait until she's eighteen. But the real answer is, you wait for her."

The funeral service at Holy Rosary was for a firefighter who hadn't been found. Since neither Eileen nor Aidan had known him personally, it wouldn't be right for them to take up a seat in the church. They stood in formation as the coffin was brought in, and when the doors closed and the Mass began, they went to Delia's.

They found Delia and Maggie in the kitchen. Maggie was filling the coffeemaker with water. She greeted them, her eyes lingering on Aidan. Eileen willed her not to ask him how he was doing. Something had sunk in of their conversation in the firehouse, because Maggie turned away and starting scooping coffee.

"Hey, how's Nathaniel?" Eileen asked. "I haven't seen him in weeks."

"Not so well," Delia said.

"Is he sick?" Aidan asked.

Delia shook her head as she explained that all of the stories on the news of the posters of the missing had hit him hard. The descriptions of what clothes they wore, the jewelry and tattoos. He looked at them and pitied the hope.

Him, as he said, of all people.

"He told me he's planning to sit shiva for his brother," Delia said. "Next week or the week after."

Eileen went still. The myth of Nathaniel's brother was impossible to separate from Nathaniel himself. All of them, she and Sean, and Sean's kids and her own daughter, had grown up on it. The lost boy.

Maggie started the coffeemaker and turned around, leaning against the counter.

"He gave me a book when I left for Ireland," Maggie said. "*Schindler's Ark* by Thomas Keneally."

Tucked between the pages, Maggie explained, was a copy of an old photograph of two dark-haired boys, one little, one much taller. On the back, in his careful penmanship, Nathaniel had written, *Mikolaj Kwiatkowski*, a sentence in Polish and beneath it, his phone number.

There was a separate note to her on a slip of paper.

Dear Maggie,

Please look.

Your friend,
Nathaniel

"And the thing is, I did. I *do*," Maggie said. "He would be an old man now, but I look for the little boy." Abruptly, she left the room.

Eileen wanted to be anywhere else. Back outside the church, at the funeral. At the Pit.

She thought it might have been the most she had ever heard Maggie say at once.

"Yeah," Aidan said. "When you don't know where someone is, you look for them."

"You leave her alone, Aidan. Enough." Delia spoke quietly. "*Enough.*"

Did Delia know? Eileen thought Maggie might very well have told her.

"With Nathaniel, his brother — would we go?" Aidan asked without meeting Delia's eyes.

"No," Delia said. "Just me."

He nodded, relieved.

"You'll come to Nathaniel's funeral, though, no matter what firemen are being buried that day. He'll be gone in six months," Delia said. "If that."

"Hey, Gran —" Aidan started to say, but then Maggie came back to the kitchen, startling all of them.

"This is it." She held up a white-edged photograph. "I probably shouldn't put a hole in it, but —" She pinned it to the bulletin board next to the little rosary. "Tell him that we still look," she said. "Or I'll go visit him and tell him myself."

"I'm going over there later," Delia said.

From her seat, Eileen could only make out their shapes, tall boy, small boy. Nobody but their family would ever see the photo there, but at the same time, the gesture was oddly hopeful.

Nobody spoke for several minutes, then Brendan and Rose came into the kitchen.

"Nancy Drew said you were probably here," Brendan said as he sat down at the table. Rose bent over and hugged Aidan, who pulled away, patting her hand.

She sat down in the chair next to his.

Aidan asked Brendan, "Why aren't you down at the site?"

"I'm taking a break." Brendan ran a hand through his hair. "They don't need as many of us now."

"Will you be going back to California, then?" Delia asked.

Brendan shook his head. "Not yet."

"When will they start filming your movie again?" Rose asked.

"They started up weeks ago. It's not New York. Life out there got back to normal much faster," he said. "Well, normal for L.A."

Eileen thought the rest of the family looked as surprised as she was.

"What about your part?" Delia asked.

"I told Eddie to recast me. We hadn't shot much. Right now I'm in a minute of film. I figured, what if I get out there and then I have to leave again? It's okay."

Leave, Eileen thought, if they find Noelle.

"Isabel told me that her dad's service is probably going to be next week anyway. You have to be here for that," Aidan said.

"When did you see Isabel?" Rose asked.

"I showed her around the site last week." Aidan frowned at the table.

Eileen waited for Rose to tease him, but she said nothing.

"How are they doing?" Delia asked.

Aidan shrugged. "Isabel's mom still wanted to wait, but Isabel put her foot down and said that they had to do this before Christmas. She's going to ask if you can sing, Rosie."

Rose nodded. "Sure."

Rose had sung at a service early on. Eileen couldn't remember whose it was, but since then she'd been in demand for the funerals. "Wild Mountain Thyme." "The Parting Glass." "Danny Boy," of course.

Maggie set mugs of coffee in front of her and Aidan.

"What about me?" Rose asked.

"Wait until college, when you really need it." Maggie sat down next to Brendan and brushed his hair behind his ear.

"You need a haircut," she said.

Brendan pushed her hand way. "Hey, I'm a Californian now."

"I might not even go to college," Rose said, raising her voice. "I was thinking I might take the test for the fire department."

"I might become a priest," Brendan said.

"I can run into burning buildings," Rose said. "You can't give up girls."

Brendan grinned. "Sex. You mean I can't give up sex."

Rose laughed but Aidan glared. "Don't talk like that in front of her."

"She's not five. She knows what sex is," Brendan said.

"It's true," Rose affirmed.

"Both of you knock it off," Delia said. She got up from the table and chose an apple from the basket on the counter.

"College credits are a requirement for the job now, Rose," Eileen said. "Lucky for me, they didn't used to be."

"What about being an EMT?" Aidan said. "You should look into that."

Eileen thought that was a far better idea but still couldn't quite see Rose fitting into either profession. But, hell, she was only seventeen.

Rose shrugged. "Maybe."

"There's a service at three o'clock today at St. Stephen's, by the BQE. You're coming, Aunt Eileen, right?" Aidan asked.

"I'm going home after this," Eileen said defensively. "I told Quinn I'd spring her from school early and we'd go to the movies."

"Bring her to the church." Aidan sat up straight. "The ranks are stretched thin enough. It's good of the departments from out of state to come and all, but our guys should have as many of their own in the crowd as possible. Quinn's not a baby. She can handle it."

"She's young enough," Delia said without looking up from the apple. "She should get to see her mother for a few consecutive hours and not at a funeral."

Eileen wasn't sure if she was being complimented or criticized for being too busy. She let it go, like with Madd. Quinn had reported that her father kept reminding her that no matter what you see on the news, firefighters weren't the only rescue workers who died. Twenty-three cops. Thirty-seven Port Authority police. Eileen was tempted to tell her daughter to point out that the FDNY still won by a landslide: 343.

"I have two funerals the Friday after Thanksgiving. How's that?" she said. "Both guys I knew. One I worked with a couple of years ago and the other was my first captain."

Delia turned from the counter. "You mean the first firehouse you were ever at, when you were still rotating?" She set the knife down.

"No, my first permanent house," Eileen said. "The one Sean got me into."

"He did?" Aidan sounded pleased.

"He never said so, but I figured he asked around about who wouldn't put up with any bullshit. Not too many of the guys were happy about getting a woman firefighter." She looked at Rose pointedly.

"That was decades ago," Aidan said. "Nobody gives a damn anymore."

"Things are better, but they could hardly be worse," Eileen said. "Sean did a good job, though. My first night, a couple of the guys pulled some shit, and the next morning, Cap locked the whole company in the kitchen and told them, not in front of me, I heard about it later — let me see if I can get his exact words — he told them that I had the right to prove I could do the job, and if they kept it up, he would transfer each and every one of them out to Staten Island. He tells them, You can take a fucking boat to work, then sit around playing Boggle all day." Eileen laughed.

"And he's dead," Rose said wistfully.

"No," Delia said. She gripped the counter. Her face was suddenly pale. "I looked on the list. There was no O'Hagan killed."

"It's not O'Hagan," Eileen said. "I never had a captain named O'Hagan. It's Phelan. Flynn Phelan. In-like-Flynn. That's what they called him."

"That was his stepfather's last name. I didn't think —" Delia drew a ragged breath. "He's dead?"

"Yeah. They haven't found him." Eileen fixed her eyes on Delia. "Did you know him?"

"He lived here a long time ago." Delia still had hold of the counter.

"In the neighborhood?" Maggie asked.

Delia didn't answer. She was breathing with effort.

Brendan jumped up. "Hey, Gran, maybe you should sit down."

He brought her his chair and Aidan stood up too, probably pissed at himself for not thinking of it first. Eileen didn't move, assuming Delia would have more patience with her grandsons.

Aidan crouched by the chair. "Are you having chest pains?"

"No, don't be ridiculous. Boys, both of you, sit down."

Her color was better. Aidan and Brendan backed off and returned to the table. Maggie put her cell phone back in her pocket.

"Where was he, Eileen? He had to be retired, no?" Delia asked.

"He was. But he was at MetroTech for something," Eileen continued. "A bunch of guys who were at headquarters ran in over the Brooklyn Bridge when the first tower got hit. Captain Phelan went to look for his son. I ended up in the ER with him that morning. I didn't know who he was until later."

"His mother?" Delia asks. "Flynn's mother, is she still alive?"

Eileen shrugged. "Cap had to be in his sixties. I guess she *could* be."

"She's my age," Delia said. She stood up and resumed slicing the apple.

Eighty-three, Eileen thought. She glanced at Maggie and saw from her expression that she was doing the same math. The math of mothers and daughters and how long a life might be. *Wait for her.*

Delia brought the bowl of apple slices to the table and set it in front of Aidan. As she moved away, Maggie looked up at her.

"Cabbage leaves," she said.

Delia said softly, "Claire."

The pumper was parked in the street outside Holy Rosary. A single row of FDNYs were lined up in the street. Behind them were three lines of firefighters in out-of-state uniforms. Eileen wasn't sure where they were from. It was good of them to come so close to Thanksgiving.

Rose had run home to fetch Norah, and she and Aoife were both in the crowd of civilians standing outside the church.

The FDNY pipe and drum band had been dividing and dividing itself among the funerals in order to give every man his due. Today four pipers were poised to play. The church bells tolled and the crowd quieted. The church doors opened and the assembled firefighters saluted as the pallbearers started down the steps. The pipers began to play "Going Home."

A dark-haired woman appeared at the top of the steps with a similarly dark-haired little girl and boy on either side of her. She was ashen, but dry-eyed. The children looked to be between the ages of five and eight. The girl, who was older, held the helmet.

Eileen tensed. Most churches, it seemed, had steep steps. At nearly every funeral Eileen had been to since September, she had waited, hardly breathing, yet the women, somehow, never fell down.

Reliable's funeral home was packed for evening visitation, which was from seven to nine p.m.

The wake was being held on one day instead of two because there were so many funerals in the neighborhood. From what Eileen had heard, the director of the funeral home gently suggested the shorter wake to all the families.

The rest of her family went in the afternoon, but Eileen had two funeral Masses to go to in the morning, both guys she knew, and Aidan had three wakes in the afternoon, all on Long Island. She and Aidan decided they'd go together in the evening, and Maggie waited to go with them.

Eileen and Aidan were in their dress uniforms, and when they walked in, the crowd quieted and parted as they approached.

Maggie poked Aidan in the side. "Now the Red Sea, Moses."

"Shut up," he said, but his mouth lifted.

Eileen got a little hope out of it. Maybe Maggie, as the outsider, could get him out of his head for a while after all. Aidan still wasn't listening to his mother's pleas to rest. Rose had a solo in some memorial concert held at her school, and he didn't go. Eileen didn't blame him for not wanting to listen to a bunch of teenagers sing "Stand by Me" and "Fire and Rain." But it had been a big deal to Rose, and according to Norah, the principal had been hoping to have an actual fireman there.

Nice that nobody in her own family thought to ask her.

Lizzie Lehane stood next to the closed coffin, clutching a handkerchief. A photograph of her brother as a young man was propped on an easel beside it. Amred stood in front of the firehouse, a camera around his neck, smiling shyly, his posture self-conscious, awkward.

Amred, who had been out the door, camera in hand, minutes after hearing the very first news report, when it was still an accident of bizarre and tremendous proportions.

"It's the city!" Lizzie apparently had called after him, astonished because Amred hardly ever left Brooklyn.

"This is the big one," he'd said, knowing, of course, that this would be precisely the way firefighters in firehouses in all the boroughs were putting it.

Amred, who got to the World Trade before nine-thirty and started snapping photographs.

Amred, who had a way, firefighters said, of getting close to the action while remaining invisible. The day after a good fire, Amred would turn up at firehouses with a box of cookies or a cake from Agnello's (he knew well the firehouse rule: Always come knocking with your elbows) and a roll of film he'd just developed. The photos would be incredible, yet afterward nobody could remember him being there. He was eighty-three and showed no signs of slowing down.

Amred, killed in the collapses, his camera found beneath him, unscathed.

Maggie thought this was amazing, but Aidan was unimpressed. That was the way of the Pit. The camera should have been bagged and tagged as evidence, since the site was technically a crime scene, but Amred was found by guys from Brooklyn. His body could not be identified by sight, but his camera had his name on it.

One of the firemen took it. It was not like Amred could've caught the terrorists on film running from the scene, Aidan quoted the firefighter as saying; the cocksucking motherfuckers were in pieces just like the people they killed. The fireman brought the camera to the Glory Devlins, as was proper, since Amred was their buff.

As firefighters who'd grown up in the neighborhood, Eileen and Aidan went together, in dress uniform, to tell Lizzie that her brother had been found. Aidan had handed her the camera, the film still inside it.

There was a line for the casket, but people stepped aside for them. Aidan ignored them, but Eileen nodded her thanks.

Lizzie stood up straight, her face lighting with pride. She glanced at the coffin as if she wanted to tell her brother who had come to pay their respects.

Lizzie clutched Maggie's hand first.

"The ball field named for my dad at the park," Maggie said. "That wouldn't have happened without Amred."

Eileen knew this was true. Amred started the petition a year after Sean was killed, which was easy to forget, since the firehouse took over the fundraising efforts.

"He never got over it," Lizzie said. "Never. He always said Sean would have gone all the way to the top." She looked at Aidan and smiled.

Aidan lowered his eyes.

"Amred always wanted to open a museum for the Brooklyn fire department," Lizzie said. "I know there's the museum in the city, but he wanted one for just Brooklyn. Maybe a gallery. He had so many pictures. There are a few nice ones of Sean. I can't look at the ones from . . . from 9/11 yet."

Aidan's jaw was working. Maggie reached a hand toward him but Eileen grabbed her elbow and shook her head. Maggie crossed her arms over her chest.

"It's way too soon," Aidan said.

"I'll have to do it," Lizzie said.

Eileen didn't know if she meant open a museum, which was hard to imagine, or simply go through the pictures. She stepped up and shook Lizzie's hand. "I'm sorry for your loss."

Quick was best, she'd learned.

Usually at a wake they would linger, but as if they'd agreed ahead of time, they headed for the door. The three of them were almost out of the room when Eileen stopped.

"Fuck," she muttered. "Wait here."

She left her niece and nephew staring after her.

Eileen bypassed the line without a glance. The man talking to Lizzie quickly stepped back, and Lizzie looked at her expectantly, as though she'd been hoping for something more.

Eileen told her that at least a dozen guys from Brooklyn spotted Amred around the command center, snapping away like mad. Every single one reported telling Amred the same thing:

Get out of here, you dumb fuck.

For all of Amred's admiration of New York City firefighters, for all the guys who scorned it, mocked it, fed off it, ignored it, Eileen wanted Lizzie to know, she had to know, that now her brother was being talked about in firehouses all over Brooklyn. In the kitchens. They were talking about that day, how Amred was there, and all the days he was there, never asking for anything but to see the action up close. Firefighters were saying that Amred Lehane was the best. The best of his kind.

Without discussing it beforehand, she and Maggie and Aidan headed across the street to Lehane's. Through the first beer, they talked about Norah and the fire widows.

Eileen said she was trying to give the girls other names too, now that Norah was back to work full time. Even though Irish Dreams was hardly busy, because nobody wanted to fly.

"If they go out of business because of this, after everything Mom's worked for, then, Jesus." Aidan frowned into his beer.

"Mom thinks a lot of people are going to want to go to Ireland next year," Maggie said. "Pilgrimage."

"Are you going back?" Aidan asked.

"Aunt Aoife's going to want Noelle to be buried at home, not here. I don't think Declan will say anything. Since they weren't married yet, he can't argue, really."

Aidan didn't answer.

"You don't think they're going to find her, do you?" Maggie said.

"No." Aidan drank from his beer.

Eileen supposed the lines around his eyes would disappear when he started getting more sleep. But perhaps not. He was twenty-seven years old. At twenty-seven, Sean had only eight years to live.

"I know you'll come to Ireland then, for the funeral or the service," Maggie said to Aidan. "But you should maybe stay for a bit."

"I'm not going on vacation."

"I didn't mean that you'd take a vacation, for fun," Maggie said. "But it might not be a bad idea to spend a few days."

Eileen was about to jump in, head off the coming argument.

"Maybe in a few months," Aidan said, surprising Eileen, and Maggie too, because her eyebrows went up.

She only nodded, though.

"More than a few," he added. "Maybe in the summer. It'd be nice to get away from the heat."

Eileen almost laughed. Aidan loved the beach. He planned to buy a boat and often talked about buying a house in Breezy Point someday.

"Maybe in August," Maggie said, so softly Eileen almost didn't hear her.

"Maybe," he answered.

They were silent for a moment. The bartender came over with more beers. "From the guy over there."

The three of them turned to a man sitting at the bar. He was white-haired, clearly Irish. He raised his glass, and Aidan did the same back.

"Nice of him to include me even though I'm not in uniform," Maggie said.

"Hey, Maggie, listen," Aidan said. "You heard we found Brian Grady? They positively ID'd him yesterday."

"Mom told me. It was in the paper too," Maggie said. "I left Danny a message at his dad's house, but I don't expect he'll get back to me."

"Yeah, he's not in a place to do that right now," Aidan said. "I was in the crew that found him. Did you know that?"

Maggie shook her head.

Aidan hadn't said anything to her, but Eileen heard the story going around the Pit. A crew was digging when they saw the yellow stripe of a turnout coat. They kept going until they saw the letters GR. Then some tools marked with Brian's company were uncovered. All work stopped while the company and Chief Grady were called. When he and Danny arrived, the guys who'd made the find officially stepped off, except for Aidan, who asked to stay. Danny said he could.

Eileen understood. It wasn't just that Aidan and Danny were buddies from the neighborhood. Aidan wanted to be there because of the little girl neither he nor Brian had ever seen, and now Brian never would. He wanted to tell his niece someday that he helped bring one of her uncles out.

Kaitlyn, Eileen thought. The name had not left her head since Maggie said it.

"I'm glad you were there," Maggie said quietly.

"Danny was saying he's got a job ahead of him, with the boys," Aidan said. "Separating the stuff in the press from what Kev and Brian were really like. But that's true for everybody, right?"

The estimate, Eileen had read, was over one thousand. One thousand children of the FDNY who had lost a father.

"The hero stuff?" Maggie said uncertainly. "I'd say they were."

"Call them heroes, yeah," Aidan said. "But not fucking saints."

"They were good guys," Eileen said, "but not a halo among them."

The press kept pushing the idea that the firefighters ran into the buildings heedless of the danger. That phrase. The guys had been repeating it around the firehouse: I'm going down the basement *heedless of the danger*. I'm cooking these meatballs *heedless of the danger*. I'm cleaning these tools *heedless of the danger*.

In speaking of the courage it took to run into burning buildings, the press made it sound like firefighters didn't give a fuck about "the danger," whether it came from a smoldering hardware store that looked like an easy job or two skyscrapers hit by airplanes.

But the guys on 9/11 had not died gladly. Neither had Sean.

Eileen had been thinking a lot about how she'd told Mrs. Jimenez that if she'd not stolen Sean's money, his life might have gone differently.

In altering Sean's fate, Eileen had always imagined sparing Delia the loss of her child, freeing Norah from widowhood and saving herself from missing every single day the person she'd loved best until her daughter was born. And that was different. Quinn was a whole other category.

Until recently, though, Eileen had not considered what Sean would have done if he was given the choice of dying at thirty-five or driving out of Brooklyn into a much longer life. Presented with it at twenty years old, he would have gone away. What young guy wouldn't? But suppose it was the night before the fire, when Sean had been a husband for eleven years and a father for ten?

Eileen looked now at her niece and nephew, both coming up on thirty, their lives on the courses they'd chosen, or found themselves on. She thought of Brendan and Rose, still starting out, and of Norah, who had planned to stay in New York for a year and ended up spending a lifetime, most of it grieving.

Sean would not have chosen a life without her, a life in which his kids never existed. And he would not have run from the fire that killed him, even if he had been told it would.

The whole job was the pull between knowing you could get killed and thinking you'll always find the way out. Knowing what will happen if you don't. Going in anyway.

On ordinary days, nobody gave it much thought. And that, Eileen thought, was what you didn't understand unless you did the job yourself.

The counselors who were assigned to the firehouses didn't get it. Are you having nightmares about September 11? This was always their opening question. Nightmares and flashbacks were supposed to be the worst September 11 symptoms.

But over and over, Eileen dreamed about September 10.

The day is quiet as the whole summer has been quiet. O'Mara says, as he has a hundred times since August, Something big's coming, I can feel it in my bones, something big. And Bonafedes growls, Say that one more time, Billy boy, and I will choke you to death with one hand. They catch a couple easy jobs, nothing much, nothing to write home about.

Late in the afternoon, they go to Key Food to shop for the meal. The dog jumps on the rig. She's a terrier–sewer rat hybrid who'd turned up at the firehouse a few months ago. Eileen and Jimenez the probie and Killian and Ayres move through the supermarket's aisles at peace. Nobody sees them and begins to cry. Nobody comes up and says, You're saints, you're heroes, God bless you, and thank you, thank you, thank you. An old lady at the checkout clutching a can of Pledge and a five-dollar bill leans away from them, wrinkling her nose, because, yeah, they

do stink, not of corpses and gray dust, but only the way they are supposed to, of black smoke from a good fire and garlic and something
else, something like salt, like the sea.

And they jump back on the rig with pork chops for the meal and
the dog lunges for the shopping bag and Rowley says, I'm going to kill
that fucking thing, and Smithick gives the dog an M&M, laughing,
and they are all laughing, and it is a good day.

In the dream, Eileen wakes to find a pristine blue and yellow morning, the most beautiful day in the history of New York City. A Tuesday.
Always Tuesday.

CHAPTER SEVEN

Katie McKenna

September 10, 2012

KATIE HESITATED on the sidewalk, studying the handsome three-story brick house that looked like neither the cloistered convent it used to be nor the museum it now was. The black iron gate was open, as was the front door. The tall windows were raised, and from inside came the murmur of a speech, or perhaps a prayer.

The website for the Brooklyn Firefighters Museum advertised a brief memorial program for firefighters and their families. She guessed it was on the tenth for the sake of the families who wanted to go to ceremonies at Ground Zero. It started at one o'clock and it was nearly one-thirty. She had procrastinated too long before setting out.

Katie told herself she had to go inside the museum to justify missing class only two weeks into the semester. She should go in because she'd taken the trouble to wear a new skirt. It was red and gold plaid, not the sort of thing she often wore, but she'd bought it for today because it looked like a kilt, and that seemed appropriate for the occasion. She'd decided on a T-shirt instead of a blouse, and her black shoes with the square heel that she'd bought because they reminded her of an Irish hard shoe, from when she'd taken step-dancing as a kid. Only after she escaped it did she get sentimental over Irish dancing, which had made her feel like she was trying to stand still and fling herself apart at the same time.

She walked up the front steps and into a vestibule between the outside door and an inner door. On a table, a book lay open for guests to sign. After picking up the pen, she paused. Long ago, she'd stopped hyphenating her last name and usually gave it little thought, except this time of year.

Katie R. McKenna.

A compromise. She set the pen down. There was a mirror on the wall above the book. As a kid, she'd played a trick with mirrors. She took off her glasses and stared at her reflection until it began to slip and blur, rearranging itself to form other features. She tried to keep her reflection still, like a photograph, but it was always fleeting, gone with a blink that she tried to hold back as long as possible. When it came, the unstoppable blink, Katie was left with her own face. Freckled, but lightly. The blue eyes and very dark hair that got her labeled Black Irish. She heard that one a lot.

Katie turned from the mirror. She left her glasses off and put them away, even though nobody here knew her, with or without them. She felt better seeing less well, as if her own blurry vision would be transferred to those looking at her, letting her hide in plain sight.

"You okay?"

A whisper.

Katie turned to see a girl of about her own age, standing behind her and carrying a guitar case.

"Oh, I'm sorry! I thought you were a kid." She laughed softly. A heavy auburn braid hung over her shoulder, its tip nearly touching the belt of her jeans.

"It happens," Katie said.

The skirt probably made her look like an overdeveloped sixth-grader. She should have worn all black.

The redhead hoisted the guitar case. "I've got to get this to the talent, who brought the wrong guitar. Sorry again."

"Rose O'Reilly?" Katie said without thinking.

"Yes, Rose is singing. Do you know her?"

Katie shook her head. "Just from her website. I've never heard her sing in person."

"She's just going to do a couple of songs. They want to keep the program short since the speeches and things went on too long last year."

Her tone, as she spoke, had grown more absent. She reached up and touched her braid, tugging it as though she were ringing a bell.

"Do you know any firefighters?" she asked.

"No," Katie said. "If that's okay, I mean —"

"Oh, sure." She hefted the guitar case again. "I'd better move it. I'm all the entourage Rose has. Stay. Look around."

She walked into the hallway and stopped, turning to stare for a moment before continuing on, practically running.

Katie stepped forward and then hesitated.

To the left was the gathering. A man with a pronounced Brooklyn accent was speaking. The rows of white chairs were filled. Most of the men wore blue dress uniforms. More firefighters stood in the back of the room, including a few bagpipers.

"— and as we commemorate the eleventh anniversary of September 11, this museum stands as a testament that the FDNY has a long and storied past. Before the FDNY, we had the BFD. The Brooklyn Fire Department, when we were our own city, before the Great Mistake of '98 . . ."

Katie wasn't about to stand conspicuously in the back of the room. She went instead through the open door across the hall and into an office with a small desk. Immediately, she envied whoever got to use it. There was a fireplace and, on either side of it, built-in bookshelves. She went over to check out the books and saw that they were all about the FDNY, or September 11, or the FDNY *and* September 11. *Report from Engine Company 82. 102 Minutes: The Unforgettable Story of the Fight to Survive Inside the Twin Towers. Brooklyn Firefighters: Photographs by Amred Lehane.* Katie ran her finger over the orange letters of the title.

"— now Rose O'Reilly, daughter, sister and niece of New York City firefighters, is going to sing for us."

Katie crept closer to the doorway, almost tiptoeing.

Rose began to speak. "I'd like to dedicate this song to my father, Sean O'Reilly, and to my aunt and my brother, who hasn't been thrilled by all the love from the press —"

The crowd laughed.

Aidan O'Reilly, Katie thought. *Eileen O'Reilly.*

"— even though I've finally gotten him to admit that without the attention, this place never would have happened. I can't leave out our black sheep, Brendan, who went and became an EMT. I am not going to make the joke about how at least he's not a cop —"

Again the crowd laughed.

"— not today, when we're remembering everybody who lost their lives that morning and those who are now losing their lives to illness. But given where we are, this is especially for all the members of the FDNY who have made the ultimate sacrifice, long before and long after September 11.

"First, I'm going to start with a song that Mary Fahl wrote for the FDNY, about 9/11," Rose said. "Many of you will probably recognize the tune as 'On Raglan Road.' It's called "'The Dawning of the Day.'"

Rose began to sing.

Katie slipped out to the hallway and went into the next room. It was unfurnished. Framed photographs hung on the white walls, hemmed by the molding. More were presented on easels. Through an open pocket door, she could see another room, much the same. She looked up at the two photographs displayed on the mantelpiece and stepped closer to see them better.

The photo on the left was a black-and-white shot of a fireman standing beside the open door of a fire truck, as though he'd just jumped down, his gaze intent, not aware of the camera. Beside it was a photograph of Aidan O'Reilly on September 11, leading a bleeding woman away from the burning towers, which appeared in a corner of the frame. Because this photo was in color, his blue eyes were a focal point.

Rose was singing "Wild Mountain Thyme."

Squinting, Katie read the label next to the photo, which told the story of its discovery in 2007, on a roll of film found among the belongings of the photographer's sister after her death. The photographer himself had been killed in the collapses. When the picture was first published, Aidan O'Reilly was misidentified as a firefighter who had been killed, and this was taken as fact for almost a day, before he stepped forward. In the one interview he gave, he said he did so only so the press would stop bothering the family of the other firefighter.

Katie recalled that she'd read the interview quickly and dispassionately, though with some of her old resentment for the way the deaths of the firefighters were made out to be the main event of the attacks.

Rose announced "The Parting Glass."

Katie knew that would be the last song. It always was. When the song ended and the applause finished, Rose thanked everybody for coming. The museum was open, she reminded them, as was the garden. Chairs scraped back. A burst of conversation began.

Katie slipped out the front door, not daring to peek in the room. At the bottom of the stairs, she turned right and stepped onto a cobblestone walk that she assumed led to the back of the house and the garden. She was not brave enough to stand and watch the crowd enter the hallway, but she was not such a coward that she would leave altogether.

She rounded the corner of the house and stopped when she saw a side door that was ajar. Distracted by her own curiosity, she opened it wider and looked inside, where she saw a narrow, unlit room. The museum was clearly using the space for storage. Stacks of boxes lined the wall. Shovels, rakes and other gardening supplies hung from hooks.

Katie stepped in. At the far end of the room was a window with a heavy mesh screen, like a confessional in 1950s movies about the Catholic Church. It was blocked by a dark wood panel from the other side. Katie realized what it was. She'd read about the convent on the museum's website. The cloistered nuns inside would open it to speak to visitors. Beneath the screen was the turn. Katie went over and gave the cabinet a spin.

When she heard two voices outside, she glanced around the room for a way out besides the door she'd entered from. A rectangle of sunlight fell across the wooden floor. Rose O'Reilly came in, and behind her the redhead with the braid.

"We saw you duck in here," Rose said, "and we were wondering if you could settle a bet?"

"A bet?" Katie repeated.

"I believe you saw my tall cousin on the way in?" She nodded at the redhead. "Quinn said you were even smaller than me, and I said that was hard to believe, so we've come to find out who's right."

"Five-foot-seven is a perfectly average height," Quinn said. "Anyone over five-five looks like a giant to you, that's all."

Katie took a step back. "Well . . ."

"I prefer 'small' to 'short,' even though one of my best friends says it makes me sound like an elf."

Quinn laughed. "Justin?"

"Who else?" Rose said. "It's dark in here. Where's the light?"

"Are you blind?" Quinn turned around and flipped a switch that Katie hadn't noticed. A dull yellow light filled the room.

"Not much better," Rose said. "And no, I'm not blind. I'm not the one mistaking adults for children." She turned to Katie. "You must be — how old? Twenty?"

"Yes," Katie said.

Rose's blue eyes did not leave Katie's face. Katie stared back.

Rose sighed. "I'm getting old. Lucky I'm a Sagittarius. We don't dwell on the past. I'm going to guess from your inquisitive nature, poking around in here and all, that you're a Leo?"

"No," Katie said.

Quinn laughed. "Nice."

"I'm a Virgo," Katie said.

Rose frowned. "Ah, but on the cusp?"

"The cusp of what?" Katie asked, confused.

"Of *Leo*. You're on the edge, right after Leo, just into Virgo. Your birthstone is peridot, not sapphire. For which I'm sorry. Sapphires are much prettier."

Both Rose and Quinn were looking at her expectantly, but Katie could not bring herself to surrender her birth date.

She showed them her bare fingers. "I don't exactly wear a lot of jewelry. My ears aren't even pierced. I can't say I ever minded peridot."

Rose and Quinn exchanged a look. Rose lowered her chin, but so slightly that Katie could not be sure it was a nod.

"Well," Rose finally said, "how did you hear about the museum?"

"I saw the event posting on your website," Katie said. As soon as the words were out, she wished she'd thought of a lie.

"A fan!" Rose said. "Well, I won't make you ask for my autograph, ah — I'm sorry, what's your name?"

You tell me, Katie thought.

Katie knew the story of Kaitlyn. Her father wanted to name her Antonia, in the Italian-American tradition, where the first daughter is named for the paternal grandmother. Her mother, though, didn't think it matched their last name, and she was also sure it would be shortened to Toni. They'd chosen Kaitlyn from a baby-name book, in spite of her mother's worry that it was too popular.

And it was. She'd never been the only Kaitlyn in her class. She wished they'd kept looking.

Katie sometimes Googled her name. "Katie McKenna" brought up her Facebook page. Her profile picture was of herself and her mother standing in front of a pub in Ireland called Rourke's, though she'd cropped out the sign. The picture was Katie's favorite, even if her father had been standing a bit too far away, and even though she clearly recalled the thought she had in the moment before he clicked: Rourke's isn't my pub. Sometimes, like a child playing hide-and-seek, she took that picture down and put up an image of the Book of Kells, or something similar.

If she went more official, up came a *Newsday* article that named Kaitlyn Rourke-McKenna as the daughter of Laurel Rourke-McKenna, who was among the missing in the World Trade Center. She was Kaitlyn McKenna in an article about her father and Emma's upcoming wedding — "9/11 Widow and Widower Find Happiness Again."

"Katie," she said.

Quinn looked sideways at Rose, who only smoothed the skirt of her black dress.

"Well, if you haven't seen the garden yet, Katie, you should take a look."

A low buzz. Katie glanced at her own bag, but Quinn was reaching into her back pocket. She looked at her phone.

"Text from my mom."

"Your mother can text now?" Rose laughed.

"Yeah, she finally figured it out. But she spells all the words out. *We are heading back to Delia's. Where are you?*" Quinn laughed.

"We did disappear on them," Rose said. "Bad news, your mom's pissed off. Good news, Quinn, you won the bet. Katie is smaller than me."

As far as Katie could see, subtracting for shoes, she and Rose were just about the same size.

Reconnaissance.

That was what Katie had told herself when she got on the F train to come here, a street map of Brooklyn tucked in her bag because she'd never ventured this deeply into the borough before. Before she could think of an exit line, Rose said, "Hey, Quinn, maybe you should head over to Gran's."

"Sure."

Why? Katie thought with a touch of panic. Why send her away? She felt less conspicuous as one of three, even if it was illusory, since she was the object of their attention.

Rose added, "Can you please do me a big favor and grab my guitars and take them over there?"

"Got it." Quinn smiled at Katie and ducked out the door.

Rose went outside after her. "Quinnie! Wait a sec!"

Katie glanced around the room again, hoping she would spot another door.

Instead, she saw a display of photographs encased in glass. Many were daguerreotypes of unsmiling men and women, some middle-aged, some young, and there were also black-and-white Kodaks. Nothing in color.

She wheeled around when Rose burst back in.

"I had to beg Quinn not to tell my brothers that I brought the wrong guitar. I'll be twenty-nine in a couple of months," she said, "but once the youngest, always the youngest, you know?"

"I'm an only child," Katie said.

Rose didn't seem upset, the way people usually were. What a shame! Why? What happened?

"Oldests and onlies are supposed to be the smart ones," Rose said. "The youngests are dumb but charming."

"Well, I'm not an only anymore," Katie amended. She felt her face heat but Rose didn't laugh. She waited.

"When I was thirteen, my dad and stepmom had a baby, and then a year later, another one."

"Brothers? Sisters?"

"Boys," Katie said. "I'm away at school, so I don't get to see them much. I know I just made it sound like I forgot them. I didn't. The kids are . . . Emma's. And my father's, of course. Brown eyes. They both look just like him."

She told herself to stop babbling. Though she hadn't meant it that way, it sounded like an invitation for Rose to comment on the color of Katie's eyes.

Indeed, Rose started to say something, but Katie, flustered, interrupted.

"What's with these pictures? Do you know?"

"Those, yes," Rose said. "The nuns were allowed to bring one picture with them when they entered. But in true Catholic Church fashion, there were rules attached that were probably totally the whim of the mother superior. The sisters weren't allowed to keep them in their cells." Rose stepped up beside her. "Look."

She pointed to a sepia photo of two little boys. She tapped the glass.

"This one the nun kept with her. When she died, they found it, along with instructions that she be buried with it. Obviously, they weren't followed." Rose tucked her hand in her sleeve and used it to polish the glass where she'd touched it.

Katie studied the photo. The boys were both under six years old and almost certainly brothers.

"My mom wants these photos to be their own exhibit. The history of the convent and all. Some of her fellow board members want to keep it strictly about the fire department. Bit of infighting going on."

Norah O'Reilly, Katie thought.

"But I can tell you this," Rose said, grinning. "Mama Bear will win."

The silly nickname pierced Katie. "I tried, Kit-Kat," her own mother said once, about being a stay-at-home mom. "Lasted six whole months. I nearly went nuts. No offense."

Katie had laughed. Nobody else's mother talked like hers.

"She's determined," Rose said. "And sort of dating the museum's president, not that she'll admit it."

"Sort of?" Katie said.

"The president of this nonprofit organization." Rose waved a hand. "It's all-volunteer, so they're not violating any code of conduct. It's pretty funny. She's been in this country most of her life but she's still Irish enough to pretend nothing's going on," Rose said. "Stephen is a widower. He and his wife lost their sons on 9/11, and then Mrs. Crowley died a couple of years later."

"They were firemen?" Katie asked.

"Yes. And Stephen was. At his wife's funeral, a lot of people said she died of a broken heart. Mom said that was ridiculous. Nobody dies of grief. The only people who say that are the people who've never grieved. Otherwise, they'd know it wasn't so easy. You don't get to just die."

Katie nodded, uncertain if Rose was waiting for her to ask how her mother could know this. But then Rose continued, "Mom was planning a trip to Ireland for the Crowleys through her travel agency. They never made it. About a year after his wife's funeral, Stephen started going to Irish Dreams, to discuss taking a trip by himself or maybe with his daughter. It took my mom a while to catch on that he was visiting her. Then they both got involved with the museum, and there you go. We all wish she'd marry him."

"She won't?" Katie asked.

"She says it's too late, but I think it's because she doesn't want to leave her sister alone. My aunt lives with her," Rose said. "Her daughter died on September 11."

Noelle Byrne, Katie thought.

Katie fidgeted in the silence that might have simply been a respectful pause and not an invitation to share. Years ago, people used to do that whenever 9/11 was mentioned.

"Aunt Aoife came over from Ireland after, and she never went back, not to stay."

"On September 11 . . ." Katie reached up to take her glasses off, then remembered she wasn't wearing them.

"Yes?" Rose asked.

"My friend's father was killed."

Owney's face came quickly to mind. Nice save, she imagined him saying with a quirk of a smile.

"After 9/11, he and his mother kept moving," Katie said. "They spent the off-season living in empty houses in the Hamptons. Sometimes his mom was caretaking, and other times she was renting. You can find decent rents in the off-season."

"You too?" Rose asked.

"Me too?" Katie repeated.

"I mean, you're from the Hamptons?" Rose asked. She probably thought that Katie and Owney were neighbors or former high school classmates.

"We lived in Manhattan until I was nine. Then we were in Southampton for a couple years, and now my dad and stepmother are in Sag Harbor. I'm *not* from Long Island. I'm from the city."

"Hey, sure, if you were nine before you left," Rose said agreeably, holding up a conciliatory hand. "No Long Islanders here."

Katie flushed. She hadn't meant to sound quite so vehement. But it was true that when she drove to the house in Sag Harbor, in spite of the road she was on, some part of her expected to arrive, not at the pretty white house with black shutters and generous front porch, but their building on the Upper West Side. She would take the elevator up to apartment 6R. The five rooms would be unchanged, with throw rugs in blue and green on the hardwood floors, black-and-white prints of city scenes on the walls, and the small terrace overlooking the court-yard that her mother always cited when her father argued they needed a house with a backyard.

"Just so you know, Quinn's very good at keeping secrets. She's got the blood of a pretty crooked cop running through her veins."

Quinn was not, Rose surely meant, at this very moment telling every O'Reilly at her grandmother's house about the twenty-year-old Virgo she and Rose ran into at the FDNY museum.

Before Katie could formulate a response, Rose said, "I'm engaged."

She held out her left hand.

Katie, confused, looked down. On her ring finger Rose wore a clad-dagh ring, heart out. Left hand meant she was taken, Katie knew. Heart out meant unmarried.

"Oh. Congratulations."

"Right now this is my engagement ring, but on our wedding day" — Rose slipped the ring off and turned it right side up — "Xavier will pop it off, turn it around and slip it back on. Zave is a filmmaker. He writes and directs. We're broke." She put the ring back on upside down.

"Part of me wants to walk down the aisle alone, but my oldest brother would be very hurt. He's got three sons, and he jokes that he's fine with that because I wore him out. I think he really wants a girl, though. We all think they'll give it one more try. That's the joke, Aidan says. Once you're outnumbered, you might as well keep going."

Katie nearly second-guessed her assumption that Rose knew she was talking to someone whose parents had not been able to have children. But most people were that casual about having babies. They could be. Perhaps she was wrong to expect any O'Reilly to understand the other side of the story. Katie pushed aside her disappointment.

"Aidan deserves this moment, if he wants it. He's never disappeared on me," Rose said.

Who had? Katie looked at her, but Rose didn't turn.

January 2012

Eanáir. Fuar. Sneachta. Geimhreadh.

The Irish words turned to frost as Katie whispered them, alone on the path that cut through the center of campus.

January. Cold. Snow. Winter.

After Beginning Irish, when the teacher's accent and her own enthusiasm were still fresh, Katie always felt as if she might yet piece the whole language together. In this flush of confidence, she liked to speak out loud. Usually, after about an hour, she was back to the reality of long words stuffed with consonants and a grammatical structure whose rules sounded simple, but proved baffling when applied to actual sentences.

Leabhar. Peann luaidhe. Múinteoir.

She could almost see the syllables in the blue winter light.

Book. Pencil. Teacher.

Since she'd tried to learn Irish as a child, returning to it at nineteen gave her a strange sense that she had indeed once spoken it, but let it fall away.

Though she kept her voice to a whisper, Katie could have shouted and nobody would have heard. It was early afternoon, January 6, the Feast of the Epiphany. Since winter intersession classes didn't begin until next week, the campus was almost entirely deserted. She had come back early because, since mid-December, she'd been taking Beginning Irish at the McNally Irish-American Heritage Center, which was a fifteen-minute drive from the college.

Katie was walking swiftly from the parking lot to her on-campus apartment, where she had a bedroom to herself but shared the rest of the space with three other girls.

She left the path and cut across the lawn where, according to a photo on the website, students had friendly snowball fights in the winter, and in the spring sat reading and strumming guitars. Katie, now midway through her sophomore year, had never seen anybody do either. The school drew its student body from neighboring towns along the Hudson River, and many students retreated to their parents' houses from Friday afternoon through Sunday evening. On weekends, Katie often felt like an orphan abandoned at a boarding school over the holidays. "Campus life" was not something she'd thought to ask about. But then, she'd never seen the school until after she got her acceptance letter.

The three-day-old snow was hard-packed, and Katie's boots did not leave a trace as she walked. She thought it fitting on this day when she was seriously considering that she should indeed disappear. That is, transfer out of this quaint, decent college in upstate New York, where she would probably choose English literature as a major next semester when she had no choice but to declare one.

Her college GPA was high enough to nullify the grades she'd earned during her junior year of high school, those C's and D's that canceled the life she'd been headed for, at least in theory, since kindergarten. Columbia. NYU. Vassar. Stanford. Johns Hopkins.

Today as she was leaving class, Katie had stopped, one arm in her coat, to ask the receptionist-registrar if the class on *Dubliners* was filled yet. She hadn't planned on taking it, but the thought of the coming semester, which would include math for non–math majors and biology, made her pause.

Dubliners was still open, Mrs. O'Dea said, and then offhandedly asked if Katie wanted her to email a list of schools that offered Irish studies as a major. McNally's liked to keep people paying for its classes, Mrs. O'Dea added, but Katie was young. Her interest in Irish culture seemed to be more than a hobby. Get a degree. Make it pay.

"Yes," Katie managed to say. "Send me the list, please."

That moment, Katie thought now, was like the morning after a bad hangover, when you open your eyes and sit up, stunned to be cured.

She started hurrying, not because of the cold but because she hoped that Mrs. O'Dea had sent the email already.

Back on the path, Katie rounded the corner, skirting a patch of ice, and then she stopped, confused at the sight of her father pacing back and forth in front of her door. On Friday afternoons the restaurant was open; he should be at work. Then, panic. Ben and Will. If it were Emma, her father would have stayed with the boys and sent one of his cousins to pick her up.

She'd turned her phone off for class and hadn't bothered to turn it back on. How long had he been waiting in the cold? She passed by him and unlocked her door. He followed her inside, rubbing his gloved hands together, as she shut the door and leaned against it.

"Who is it?"

As soon as she spoke, Katie realized that there was only one reason, besides a recent accident or death, that he would have driven two hours to see her, unannounced.

"Katie —"

"They found more of Mommy," Katie said.

Her father nodded. Katie nodded once. She started to unbutton her coat, but stopped.

"Something they've had, or —?"

"Something they've retested."

Retested, he meant, against the DNA sample her grandmother had given, or maybe from whatever they'd culled from her mother's toothbrush, which they'd handed over in a Ziploc the week after. *Laurel Rourke-McKenna.* No brothers. No sisters. Abandoned by her father when she was six. Her only child a procured daughter, though she'd always sworn it did not matter.

We waited so long. It's love that matters, not blood.

At least it had not mattered until her mother was lost in the city and blood was the only thing that would find her.

"You didn't have to drive all the way up here to tell me," Katie said.

"Of course I did." He cleared his throat.

Emma must have made him. He looked tired. She never thought of him as aging, except when she considered her mother, who had been forty-six when she died. Her father was now fifty-seven.

"Katie?"

"Closure," she said, borrowing a word from the old days.

They arrived back in Sag Harbor at four o'clock in the afternoon. Ben and Will had been sent to a neighbor's for a playdate.

Katie hefted her backpack, in which she'd hastily tossed enough clothes for the weekend, and said, "Well, I'll just —"

Her father and Emma exchanged a look.

"We'd like to talk before the boys come home," her father said.

Katie held back her sigh and perched in an armchair, and her father and Emma settled on the couch.

"Emma and I were thinking that we shouldn't have a service. We'll just take care of it ourselves."

"You were *thinking?*" Katie said. "She was my mother."

Twice already they'd had the grave opened to bury keepsake urns, pretty little boxes used to divide ashes among family members. The casket from November 2001 held her mother's locket with Katie's baby picture in it, a silk scarf that had been an anniversary gift and a selection of photographs.

"And she was my wife," he said.

"Charlie," Emma said, nearly whispering.

Considerate, patient Emma. She liked to talk things through, and she often repeated what was said to her as proof that she was listening.

Katie marveled at how selective her father's memory had grown. He seemed to have forgotten that they'd lived in an apartment where the sound of her parents' raised voices was as constant and unremarkable as the footfall of their upstairs neighbor or sirens wailing outside.

"Okay. I understand what you're saying. You're over eighteen now," he said. "You let us know what you decide to do, then."

Katie nearly said, Hey, no, wait. But she caught herself. She looked at Emma, expecting her to protest.

But Emma nodded. "Maybe it's better this way."

Wordlessly, Katie left the living room and headed upstairs. She should not have come back here, but there was no way she could have told her father that when he'd driven two hours to fetch her.

The boys' baby pictures lined the wall going up the stairs. Her mother used to make fun of people who'd decorated their homes that way. A sincere lack of imagination, she'd called it. Katie spent more time than she should have scripting her mother's reaction to her own photo, which was on a shelf in the family room. Beside it, in a matching silver frame, was a picture of Emma's husband Philip, who'd called to say that everyone in his office was evacuating and he was about to start down the stairs.

Katie's bedroom was on the third floor. The staircase was hidden behind a door that she'd initially thought was a closet until the real estate agent opened it with a flourish. Later, when asked for her opinion, Katie said she loved the house, but she meant she loved that door.

Katie's bed was in the corner, beneath the slanted ceiling. She crawled under her blue quilt and simply lay there, fighting the strong arm that was clamped around her waist, pulling her into the past.

The first time, there had been a congratulatory feel, as if her mother had been wandering in circles around lower Manhattan and could, at last, sit down. The second time, what they'd found had been recently discovered in some bit of road that had been paved over.

Katie got out of bed, turned on her computer and opened her email. She typed "O" and clicked owney.zinn@gmail.com when it popped up.

Owney, who had just turned twenty-one, was spending this winter break in East Hampton with his mother. They were living in an eight-bedroom house on the beach, caretaking for the owner, who would not put a big toe on Long Island until Memorial Day weekend.

As children, Katie and Owney used to see each other once a year at the Bentley & Sackett Christmas party. He and his parents had never been at any of the barbecues held up in Westchester at the enormous houses with backyard pools. Violet was a secretary. She'd been in the group of six whom her mother gave permission to leave after WTC 1 was hit, when they were merely witnesses to the catastrophic accident across the way. No one knew why Laurel didn't go with them.

Though she saved Owney's mother, Laurel could do nothing for his father, across the way in the North Tower, above the fire.

Owney's father, Gray (born Gary) Zinn, had been a painter and sculptor with a residency in unused office space in the North Tower, leased by an arts organization with a long name Katie could never recall. Violet, who was a poet, was the one who'd heard about the residency and suggested her husband apply.

Katie could still recall her surprise the day she and Owney ran into each other by chance in Sag Harbor. They'd both tagged along with their parents on errands as a way to get to BookMarks, the used-book store by the supermarket. It was only weeks after her father and Emma's October wedding. Autumn was slipping into winter. Those in town were there to stay. She'd been twelve, and Owney thirteen. They were both browsing Fiction, not Young Adult.

"Read this," she heard.

Katie turned with her hand out and took the book, *The Quicken Tree*. She read the description on the jacket flap and then looked up.

"You too?" she said.

"There's a lot of us here," he said.

And Katie imagined a whole network of half orphans on the East End, refugees from the city. Indeed, an entire community of families like hers who'd lived in spaces the size of attics, with Manhattan at large for compensation, and who, in the acrid, final months of 2001, fled to a place nobody would think of attacking, trading the city for houses where they could lose each other around corners, down hallways, up staircases, gaining through grief a measure of autonomy.

She'd once said to Owney that it was a pity the second identification had not come after college applications were safely in. But the call came only two weeks into Katie's junior year of high school, the year colleges judge you by. Katie had never paid much attention to this warning, which began the moment high school commenced and increased in pitch throughout her sophomore year.

The day after her mother's third funeral, Katie cut her afternoon classes for the first time. While walking away from the building, she saw, in the park across the street, a group of kids she'd barely ever noticed, except to roll her eyes when they gave joke answers to questions in class. The jokes were not even close to clever. That day, Katie went to the movies. The next time she cut class, she joined them.

The group of six existed in a kind of netherworld at the school, not popular, not jocks, neither brains nor delinquents. Misfits, Katie supposed, might be the best word.

At first they accepted Katie with amusement, for the tourist she was, but took her more seriously after she demonstrated an almost uncanny ability to buy beer without getting carded. Her height was an advantage, she explained. She wore jackets one size too big and kept them zipped. The bored clerks at delis and 7-Elevens assumed that no fourteen-year-old would be bold enough to put a six-pack on the counter without giggling. It didn't work all the time, but her success rate was impressive.

Even when they were ostensibly friends, Katie saw the group collectively, barely able to tell one from the other. Her teachers sounded like the grown-ups in Charlie Brown cartoons. She took the SATs with a hangover that made her feel like she was on a roller coaster every time she raised her head to ponder an answer. She ignored her curfew. When her father lectured her, she had to sit on her hands to keep from biting her nails, because even in the middle of rebellion, she felt the pull of pity.

He probably told Emma that things had changed after Laurel died. Maybe he really thought so. He had been the one to pick up Katie after school. He'd cooked dinner, enlisting her assistance with simple chopping and slicing, carefully explaining why they were changing up the recipe. At least a couple of nights a week, the two of them ate alone. As Katie got older, he was more likely to order in than cook, and when he did, he no longer asked her to help. She blamed herself, certain he'd figured out that cooking bored her. Katie recalled his unhappiness as an almost palpable thing. Its exact start she could not date, but surely long before that final summer.

After the boys were born, Katie began to understand that it had not been just the failing marriage but a more complete dissatisfaction. Her otherness did not distance him; her singularity did. A lone daughter was not the family he had imagined.

As a widower, her father had not merely started over. It was like he'd gone back to his twenties and corrected the mistakes he'd made in choosing his career, in choosing his wife. He reset his entire life.

All that work, and his peace was being disrupted terribly by the blue-eyed teenager who lived under the eaves of his beautiful home.

It was Owney who pulled Katie back from her ledge. He had been warning her for months that she needed to quit her new friends.

Still, he was the one she called at two a.m. one Saturday morning, late in June, a few weeks after the end of the school year. Panic was rapidly sobering her up. She was somewhere in Queens, she told him. In a strange house. She'd been at a party and this guy said he knew a better party. She'd left with him. Owney calmly told her to find a piece of mail and look at the address. She did, and read it to him over the phone. She stayed at the front window, casting nervous glances at the sleeping forms sprawled on the living room floor. It was more than an hour before a car came slowly up the block and stopped in front of the house. Katie practically dove into the passenger seat. Owney waited until she'd buckled her seat belt before driving away.

Now, from beneath the covers, Katie sent Owney an IM.

How do you have a funeral for a toe bone?

It took him ten minutes to respond.

Big toe is Methodist. Keep a stiff upper lip. Second toe Jewish. Do it right away. Next, Catholic. Get a priest to bless it. Next Hare Krishna. Airport joke too obvious & in bad taste. Little toe, hippie. Hire girl singer-songwriter.
No really?
Ashes. Scatter.

By eleven o'clock, the house had settled. Emma and her father were morning people, as her mother had been. Katie, though, had always been a night person, even as a toddler, which had frustrated her parents greatly. They told stories of her at age two, wide awake and calling to them as late as ten o'clock at night.

She was on her computer, Googling the colleges in Mrs. O'Dea's email, browsing their websites. Admissions. Academics. Photo Gallery. Campus Map. Ask an Alum.

Owney was a night person too, so Katie was not surprised when her phone buzzed and she saw a text from him saying he was in front of the house.

Katie crept downstairs to let him in. Owney took off his sneakers and followed Katie up the steps, carefully placing his feet exactly where she put hers, which impressed her, since he never had any call for slyness, given his mother.

In her room, Owney settled on her bed and crossed his arms loosely over his stomach.

Katie leaned against the door. "Remember that time I was in love with you?"

He laughed.

"I should have slept with you," she said.

They had been a couple only briefly, in the time after Queens.

In the crackdown, only he was allowed to visit, because her father liked him. They started dating, in a way, since she was not allowed out on weekends. After more than a month of house arrest, which she found oddly restful, her father eventually let her go to Owney's, which at that time was a three-story house in Montauk, minutes from the beach. The owner, burned once by partiers, let Violet stay at a winter rent.

His mother was seeing someone then and she was gone a lot. Katie and Owney wandered the house, choosing whichever bedroom struck them. Lighting. The view. A queen-size bed. A balcony.

But again and again, Katie pushed his hand away when he reached for the button on her jeans. Finally, he asked, "Do you think you inherited some gene that short-circuits birth control?"

"You don't give away a baby you were trying to conceive."

He pointed out that her birth parents had probably not used anything.

After two months, near the end of the summer, Katie said they should break it off. He was going away to college; he should start out at school unencumbered. She had not meant it, but Owney agreed they should split. It had been a mistake for him to think she was ready, so recently returned from her wild months.

Now Owney laughed from his place on her bed. "Maybe we give it another shot when you're old enough to drink and I can take you out for real."

"Great. It's a date for a year and seven months from now." Katie moved to sit on the edge of her bed. "I told Dad and Emma that we'll cremate and that I'd take care of the ashes myself."

Her father and Emma had nodded somberly, barely able to mask their relief. Very few of her mother's friends would have come to another service. Laurel Rourke-McKenna had not been lonely in life, and Katie was not sure how she had ended up so in death. She supposed it was simply going on too long.

"Okay," Owney said, "next is to get yourself listed as next of kin. Then tell them you don't want to be notified anymore."

His mother had done just this. Violet preferred to imagine that her husband had simply vanished into the day's beautiful sky.

Owney was certain that he had jumped. Gray's work in the last year of his life had been about fire and flight. Premonition, Owney believed. Only he had seen the pieces that were meant for an exhibit set for spring 2002, and he was now working to re-create them from memory. Last year, he had begun sketching from notes he took a long time ago. Owney wanted proof.

When he was younger, he'd resembled Violet, with his dark hair and the kind of slenderness that made him seem almost fragile, like the survivor of a childhood illness. But it seemed that with each year out from September 11 he looked more and more like Gray, gaining inches of height and a new solidity. Katie imagined it happening the more confident Owney grew in reviving what had been destroyed, as if his father wanted to bequeath to his son the kind of hands that could manage the work. His eyes were the same light blue as his father's, but Gray's vision had been perfect. Katie would not be surprised if Owney suddenly tossed off his glasses one day and, from across the room, began counting the freckles on her nose.

"And while you're at it," Owney said hesitantly, "I think it's time to ask for your birth mother's information."

Katie touched her hair and then let her hand flutter to her lap. "Some stranger can't replace my mother. It's not getting her back. You're living vicariously."

"Maybe," he said, surprising her. She'd thought he would laugh.

"You're not getting Laurel back. But, something."

"A woman who wants nothing to do with me, or a woman who tries to act like she *is* my mother."

"Something. Better than a blank," Owney said. "At least find out from the lawyer if she even wants to be in touch with you," he said. "And I'm tired of the Bartleby answer."

This time she did laugh through her tightening throat. *I would prefer not to.*

Katie had spent her eighteenth birthday turning away from her father's expectant gaze and small encouraging smiles. It was evening before Katie realized that he wanted her to ask for the paperwork so he could be rid of the burden of knowing.

Katie looked down at her folded hands.

The thought of arranging a meeting, either over the phone or by email, left her shaking. She could not imagine walking into a room knowing that she was about to see the woman whose body she'd once shared. The nervousness was so intense, Katie wasn't sure if it was like the thought of coming face-to-face with a monster or somebody terribly famous.

"You chase after your own reflection," Owney said. "I don't think you know you're doing it. We pass store windows and you turn and look every time."

Katie felt her face flush. "I'm a raging narcissist, that's all. Now you know."

He laughed. "Hell, we can probably guess her first name. Maureen? Mary? Tara?"

"Margaret."

"Right, Margaret," Owney said. "Deirdre. Shannon."

Katie stood up and went to her bookshelves. Like most photography books, it was broad and did not align with the neighboring novels. It was in plain sight on the third shelf from the top, the last one she could reach without a chair.

Katie ran a finger down the spine. In orange type, *Brooklyn Firefighters: Photographs by Amred Lehane*. She slid it off the shelf and went to stand beside the bed. She held it up for Owney to see.

The firefighter on the cover was standing in front of a fire truck, grinning at the camera. He appeared to be around thirty or so, and his eyes were very blue.

She climbed on the bed and sat next to Owney, her shoulder touching his. She opened the book to page 42.

"See, this is the cover image? And here he is, dead." She brushed her hand over the image on page 43, which was a black-and-white shot of a covered body on a stretcher being carried by a contingent of grim firemen. Only the big fireman's boots were showing.

"On 9/11?" Owney leaned over to get a better look.

"No, no. Sean O'Reilly was killed in 1983," she said.

"1983? Okay."

"I think he's my grandfather."

Owney was hard to surprise. But his eyebrows went fully up and he pulled back from her as though she'd threatened to bite him.

Katie flipped to another page. Page 48, a firefighter on 9/11. She tapped the picture.

Owney leaned forward. "I've seen that one."

"This is the one that came out years after 9/11. Aidan O'Reilly is Sean O'Reilly's son."

"Right, fine," Owney said. "But why do you think he's your father?"

"I don't," Katie said. "I think he's my uncle."

Owney waited as Katie turned back several pages, stopping at a picture of Sean O'Reilly's funeral. The coffin was being carried down the steps of a church. Behind it was Sean's wife, and two boys stood on either side of her. Aidan, the 9/11 fireman at eight years old, and Brendan, who was four.

"You can't tell, but the wife, Norah — that's her name, Norah — she was pregnant. She had a baby girl in December."

"A baby born in 1983 would not be anywhere near old enough to be your birth mother."

"I'm bad at math but not that bad," Katie said. She placed a finger on the woman with white hair behind the widow. "This is Sean's mother." She moved her finger to the girl standing in front of her grandmother, whose face was turned away from the camera.

"This is Maggie O'Reilly. She was nine years old."

"So, old enough," Owney said.

Katie nodded and tapped the picture.

"Hey, you didn't just open this book and pick some random Irish family to join, did you?"

He tried to say it lightly, but she read the concern in his expression.

Katie closed the book and moved back to sit cross-legged in the center of the bed so she could see Owney's face as she told him how she'd gone into BookMarks and passed the table of 9/11 books that were out for the anniversary. *Brooklyn Firefighters* was not one she would ever touch, but a glimpse of the fireman on the cover made her stop and stare. He looked familiar.

"I opened the book and read that his name is Sean O'Reilly, his son is that fireman from a lost roll of film, and the photographer was killed on 9/11, and it's all very, very sad."

Owney shook his head. "Kate — not following."

"That would have been it. I would have put the book down and walked away, question answered, except, once, I got this phone call."

Katie let the silence build as she tried to think of a first sentence.

"The night of September 11, friends of my parents' made up a flier. They put a picture of my mother on it and our phone number."

Over the next few weeks, strangers called their apartment. Men and women both cried as they said they were sorry. Some people were crazy or drunk, saying things like she'd run away to Florida, or if she'd been home with her kid, she wouldn't be dead.

Katie was told not to answer the phone, but her father was afraid to change the number even after it was clear her mother was not coming home. There was always the chance they'd hear from somebody who could tell them where she'd been at any point in the morning.

Her father started falling asleep on the couch by nine o'clock every night. Katie didn't think about it then, but she wondered now if he'd been taking something. She'd be wide awake until at least midnight, wandering the rooms of their apartment or sitting outside on the terrace. That winter was strangely warm, as though it were going to stay September forever.

"Yeah, I remember," Owney said. "It didn't get cold until Christmas Eve."

By early December, her father had secured the rental house in Southampton. Katie had already packed her books in boxes, shaking each one before she put it in. She could not help but wonder if her mother really had run away from home. Perhaps she'd hidden a note.

One night when her father was asleep, the phone rang. Katie answered. A woman asked for Charlie McKenna.

Carrying the phone out onto the terrace, Katie said he was busy and offered to take a message. The woman said she was sorry about Laurel.

"The strangers and the crazy people almost all called her Laura. But this woman said *Laurel*. I thought she must be a law school or college friend," Katie said. "I didn't ask for her name. I guess it didn't seem important. We talked for a few minutes."

Telling the story out loud was like describing a dream.

"The woman said she'd read in the paper that we'd gotten back from Ireland not long before 9/11. She asked if we were there over my birthday.

"I told her yes. We always went on vacation for my birthday. Ireland was supposed to be saved for when I turned ten, but that spring, my mother all of a sudden decided we shouldn't wait. So we went a year early. I said that I wished we'd never left. She told me her mother was from Ireland and that her dad died when she was nine. After his death, she'd wanted to move to Galway, but her mother said no."

Her father, she said, was a fireman who was killed in a hardware store fire in Brooklyn. He was the only one who died that day. She told Katie that she'd miss her mother forever, but after a while she'd be able to re-member her without thinking of how it happened.

"Everybody else kept giving me that 'time will heal' bullshit. But she explained *how* time might heal. Your memory of the death gets sepa-rated from all your other memories."

"Do you even know if your parents met your birth mother?" Owney asked.

"I have no idea. Before 9/11, I was too young to be told anything. Af-ter that, I never asked. I didn't want to hurt my dad's feelings," Katie said. She had not wanted him to think she was looking to defect to an-other family, should she find them.

"If they all knew each other's names, it probably was her," Owney said. "Your birth mother could have seen it in the papers. But why would you think she's this fireman's daughter?"

Katie picked up the book again and opened it to the picture of Sean O'Reilly's funeral. She passed it to Owney so he could read the para-graph on the page.

She watched his expression change as he read the words.

Firefighter Sean O'Reilly, the only firefighter killed in a fire at Lenny's hardware store on Flatbush Avenue. His wife, Norah O'Reilly, was a na-tive of Ireland.

"Okay, that's why," Owney said.

"She never said 'Lenny's.' An old friend of my mother's might know my birthday, and it's a safe bet that Sean O'Reilly wasn't the only fireman married to an Irishwoman."

Owney slowly closed the book and tossed it across the bed.

"Do you look like this Maggie O'Reilly?"

"I can't find her, Own. I maybe look a little like Rose, the younger sister. Our coloring's the same, but she's really pretty." Katie ran a finger from her forehead to her chin, which she tapped once. "When I Google 'Maggie O'Reilly' or 'Margaret O'Reilly,' a lot of stuff comes up but nothing that fits. The name is too common."

"If it was your birth mother who called, did she break the law?"

"No," Katie said, affronted. Then, less certainly, "I don't know. I don't care. It was right after 9/11. Nobody was in their right mind. Anyway, it was at night. She asked for my dad, not me."

Owney nodded, a concession. Then he asked quietly, "How come you never told me any of this?"

"It all happened after we — when we weren't talking."

Six months had passed after their breakup before Owney texted her. *KT?*

"Then, when we were talking again, I'd known too long to say it out loud," she said.

"It was a secret by then," he said.

Something in his tone, or perhaps just that he had understood so readily, made Katie wonder what things he had never told her.

"Yes," Katie said. "And I didn't want you bugging me to find out for sure."

"Like I'm doing now," he said unapologetically. "If you're waiting for everything with your mother — and I mean Laurel — to be settled, you know they might never stop finding her."

Katie returned the book to the shelf and knelt beside the bed. She pressed her face into the mattress before tipping her head back to look up at him. She envied Owney's ability to simply leave his father wherever he was, and his belief that it was not abandonment but the only way forward.

"Sometimes I think I want to marry you because you have such a funny name."

Owney laughed and opened his arms to her. Katie got up, crawled across the bed and laid her head on his chest. His arms came up around her.

Late Sunday night, Katie was online, reading admissions requirements for the schools with Irish studies programs that interested her. The thought of writing an admissions essay again was depressing. She'd done a coward's job the first time, ignoring her guidance counselor's hesitant suggestion that she write about "her loss."

She scorned the idea, not because she believed it wouldn't work, but because she thought it probably would. She didn't want to be admitted to college on sympathy.

Her phone buzzed and she jumped and scooped it up. Owney.

I'm here.

Owney had called this afternoon and asked if she wanted to go to Brooklyn with him. He had done some Internet searching himself. The sister of the photographer of *Brooklyn Firefighters* had owned a bar in Brooklyn, in Cross Hill. It was still there and still called Lehane's.

The photographer had spent decades taking pictures of the neighborhood firefighters. The fire company where Sean O'Reilly worked was near the bar.

Katie refused. She wasn't twenty-one.

Owney didn't point out that her age had never stopped her before. He asked if she minded if he went by himself, adding that it might even be better. Nobody could tell the family that a young woman had been asking questions about them. Katie told him he could do whatever he wanted.

When Katie opened the front door, Owney already had his sneakers off.

Again they crept through the quiet house. Katie shut her bedroom door, and when she turned around, Owney was sitting on her bed, leaning forward.

"The bartender at Lehane's knows the family."

Katie sat down at her desk.

"He's new to the neighborhood, but he says they're 'old stock.' That's how he put it. They've been there forever."

"They're still there?"

"Sean O'Reilly's widow and his mother are, and the younger sister."

"Rose." Katie gnawed on her thumbnail. "Did he know Maggie?"

"No," Owney said. "But he told me I should come in around six o'clock when the firemen get off work, or on a Saturday when there's a Mets game on. But . . ."

"What is it?" Katie asked, certain he was about to repeat some rumor about Maggie O'Reilly.

Cystic fibrosis, hemochromatosis, celiac disease, Tay-Sachs, schizophrenia.

What Katie found when she Googled "diseases that run in Irish families."

Schizophrenia. Average age of onset, eighteen to twenty-five.

Someone mentally ill might not appear in an Internet search, because she had no career. She might not be mentioned on siblings' Facebook pages, or talked about at all.

"Sean O'Reilly's wife lost a niece on 9/11. If this *is* your birth family, she'd have been Maggie O'Reilly's first cousin."

Katie tried to absorb that. It had never occurred to her that her 9/11 losses might extend beyond her mother.

"Did you get this cousin's name?" she asked.

"The guy said he remembers that she was Noelle, because she worked for some theater that had a fundraiser in her memory at the bar around Christmas. He couldn't remember her last name."

"Did you do any searching?"

"I figured that was up to you."

Katie swiveled her chair to face her laptop. *Noelle, O'Reilly, 9/11, September 11.*

She read the visible lines of the first link.

Noelle Byrne, a native of Ballyineen, Co. Galway, who moved to
New York several years ago . . .

Katie opened the link and it brought up a September 13, 2001, edi-
tion of a newspaper called the *Ivehusheen Herald*, which filled the whole
screen.

. . . is missing and feared dead in the terror attacks on the World
Trade Center complex in Manhattan. Twenty-nine-year-old Noelle
is the only daughter of Peter and Aoife Byrne. She did not work in
either of the twin towers, but had an early-morning meeting in the
South building. Cathal Mulryan, identified as Ms. Byrne's uncle,
said that the family fears the worst.

A spokesman for the Kilmaren College has confirmed that
graduate student and teaching assistant Magdalena O'Reilly (pictured left), from Brooklyn, New York, is a cousin of Ms. Byrne's.
Ms. O'Reilly has been studying in Ireland and is a candidate for
a master's degree in Irish literature. She could not be reached for
comment and is said to be at her grandparents' home waiting for
news.

Pictured left. Katie shifted her gaze. Only the edge of the photo was
showing. Sliding the screen was like drawing back a curtain.

The photo had been taken in an office. She was seated at a desk and
there were bookshelves behind her. Magdalena O'Reilly. Long brown
hair and blue eyes in an intelligent face. Only the hint of a smile. A pair
of glasses in her hand.

What Owney didn't understand was her holding back. It was fear
of rejection, fear of what she might find. Of course it was. But the
thing was, after reading about them in the book and her subsequent
cyber-stalking, Katie wanted them. The O'Reillys. She wanted the
well of bravery, and Norah from Ireland, a great-grandmother, and

the beauty of Rose's voice. She didn't want to relinquish them and begin again.

Owney got up off the bed and came to stand behind her. He brushed his palm against her shoulder. She reached up and took his hand.

The story was that Katie had not been able to handle it the second time they found her mother. She'd gotten lost for a little while. This was surely what Emma confided to her friends, and what her father would say if he spoke of it, which he probably did not.

But Katie had never tried to explain, even to Owney, how often she'd stared at women with dark hair and blue eyes when she was a child.

After 9/11, though, Katie had looked for Laurel. There was even a name for it: searching behavior. The grieving believe they glimpse their loved one among the living. Two rows ahead at the movie theater. In the next car while stopped at a red light. At a restaurant, ensconced with another family.

If one fragment of bone was a symbol, proof that Laurel Rourke-McKenna had not used the chaos of September 11 to start a new life, a fantasy Katie had occasionally indulged in, two fragments meant that there were hundreds more. Thousands? Katie began to understand for the first time that her mother had not only died, she'd had a death.

Yet this was not the reason Katie cut class for the first time. In the classroom across the hall, Katie had caught a glimpse of a new teacher who was petite with dark hair and fair skin. Three steps closer and Katie saw only a superficial resemblance between her and the teacher, who was far too young anyway. But logic always arrived too late to stop the surge of adrenaline. As her heartbeat calmed and her breathing slowed, Katie realized that she was no longer looking for the mother she'd known. No, she was back to searching for a stranger with a familiar face. She'd turned and walked out of the school.

Owney squeezed her hand. She squeezed back and pulled her hand away.

Katie gazed at Magdalena's — Maggie's — picture and understood that she was always going to know her first mother's face as soon as she saw it. As though she were remembering.

Rose led Katie outside to the garden.

The few people wandering around did not even glance at them. The leaves were beginning to show a hint of autumn color and there were flowers in bloom, mostly orange and dark purple. She and Rose paused at the saint's statue in the center. The statue used to be out front, Rose told her, but it had been moved now that the house was no longer a convent. The convent had closed in 2005 after the last two nuns died within a month of each other.

Rose started walking and Katie kept pace.

"Where do you go to school?" Rose asked. There was some hesitancy in her voice, as though Katie were a deer she didn't want to startle.

"Not too far from here," Katie said.

Rose was silent, obviously waiting for her to continue. When she didn't, Rose asked, "What's your major? God, I sound like my mother."

"Irish studies. You can choose a focus on literature or history, and I think I'm going to do the history track."

Rose nodded. "I guess you want to teach, then?"

"Maybe." Katie shrugged.

"You want to walk around all day talking about Ireland?"

"Maybe." Katie laughed.

Rose made a noise low in her throat. "Were your parents really into the Irish thing?"

"No, not really. When I was eight, my mom decided I needed to do more on the weekends than sit around reading. She wanted to sign me up for this softball league that played on Saturdays in Central Park, or horseback riding. I asked if I could take step-dancing instead."

"I did that. I wasn't competitive, but I liked it."

"I sucked." Katie remembered her disappointment, like she'd failed some kind of test. "But Mom wouldn't let me just quit. She said to pick another class. I switched to Irish Language for Kids instead. The teacher went into Irish history a little bit, about how the language was against the law and all that," Katie said. "That's how I got interested."

"Did you know you were Irish? Or did you guess?" Rose asked.

"I knew," Katie said. "That was the one thing I knew for sure."

She and Rose walked in silence for a few minutes, until they came to a bench set in a half circle of three evergreens. The garden was empty now, and Katie could hear nothing beyond the wall. She and Rose might have been the only two people in Brooklyn.

Rose sat, and so Katie sat beside her.

"Sometimes I wish I still did drugs," Rose said.

"Me too."

Rose laughed. "It's like that, then."

"In high school, for a little while."

"I'm sorry things had to be this way," Rose said.

"They are this way. I don't know if they had to be."

"That's not a question I can answer."

Katie traced the squares on her skirt. She was not surprised when Rose spoke. Rose had, Katie had already learned, a knack for taking the measure of a silence, and ending it just before it became uncomfortable.

"Xavier and me might have our ceremony here in the garden," Rose said. "I'm getting married on a Thursday. My grandmother asks me, What about people who have to work? I said, Gran, my friends are all actors and singers and writers. They've got the kind of day jobs they can handle with hangovers. She said I should get a better class of friends. She was mostly kidding. Me and Zave are moving in with her. She lost her best friend the January after 9/11 — that was Nathaniel — and a few years ago, another friend from the neighborhood whose son was killed on 9/11 died. Gran's by herself now. She'll be ninety-four in a month."

Delia O'Reilly.

"She's, uh, alert?" Katie said, realizing immediately that it was a dumb question.

"Sure. She's more with it than me. My niece once asked her how long she was going to live, and Gran said she was a vampire and was never going to die."

"Your niece?"

"My other brother's daughter."

"Brendan has a daughter?"

"He keeps her off his Facebook page. Offline altogether. A thing with her mom. She's — how do I put this politely? Kinda batshit," Rose said. "She took off and Bren got custody."

"How old is she?"

"Five," Rose said.

Rose was probably great with her. Katie could imagine her slipping her niece and nephews Hershey's Kisses behind their mothers' backs. When she babysat, she probably hurried the kids to bed only when the key turned in the lock. When Brendan's daughter became a teenager, Rose would be there to dispense funny, inappropriate advice.

But that was still about ten years away. Katie might be casting Rose in a role meant for a much younger aunt.

"Things are fine," Rose added. "Bren's overcautious. I'm not actually convinced the woman can read."

Katie thought that was a little harsh, and although she didn't say it out loud, her expression must have shown what she was thinking.

"Trust me. It's the best thing that could have happened," Rose said. "She's way better off with my brother." Her tone closed the subject.

Katie wished it hadn't. Then she could say, Yes, isn't that how it works? Walking away is not the act of a bad or indifferent mother, but a good one. The very act of doing so is transformative. But again, Rose was not the one to put that question to.

"You're going to take care of your grandmother?" Katie asked.

"More like the other way around," Rose said. "I'm kidding. Sorta. We're paying rent. We offered her market value — okay, a little below, that's sixteen hundred a month — for the rooms on the third floor, and she asked if we'd both gone insane. Aidan and Xavier might put in a kitchen. Gran says we can use hers. I said, Then we're just living with you, and she said, Fine, then you're just living with me. Can't wait to see how this goes."

Katie laughed.

"Truth is, she'd rather it were my sister," Rose said. "She lived with her for a few months. In the summer of '92."

"Did your mother kick her out or something?"

"God, no. But she was nineteen, sharing a room with me. Needed her privacy, I guess."

"Why?" Katie tried to keep her tone light. "Did she have a boyfriend?"

"Yes."

"Was he nice?"

Rose was silent for so long Katie didn't think she was going to answer. Then she half smiled. "He used to call me Roses."

Katie slouched on the bench. That did not sound like a jerk. He did not sound like an arsonist, walking away without looking back. Only rarely had Katie pictured a couple still together at the time she was born. But if so, then she'd been given up by two people, not just one.

She pressed her temple, as though trying to dislodge the thought.

"Does she ever come back to New York?" Katie asked.

Rose was watching her carefully. "Maggie's lived in Ireland for a long time. Hasn't been back to the States for any long stretch since after September 11, when she stayed for a couple of months. Last year, she took a position at the school where she got her degree. Head of the English Department. She teaches Irish literature. It's not far from where Mom's from, in Galway."

"Galway," Katie said.

At home in New York, strangers had often looked at her brown-eyed father and hazel-eyed mother and asked where Katie had gotten her eyes. Who had passed down that shade of blue? But they never suggested Katie did not originally belong to them. The Irish, though, did just that.

Waitresses and tour guides and the women showing them to their rooms in the bed and breakfasts saw Katie and said:

She's got the postman's eyes, I think!
This one doesn't look like a Yank at all.
Lord love her, but she's got the map of Ireland on her face.
You'd better put that one back where you found her.

Once, the three of them were in the back seat of a cab in Dublin, stopped in traffic. The driver peered in the rearview mirror.

"Are you sure she's yours, with those eyes?"

Katie's mother answered, "We bought her from the Gypsies."

"The faeries, it would be," the cabbie said. "A changeling, that one."

Her mother laughed, but her father turned his head away.

A changeling, Katie later learned, was a faerie's child meant to take the place of a stolen human child.

The afternoon before her birthday, she and her mother went to a pub for lunch while her father "relaxed at the hotel." Katie knew that meant he was shopping for her gift.

Katie waited until after the waitress took their order.

"Do you know if my birth mother has blue eyes?"

Her mother had been smiling, about to say something. She sat back abruptly.

"Dad and I have explained that we'll talk about this when you're eighteen, not before."

"What does it matter if you tell me what color her eyes are?"

"Your mother's eyes are hazel." She tapped her temple with one finger.

"Did you get to meet her, or did she meet only the lawyer?" Katie asked.

"When it's time, we will talk about this." She put her hand over Katie's hand.

"Was I born in Ireland?"

"Born *here*? Of course not. You were born in New York, like me and Daddy."

"Did she have the map of Ireland on her face?" Katie asked.

Her mother gazed at her and then withdrew her hand. "Yes."

In one of Katie's worst 9/11 nightmares, her mother calls from the office and says that she is about to start down the stairs. It will take hours, but don't worry. She will get out. Eventually she'll make it home.

Katie asks, "What's my mother's name?"

On the bench, Katie sat still and Rose did too, simply waiting. It was like they were together in a car, companionably trapped.

Katie wanted to ask what August 27, 2010, had been like for the O'Reillys. That is, if they'd been aware of her eighteenth birthday and its significance, legally. The secret's expiration date. Maybe Maggie alone understood.

"I keep wondering," Katie said, "what it's like to be dreading a phone call for two years."

"Or waiting for twenty," Rose said.

Katie looked at her, but there was no hint of humor in her expression.

"My wedding is on April 8," Rose said. "Maggie teaches a lot of summers, but she can take off if she wants to. But that's my busiest time of year, and Xavier's too. Also, it's hot as fuck in this city. The week after Christmas was another option, but a lot of our friends are from out of town. They go home for the holidays through New Year's. We would make our families and whichever friends can afford it fly to Ireland, but my grandmother can't travel. And this April is the thirtieth anniversary of my father's death. We're going to have a second wake for him. It was Aunt Eileen's idea.

"My sister would fly home for my wedding no matter when I set the date. She would rearrange a million things at work and she'll come. But why make her go back and forth twice within a few months? Mama Bear said, Well, Miss Picky, if not Christmas, if not summer, then there is no reason, after three decades, to keep April a sad month."

"Maggie's coming in April."

"Maggie's coming in April."

April, Katie thought, as though the month were a foreign country.

"They'll be here for at least a week," Rose said.

"She's married?"

"Yes."

"Does she have kids?"

"No."

The disappointment cut more than Katie would have guessed. She'd wanted to ask what Maggie O'Reilly named the children she kept.

Rose had answered with some hesitation. Because the information wasn't quite hers to give? But Katie thought there was something else there, an acknowledgment that though the answer was simple, the question was not.

"The invitations are going to be cheap and handwritten. Aside from the ceremonies and the color of my dress, there won't be much difference between the wake and the wedding."

"In ancient Ireland, wedding dresses were blue," Katie said.

"Really? I never heard that." Rose sounded pleased. "Maybe I'll do it."

If I'm invited, Katie thought, if that's what you're saying, maybe I'll come.

Katie knew, and she sensed Rose did as well, that they had reached the end of their meeting. A hug would have felt wrong — taking things too far — and Katie was relieved when Rose offered her hand. Their handshake was brief, though Rose squeezed lightly before she let go.

Katie wanted to press her palm to Rose's palm to see if, indeed, from one angle, her hand would be hidden by Rose's and, from another, Rose's would be hidden by hers.

Katie went straight to the subway, walking intently with her eyes downcast, as if she were wary of broken squares of sidewalk. She'd planned to case the neighborhood after leaving the museum, maybe walk by Sean O'Reilly's firehouse and Lehane's, but now she wanted only to leave. Never before had she been recognized by her features. By coming here, she had taken the dare and she had been called out.

Katie got off the F train at Carroll Street, one stop past where she would catch the bus to Red Hook. It meant a much longer walk, but she had the rest of the afternoon free.

Rose had not asked for her contact information, which surely meant she knew how to find Katie online. She was certain, though, that Rose did not have any idea where she lived.

Katie walked down the narrow sidewalks, passing rows of brownstones. She reached Sacred Hearts and St. Stephen, a huge Catholic church that she kept meaning to go into, just to see it. Not today. She crossed Hicks Street and climbed the wide, awkwardly spaced steps of the overpass that led from pretty Carroll Gardens into the far more spare Red Hook. If she'd lived here as a child, she would have pretended it was a bridge and the humming Brooklyn-Queens Expressway below was a river. Indeed, the overpass felt a bit like the door to the stairway to her Sag Harbor bedroom.

These days, everybody moved to Brooklyn. It should be no big deal that she had too. The Irish studies track at Lyons College in Brooklyn Heights was well established; it offered cultural events in and around New York City as part of the curriculum. Really, she might well have chosen it anyway. That it had no on-campus housing had given her pause, but only briefly. She decided she was more suited to being a neighbor than a roommate anyway. Her father had not been happy about it, though he was the one constantly cautioning her not to waste what he delicately called her "inheritance."

Katie asked him to Google Red Hook so he could read for himself that it was set to be the next big neighborhood, in spite of being so far from the subway. She'd rented a one-bedroom for a good deal less than a studio closer to the college.

She'd kept her car but was considering selling it. Walking almost everywhere was helping her learn Brooklyn, which she'd found unexpectedly foreign. She'd hoped for an innate familiarity, asserting a life that might have been. It seemed, though, that Brooklyn was a place she'd have to learn the way she would anywhere she chose to live.

Her apartment was on the second floor of a three-story building near Coffey Park. Across the street was an abandoned warehouse that had once been a brewery, according to her landlady, who lived on the ground floor.

Katie entered her apartment and shut the door, leaning against it, listening to the silence the way some might listen to a piece of music. The apartment had a galley kitchen against the brick wall and a bedroom that overlooked a weedy backyard. The couple upstairs, who'd been in New York for less than a year, told Katie they were hoping to persuade the landlady to let them plant a vegetable garden. Katie had often seen the woman out there after dark, smoking, and doubted the vegetable garden would happen. But she encouraged the couple to ask anyway. They believed they were going to get just what they wanted from New York. That was nice.

She had been in her apartment for three months, but so far Katie had bought only a desk, a bed, a bureau, two bookcases and, instead of a couch, an easy chair that looked adrift in the long room. All summer, she had not had a single visitor, though that would change tomorrow when Owney came.

Katie changed into jeans. She stuffed the skirt she had on into her laundry bag, though she might as well have thrown it out. She'd never wear it again. Next she checked her email, rubbing her eyes, which felt heavy, as if she'd been crying or awake all night. Nothing beyond the usual stuff, but surely Rose had already contacted Maggie. In Ireland it was almost nine o'clock at night. Perhaps Quinn could keep a secret, but Katie assumed Rose could not, and wouldn't even try. She didn't want her to. If Maggie did write to her, after midnight New York time, Katie resolved not to answer until September 12.

Last year, for the tenth anniversary, Katie had visited Owney at his college, and they'd spent most of the day reading, her on his bed, him on his absent roommate's.

Katie wasn't sure yet what they'd do tomorrow. Owney had never gone to the reading of the names, and she went only the first year. She'd stood beside her father, holding a picture of her mother and constantly pushing her hair out of her eyes in that awful, incessant wind. She'd refused to go again.

Impulsively, Katie took her keys out of her bag and grabbed her phone. She slipped into the hallway and listened for a moment, but she saw and heard no one. Still, she climbed the stairs quietly and went to the door at the end of the hall, which was supposed to be locked. The lock was broken, probably on purpose. She climbed the narrow steps to the roof and cautiously opened the door. The roof, with its ledge as high as her waist, was empty. She had not come up here often, too nervous about getting trapped, even given the broken door. She imagined herself having to call 911 and enduring the embarrassment of a rescue.

Katie picked up a stray brick and put it in front of the door, propping it open, and tested the doorknob for good measure. It was loose. Though total disrepair would have been bad, she liked that the building was rundown. It was better than the tidiness of Sag Harbor.

Katie went to the edge of the roof. Across the water, the Manhattan skyline looked like a painting. It was hard to believe she had lived there once and was made to run away.

The sky was not dark enough to properly see the Tribute in Light. But tomorrow evening, she and Owney could come up here and look. At first he would refuse. He would say there was no point. His father was dead every day. But Katie would insist.

She also intended to suggest that he break the pattern his own mother set in motion eleven years ago, this drifting in and out of strangers' second homes. Move to Brooklyn.

Katie rubbed her arms. Autumn had definitely arrived to stay.

September is the saddest month. Not April.

April, Katie thought, had only ever meant the start of spring and usually Easter Sunday. Though Katie has read plenty about identity issues, medical concerns, feelings of abandonment, fear of rejection, fear of reunion, unrealistic expectations, she never once realized that she had two calendars to consider. That is, two calendars with only August 27 in common.

Katie felt as if she'd spent the morning trying to solve a riddle.

There is the woman who gave birth to you and the woman who raised you for nine years and they cannot both be your mother, but they are both your mother. Who is your real mother?

Perhaps it wasn't a matter of DNA or love, or the weight of twenty years apart.

Katie might have to split her loyalty between the living and the dead.

If she had met Maggie O'Reilly today, she would have had the obvious questions ready. Why did you have me? Why didn't you try to keep me? Were you ever sorry?

Katie had not thought of what she might say to the rest of the family. But the casual way Rose spoke about the rest of the family made Katie understand that the O'Reillys were real, with whole lives outside of the bits of biography Katie had culled from the Internet. Lives that intersected with her own beginning.

Katie wanted to learn, as well, about April 5, 1983, in a way she had not when she first read about Sean O'Reilly's death. Despite knowing that he might be her grandfather, Katie skimmed over what had happened to him. She wouldn't do that again. The day of the week, the color of the sky, how the fire started, why he couldn't be saved. It was not curiosity. She wanted to know the facts, the way you do when something will soon be yours. And Katie also wanted to know if, for Maggie O'Reilly, losing her father had somehow made it easier to walk away.

She had from September to April to find a way to ask.

Acknowledgments

THANK YOU to my agent, Caryn Karmatz Rudy, for her belief in what *Ashes of Fiery Weather* could become, and to my editor, Lauren Wein, whose vision for the book brought the story to a place I could not have taken it on my own.

I want to thank the team at Houghton Mifflin Harcourt, especially Pilar Garcia-Brown, for her insightful comments on the manuscript, and Larry Cooper, for the acumen of his manuscript editing.

I am grateful to my parents for never suggesting I "do something" with my B.A. in English. That is, they never said to choose a profession more practical than that of novelist. Not once, through two unsold novels and twenty years of writing, did they tell me to become, instead, another person.

Thank you to the two people who have always been on either side of me, my sisters, Jennifer and Elizabeth; to my brother-in-law, Alex; and to my nieces and nephews, Eddie, Meghan, Nick, Lily, Kristen and Michael.

There is too much to say to my husband, Travis, so just one word: February.

Our son was born when I had about one hundred coherent pages of this book, and he was almost three when I finished the first draft. Before, I used to lean on the novel-as-child metaphor. It was comforting. It made sense. After, I discovered that it is neither accurate nor fair.

Liam, there is only you.

Thank you to the men and women of the FDNY, particularly my father, uncles and cousin, and the fire families of New York, who suffered unprecedented losses on September 11, and in its aftermath called on the traits that have always been there — resilience, courage and compassion. And, eventually, humor. This book is for you, for us.